the Dream Merchant Saga

BOOK FOUR
Sin

Written by
L.T. Suzuki
in collaboration with
Nia Suzuki-White

Book Cover, graphic design and layout:
Scott White
Shinobi Creative Productions
www.shinobicreativeproductions.com

Note for Librarians:
A cataloguing record for this book is available from the Library and Archives
Canada at: www.collectionscanada.ca/amicus/index-e.html

ISBN 978-0-9921265-1-3

Dedications

To my dear friends,
Anna H., Lauren M., and Melody M.!

Thank you for all your love and support
throughout the journey we've shared.

Nia

To all the fans who kept asking,
"When is the next story ready?".

Well, here it is, with one more novel to follow!
Thank you for your loyal support and words
of encouragement that keep me writing.

Lorna

Contents

1

Jibber-Jabber

CLANK! SCRA-A-A-APE!

Rose's breath snagged in the back of her throat. The clash of swords echoing through the air turned the blood in her veins to ice.

This was not the time for cowardice, nor did she have time to daintily glide down the stairs of the castle keep, as a princess should. Hiking up the hem of her gown, she dashed through the main hall. The mad pounding of her heart thundered in her ears to mute the harsh din of steel grating against steel.

Due to Rose's misadventures of late, she had become all too familiar with the horrific sounds of battle. It set her nerves on edge, and even more so upon hearing Tag cry out. His frantic words sounded from the courtyard, filling her heart with dread.

Tag raised his weapon to block the blow meant for his head. His arms throbbed, aching to the bones from the jarring impact.

"I'm not dead *yet!*" scoffed Tag. "Try harder!"

"Do not provoke me, boy!" snarled his adversary. Dressed in a full stand of armour, an angry voice reverberated through the grated visor of a helmed head. "You are not dead because I was not yet trying!"

Bellowing like a madman, his sword slammed against Tag's. Bearing down with all his might, he pressed against the broad edge of the young man's weapon.

Rather than yielding to this formidable opponent, Tag mustered all his strength to push this rival off. He groaned; staggering back as the knight's foot came up, smashing into his midriff. The well-placed kick forced Tag to double over. He stumbled, tripping over the low boxwood hedge lining the courtyard. Through clenched teeth, a painful groan gushed out with the air knocked from his lungs.

Having opted to do battle without the protection and burden of heavy armour, save for a vest of mail, this knight-in-training believed, like the Elves, agility would work to his advantage.

Instead, *unlike* the Elfkind, Tag fell gracelessly. Somersaulting over the hedgerow, he landed clumsily. Sprawled out flat on his back, the stones and pebbles bit through the protective mail, pressing into his flesh as he hit the ground hard.

From the corner of his eye, Tag caught a fleeting glimpse of Princess Rose. There was that unmistakable look of terror etched upon her face as she bounded down the stairs of the keep, shouting, *"STOP!"*

Her orders to halt went unheeded. Tag's assailant was determined to see it through, to put this young whelp soundly in his place.

With the telltale rattle of mail and the ominous clatter of steel armour on the offensive, the knight brandished his sword with utmost purpose. Hoisting this weapon on high, he was determined to bring this battle to an end.

Before he could deliver the defining blow, with a loud *'CLANK'*, Tag's assailant staggered back. Momentarily stunned by an unexpected strike, a fist-sized rock jettisoned by Rose's hand had struck him spot-on. It bashed the side of his helmeted head.

Throwing herself over Tag's chest, she cried out, "Mercy! I beg of you!"

The knight lowered his weapon as he regained his composure. Being the recipient of her dangerously accurate aim, the blow had effectively broken his singular drive and focused concentration.

"You dare attack my friend?" Rose positioned herself between this brazen adversary and Tag as she shouted her demand: "Show your face, sir, so I may deal with you accordingly!"

"As you wish, my lady." The man's words were contrite as he bowed in respect to Princess Rose.

He swung the blade about with a flick of his wrist. In one fluid motion, the length of deadly steel slithered through the locket to sheath this sword into its scabbard once more. The knight removed his steel helm, as the impact of the rock had dented the visor, preventing him from lifting it smoothly to reveal his identity to her.

With a single, disapproving glance at this suddenly familiar face, Rose scowled in annoyance. She pushed off of Tag, unceremoniously knocking him back onto the ground as she snapped, "Cankles Moron! I should have known it was you!"

"It is *Myron Kendall*, my lady."

He corrected her for the umpteenth time, even knowing that it was probably all for naught. This particular princess was never known for her ability to recollect faces and names, unless there were dire consequences in not doing so, or that face and name were attached to a prominent title and great wealth.

"Cankles, Kendall! Moron, Myron! It matters not! You know bloody well whom I am speaking of, you rogue of a knight!" Rose shook an admonishing finger at him. "Just what did you think you were doing, bashing Tag about like that?"

"I didn't think you cared," teased Tag. Giving her a coy smile, he stared with raised eyebrows at Rose. It was obvious there was genuine concern in her voice.

"*Care?* About you? Think again! Wipe that smug grin from your face, you fool!" Her balled fist punched his arm. "You were appointed as my personal bodyguard. You are no good to me dead. And stop speaking like a common commoner! It is 'I *did not* think you cared', you knave!"

"You speak in jest!" protested Tag.

"Enough of this lazy talk you have adopted from this man when we knew him as Cankles. Sadly, you have regressed, both socially and mentally, in doing so!"

"You're royalty, Princess. You're expected to speak in a formal manner. For me, I'm as common as they come. Contracted words suit me just fine, when the occasion calls for it."

"It is never called for. And as insignificant as it seems to you, it is what separates *us* from *them*." Rose's eyes narrowed in resentment as she scrutinized Tag, and then glanced at a woman rushing by to deliver a basket of duck eggs to the palace kitchen. "Now, enough of this craziness before you drive me mad with all your jibber-jabber!"

"No craziness intended, my lady," assured Myron, bowing his head in apology.

"We were merely doing some intensive training," stated Tag. In a disgruntled huff, he picked up the sword that was knocked from his grasp. "And no disrespect to our friend, but who said *he* was bashing *me*?"

"Do you think me blind? It was *you*, not him, flopping about like a fish on dry land." Rose's index finger pointed accusingly first at Tag, before judiciously jabbing her thumb over her shoulder toward Sir Myron Kendall. "And had I known it was our friend delivering this sound thrashing you were probably deserving of, I would not have intervened on your behalf."

"Intervened?" snorted Tag. His eyes rolled in frustration as he shook his head. "I was doing fine before you came along to *interfere*."

"He speaks the truth, my lady. The young sir was holding his own and doing so quite nicely," stated Myron, nodding in agreement, "until he tripped over the hedge, that is."

"I am all too familiar with tripping and Tag did not trip! You kicked him over, plain and simple!"

"So, it was a combination of both and a bit of bad timing to boot," conceded Myron.

"More like your boot to Tag's midriff. Ultimately, he was the big loser in this little contest." Rose shook her head in disgrace as she chided him, "For shame, Tag Yairet, for shame!"

"If the young man's wisdom serves him well, losing should make Tag better, not bitter," responded Myron.

"Absolutely," agreed Tag, nodding in gratitude to his friend. "If I were to quit now, then I would truly be a loser. Instead, my skills shall only improve, the more I learn from this accomplished knight."

"So you say, but just what were you two doing here in the first place?" interrogated Rose. Her eyes flashed with annoyance as she conducted a cursory inspection of the royal courtyard and its immaculately pruned collection of exotic shrubs and rosebushes.

Myron and Tag exchanged quizzical glances.

"What is wrong with the both of you? This is not the place for swordplay! There is an area out back, next to the stable, for knights and those in training. It is designated specifically for such high-spirited shenanigans."

"I am sorry, Princess Rose. I must admit we were a bit zealous," apologized Myron. "In the future, we shall restrict our activities to the appointed area."

"As you should!"

"And you should know, perfecting one's skill with the sword should never be taken lightly, nor should it be categorized as being something as trivial as *shenanigans*," corrected Tag. He carefully sheathed his special weapon. It was the family sword bequeathed to him upon his father's passing and returned to him by the Princess only after surviving their first quest.

"Say what you will, you ruffian, but you could have destroyed these beautiful roses with all this foolishness." She scrutinized the rows of delicate, fragrant blooms soaking up the warmth of this last day of summer sun. These roses were planted to commemorate her birth just over sixteen years ago and she was determined that they would not suffer the indignities of being trampled by these rapscallions. Upon her fleeting inspection, these flowers appeared unmolested after this pugilistic display.

"Consider it a fitting sacrifice, if I am to learn from this great knight. I must better my skills so I can keep you safe, should we be forced to join you on another one of your ill-fated misadventures." Tag was smug as he attempted to justify their actions to her.

"Keep *me* safe? I think not, Tagius Oliver Yairet!" scoffed Rose. Her amethyst eyes sparkled, as she set him straight. "I, with my scary-accurate aim, prevented this great, but demented, knight from cleaving your head in two."

"I was not actually going to cleave his head, my lady," corrected Myron. "I was merely teaching Tag how to respond in a real battle situation. Plus, it was to hone my own skills, being so rusty after all these years."

"I saw what you were doing to Tag," snipped Rose. "Believe me, you are not that rusty. You are more capable than you care to admit, and certainly more capable than Tag."

"It is kind of you to say." Myron bowed politely in response, but inwardly, he cringed.

It had been a long road to recovery. Just thinking about all these wasted years living life in both denial and forgetfulness as the village idiot of Cadboll, it was something he still struggled to come to grips with. Even with the passing of these months since the necromancer, Parru St. Mime Dragonite, had captured, tortured and cruelly restored his memory of the last great battle. It was the war that culminated in the tragic death of his captain, and Tag's father, and to this day, Myron Kendall struggled to reclaim his former life and all it once represented.

"I speak the truth," insisted Rose. "You have worked long and hard since our return, immersing yourself in a gruelling daily regimen most knights in my father's service quail at the mere thought of undertaking. As far as I am concerned, you are of sound mind. Your vim and vigour has been restored to its former glory. Your skills in battle are such that I have absolute confidence in your abilities were you to be called to war."

"And yet, in my humble opinion, I am in dire need of sharpening my skills with this blade, no pun intended." The gauntlet protecting his hand rattled as he patted the sword's hilt.

In his heart he believed, if this was indeed true, her father would have promoted him to the position of captain, or at the very least, restored him to his former role as a first officer. Instead, Myron was recognized as a knight once more, but his responsibilities were less than prestigious. He had been relegated to nothing more than that of a glorified babysitter, acting as Rose's personal bodyguard should she ever require an armed escort, alongside of Tag, to venture beyond the walls of Pepperton Palace.

"I beg to differ," countered Rose. She glanced over at Tag, attempting to intimidate him with one of her mincing stares. "It is obvious to me that this dolt is the one needing to improve his swordsmanship."

"So you say, Princess, but as unsophisticated or as unorthodox as my methods appeared to be in the past, it had been adequate, enough to ensure our survival to this very day," argued Tag.

"Adequate sounds so very… *mediocre*, less than average at that," muttered Rose. She shuddered just saying this word as she turned her pert, little nose up at him. "And nobody remembers average. No one recalls a so-so time or an ordinary meal. For this reason, I would never settle for mediocre, and if you were wise, neither should you."

"Hence the reason we were engaged in rigorous training," reminded Myron. "This young man aspires to his father's greatness. The more he practices, the greater his skills will be."

"Now, I am the one hoping you are speaking the truth," responded Rose. "But I suppose there is no harm in Tag wishing to follow in his father's esteemed footsteps, just do not get him killed in the process."

"Tag is his father's son, but he need not meet the same fate." Myron patted the young man on his shoulder. "If he is diligent with his practice and wise in incorporating effective strategy, Tag will be able to hold his own in no time."

With a sideways glance she could see that these past few months of intensive training had helped immensely to restore Myron close to his original form. He had evolved greatly from the mere shadow of a man they had originally encountered on their travels through Cadboll in the County of Wren.

A healthy diet paired with a voracious appetite and the many hours and days of ceaseless, focused training served to rebuild Myron's muscles. It also helped to recoup his strength and reclaim his capacity to remember even the smallest of details. But it was not only Myron to go through a great transformation, both physically and mentally. Tag, too, had bulked up considerably with these months of training side-by-side with this knight, but mentally? There were moments when Tag's logic and reasoning made him sound wiser than men twice his age. And then, this young man would say or do something that left her questioning the level of his maturity.

Too often of late, Tag had thought nothing of verbally putting the Princess in her place, and doing so with unusual zeal. It was a situation that did not sit well with Rose. She was a genuine princess after all, and though Tag had always been her dearest friend, he was still a commoner and merely a knight-in-training! In her opinion, he was either too stupid or too immature to truly appreciate that her title alone held more sway and far greater power than his lowly station would ever afford him in the big scheme of things that truly mattered.

Rose stared wistfully at Tag. Whatever the case, he was definitely not the same gangly boy she grew up with; the awkward youth who had embarked on that ill-fated adventure early in the spring. Under Myron's tutelage, as well as incorporating what he had learned from Lord Rainus Silverthorn during their mission that saw them run the gauntlet to survive the dragon-infested lands to the north, Tag had continued to grow. Whatever the case, Rose came to the conclusion Tag's mind was not keeping in step with his increasing brawn.

It was when he'd hoist his sword, preparing for mock battle against Myron or the other knights that she could not help but notice his strong hands and those well-defined muscles that swelled and flexed with each movement, no matter how subtle.

"What are you gawking at?" questioned Tag. Feeling the intense scrutiny of her discriminating eyes, he lifted his arms to check if he had ripped his tunic during this latest bout of energetic swordplay.

"A princess does not gawk! And if I were, you are certainly not gawk-worthy!" Rose's cheeks burned with embarrassment as she averted her eyes.

"So you say!" chuckled Tag, delighting in her discomfiture.

"If you must know, I could not help but notice that you are covered in dirt and you reek of sweat."

To Rose's disgust, Tag lifted one arm to take a deliberate whiff of his armpit as he blotted away the fine patina of perspiration beading his forehead.

"Oh… I suppose I am too manly for your royal liking."

"You are too *something* for anybody's liking," stated Rose, her nose wrinkling in repulsion. "But know this, you insolent fool, even a swine is well acquainted with dirt and reeking of a foul stink."

"Between a pig and a man, there is a big difference in the type of dirt and the kind of stink. And at least your lovely handmaiden is not put off by my *manliness*," quipped Tag. He winked at Myron as though this was something only another man could understand or appreciate.

"Oh, come now!" snapped Rose. "Look at her lowly station in life! Gwendolyn –"

"For pity's sake!" grumbled Tag. With a dismal shake of his head, he corrected the Princess. "Her name is Evelyn and you bloody well know it!"

"Fine!" snorted Rose. "As I was saying, *that girl* is able to overlook these things only because she is used to dirt, sweat and all manner of things that reek, you included."

Tag's hands flew up in resignation. During the struggles of their shared adventures, he was certain this spoiled royal had shed the worst of her irritating traits. However, by her very words, he knew old habits were hard to break while new habits were even harder to assimilate as her own.

Heaving a disheartened sigh, Tag grumbled, "It is interesting to see how some things never change, no matter how much change is desired."

Ignoring his biting comment, Rose considered this unlikely pairing of servant girl and knight-to-be. Her eyes narrowed in resentment… or was it jealousy?

This growing relationship between the two was fast becoming a real conundrum to her, a regular mystery for the ages. Whatever it was her personal handmaiden found appealing about this incorrigible lout, and whatever he found enchanting about this ordinary looking girl from extraordinarily ordinary circumstances, it only served to perplex Rose.

Whatever the case, she knew for certain that dirt and sweat had no place in her privileged life. And thinking back, one of the wishes she should have made when the Dreamstone was still in her possession was to be gifted with the Elves' ability to repel all forms of dirt and to be done with the whole messy business of sweating when made to toil in menial hardship. If she had her way, she would always smell of the delightful fragrance distilled from the attar of roses, no matter how dire the situation she was faced with. Or if she did sweat, the beads of perspiration would be like glistening jewels infused with a rose-scented perfume. That would have been perfect!

Tag snapped his fingers before Rose's vacant eyes. "Are you even listening to me? I said change is desired."

"Well, there you go then! I have no desire to change and no need to, so why should I?" grunted Rose. Her slight shoulders shrugged with indifference. "And as I said before, dirt and sweat are synonymous with that girl, so it is no big deal to her!"

A broad smile creased Tag's handsome face as he mulled over Rose's agitated words. "If dirt and sweat are the hallmarks of an honest, hardworking individual, then Evelyn is imbued with good wisdom and fine taste, not to mention knowing the virtues of hard work and how it can develop one's good character."

"Or that servant has lowered expectations, lacking the wisdom to know the smart individual can prosper from the hard work of others, than to get dirty himself, or herself, in this case."

Tag unleashed a dreary sigh. "You are hopeless, Princess."

Rose's perfect brows arched up in response. It was with an equal measure of surprise and anger.

Myron raised his hands in a gesture for calm as he stepped in between the two quarrelsome friends. "Stay your tongue, both of you, before you regret your words! Once said, you cannot take them back."

Tag nodded in agreement, relieved that even now, as Sir Myron Kendall, this man continued to be the voice of reason. "I suppose I am the hopeless one, believing in change when none is forthcoming."

"And I am hopeful that you will one day come to see that perfection does not require change," offered Rose, her words terse. "In fact, perfection is its own reward."

Before Tag could issue another frustrated sigh or utter derogatory words to counter her comment, Myron seized the young man by his shoulders, steering him away. "Enough said. It is time to resume our training."

"Yes, but take your swordplay elsewhere," ordered Rose, waving them away from the courtyard. "I will not allow my beautiful roses to be subjected to your brand of roughhousing."

"Worry not," said Tag. "We shall resume our training around the back."

"Brilliant, for that is where you belong; neither to be seen nor to be heard!" Rose shouted over her shoulder as she retired into the palace. "So keep your voices down this time. Unless one of you is hurt or dying, I do not want to make another mad dash out here all for naught."

"Yes, yes!" Tag responded with a shake of his head as he and Myron marched away from the courtyard.

"Answer me this, my friend," requested Myron, pondering a mystery as Rose retreated from their sight. "How is it that she has the capacity to recall your name in its entirety, and yet, she struggles to remember my name, which is not that different from what she was calling me before?"

"Therein lies the problem, my friend. You know Princess Rose is easily confused."

"She is?"

"Well, either that, or she is just an idiot," replied Tag. "In truth, I prefer to believe she is easily confused, but then again, perhaps I am the idiot for wanting to believe that to be so."

"It is not even the noon hour and already this day has gone awry. I must retire to my bedchamber; find respite from the doldrums of this existence that has become my life," Rose muttered beneath her breath.

Climbing the stairs, she made her way to her room, and with each step, she grew more agitated. She regretted rushing to Tag's aid, for it was neither wanted nor needed. Dashing down these stairs in a bid to help was pointless, and now, Rose had to climb them once more to reach her private sanctuary. It was bad enough to have made the needless trek, but adding insult to injury, for all her effort, instead of being thanked, she was verbally accosted by Tag. Plus, his constant nagging about her need to change made no sense.

"Why must I change? Perfection is a quality that should not be tampered with," Rose grumbled, as she reached the top of the stairs.

These months of physical inactivity wreaked havoc on her body. She rubbed the aching burn from her thighs brought on by the exertion of ascending the grand staircase after her mad dash.

"So my stamina is somewhat lagging and I will admit my forthright nature can be off-putting to the few who do not appreciate my candidness or honesty, but people should really learn to conform. They should change to fit my needs. After all, I am a member of one of the most respected houses in this realm."

With great pride, Rose straightened her back. She inhaled a deep breath, slowly exhaling to clear her mind and gather her composure. Brushing off the traces of dirt, she smoothed away the creases that formed on her gown during her brief sprint.

"A princess must look presentable at all times." She repositioned the tiara on the crown of her head just so, raising her chin to assume a regal air. "Much better!"

She glided through the corridor toward her bedchamber. Standing in front of the large door, she pushed it open.

A surge of heat and light repelled Rose. Squinting, her eyes adjusted to the brilliant sun flooding through the windows. With the shutters wide-open, the thick panes of glass worked to intensify the sunlight glowing defiantly on this final day of summer. It shone upon the goose down counterpane covering her bed, stretching across the floor to illuminate the tapestry-adorned walls. Stepping inside, the stifling temperature and humidity that built up during her brief absence assaulted her senses. She felt like a delicate flower wilting in the sweltering heat of a blistering hot desert.

"Oh, my! This is much too warm for my liking." Rose marched through the heavy air toward the sunlit windows. "Some fresh air should remedy this hideous condition."

Yanking the windows wide open, she breathed in the morning air. Closing her eyes, Rose basked in the glow of the sun, its heat now tempered by a cool breeze to herald the coming of autumn. This swirling gust of air was invigorating as it swept through her stuffy quarters, causing the curtains draped over the head of the canopy bed to ripple, billowing like the sails of a tall ship.

Rose's eyes snapped open.

An ear-piercing '*screeee*', a burst of wind and the blur of a dark shadow winging her way forced the Princess to drop on all fours. She yelped in surprise as a falcon skimmed overhead, swooping into her bedchamber. Rose spun about, watching as the raptor alighted upon the railed footrest of her bed.

"Get out, you filthy beast!" shooed Rose, pointing to the open window to show the way.

Rather than flying to freedom, the bird cocked its head, watching the human flapping her arms about as though she was trying to take flight.

Rose snatched up a velvet cushion from a nearby chair. Using it as a shield in case the bird attacked, she waved it about to scare the creature off.

In response, the falcon merely ruffled its feathers, its beak clacking as if annoyed by this mortal's actions.

Sensing this bird knew a soft cushion posed no real threat; Rose reached for a sandal. She slipped it off her left foot. Weighing it in her right hand, Rose took aim, preparing to launch it at the bird. Just as she drew back her arm to lob the footwear at her quarry, the falcon cried out.

A great, white light swelled from within this raptor. The brilliance momentarily blinded Rose, causing her to drop her intended weapon. She crouched down, trying to protect herself from this peril and to shield her eyes from the intensity of this glare.

Just as quickly as it appeared, the great light vanished.

Rose blinked hard, fighting to regain her vision that was now obscured by blobs of phantom light dancing before her. It was like staring into the black of night when a bolt of lightning shatters the sky, its white light searing the retinas with its brilliance. These smears of light followed every movement of her eyes as she tried to focus on the menacing presence before her. Pressing her hands over her eyelids, in this enforced darkness these blobs of light grew more intense. Rose rubbed her eyes, blinking until the spectres were vanquished from her sight. The world became clear once more.

Glancing to her side, Rose spied her brocade sandal lying on the floor. Snatching it up into her hand, she sprang onto her feet. Hoisting this weapon, she was poised to launch an offensive.

"Stop, Princess!"

Rose gasped. Her eyes opened wide in astonishment.

2

The Calm Before the Storm

"You are lucky I did not kill you!" admonished Rose. Lowering her throwing arm, she slipped the sandal onto her foot.

"Indeed!" Loken nodded. He breathed a sigh of relief, watching as she darted over to the dresser.

Rose threw open the lid of a simple wooden container resting beside a much larger, ornate jewellery box. She snatched up her sling and the suede bag containing ammunition. Tucking these items into the sash of her dress, she was now prepared should another threatening situation arise.

"Consider this fair warning, Loken."

Hovering before her, the shape-shifting Sprite bowed in respect. "I forgot about your deadly aim. I shall be more careful, should there be a next time."

"No doubt, for I have met my mark on more than one occasion where you are concerned," she reminded him. Rose offered the little being a smug grin, squinting as his aura glowed brightly now that he had been restored to his former glory. "A knock on that puny noddle of yours is probably the reason for your lapse in memory."

"My head and memory are quite fine now," assured Loken. Alighting upon the great, oak dresser, he paced to and fro as he gathered his thoughts. "It was my eagerness to get here, and in one piece, that caused this momentary bout of forgetfulness."

Rose leaned forward, scrutinizing his worried face. Those sinister amber eyes she once found so unnerving when Loken was Dragonite's minion no longer burned with malice. Instead, they were a dazzling blue, but by the glint in his eyes and the furrowing of his brows, she knew something was posing a great vexation to his spirit.

"So what brings you here? The Fairy's Vale is not an easy trek for one so small."

"Hence the reason I adopted the form of a falcon to deliver me with haste." In pensive thought, the Sprite's index finger tapped his chin as he carefully considered his words. "And I made this journey for good reason, Princess Rose. I have urgent news to share; ill tidings from the north."

"North?" gulped Rose. Her heart dropped into the pit of her stomach as she thought on the ferocious dragons, large and small, that menaced them throughout their last quest. These beasts suddenly rampaged with deadly abandon through her fecund imagination. "As in the Fire Rim Mountain Range, north?"

"Not *that* far north, my lady. I am speaking of the happenings in the Woodland Glade."

"Rainus Silverthorn's domain?"

"Precisely!"

"I am *not* an Elf maiden, though I can be mistaken for one. So tell me this, little Sprite: this is Fleetwood, why would this matter concern me?"

"Compassion, my lady."

"And I am full of it, compassion that is, but truly! Why would the affairs of the Elfkind concern me?"

"I sensed a measure of genuine compassion, a change of heart, during the last quest. I assumed you would care enough to take appropriate action; hasten to Lord Silverthorn's aid during his most desperate hour."

Rose merely frowned in confusion as she grumbled in protest, "What is it with everyone and this desire to see me change?"

"Change, or not, is this not what friends do for each other? Come to the aid of her fellow comrades during times such as this?"

"Such as what? And I would say Lord Silverthorn is more of a friendly *acquaintance* than a true friend. Surely the great Elf Lord has others he regards as genuine friends, much closer allies than I will ever be?"

"A true measure of friendship is defined by the sacrifices one is willing to make for the said friend," responded Loken. "If I recall correctly, did not Lord Silverthorn and his people willingly sacrifice life and limb to see you safely delivered through those lands to the north? Did he not grant you safe passage through territories inhabited by the great and terrible dragons?"

"He helped."

"And before that, did he not come to your aid when the Sorcerer and his army of mimes laid siege to you and your comrades, ambushing you as you journeyed through Dragonite's domain?"

"Are you trying to make me feel guilty?"

"I am desperately trying to appeal to your conscience and sense of goodwill, my lady."

"My conscience warns me to be leery of you, and to be prudent of where I dispense my goodwill, especially where you are concerned."

"Just keep in mind, I am not the one seeking your goodwill, however, I can understand your reluctance," admitted Loken, with a judicious nod of his head. "My past actions leave much to be desired, but in my own defence, my intentions were always honourable, where my beloved Celia is concerned. You know that."

"I suppose."

"So, you will help Lord Silverthorn and his people?"

"That depends," said Rose.

"On what?"

"Just what is this news you bring? And what makes you believe I can be of any help to them, when it is obvious the Elves cannot even help themselves, ergo your presence?"

"Sometimes, it can be cleansing to the soul for one to right a wrong," replied Loken.

"Well then, I recommend that you go stand under a great, rushing waterfall, perhaps the Devil's Tears to the north will do, for you still have a whole lot of soul-cleansing to do."

"I was speaking of you, Princess Rose!"

"Me?" Her eyes flashed a deep amethyst as her annoyance grew. "My soul is plenty clean; sparkling clean to be exact!"

"No disrespect, my lady, but I beg to differ. I am confident your soul is feeling a little tarnished after your dealings with the Dream Merchant."

"That Wizard tricked me! All my woes, and those affected by my efforts to make life better, were his doing!"

"You mean to say, efforts to better *your* life," corrected Loken, with a roll of his eyes.

"That is besides the point!" Rose stamped her feet like a spoiled child. "You have yet to explain any of this and why I should be drawn into the troubles besetting the Elves."

"*Troubles?* It is nothing as trivial as that!" Loken's anxious pacing came to a halt as he spun on his heels to confront this mortal. "The Elves are *dying* as we speak!"

"No! That is not possible," argued Rose, dismissing the Sprite's words with a wave of her hand. "The Elves are long-lived, immortal even by mankind's standards. Those beings do not just die! They can be killed, but it is not as though they just keel over and die of sickness or old age."

"So I thought, but I speak the truth! I have no reason to lie or to embellish about this matter that plagues them now. In fact, where is the young master? Where is Tagius Yairet, and Sir Myron Kendall, too? They both should be privy to this ill news."

"Step lively, gentlemen!" ordered Rose, as she ushered Tag and Myron through the long corridor. "Do keep up."

"I'd be livelier if I knew what you wanted from us," grumbled Tag. He was growing more suspicious, especially after she referred to him as a *gentleman* rather than a rogue or a rapscallion.

"Patience, Tag," urged Myron. "We shall find out soon enough."

"You will, indeed," assured Rose. "We have an unexpected visitor waiting to meet with us."

Pushing open the double doors into the grand meeting hall, even a whisper echoed due to the high, vaulted ceiling. Peering inside, their eyes were met by a heavy oak table that stretched across almost the entire length of this cavernous chamber. Surrounding the table were fifty ornately carved, sturdy oak chairs and a matching armchair at each end of the table. These two special seats were reserved for the King and Queen of Fleetwood, but for now, each chair was vacant and neatly tucked into its place, pushed up against the edge of the table.

There was not a single lit candle, so the gloom was broken at even intervals by the light streaming through the bank of tall, narrow windows lining the west wall of the chamber.

"Get in! This is not the time to be dragging your feet." Rose steered Tag and Myron into the room.

"Why should we be enthusiastic about this when we have no idea what you're up to?" responded Tag.

"Who said I was up to anything?"

Peeking into the corridor to make sure there were no unwanted eyes or ears lurking about, Rose closed the double doors behind them. She rushed over to the windows, pulling the heavy drapes shut so darkness enveloped the room. The seams of light seeping through the crack between the double doors and peeking over the rods of the closed drapes provided the only source of illumination in this otherwise black chamber.

"If you are not up to anything, then why all the secrecy, my lady?" queried Myron, squinting in hopes his eyes would adapt faster to this enforced gloom.

"Because it is necessary, but trust me when I say there is no need to worry."

"Then why do I feel greatly worried?" Tag muttered to Myron, groaning in pain as his knee caught the leg of a chair as he attempted to manoeuvre in the darkness. "Can we get some light in here, even a single candle, Princess?"

"Be patient! I am getting to it."

Cautiously shuffling forward, Rose extended her hands. She groped about, her fingertips grazing several chairs as she made her way around the table. These obstacles repeatedly forced her to adjust her course.

"Why didn't you just leave the doors and drapes open?" asked Tag.

"I told you, we require a level of privacy," grumbled Rose.

"There is no point now in discussing what should or should not have been done. It is no longer relevant," said Myron, pointedly. "So why this urgency and secrecy, my lady? Why did you call for this meeting?"

"I am not the one requesting this meeting. And I take it, you already forgot that I had said we have an unexpected guest?"

"Enough with the games!" snapped Tag. "Who is this guest? And where is she now?"

"The 'she' is a 'he' and he is in this very room, as we speak." Rose's tone was smug.

Simultaneously, Myron and Tag drew their swords. Their anxious eyes searched the darkness for this so-called *guest*.

"No need for hostility!" shouted an agitated voice.

"Who said that?" asked Myron. He glanced about, searching for the source of these disembodied words amplified by the cavernous space.

In response, a white light swelled from beneath the table. This radiant sphere grew brighter as it floated toward the trio. "I come in peace, with no desire to leave in pieces. Away with those swords, if you please!"

"Loken?" called Tag. He squinted as he stared at this bright, hovering orb. "Is that you?"

"Yes, young Master Yairet! And I come with ill news." Loken nodded in approval upon hearing the blades slither back into their respective scabbards.

"Ill news, you say?" said Myron.

"Yes! And thank you for answering my call in an expedient manner. This news must be shared immediately," insisted Loken, eager to get this meeting underway. "Are you certain none will disturb us in here, Princess? For what news I bear can prove treacherous in the hands of the unscrupulous."

"We will not be disturbed," assured Rose. Assuming the seat at the head of the table that was reserved for her father, she motioned to Tag and Myron to sit in the chairs to her immediate left and right. "There are no spies or characters of ill-repute lurking in the halls of Pepperton Palace. Nor is my father expecting delegates or ambassadors from lands far and away from here, so not even the cleaning staff will be expected any time soon."

"Then let our meeting commence," said Loken, alighting upon the table.

"So what brings you to Fleetwood, my friend?" questioned Tag.

"I come on behalf of Lord Rainus Silverthorn."

"Hold on here!" Rose's arms crossed her chest in annoyance and anger as she confronted the Sprite. "You said nothing about coming here on the Elf Lord's *behalf.* You merely said you had some ill news to share on happenings in the Woodland Glade."

"You were too busy denouncing and denying my presence from the start to allow me to fully explain, my lady." Loken's wings rattled with indignation upon being subjected to her haughty tone.

Before she had a chance to dispute these words, Myron raised his right hand, motioning for silence. "With all due respect, my lady, allow Loken to speak freely. Exactly what is this news you bring from Lord Silverthorn?"

Loken bowed in appreciation to the knight. "I digress, my friends. Something terrible has befallen the Elves."

"You claimed they are dying," reminded Rose, with a doubtful roll of her eyes.

"Say again!" gasped Tag. His back stiffened upon hearing these ominous words. "The Elves are under attack?"

"If it were only that simple, young master," responded Loken. "If that was so, the Elves would be able to repel a physical attack, and do so with relative ease, being the skilled warriors that they are."

"Your words are rather troubling. Exactly what are you saying?" Leaning forward to learn more, Myron peered down at Loken.

"I am saying it is something far more insidious than an outright attack! An invisible killer is at large, Sir Kendall!"

"A stealthy assassin that moves in the shadows?" Tag wondered aloud; perplexed by Loken's strange and foreboding words.

"Even a trained assassin would be easier to deal with," answered Loken. He heaved a weary sigh as he continued on, "This invisible killer I speak of has already taken the lives of four Elves when I departed from the Woodland Glade. It will only be a matter of time before more die."

"The manner of death," probed Myron, "just how did these Elves meet their demise?"

"They had fallen to a mysterious sickness!" The Sprite's words were spoken with conviction. "It was most curious... In a matter of days after being stricken with this terrible malady, they wasted away, eventually losing their will to live."

"That makes no sense, Loken," rebuked Rose, dismissing his words. "Even I know the Elves do not fall to sickness and pestilence, as human beings do."

"She is quite correct," agreed Tag. "Their longevity, and their ability to avoid all manner of illnesses, are what separates the race of Elves from us mere mortals."

"This is what makes it so insidious, mysterious and all the more deadly," stated Loken. "Lord Silverthorn cannot make sense of it. Through the ages the Elves have had the power to heal wounds... broken bones... torn flesh and so on. But this... This is something terrible and new."

More so than Princess Rose, Tag and Myron listened intently, eager to hear more.

The tiny being unleashed a troubled sigh as he continued on, "The Elves lack the ability to heal from illness. Throughout their long history in this realm, they had never fallen to sickness, so there was never a need for this ability or knowledge."

"Hence, the inability to treat or concoct medicinal remedies to heal whatever this is," determined Myron. "It is beyond their ken."

Loken nodded in confirmation.

"Strangely enough, for some reason, this explanation made absolute sense to me," confided Rose.

"What are the symptoms?" questioned Tag.

"If I remember correctly, Lord Silverthorn claimed it was the same for the four that had eventually succumbed. First, there was a profound lack of appetite that was accompanied by a severe bout of the chills. This condition gradually changed, manifesting into a great heat that consumed the body and confused the mind, as though the body and brain were cooking from the inside out."

"A raging fever," assessed Myron.

"A terrible and all consuming fever! I can only compare it to a malady that befalls the race of man from time to time," disclosed Loken. "Where the elderly, the young and those already weakened by illness can easily fall victim to the sickness, even dying when the fever is too much, the average person tends to survive."

"But not so with the Elves," surmised Tag.

"Yes! In this case, each Elf to show symptoms eventually perished.

The ravages of this fever proved devastating. To date, all the deaths in the Enchanted Forest can be attributed to this condition. Once the cessation to eat and drink sets in, they are weakened by this loss of appetite, making them all the more vulnerable to the deadly powers of this fever."

"Aside from the four that died, others have been stricken by this same mystery illness?" asked Myron.

"Indeed, Sir Kendall! Whatever it is, this dreadful ailment does not discriminate between men and women or the young and the old. At last count, nine more, including Lady Valara Silverthorn, were showing early symptoms upon my departure from Driven Hill."

"The poor dear!" gasped Rose. She was genuinely surprised by this news.

"Indeed!" Loken nodded.

"Have there been signs of this same illness afflicting human beings living along the outskirts of the Elves' forest?" questioned Myron. "Perhaps it had spread from men living in Axalon to the Elves?"

"My beloved Celia and her troops of Fairies reported that nothing out of the ordinary was noticed on their nightly forays to collect teeth," answered Loken. "The odd sniffle or cough that is common this time of year for the mortals, but nothing that resembles the harbinger of death as it has become for the Elves."

"And Lord Silverthorn, has he taken ill, too?" asked Tag.

"Not yet, but he is stricken with grief; burdened by the weight of this troubling situation that has blackened the very heart of his realm," revealed Loken. "As best as I could tell, he seemed no different, but that can change abruptly."

"And this is why you, rather than Lord Silverthorn, came here seeking our help," determined Myron.

"Yes! He dare not leave his wife's side as she fights against this deadly ailment that has claimed the others so mercilessly."

"Understandably so, Loken," said Tag.

"So what are we expected to do about this?" asked Rose. Her slight shoulders rolled in a shrug.

Loken launched into the air, hovering before her disgruntled face. "Human beings, by design, are frail creatures, easily falling victim to sickness, and yet, your race has proven to be very resourceful. You have found ways to remedy some of what plagues your kind."

"And insulting us by pointing out how *frail* we are is supposed to accomplish what?" grumbled Rose. "For I am hardly inspired to lend aid, if that is what you seek from me."

"Lord Silverthorn, not Loken, is seeking *our* help," reminded

Myron. "I cannot speak for the others, but I owe Rainus Silverthorn and his people my very life. I am indebted to them. Lady Silverthorn stood watch over me as I healed from the terrible wounds inflicted by the Sorcerer. She never gave up hope that I would recover from my injuries, therefore, I will do whatever I can to help them, for it is the right and proper thing to do."

"But what makes you believe we can even help the Elves?" questioned Rose.

"It stands to reason that if the Elves never had cause to develop medicinal remedies as we have, they would not know of the plants with the healing properties that can help to alleviate even something as simple as the ordinary cold, never mind finding relief from something worse that brings on fever or inflammation of joints and muscles," replied Myron.

"I know it is not as bold or daring as engaging in open warfare against armed adversaries, but this enemy is very real to the Elves," stated Loken. "If you possess the means, a medicinal tincture perhaps, in your apothecaries that can help to alleviate this fever, thereby perhaps circumventing death, then you must go to Lord Silverthorn. Deliver this possible cure, and do so immediately!"

"I believe we have a medicine that can possibly help to ease their suffering," said Myron.

"Yes, one derived from the bark of the willow," added Tag.

"That is all well and good," commented Rose, "but there is nothing to say this medicine will work on an Elf."

"Well, we won't know until we try," responded Tag.

"Yes, it is better to do something, even if we fail, than to do nothing at all," said Myron.

"Good intentions are fine and dandy, but wasting time and energy on a lost cause is just plain foolish," argued Rose.

"I agree with Myron," countered Tag. "You speak in haste to call it a lost cause. We cannot idly stand by, doing nothing when we hold the possible remedy to what is killing them."

"Then I shall wish you both well on this mission," offered Rose, waving farewell to her two friends.

"Surely you feel some responsibility in all of this, my lady?" With an unyielding stare that seemed to pierce straight through her heart, Loken scrutinized this mortal.

"Why would I? And why should we even believe in the words of a Pooka?" queried Rose.

"A *Sprite*, a shape-shifting one," corrected Loken. "There is something so derogatory about being called a Pooka, especially when it is being said by you."

"So you say, but you have yet to explain why I should feel any responsibility in this sorry state of affairs to beset those in the Enchanted Forest."

"Because rumours abound that this illness to afflict Lord Silverthorn's people is due to you, Princess Rose," informed Loken.

"Me?" Rose gasped, appalled by this accusation. "Rumours, indeed! I have not set foot in that forest since I was tricked into accepting the magic crystal."

"Master Agincor did not deceive you, Princess. You were the one to engage the Dream Merchant, striking up that little deal that went so totally wrong," reminded Tag.

"Aha! Then Pancecelia Feldspar is the guilty one," decided Rose, as she pointed an accusing finger at Loken, for he was guilty by association. "The Queen of the Tooth Fairies, your ladylove, tricked me! She was the one to tell me about Silas Agincor in the first place."

Loken looked aghast, dismayed by these damning words.

"True, Queen Pancecelia did tell you about the Dream Merchant. Alas, you were the one to act upon your whim, Princess," reminded Tag. "No one forced you to strike up a deal with the Wizard, a deal that continues to hold sway over your parents and resulted in a cavalcade of disasters along the way to reclaim the cursed crystal that was entrusted to you."

"Hold on here! Allow me to be the voice of reason." Rose spoke with all seriousness.

"You?" Tag's tone was incredulous as he chortled, "I think not!"

Rose raised her hands in surrender, motioning for silence from all as the evidence presented thus far placed the responsibility squarely on her shoulders. "I highly recommend that rather than assigning blame, our time is better spent coming to Lord Silverthorn's aid."

"What do you know?" Loken's eyes opened wide in dismay. "She actually does sound reasonable!"

"What she suggests is the most prudent thing to do, but tell us, Loken, for I must know; just how is Princess Rose being implicated in this strange turn of events?" queried Tag.

"As I said, it is only a rumour, but by all accounts, it seems grounded in truth."

"Go on, then," urged Myron. "Tell us more."

"In my defence," interjected Rose, her words indignant as she spoke, "rumours, whether grounded in truth or not, are still rumours until proven otherwise."

"Fair enough," agreed Tag, as he motioned for her to calm down.

"Now, go on, Loken. Tell us what you've heard."

The Sprite drew a deep breath, gathering his thoughts before sharing in the details he had discovered prior to his departure from the Enchanted Forest.

"Never in the long and illustrious history of the Elfkind had a catastrophe of this nature plagued these people. Sickness is unheard of, but since the Sorcerer, Parru St. Mime Dragonite, had vanished during the last ill-fated mission that almost got us killed, our realm has been strangely quiet."

"But quiet is good," stated Rose. "I like quiet."

"In most cases, yes, it is a good thing." Loken nodded in agreement. "However, this was like the calm before a cataclysmic storm. From out of nowhere, the Elves began to fall ill. A dark energy seems to emanate from their forest."

"What dark energy?" Tag frowned upon hearing this news.

"Hey… You said nothing about an energy, dark or otherwise," reminded Rose.

"At the risk of repeating myself, I felt it was prudent to wait until all concerned parties had gathered before sharing in the details, lest I be accused of chewing off your royal ears needlessly, my lady," explained Loken.

Myron pressed a finger to his lips, gesturing for silence from the Princess as he nodded at Loken, urging him to continue. "So, you say the trees are dying?"

"The trees are alive, but they are not *living* as they were before." In demonstration, Loken's tiny arms waved about like the vine-like branches of a willow caught in a windstorm.

The trio of friends frowned upon hearing this disturbing news.

"Now *this*, I do not understand," admitted Rose, as she stared at the Sprite's performance.

"Loken, are you saying the trees are very much alive, but just not as *animated* as they once were?" questioned Myron, thinking back on how Tag was accosted by a great willow tree after he had urinated against its trunk.

"Yes, but it is more than that!"

"As far as I am concerned, those trees were much too animated to begin with," sniffed Rose. "Not only did a willow tree attack us with fervour, hoisting us dangerously high into its crown, it deliberately oozed sticky sap all over us. It was nothing short of disgusting!"

"That old willow did so for good reason, thanks to my ignorance at the time," reminded Tag. "But allow Loken to continue."

"Thank you, Master Yairet."

"Please, just call me Tag."

"As you wish." Loken nodded to the young man. "As I was saying, Tag, not only have the trees grown quiet, the leaves are falling."

"Is it not that time of the year?" probed Rose. "With the golding of the leaves throughout the realm, they do tend to fall with the coming of autumn."

"True, but we have yet to experience the first frost of the season, my lady. And even so, how do we account for the evergreens? Many of the fir and pine trees in and around the Elf community of Driven Hill are dropping their needles as though they, too, are gripped by an illness that not even the healing powers of the Elves and the natural energy surging through that forest can remedy."

"Perhaps the well-being of the forest is tied directly to that of the Elves?" offered Tag. "If their welfare is in jeopardy, it is being reflected in the very place they have resided in for an eon."

"It makes sense. If one's hand becomes infected from a wound, then eventually, it can poison the entire body," reasoned Myron. "It would stand to reason, for the Elves are one with nature."

"Thank you for that disgusting analogy, but it still does not explain why rumours abound that *I* am to blame for any this," said Rose.

"I was getting to that, my lady," responded Loken. "As I said, it was like the calm before a great storm. There is mounting fear that the Sorcerer was not killed. Instead, that madman was merely grievously injured by Tag's sword. This lull in activity on his part could have been due to Dragonite's need to convalesce from the wounds inflicted upon him."

Myron's brows arched up in surprise as he pondered this possibility.

"Aha!" Rose's hand slapped her thigh in glee. "So the demented, mime-loving Sorcerer is to blame for this, not me!"

"I beg to differ, Princess. It stands to reason that the Sorcerer would not be hell-bent on revenge had he not been drawn to the Dreamstone to begin with," reminded Myron. "Dragonite would have likely given you a wide berth, if not totally ignored you, had he not known you were venturing into his domain with the magic crystal in your possession."

"Then you, Loken, are the one to blame for this malady inflicting the Elves!" Rose pointed an accusing finger at the Sprite.

"Say again!" gasped Loken.

"This is entirely your fault, you little mischief-maker!" declared Rose.

In a brilliant flash of light, Loken morphed in accordance to his mood. Rose shrieked in fright as the Sprite transmogrified into a huge, ebony serpent. Before she could flee the room, Loken's tail whipped around her ankles. His scaly body slithered, coiling around her to prevent Rose from escaping. Constricting her frantic movements, he hissed in resentment.

Instead of apologizing, Rose's fear erupted into anger as she defied Loken, struggling against his reptilian form.

"You heard me, you troublemaker! If you had not eavesdropped on us in the first place when we were in Lord Silverthorn's company to report to Dragonite that I was in possession of the Dreamstone, then none of this would have happened!"

"None of this would have happened if *you* had not struck up a deal from the start with the Dream Merchant," countered Loken. His sinewy muscles contracted, squeezing around Rose as she foolishly stoked his growing ire with her desperate accusations.

"Loken does have a good point," said Tag, as he motioned for the Sprite to return to his usual form, "however, acting in anger will solve nothing. For now, allow cooler heads to prevail."

Hissing loudly, his scales rattled in resentment. In a flash of light, Loken morphed. Hovering before Rose, his wings quivered with annoyance.

Rose shook an angry fist at Loken before shooting a blistering stare in Tag's direction.

"This is a bunch of malarkey! You are supposed to be my closest friend!" Turning on Tag, Rose jabbed an index finger against his chest. "Whatever happened to being on my side?"

"As your closest friend, I *am* on your side! I just mean to keep you humble *and* honest in doing so. I would be doing you a grave disservice if I failed to make you see reason by feeding your delusion that you had no hand in any of this."

"Humble? I am a princess! I should not even know what that word means! As for being honest, *Honesty* should have been my middle name!"

"If you mean to be a just and fair ruler, then being humble has a proper place in your life."

"With friends like you, Tag, who needs enemies," grumbled Rose. "At this moment, I would prefer to gouge out my eyes with a rusty spoon than to hear you lecture me."

"Now, now! I believe you are exaggerating, my lady," commented Myron, casually dismissing her words.

"Oh, lovely! Not only am I accused of not being humble, but now I am exaggerating, too? Well, I think not! Were I not already so humble, I do not exaggerate when I say that any other princess would see fit to have you two thrown into a smelly dungeon for speaking as you do now!"

"Stop it with your little tirade. You know I speak the truth," rebuked

Tag. "All I am saying is that you should take some responsibility for your actions."

"As should you, you rapscallion of a knave!" snipped Rose, turning her nose up at her lifelong friend.

"Of course I do!"

"Well, if that is so, then why have you not acknowledged your share of responsibility in this whole little nightmare come true?" The toe of Rose's sandal tapped impatiently on the floor as she glared at Tag.

"What are you speaking of, Princess Rose?" questioned Myron. "You know, as well as I do, this young sir has always been accountable for his words and actions."

"Two peas in pod! That is what you two ruffians are!" snapped Rose, as she shook an admonishing finger at the knight and his partner in crime. "I might have been the one to initiate the first quest, but Tag was the one who failed to see the last quest to its proper end! If you, Sir Kendall, had stopped for a moment to consider Tag's actions, you know he is just as responsible for what is happening in the Enchanted Forest as I am, if I am even to be blamed for any of this."

"Your words truly confound me, my lady," sighed Myron, shaking his head in confusion.

"No more so than yours, in general, serves to baffle me, sir! Even in the state you are in now, as a gallant knight than a fool of an idiot, you still continue to confound and baffle me," rebuked Rose. "Perhaps even more so these days than ever before!"

Tag raised his hands, motioning for Rose and Myron to stop this bickering. "She is right... I am to blame."

"I am?" Her eyes narrowed as she stared suspiciously at Tag. "You are?"

"Yes, Princess! If I had only taken appropriate measures to ensure the Sorcerer was truly dead before he disappeared, perhaps none of this would be happening now. If there is a chance that Dragonite had survived, it would make sense he would exact his revenge when he was ready to do so."

"I was there, Tag! You had run your sword clean through that necromancer. What more could you have done?" Myron spoke with utmost conviction. "We all believed that madman had met his demise when he vanished with the magic crystal in his clutches."

"I suppose it was wishful thinking on my part in wanting to believe the Sorcerer had been destroyed," admitted Rose. "I believed the dark magic he would unleash when he roamed the lands with his army of mimes having come to a stop was a good omen. Perhaps it is as Loken says, it is merely the proverbial calm before the storm."

"It was natural for all to assume Dragonite had met his end during our last confrontation," concluded Myron.

"And now, it could well be that we had all assumed wrong," added Tag, with a disheartened sigh.

"So you, too, believe Dragonite has returned, employing the powers of the Dreamstone to unleash his dark magic on the Elves?" questioned Loken.

"What else can it be?" responded Tag. "Dragonite was hardly the type to spread good cheer. Dispensing a good dose of the forbidden arts is more in line with what that madman would do."

"But why Lord Silverthorn and his people, if the Sorcerer means to exact revenge on me, I mean, us?" questioned Rose, eager to share the blame.

"Perhaps he lashes out at the Elves for coming to your aid," suggested Loken.

"That cannot be a good thing," said Tag. "If this is true, it will only be a matter of time before he attacks the Dwarves and Trolls; perhaps even you and Pancecelia Feldspar for helping us, too."

Loken's wings thrummed loudly at the thought of this. "My dear Celia… I left her to deliver this message. She may be in grave danger as we speak! The entire Fairy's Vale may be in jeopardy!"

"Remain calm, my friend. Before we jump to any conclusion or consider the worst, we should conduct a thorough investigation," recommended Myron.

"We?" repeated Rose. Her perfect brows furrowed in confusion. "What do you mean, *we* investigate?"

"Of course, we," stated Tag, pointing at her, and then Myron before jabbing a thumb against his chest, "as in the three of us."

"Can you not conduct this investigation without me? Just do so on my behalf?" asked Rose.

"Are you serious, my lady?" Myron stared with raised eyebrows at her.

"You heard me. And when you are done, you can both report back to me when you know what is what, and what can be done, if anything, to rectify the matter."

"Believe me, I am confident we would cover more ground and accomplish this task much faster and with far less hassle without you tagging along and complaining the whole way," answered Tag.

"There you go then!" said Rose.

"But if all these ill omens are due to that Dreamstone, then you are the only one with the power to reclaim the crystal, returning it to its rightful owner to put an end to this calamity," added Tag.

Rose's shoulders drooped upon hearing this.

"Tag is quite correct, my lady," stated Myron "If indeed Dragonite has returned and the dark magic is a manifestation of the Dreamstone, we shall need you by our side."

"Another mission?" muttered Rose.

"A very necessary one, Princess," assured Tag. "But if there is a chance the Sorcerer is not behind this horrific event, then consider this a goodwill mission on your part."

"How so?"

"If the medicines you deliver from your royal apothecary prove beneficial to our Elf friends, you shall long be hailed a hero to Lord Silverthorn and his people," answered Tag. "Undoubtedly, minstrels will compose great ballads about you to regale the people, far and wide, to last through memory and time."

"You think?" Her eyes sparkled at the mere thought of being immortalized in such grand fashion.

"Trust me when we say your compassion will become legendary," added Myron.

"A little adulation suits me just fine!" Rose nodded in approval. "And who knows? Perhaps this will have nothing at all to do with me or the Dreamstone."

"Let's hope," agreed Tag.

"So, you are willing to come to the aid of the Elves?" asked Loken.

"It would be a sin not to," answered Tag.

"Very good!" Loken flew to the open window, eager to be on the move. "Time is of the essence!"

"We leave immediately," announced Myron. "But first, we will gather what we need, medicine included, and then we shall be on our way once I ready our mounts."

"Immediately?" Rose's shoulders drooped even more, as though an invisible, but heavy burden had been hoisted upon her. "I need time to properly prepare for such an expedition."

"There is no time to lose, Princess. Gather only what is necessary. You do not need to bring your entire wardrobe, so it shouldn't take you long to get ready," said Tag.

"And just what will you be doing while I get myself sorted out?" questioned Rose.

"I shall pay a little visit to Evelyn," informed Tag.

"Truly?" The roll of her eyes was followed by a loud snort of derision. "Must you see her in person? Can you not just leave that girl a farewell note?"

"I was going to ask her to pack some provisions for us; food and drink to sustain us on this mission," stated Tag. "But now that you mention it, I should do the gentlemanly thing; bid the fair lady a fond farewell, and do so in person."

"Oh, huzzah!" grunted Rose, waving him off. "Just do not make her sick with all your sappy, sentimental nonsense before she has had a chance to prepare our food."

They watched as Rose concluded this order with a juvenile display. She thrust an index finger into her throat, pretending to gag in response.

"Are you jealous?" teased Tag. A satisfied grin creased his face as he scrutinized her agitated scowl of disapproval.

"Are you an arrogant idiot?" snipped Rose.

"Just making an observation."

"Well, allow me to do you a favour by plucking out your eyes, for they observed wrong! And come to think of it, I will be needing my handmaiden to help me prepare for this little jaunt we are about to embark on."

"What are you talking about now?" Tag groaned.

"You heard me! Send what's-her-name to my bedchamber, immediately! She was quite proficient at readying me the last time, surely she can be just as proficient and expedient the second time around."

"And just who will prepare our food, if not Evelyn?" questioned Tag, his face glowing red with mounting annoyance.

"Make yourself useful and do it yourself. But then again, we shall all run the risk of falling ill, so never mind."

"Then whom do you propose I assign to this task?"

"Mildred will do."

"And if she is too busy?" asked Tag.

"She is never too busy where I am concerned, but that other woman; the tall, skinny one, will do. You know whom I speak of."

"What is wrong with you?" grunted Tag, shaking his head in disgust. He was absolutely frustrated, just knowing that Rose did indeed know her servants' names, but chose to play the *I'm-not-forgetful, I'm-just-too-busy-to-remember* hand than to address them properly.

Myron intervened. Sensing tempers were about to flare once more he stepped in between them. The knight gently steered Rose toward the double doors, opening them to send the Princess on her way.

"Time is a precious commodity we cannot waste, my dear friends. While you pack and Tag sees to our provisions, I shall gather our weapons and horses. We shall meet in the courtyard," instructed Myron. He then waved Tag on his way with one hand as the other motioned to their guest. Flexing his index finger, he invited the Sprite to follow him. "Come with me, Loken. We shall talk more on this matter while I make preparations."

Loken alighted upon Myron's right shoulder. Holding on to the edge of the collared tunic the knight wore, the Sprite leaned to and fro as a counterbalance to the knight's gait as he quickly marched away with deliberate strides.

In a disgruntled huff, Rose stomped off. Believing that taking a parting glance would only be misconstrued for her caring, she resisted the urge to peek over her shoulder to watch Tag's departure, and if indeed he was on his way to pay Evelyn a visit. Her angry steps resounded through the main hall as she marched right by the library.

Rose came to a sudden stop.

Taking two steps back, she turned on her heels. She stood before the open doors to this sanctuary lined by tall shelves filled with leather-bound books of all descriptions. With balled fists quivering in resentment, her foul demeanour barely garnered a curious glance from her parents when she stormed by. And even now, as she stood fuming before them at the entranceway, it did nothing to solicit even passing interest from her mother and father.

Before Rose had foolishly dealt away the love of her parents in exchange for the Dreamstone that promised to grant her all the things she ever desired, such a display on her part would draw far more attention than she ever wanted.

Between a doting, overindulgent father and her loving, but controlling, overprotective mother, both her parents claimed to be doing their part in a bid to tailor her into a right and proper princess, one truly worthy of ruling the great kingdom of Fleetwood.

It was attention Rose despised, until now...

She learned from a young age exactly how to manipulate her father in order to undermine her mother's efforts to discipline her. But Rose found out too late all this controlling, fussing and grooming was their way of showing their love. They cared enough about her to enforce rules and assign responsibilities to shape her into the best possible person she can be.

And how things had changed once she got what she wished for. The hardships she endured, no thanks to Pancecelia Feldspar were compounded by her dealings with the Wizard, Silas Agincor.

Rose grunted in utter annoyance, muttering beneath her breath, "Dream Merchant indeed! That cunning Wizard was more a purveyor of nightmares than dreams."

Not only did the transaction with Pancecelia thoroughly test her mettle, her dealings with the so-called Dream Merchant made an already bad situation worse. Her mother and father failed to recognize their own daughter at the start of this misadventure thanks to the

Queen of the Tooth Fairies, but because of her foolish dealings with this particular Wizard, she was now deprived of parental love, too. This particular curse remained and would continue until she was able to return the magic crystal back to Silas Agincor.

The only consolation on embarking on the initial quest was that in the end, she was able to break the curse invoked by Pancecelia Feldspar.

When Rose finally found her heart, in this case, her sense of compassion and came to understand how her self-indulgent, self-absorbed sense of entitlement shaped how others viewed her, it was the first step to undoing Pancecelia's curse.

It was enough to allow her parents to recognize her once more as their daughter upon her return to Fleetwood, than the hag they had initially driven out, but the attention she garnered was nothing short of neglect. Rose's attempts to break the Wizard's curse failed once again when the wounded Sorcerer vanished with her Dreamstone in his clutches during their last ill-fated quest.

Without the magic crystal in her possession the King and Queen merely acknowledged her as their daughter and their only heir to the throne, but that was the extent of it. It was just enough to prevent them from driving Rose out of her rightful home, but nothing was the same from that day forward.

Absent was the love she now craved. Instead, this love and devotion was replaced by minimal, familial concern. It went only as far as accommodating her so this public display of parental care would not be questioned by their peers. As far as they were concerned it was more important in the big scheme of things to maintain the wealth and power that comes along with the family name and royal title.

Rose's failed attempts to return the Dreamstone to Silas Agincor merely tempered their lack of love to justifiable indifference. And it was this apathy that now drove the Princess mad, pushing her into a state of despair.

She stood at the open doorway to the library.

Rose's presence was not menacing, but she did brood like a dark storm cloud threatening to obliterate the sun and its light that brightened her parents' day. With indignation, her arms folded across her chest as she glared at them, waiting for some kind of reaction or invitation to come forth and speak her mind.

Instead, her mother, Queen Beatrice continued with her embroidery while her father, King William did not even peer up from the periodical he was reading as he caught up on the latest news as well as the contestants' standings at a jousting tournament hosted by a neighbouring county.

It was only when Rose cleared her throat with a very loud and unladylike *harrumph* did she finally manage to solicit their attention.

"Yes, my daughter? What is it now?" Beatrice barely managed to pull her eyes away from her embroidery hoop as William merely grunted his acknowledgement that she was indeed standing there. But even at that, the King continued to read, holding up the large sheet of parchment even higher to block out the sight of his irate daughter as she stewed in the juices of growing resentment and frustration.

Rose marched right up to the table where her parents were seated. Rather than her usual dainty steps, her loud stomping served to punctuate her mounting annoyance.

Having enjoyed their morning tea and biscuits in the solitude of the grand library, her parents quickly slipped back into their uncaring demeanour. They hoped they would not be subjected to Rose's whining or latest complaints.

With a loud thump, her clenched fist smacked down on the table to send the tea service rattling. Rose snapped, "I will not be ignored!"

In reluctant response, her parents simultaneously wheezed out a sigh of resignation, for it was obvious their daughter was not going to leave them be until she got what she came for.

Queen Beatrice lowered the embroidery hoop as her husband peeked over the publication he was perusing.

"Your mother did say, *'what is it'*," reminded William. "What do you wish to complain about now?"

"Who said I was going to complain?" grumbled Rose. Her eyes narrowed in resentment as she endured his scathing tone.

"It is what you do best, my dear," reminded her mother. "So what is it? Spit it out. Do so now, so we can get back to our work."

"Back to work? You are embroidering while Father is reading that daily rag of arguably honest and rather trivial news."

"I beg to differ," countered William. "I am keeping in touch with the common man and what is making news beyond the walls of this palatial setting you are lucky to call home."

"So you say!"

"What brings you here?" questioned Beatrice.

"Brings *me* here? I live here!"

"I mean to say, what brings you here to disturb us in the solitude of this library."

"Oh…" Rose's feet shuffled about nervously. "I wanted to let you and Father know that I am being called upon to undertake another deadly quest, far from the safety of Fleetwood."

"Brilliant!" praised Beatrice.

William folded the parchment he was reading, placing it on the table as he addressed her. "Well, good on you, Rose-alyn! Another opportunity to build your character and to see what this great, big world has to offer."

"What?" gasped Rose. "Did you not hear me? I said, *deadly* quest, not a leisurely afternoon romp in the countryside. Truth be told, I can die this time."

The Queen's face flushed red. Her nose crinkled as she giggled in response. "You exaggerate, Rose. You will only die if you are not careful. Are you saying that you will *not* be careful this time?"

"Of course I plan to be careful, but accidents do happen."

"Then you must take extra care," advised William, his words matter-of-fact.

"But an accident is called an accident for good reason."

"So you say, Rose, but if you travel in fear of an accident occurring, why not take along your friend, Tagius Yairet?" suggested her mother. "I am confident the young man has no qualms about keeping you safe. I understand he has become quite handy with the sword."

"And Sir Myron Kendall, too," offered up her father.

"That's it? You will appoint only two for this task?"

"It would not be prudent of me to assign an entire battalion of knights and soldiers, forcing them to abandon their posts here so you may gallivant about. In my opinion, Sir Kendall seems quite capable now. Take him along with you. Put that knight to good use!"

"But – "

"But nothing," assured William, with a wave of his hand to dismiss her. "It is the least we can do."

"Yes… it is," agreed Rose. She unleashed another dreary sigh.

"Very good then," said Beatrice, as she waved her daughter off. "Farewell, my dear!"

"Is that all you can say?" questioned Rose, her heart sinking with this blatant show of indifference.

"Oh, yes! And do be careful," added her father. With a loud snap, he unfurled the sheets of heavy parchment as he resumed reading.

"And do not forget, Rose," said her mother, "as you failed to return on your sixteen birthday celebration with a prospective groom and you declined our offer of matchmaking, should you *not* die during this quest, then you should get busy."

"Busy? How so?"

"Somewhere along your travels it will serve you well to find a suitable candidate for betrothal before you age further, becoming an undesirable spinster."

Rose's mouth drooped open, absolutely gobsmacked by her mother's suggestion.

Her father peered over the periodical to add, "And make sure he comes with a worthy title, a suitable pedigree and wealth comparable to ours, for there is no point in marrying below your station in life. It shall only defeat the purpose of being a princess by adding to our burden rather than increasing our wealth and power."

Without their peers or servants present to observe and gossip about this exchange, there was no need for diplomacy or for them to put on an appropriate show of propriety. Instead of embracing their daughter in a fond farewell or pleading her to stay for her own safety, King William resumed reading while his wife continued with her fine stitch work.

Rose felt her lower lip quivering in a sad pout. Where before it would melt her father's heart, enough to absolve her of whatever punishment her mother felt appropriate for the occasion, she knew the curse was still at work. Though her sadness was genuine, in their present state, her parents would remain unmoved, even annoyed, by this pathetic display.

With a sigh of resignation that failed to garner a second glance, Rose turned away, abandoning her parents to matters of greater concern. Her heart was now as heavy as her sullen mood, but she knew it would hold no sway over their cursed disposition.

She trudged up the grand staircase toward her bedchamber. This latest interaction only served to steel her resolve to complete this mission, thereby undoing the Dream Merchant's curse once and for all. If she can help the Elves, and at the same time, possibly reclaim the Dreamstone to break the foul magic holding power over her parents, then the end results will be positive all the way around.

With determined steps, she marched back to her bedchamber. Rose imagined how things were sure to be once this curse was lifted. She will no longer have free run of the palace, nor will she be able to freely come and go. Her parents will undoubtedly reintroduce curfews and enforce protocols, having certain expectations she was to meet and exceed. She'd also be weaned from her propensity of eating dessert first, before consuming the main course and starting her morning meals with those dreadful prunes she so hated, but her mother deemed a healthy part of every person's dietary regimen.

It promised to be a great sacrifice, but a worthy one indeed, once she is able to bask in her parents' love and adoration, than to wallow in their growing contempt and apathy.

Heading down the gloomy hallway, as Rose neared her room a seam of light caught her eyes. The door to her bedchamber was cracked open, left ajar by an unknown intruder.

Pressing an ear to the door, Rose listened. Inside, she can hear someone rummaging about. This was followed by the sounds of light footsteps crossing the room, and then the squeak of hinges as the doors to her wardrobe cracked open.

Knowing the domestic staff had become as indifferent to her as her parents were, none would come running if she summoned them. And if they did, they'd likely arrive well after calamity struck. Rose drew a deep breath, mustering her courage. She knew it was in her best interest to act and she'd have no choice but to act on her own, and quickly, if she meant to catch this culprit.

'I will not be taken by surprise this time,' thought Rose.

Removing the sling she had discreetly tucked into the sash of her dress upon Loken's unexpected arrival, Rose hastily plucked a steel ball from the suede pouch that dangled at her side. Though she failed to reclaim the Dreamstone during the last quest, she had still managed to salvage her weapon and this bag of stainless steel balls from the Sorcerer's lair upon their departure.

Pressing her hand lightly against the pouch, she felt the missing ball being magically replaced by another to keep her armed with a never-ending supply of ammunition. It was just another sign the Dream Merchant's powers were still at work and as potent as ever.

Rose listened.

A high-pitched *'creeeak'* sounded from inside as the double doors to her wardrobe were pulled wide open. Someone was definitely snooping around and she was not about to stand for this brazen act of invasion on her privacy!

Resting the steel ball in the cradle of the sling, Rose was now ready to mount an assault. Peering inside, the culprit that dared to trespass into her room had mysteriously vanished. Glancing about, she spied upon several drawers that remained open, including the one on her nightstand next to the bed.

With hushed steps, Rose crept into the bedchamber. Her breath hitched in the back of her throat when the dresses hanging in her wardrobe stirred. The villain was deep inside, searching about for something of grave importance.

With a twist of her wrist, she set her weapon into motion. The sling whirred, spinning ever faster as she prepared to launch an assault.

Rose's eyes opened wide in horror as a great shadow emerged between the racks of clothing. In the parting wake of her colourful gowns, she spied upon a tall, headless figure enveloped in a dark cloak moving fast toward her!

3
Monster!

With a flick of her wrist she set the steel ball flying.

"Take that!" Rose shouted in defiance.

"OUCH!" A voice cried out from the shadows. "Bloody hell!"

The cloak that loomed ever closer suddenly collapsed to the floor as though the body it enveloped had magically vanished upon impact.

Rose set another steel ball in the cradle of her sling as she issued a warning, "The next one will go through your heart, if you dare try to attack me!"

"What is the meaning of this, my lady?" The cloak Evelyn was holding up high before her had dropped from her grasp when the small projectile, slowed by the barrier created by this wool garment, hit its mark. "I have no desire to attack you!"

"Oh… it is only you." Rose issued a sigh of relief as she lowered her weapon.

"Who were you expecting?" asked Evelyn.

The handmaiden was quick to mute her anger, hiding her displeasure at being the victim of this assault. Picking up the cloak from where it fell, she watched as the steel ball fell from the folds of the fabric. It rolled back toward Rose, passing her by to disappear under the dust ruffle of her large canopy bed.

"Truth be told, I had no idea. All I saw was a great, cloaked and headless figure coming at me."

"A *headless* figure?" Evelyn frowned in bewilderment on hearing this description.

"In the dark of the wardrobe, and the way you were holding the cloak up before you, that was exactly what you looked like! Some strange, decapitated fiend lurking in the shadows."

"I was just trying to keep the cloak from dragging on the floor," responded Evelyn, holding it up for her to see.

"That explains that, but it does not explain why you are nosing about in my bedchamber."

"No disrespect, Princess Rose… but are you daft? You were the one to summon me! Remember?" Evelyn folded the cloak before placing it on the bed, next to a pair of leather riding trousers.

"I did?"

"According to Master Yairet, he said you required my immediate assistance in preparing for this trek."

"Oh, yes… I did say that." Rose nodded as she tucked away the sling for safekeeping.

"I was merely searching your wardrobe for season appropriate outerwear when you decided to accost me."

"You could have warned me."

"Warn you? I did not even hear you sneaking into this room!"

"I beg to differ! A princess does not sneak. We glide. And even if I was, I have no need to *'sneak'* into my own room!"

"Fair enough, but when I arrived, you were not even here. I was told the three of you plan to leave immediately. I took it upon myself to get you ready for this journey, as you had requested. In your absence, I proceeded to prepare this bag for you. It contains all you will need."

Because Evelyn already knew Princess Rose would not take well to carrying a pack on her back, she prepared a special bag for this occasion. Lifting it from the floor onto the bed, Rose could see that it was designed to drape over the horse's back. The two compartments, when properly packed and evenly weighted, were meant to hang comfortably on her mount.

"Excellent! Thank you." For once, these words of praise and gratitude were not coerced from her. "But what are Tag's trousers doing here? Is it his farewell gift to you?"

Evelyn's brows furrowed in confusion. "What are you talking about, my lady?"

"Those trousers… surely they are not meant for me to don?" Rose cringed at the thought of wearing man-clothes.

"Absolutely. The chill of autumn is fast settling upon the lands. It will hardly be ideal weather for wearing dresses of any kind."

"Drat!" cursed Rose. If she were made to ride a horse in public than to be a passenger inside a stylish carriage, she had hoped to do so looking as fashionable as possible. "So I am to dress like a boy?"

"You are to dress *appropriately* for the weather and this mission. I knew you would refuse to wear wool, even though wool trousers promise to keep you warmer, but these are made of the most supple leather and lined with the finest linen," explained Evelyn, her hand running over the smooth fabric. "It will not rub and scratch against your skin as wool can and this supple, oiled leather should help to keep you dry and protect you from the cold should the rains and winds blow in from the north."

"Can I not wear them under a dress?" questioned Rose, holding the trousers up against her body.

"Of course not," giggled Evelyn. "But this simple shirt should top off these trousers nicely. As we are about the same size, it should fit you just fine."

"Hand-me-downs?" gasped Rose. She was mortified. Never before had she been made to wear second-hand apparel – *EVER!* "You expect me to wear *your* old clothes?"

"They are not *hand-me-downs*, I am only lending them to you. And they are not that old." Evelyn maintained her composure even though she had been insulted, even after she generously offered the finest pieces of her meagre wardrobe. She held up the linen shirt for Rose's consideration.

"You want *me* to wear *that?*" Rose frowned as she considered her handmaiden's lack of sensibility when it came to fashion.

"It should fit." Evelyn pointed to the other pieces she had arranged on the bed. "Worn with this vest and this oiled leather coat with the split back for the ease of riding, you shall be sufficiently warm for this quest. And should you venture farther north beyond the Elves' domain, this fine, wool cloak shall provide you with additional warmth, should you need it."

Rose drew a deep breath.

Her former self would have thought nothing of giving this girl a verbal lashing for speaking so freely to her. Instead, Rose nodded. "You are absolutely right. It makes good sense to dress appropriately, but I am not one to sacrifice fashion for comfort."

"So you will not wear what I had set out for you?" queried Evelyn. Her cheeks burned with embarrassment, thinking that her personal apparel was not good enough for a princess. "If so, I do not believe the royal seamstress can make anything worthy of your refined tastes in such short order, my lady."

Rose raised her hands, motioning for calm. "I will gladly wear all you have provided. All I am saying is that comfort and fashion are not such strange bedfellows. I shall don these clothes, but there is no reason I cannot make a fine fashion statement in the process."

Evelyn's delicate brows furrowed with curiosity. "What do you have in mind, Princess Rose? I hardly think a diamond tiara will be appropriate for the occasion, lest you mean to draw the attention of every bandit wishing to rob you during your travels."

"You will see. In the meantime, you have my permission to deliver this pack to the courtyard once you are done filling it. Tell Tag and Sir Kendall that I shall join them shortly, once I am good and ready to grace them with my presence."

"But I thought you were in a rush," said Evelyn. She thrust two pairs of thick wool socks into the pack before Rose could complain about them, demanding silk stockings in their place.

"They are the ones in a rush, but most men fail to understand that you cannot rush beauty," responded Rose, as she opened up her jewellery box to peek inside.

The tinkling jangle of the boots and belt buckles sounding from the stairs of the palace caused Tag, Myron and Loken to glance up simultaneously.

Upon meeting their eyes, Rose stopped, waiting for all to admire her fashion-conscious apparel as she struck a pose. Her Elven longbow in one hand and the quiver of arrows in the other added to the dramatic look of her new ensemble.

Not only was she adequately armed to handle potential perils, now, with the proper accents in the way of tasteful accessories she was truly dressed to kill.

Myron pushed Tag's drooping jaw shut, lightly slapping the young man's cheek to break the trance that held him in its grip.

"I see my fine sense of style, even when I am forced to dress down for this occasion, is too much for you to handle," mused Rose. She took certain pleasure in her friend's bout of profound silence as Tag gawked at her in slack-jawed wonder.

"It was not that, Princess," countered Tag, when he was finally able to find the words to speak. "In all the many years I've known you, I have never seen you in anything other than a dress or formal evening wear."

"So even now, in this humble attire, you are astounded that I am still quite fetching," surmised Rose, spinning about for Tag to admire. The sunlight glinted against the white gold necklace studded with brilliant cut diamonds that matched the earrings she wore. "I think I look quite sassy in a fashionable way, and yet, dangerous at the same time!"

"I said nothing of the sort," protested Tag. Still, he continued to stare at the silhouette of the fine leather pants hugging the curves of her hips and the high riding boots that fit to show off her shapely calves. "I was just a little… surprised."

"And I am full of surprises," confirmed Rose, electing to hear only what she wanted to hear.

"Yes, I'm just astounded to discover that under all those bolts of fabric you usually wear, you really do have legs to carry you about!" teased Tag.

"And if you keep staring at these legs, they shall kick you in your head, so you will not get so distracted by them!" threatened Rose. She scowled in annoyance, wrapping the edges of her long riding coat to better hide her form from his feasting eyes.

"I admit I was staring, but who said I was distracted?" countered Tag. He was as embarrassed as he was annoyed by her pointed words. Turning away, he pretended to be busy adjusting the cinch of his saddle as he muttered, "If anything, I was surprised by all those pieces of jewellery you're wearing."

"What about them?"

"Do you not think they're a bit over the top, considering the occasion?" Tag raised a hand to shield his eyes, pretending to be blinded by the dazzling brilliance reflected by the afternoon sun. "After all, we are going on a quest, not attending a formal gala."

"I do admit silver accessories would be a better match with the belt and boot buckles, but I do not do silver. White gold, yes, but never lowly silver! That semi-precious metal is for commoners," answered Rose, her words matter-of-fact.

"There is nothing wrong with silver, especially if one does not own pieces of gold, white or yellow," stated Loken.

"Yes, if you like things that tarnish with age and wear," pooh-poohed Rose. "Now, had I donned a diamond-encrusted tiara, then that would certainly be excessive. In my case, I am merely presenting a polished look to complement these dreary threads I am made to wear, for I am still a princess after all. I must do my utmost to look the part of a royal."

"Princess Rose does have a good point," admitted Myron.

"I do?" She smiled at the knight, appreciating his sudden sense of style even though, in her opinion, he had none himself.

"If anything, Princess Rose can barter those pieces of jewellery. Should we be away for a longer duration than we had anticipated, requiring funds for more provisions to keep us going, those jewels will come in handy," added Myron.

"Hey… that does make sense," agreed Tag, nodding in approval. "Especially as we no longer have the Dreamstone to wish for whatever we need, in case of an emergency."

"Well, that was the other reason for wearing these fine pieces." Rose lied, hoping to pacify Tag and make him believe she was being simultaneously practical and fashionable. "I prefer to keep what I have, but in a pinch, that is exactly what these pieces can be used for, as I hardly think you or Myron have the means to fund any kind of expedition, great or small."

"Excellent!" chimed in Loken, as he alighted upon Myron's shoulder. "So, we are ready to proceed."

"I am as ready as I will ever be," sighed Rose. Slipping her foot into the stirrup, Tag gave her a leg up onto her mare.

🌿🌿🌿

"I hate that stupid palace," muttered Rose.

Glancing over her shoulder, the spiral peaks of the tallest watchtowers shrank behind the hill Myron led them on.

"Why? It is not as though it can do or say anything to offend you," reasoned Tag.

"What do you know?" grumbled Rose.

"Are you sure you are not upset because your parents did not even bother to see you off?" questioned Tag.

He coaxed his mount on to keep up with Myron's steed that was setting the pace, trotting down the hillside.

"Oh, they did see me off, just not in the grand style I was hoping for," lamented Rose, turning her gaze back to the road before them. "If anything, I was not anticipating a need to venture forth from Pepperton Palace, especially to engage in another quest."

"Stay positive, Princess. Look at it this way, there was nothing keeping you there in the first place," stated Tag.

"I suppose."

"You did tell me just days after our return to Fleetwood that you were dissatisfied with your present relationship with your parents," reminded Tag. "All the more reason to engage in this quest, especially if you can set things right, once and for all."

"I must admit my parents' growing apathy has become somewhat tiresome," conceded Rose.

"I agree with the young sir. This is your chance to do something about it," added Loken, hovering before her distraught face. "Reclaim the Dreamstone, spare the Elves from further loss, and repair this botched relationship with your parents! If you do so, all will be right in your world once more."

"If it were only that easy," sighed Rose.

"Easy would be convenient, but life is seldom that way, my lady," responded Loken. His wings thrummed as he floated through the air before her.

"Yes, and much to my annoyance, I am finding that out for myself, thank you very much!"

"Consider it your penance for making that harebrained deal with the Dream Merchant in the first place," said Tag.

By his tone, Rose knew he felt no sympathy for the misery she was now made to endure.

"It is one thing to pay penance, it is another to be tortured. Clearly, to be subjected to the misery of another quest *is* torture."

"Well, for one made to suffer, you are luckier than most, my lady!" Loken offered her a comforting smile.

"You speak in jest! How can that be so?"

Hovering before her scowling face, Loken glanced over his shoulder to Myron and Tag. "There are few in this world lucky enough to have friends that are willing to subject themselves to such '*torture*' for the benefit of another."

Before Rose could agree or argue his point, the Sprite zipped away, flying right by Tag and his horse to alight upon Myron's shoulder once more.

"Keep up, Princess," ordered Tag. Tapping the heels of his boots against his steed's flanks, he urged his horse on when Myron's mount started to gallop as it neared the bottom of the hill.

"Where are we going?" questioned Rose, as she coaxed her mare on. "I thought we were in a rush."

"Yes, we are in a hurry and our ultimate destination is the Enchanted Forest," Myron called back to her over his shoulder as he pressed his mount on, "but first, a quick detour."

"What detour?" Rose shouted to be heard above the clatter of hooves beating against the hard-packed road. "We better not be making an unnecessary stop at that God-awful Gelded Pony Public Drinking House, Sir Kendall! This is not the time for libations."

"No pubs for now, Princess, just follow us," demanded Tag. "You'll find out soon enough."

Launching off Myron's shoulder, Loken flew just ahead of his stallion. They galloped by a large meadow that had been mown for the last time before the coming of the first frost. This rolling meadow, its tall grasses piled high, dried, baled and waiting to be stored in barns to feed livestock for the coming winter, looked vaguely familiar. Rose could not help but feel she had come by this way before. Rounding a bend in the road, there was a quaint cottage on a small, tree-lined plot of land. She immediately recognized this humble abode.

"What are we doing here?" asked Rose, reining her mare in as the horses trotted up to the hitching post just outside of Myron Kendall's home.

"I am picking up a few supplies we shall be in need of," responded Myron. He dismounted, tethering his steed. "I will not be long. You are welcome to come in, if you wish, my lady."

"Is that monstrosity of a puking dog and that hairball-regurgitating cat of yours inside?" questioned Rose.

Her nose wrinkled in disgust just recalling her first introduction to this man's trusty pets. Even though she was not dressed in a beautiful gown as she was before, she had no desire to be slobbered on again, nor did she wish to tread on wads of coughed up cat hair mingling with the mulched remains of mice.

"Worry not, my lady. Since remembering my true calling and identity, I have been spending more time at your father's palace than here in my family home. It was only right to be rid of my animals, than to allow them to linger here in my absence, pining for my return each day."

Rose's eyes opened wide in dismay as she gasped, "You killed your pets? I find this hard to believe, especially coming from someone like you, Sir Kendall! I was led to believe you adored those mangy creatures."

"Of course I did not kill them," assured Myron. He waved his friends on to follow him inside. "I placed them in a proper home. They now reside at a little sheep farm not far from here, with owners that have sufficient time to devote to their care than to allow them to roam wild, grow feral and suffer from neglect."

"You, of all people, should know firsthand about this state of existence, Princess!" declared Tag. "It was the best thing to do."

Standing aside, Tag allowed Rose to pass through the door first that Myron held open for them, as Loken darted inside.

Flitting through this room, the Sprite alighted upon the table. Rose stared through the motes of dust sent swirling in Loken's wake. The tiny particles danced through the beams of sunlight shining through the windows. She was pleased to see this quaint home had remained neat and tidy, still complete with the upgraded furniture, dishes and curtains she had wished for during her last visit. It had not degraded to what had been formerly Myron's dilapidated hovel of a home that was barely fit for a homeless person, let alone a distinguished knight of noble reputation.

"I see you have maintained your cottage well," praised Rose, nodding in approval.

This place had become Myron's sanctuary away from the bustling palace. He kept his home in good order, making repairs to the once rickety door and leaky roof. The windows were free of the film of grime she had difficulty seeing through before, while the shelves, floor and furniture were free of dirt and dust. Everything was in its proper place. There was not even a dirty plate or cup in the empty washbasin nor cold ashes or remnants of unburned wood in the fireplace. Even the counterpane resting upon a narrow cot that served as his bed was neatly in place. It was surprisingly immaculate for a home maintained by a single man living without a domestic staff to cater to him.

"I work at your palace, but this is still my home when time allows it," reminded Myron, pulling open a drawer to remove a near-full, cobalt blue bottle. "Of course I keep it presentable and in working order as long as I reside in this place, even if it is only from time to time."

"You were living here before, and believe me, there was no order to this house when Tag and I first came by here," reminded Rose. She ran an index finger along the windowsill, inspecting it for a layer of dust.

"Believe me, my lady, in my prior condition during our first meeting, keeping a tidy house was the least of my concerns. Scraping together enough to live on had far greater priority back then."

"Then it is a good thing your mind is no longer addled," said Rose. The pads of her index finger and thumb rubbed together, feeling for traces of dust.

Loken's eyes rolled as Tag shook his head in exasperation upon hearing her words of approval that were actually more insulting than anything else.

"Yes, well... Let us hope there is no relapse," said Myron. With forced affability, he offered her a reassuring smile. "It is something I can do without."

"A relapse? On this quest? Good gracious!" gasped Rose. "There better not be, for I need you and Tag to have your wits about you as we venture on."

"I hardly think there is reason for concern," assured Myron. "Only another severe blow to my head can cause such a profound relapse."

"Well, how about this?" asked Rose. She pointed to the empty bucket with a scrub brush in it. These cleaning tools rested in the corner of the room, hidden behind the door when propped wide open.

"What about it?" Myron stared in confusion at her.

She removed the scrub brush, picking the bucket up by its handle to pass on to the knight.

"You can wear it like a helmet, as you do not have one to protect that noggin of yours," suggested Rose.

"I think not, my lady!" Myron waved her off. "I have a proper helmet, if I need it."

"And just where is this helmet?" She stared quizzically as she scrutinized him.

"It is back at Pepperton Palace, my lady."

"And how will it protect your head, if you are here and it is there?"

"Hold on, Princess! It is not as though we are going into battle," reminded Tag. "We're off to the Enchanted Forest to lend aid to Lord Silverthorn and his people, not to engage in open warfare."

"I sense the good knight is in better condition and more prepared to guard his head than we are in minding our own," determined Loken, his knuckles rapping against his forehead. "I know if I were Sir Kendall, given his history, I'd be very protective of my noddle, with or without a helmet."

"And a helmet can be very limiting," added Myron. He staggered back, pretending to be struck by a thrown rock again. "Especially as the visor cannot be lifted properly until it is repaired."

"Oh, yes... *that* helmet," said Rose. Nodding her head in understanding, she held forth the bucket for him to accept. "Then this will have to do for now."

Tag snatched it away from her. Plunking the bucket down in the corner of the room, he tossed the scrub brush in it once more. "It will promise to be a rather undignified look, especially for this great knight. Instead, we shall keep each other safe from harm, if you are so concerned."

"A marvellous idea, young sir!" chirped Loken, as he gracefully spun through the air.

Taking up a dagger from the same drawer that stored the bottle of medicine, Myron checked the sharpness of the blade against the pad of his thumb. Satisfied, housing the blade back into the leather sheath, he fastened the dagger to his belt. Myron took a moment for a final look around, in case he was forgetting something.

"I believe I have all that we shall be in need of," announced the knight.

"Good. We should go." Tag glanced out the window at the lengthening shadows cast by the surrounding trees. They stretched lazily across the landscape as the westering sun continued on its journey, sinking lower on the horizon.

"Night will fall in a few hours. We can spend the night here, then continue on at first light," suggested Rose, hoping she'd not have to spend the night under the stars.

"We have far to go, so we should travel now while the light of day still holds. As you said, my lady, we have a few hours before darkness makes it too difficult to travel safely. That will bring us a few more hours closer to our final destination," responded Myron.

He pushed the cork tightly into the mouth of the bottle, making sure it was securely sealed before placing it into his pack.

"What is that?" asked Rose. Watching as the knight tucked away the cobalt coloured bottle.

"It is the willow tincture," answered Myron.

"I thought Tag had cleared out the supply in the royal apothecary," said Rose, her eyes narrowing in suspicion.

"I brought what I could, leaving one bottle on the shelf in case this sickness spreads south," responded Tag. "As we don't know how many more have fallen ill and how many will be stricken by this sickness by the time we arrive, we felt we should bring as much as could be spared."

"Hence, this bottle." Myron's calloused hand patted the bag he toted on his shoulder where the medicine was now safely stored away for the trek.

"We came this round-about way for just *one* measly bottle of medicine that is not even full?" asked Rose.

"And his dagger," reminded Loken.

"The dagger might come in handy along the way, but that bottle?" Rose rolled her eyes in exasperation.

"This one bottle can mean the difference between life or death for an unfortunate soul," explained Myron. "And look at it this way, Princess Rose, if we dispensed all the medicine we had and suddenly, *you* were the last one in need of a dose of this tincture, but we had run out, would you not wish we had made the effort to come this way to bring it to you?"

"When you put it like that, I suppose we did not go that far out of our way."

"Very well then," said Myron. Holding the door open, he ushered his comrades out. "We leave now."

As they mounted their steeds, Rose looked to Myron, addressing the knight. "Now that your brain is no longer *addled,* so to speak, do you still remember the way to the Enchanted Forest?"

"I do recall the general direction."

"I sense a *but* in there," determined Rose.

"As a courtesy to Loken, we shall first go the Fairy's Vale," answered Myron, as the Sprite nodded in gratitude. "After we make sure all is well in the Vale, then we will journey on through the country of Axalon. We shall reach the Woodland Glade by this route."

"We will travel the same path we had taken before, when we first set off to reclaim the Dreamstone," said Tag.

"Yes, that would be the most prudent and expedient thing to do," stated Myron. He turned his steed to the roadway as the other horses followed.

"That may be so, but do you even remember the way, for I do not," said Rose.

"There is no need to remember," replied Myron.

"Of course we need to remember, otherwise we can end up travelling in circles, lost for days on end!"

"Fear not, my lady, for there is no chance of that happening," promised the knight.

"Oh, I do fear, sir! I do fear!"

"Should my memory fail along the way, his will not," responded Myron. He pointed to the little Sprite flying before him. "Loken offered to escort us. First to the Fairy's Vale and onward, if necessary."

"Brilliant!" exclaimed Rose. "If Loken cannot get us there, then no one can."

"I shall take you on the most direct route these horses can travel to get there," vowed Loken. "When we arrive, it will be nigh on to the midnight hour. The three of you shall reside in the palace for the night, as guests of the Queen."

"What say you to that, Princess Rose?" queried Myron. "Do you think you can withstand the ride?"

"Consider me motivated," said Rose, prodding her mare on to follow. "It promises to be much better than spending the night in the wild with all manner of beasts lurking about."

Rose yawned, shifting restlessly in her saddle as the horses plodded on. They had slowed accordingly with the sun's dimming light as a velvety twilight settled across the land.

Myron glanced over his shoulder upon hearing her loud exhalation followed by the squeaking of her saddle as she squirmed about, trying to get comfortable.

"How do you fare, my lady?" questioned Myron.

"I have been better, but I can endure for a while longer. Are we almost there?"

"We are still in Fleetwood. We have barely left the County of Wren." Tag's voice tightened as he tried to hide his exasperation.

"Surely you jest!" gasped Rose.

"Once we reach that hill, we veer to the east, head through the forest," explained Loken. He pointed ahead, his aura growing brighter as the skies grew darker. "If we stay true to this course we shall arrive in the Fairy's Vale well before the midnight hour."

Rose unleashed another yawn, but it was more like a dreary sigh.

"Do not tell me you wish to stop now, my lady?" queried Myron. He peered over his shoulder once more to scrutinize her.

"Just because I yawned, it does not mean I am demanding that we stop." She waved him on to continue.

"I know you're getting weary, Princess, but perhaps it would help to tackle this trek in smaller increments by establishing easily attainable goals in getting to our final destination," offered Tag.

"Will it get us there faster?"

"No, but if anything, it will help to make the trek seem less tedious."

"That sounds wonderful to me." Rose nodded in approval.

"Then our first goal is to reach that hill."

Tag pointed to the path that branched off from the main road they had been travelling. This small trail wound up and over a hill silhouetted against the deepening sky. They squinted under the brilliant glow of the impending moon, its celestial light expanding just over the crest of the knoll to herald its arrival.

"That should be easy enough." Rose spoke with confidence. She was just grateful they were not made to walk this time, especially through this rolling countryside.

"Then follow me," invited Loken. He flew before Myron's steed, leading this small procession through the growing darkness.

Gently prodding her mare on, Rose followed behind Tag's horse. Approaching the foot of this hill, she watched as Loken's aura dimmed in the swelling light of the ascending moon.

The Sprite abruptly froze in mid-flight, hovering as Myron's left hand flashed out, clenching into a fist when his stallion became skittish. He motioned for silence, and for his comrades to come to an immediate halt.

Before she could rein her mare in, the animal instinctively slowed when the other horses came to a stop. Rose's eyes opened wide in surprise as the oddest thing appeared over the crest of the hill, backlit by the cold light of the rising moon.

Rose's gloved hand slapped over her mouth, stifling her gasp of fright.

Upon first glance, it appeared to be a large porcupine lumbering along. By the way the quills protruded, it had to be a highly agitated creature. But this was not the part that made it look strange, for as the animal presented itself in its entirety on the hilltop there was no possible way it was an ordinary porcupine.

"What the heck is that?" whispered Tag, watching as the mysterious creature slowed to a stop. Whatever it was, this *thing* was just as curious and surprised to come across these travellers. For the longest moment, the strange beast stood there, motionless as it stared back at them just as intently.

"M- mon- monster!" stammered Rose, her words spoken in a barely audible whisper.

"It can't be," said Tag. Squinting into the moonlight, he stared at the creature. "There's no such thing."

"Then what is that hideous beast?" asked Rose.

Myron had no answer, for it was a mystery to him, too. He merely pressed an index finger to his lips, motioning for her to be quiet and to remain calm.

He and Tag dismounted from their steeds, drawing their swords as the mysterious creature's shadow glided closer to them the higher the moon climbed into the sky.

Properly armed, Myron motioned for Rose to stay put while he and Tag investigated this mystery.

"I have no problem with that," whispered Rose, waving her comrades on to proceed, but not without accepting the reins of their horses first, so the animals would not bolt should this thing attack. Tightening her grip on the reins, her eyes grew wide with fear. Never before had she been witness to such a bizarre looking creature.

Shielding her eyes from the glare of the moon, she struggled to determine what nature of beast had just crested this hill. Whatever it was, this *thing* now appeared as large as a bear standing on its hind legs and just as shaggy. But this was definitely not a bear, at least, not a species she was familiar with, for this one looked as though it had taken to carrying a large porcupine upon its head.

Whatever this monstrosity was, it was a horrific sight for all to behold. Against the pale moonlight, Rose and her comrades could make out a multitude of stiff quills that stood out in the most threatening fashion from what could only be its head. Interspersed amongst these prickly protrusions were shadows of several round objects of varying sizes that only added to the mystery of what this beast could be.

With the great moon boldly silhouetting this strange aberration, its steadily growing shadow stretched down the hill toward them. Exaggerated by the angle of the celestial light and the sloping terrain, this black spectre glided forward, and with each passing second, these menacing spines lengthened, becoming as dangerously long and pointed as arrows.

Rose's mind and imagination raced as swiftly as her heart. She imagined a dark magic had conjured up a hybrid monster of sorts, like a *porcu-man* or a *man-cupine*. Whatever the manner of beast this was, it was not of this world!

"Kill it!" demanded Rose. The blood in her veins turned to ice as a horrible noise, like the braying of a choking donkey, shattered the still of the night. "Kill it, before it kills us!"

As this sinister being ambled over the crest of the hill, the rest of its form was revealed against the glow of the moon. Protruding from behind was a swayed back, like that of a stunted horse. Under this hung a rotund belly and beyond this was a rounded rump supported upon a pair of stout and distinctly equine legs! The trio watched in amazement as a long, thin tail that terminated with a tassel of long hairs flicked about. Its agitation was evident by the rapid, to-and-fro whipping of this appendage.

"Is that wh- what I th- think it is?" stammered Rose.

"I can't read your mind," muttered Tag. He squinted, staring through the glare of moonlight as he struggled to remain focused and ready for a possible altercation with this monster. "What do you think it is?"

"An abomination of nature! A... a... porcupine crossed with a... cen- centaur!" Rose gasped in disbelief. "Is that even possible?"

"I suppose anything is possible, especially with an imagination like yours - "

Tag's sentence was cut short as the creature uttered a low, guttural cry. The sound of slurping and the smacking of thick lips followed as the beast descended the hill quickly, spurred on by the sloping terrain. One arm flailed about, as if in frantic greeting. The strange being bellowed once more, this noise, distorted and filled with the intermittent sounds of slurping and munching.

"Good gracious! Do not just stand here!" Rose ordered her comrades on. "Confront the beast, before it gets too close to me, I mean, us!"

Tag and Myron crept forward, moving ever closer to the approaching beast. Tag gripped the hilt of his sword, pointing the tip of the blade toward this mysterious creature, as the 'clip-clop' of hooves grew louder.

They boldly ascended the path. In anticipation of a violent clash, Myron slowed his breathing to calm his racing heart.

An audible 'crunch' sounded from the beast, as though it had sunk its fangs into something crisp. Startled, Tag and Myron froze. They held their swords steady, poised to attack, as they prepared to face this beast.

Loken abandoned Rose to hover between them. His wings rattled nervously as he spoke in a hushed tone, "Shall I morph into a fearsome creature; one large enough to take this beast on?"

"Get back; watch over the Princess. Let us not be the ones to draw first blood," whispered Myron. "Lest we be provoked, we shall hold steady."

"As you wish," said Loken. With a nod of his head, he circled back to guard Rose. He waited, preparing to transform.

The plodding of hooves grew louder as the creature neared. Backlit by the ethereal orb rising steadily into the deepening sky, the creature was still a silhouette, a dark and mysterious shadow, whose features were yet to be revealed.

"Halt! Come no closer," ordered Tag. Hefting his sword, he was ready to attack should the beast charge at them.

"We come in peace," called Myron. "All we want is to travel through these lands in safety."

The creature brayed in protest, snorting and huffing in response to this command to halt. One hoof pawed and stomped the ground, churning up a small cloud of dust. Once more, the beast vocalized. It sounded like a horse suffering through the worst case of strangles to infect its lungs. More noises of slurping and munching followed.

A distinct 'gulp' was heard as the beast swallowed its meal. This was followed by a resounding burp as the creature thumped its chest with a balled fist.

"Get back, I say!" ordered Myron, angling the tip of his sword toward the approaching shadow.

"No need for worry, friend!" The creature raised his hands in a gesture of peace and to show he was unarmed. "I'm just as surprised as you folks are to see others out and about at this time of night."

"It speaks!" Rose was hysterical, pointing frantically at the monster. "Quickly! Kill it before it casts a spell upon us! Skewer the beast!"

"I've been called many things, but I'm no beast and I know nothin' about conjurin' up spells."

"Hey... I know that voice!" Myron squinted into the darkness as he called out, "Murkins! Is that you?"

"Yep! It's just me and my Sassy!"

"What the heck is a sassy merkin?" questioned Rose. Her tone was incredulous as she stared at the great, shadowy figure looming large before them.

"Murkins is my name!" A stout thumb jabbed his chest as he proudly took ownership of this moniker. "Always has been, and always will be! But you can call me Harry, if you like."

"*Hairy Merkins?* Now, that is a peculiar name," said Rose.

"Mind your manners, Princess," whispered Tag, as he elbowed her in the ribs.

"Ouch!" groaned Rose. Whispering to Tag, she muttered, "That was not necessary."

"Harold *Murkins* is an old friend of mine, from my days when you knew me as Cankles Mayron."

"You know him?" asked Tag, as he stared up at this hulk of a man towering before them.

"Yes! I have not seen Harold in the longest time!" Myron extended a hand, grasping Harold's wrist in warm greeting. "It is good to see you again! Let me introduce you to my friends, Tagius Yairet and Her Royal Highness, Princess Rose-alyn of Fleetwood and this Sprite is Loken of the Fairy's Vale."

"It's a pleasure to meet you all!" Harold snatched off the porcupine headpiece he was wearing before bowing politely to Myron's esteemed company. "I can't believe I'm standin' before a genuine princess."

"I cannot stand this!" exclaimed Rose. "Loken, we need more light. Even with the moon shining brightly, it is still too dark for my liking. I wish to see whom I am being made to interact with."

"Of course, Princess," replied Loken. Taking to the air, the Sprite hovered just above Myron's friend. "I can help to shed more light on this situation."

Holding his breath and forcing his wings to flutter at such a speed they hummed to maintain this position, Loken's aura intensified with this physical exertion. Glowing brightly, everyone could now better discern Harold's true stature and general appearance.

In this light the features of a large, barrel-chested man were revealed. His cloak, made from the skin of a bear that was probably the only animal large enough to adequately cover his frame, served to exaggerate his bulky size. This apparel enveloped him, accentuating his broad shoulders and giving him the appearance that there was no neck to support his head between these hefty shoulders. The bald patches showing through this large pelt spoke of the age of the cloak, as well as the use and abuse it had endured over time. An old vest made of deer hide added to the bulk beneath this apparel. The wooden toggles used to button the front of the vest were stretched tightly, straining to enclose his large chest and belly that melded into one to give him a distinct, barrel-shaped torso.

At a glance, it was obvious to Rose his trousers had seen better days. The hem on each leg was frayed and a multitude of patches of varying materials and colours seemed to be the only things keeping this apparel in one piece. By the length of worn, knotted rope holding these trousers up, it was indicative this fellow was probably too destitute to afford a buckled, leather belt.

Her eyes narrowed as she watched Harold carefully position his porcupine headpiece to conceal his thinning head of hair. The many stiff quills added greatly to Harold's height and it explained his bizarre shape when he first appeared, silhouetted against the moon. Impaled upon the erect quills were two apples that had grown too ripe for the branches to bear. Falling from the tree, the fruits were speared upon these spines. Trapped in the spaces between the quills were various nuts that had also ripened, falling in his wake as he foraged about for food on the ground. This made Rose decide that this odd fellow was far more clever than he first appeared, for utilizing this headpiece in such a manner freed his hands to carry even more foodstuffs he gathered.

As round as the moon rising up behind him, this man's face was cursed with bland features. Dark, shiny, close-set eyes and a nose that seemed too small for his large face appeared to be lost between those plump cheeks. Around a wide mouth, made all the larger by those thick, generous lips, and heavy jowls that caused his spherical visage to blend in with his stout neck, there were short, coarse bristles.

Harold's unshaven, dishevelled appearance failed to make a good first impression on Rose, and she remained wary of him, no matter his relationship to the knight in her company.

"Does this man suffer from some form of uglyism?" Rose whispered to Tag, as she continued to critically eye the behemoth of a man Myron was now embracing in a brotherly hug.

"That is a rude thing to say, Princess!" hissed Tag, his eyes rolling in frustration. "This is Myron's friend. We shall treat him with the respect he is due."

"Fine, I was just curious. I mean, look at him!" whispered Rose. With a quirk of her brows and the shifting of her eyes she urged Tag to see for himself. Her head subtly tilted in Harold's direction. "He is freakishly large! And I am being polite when I say this, but with such ordinary features to go with his gargantuan size, I am sure even a woman as plain as Mildred would not look twice at that buffoon."

"Stay your tongue!" rebuked Tag, flustered by her insulting words.

"Fine!" she snapped.

"Is somethin' wrong, my lady?" asked Harold. Not privy to their heated conversation, all he caught was her sharp retort. "Did I offend you somehow?"

"No, no!" declared Rose. She was quick to respond, preventing Tag from speaking on her behalf. "We were just…um…marvelling, yes! We were marvelling at your... choice of apparel and how very functional it is."

"Well, thanks, my lady!" responded Harold, beaming from ear to ear. "I hunted these pieces myself! And as you can see, this porcupine headpiece is especially useful for holdin' things."

Harold's left hand, already sticky with drying juices, reached up, carefully plucking up an apple impaled upon the quills. His unnaturally small, yellowed teeth sank into the fruit, making a loud *'crrrunch'*.

"Good gracious! Was it an apple we heard you eating?" asked Rose, her eyes narrowing in disbelief.

"Sure was! What else would I be eatin' that's this crispy and juicy?" queried Harold, as he munched on this mouthful.

"I thought you were a monster consuming its latest victim! Munching on an arm or chomping on a leg," explained Rose.

"I'm sorry, Harold," apologized Tag. "Princess Rose's imagination tends to run amok from time to time."

"Hey, just because I have an imagination, it does not mean that my thoughts and ideas are the wild imaginings of a person gone mad!" argued Rose, as an index finger spun by her head.

"For pity's sake, Princess! You thought Harold was a centaur-porcupine monster!" scoffed Tag. "You can't get any more insane than that!"

Rose raised an index finger to Tag, preparing to dispute this claim when the scraping of a hoof against the dusty path and a loud, disgruntled snort followed by the grinding of teeth echoed through the night.

Peering around Harold's immense form, Rose gasped, "Oh, my! You have quite the ass!"

"Princess Rose!" Myron groaned in disbelief. He ran a hand down his flustered face.

"Excuse me?" Harold's cheeks were flushed with embarrassment by her forthright words. "Is that somethin' a proper young lady should be sayin'?"

"What happened to treating people with a little respect?" admonished Tag, as he shook his head at her.

"I was speaking of that beast trailing behind him!" clarified Rose, mortified by this misunderstanding.

"Oh, I get it now!" Harold sighed in relief. "This is Sassy, and she prefers to be called a *donkey*, not a *you-know-what*, even though she's that, too!"

He tugged on the reins, forcing the donkey to amble forward. The animal eyed the strangers. Harold dwarfed the creature with his sheer size, but the assortment of packages and bags tied to the sides of this beast of burden made this little animal appear even smaller.

"Sassy can be real stubborn at times, but she's good company when we're out foragin' about, especially at night," explained Harold, scratching the donkey behind the ears.

Sassy brayed, revelling in a good scratch that helped to relieve a never-ending itch.

"Yes, I can see that," replied Tag, smiling at their interaction.

"And it is good to see an old friend again, but we must be on our way," said Myron.

"Please, stay for a while," pleaded Harold.

"We have no time for socializing," responded Rose.

"I'll build a roarin' fire. We can get warm. I can cook up a meal we can share," offered Harold, eager to chat with an old friend and to become better acquainted with new ones. "I haven't seen you in over four moons, Myron. This'll give us a chance to catch up."

"Princess Rose is quite right!" said Loken, his wings thrummed as he hovered closer to this large mortal. "We have already lost time we shall never get back."

"I am sorry," Myron apologized, clasping Harold's wrist in fond farewell. "We are on an important mission and have no time to spare on this night."

"A mission?" asked Harold. His eyes sparkled with delight. He rubbed his stubbly chin while mulling over the very meaning of this word that held so much promise of adventure. "Are you speakin' of a grand quest of sorts?"

"Yes, but how grand it will be is up for debate," said Rose. "And, as Sir Kendall had already explained, we are in a hurry. We must be on our way."

"Excellent!" exclaimed the man, slapping his thigh in delight as his startled donkey brayed in surprise. "I love quests! Never been on one myself, but I know I'd love it. So, where are we goin'?"

"We? There is no *we* in this team!" snorted Rose, as she pointed to herself, and then Tag and Myron. "There is only the three of us. Actually, three and bit, if you include the Sprite."

"True!" Harold nodded in agreement. "There's a *tea* though, in the word *team*. In fact, I've got some in my sack, if you'd be wantin' a nice little chamomile tea break before we go on our way."

"Oh, no! You, sir, will continue going that way," insisted Rose, jabbing a thumb over her shoulder to the south, "while we head to the east."

By her tone and actions, Harold sensed she was determined to venture on without his company.

"Well then… I'm supposin' it's farewell for now," bade Harold.

Disappointment tainted his voice as he watched his old friend and his new acquaintances mount up. "Just be careful out there! Last week's rain made the ducks and beavers happy, but it could make for tricky travellin', if you get my drift?"

"We shall keep that in mind, my friend," said Myron, as he steered his horse away.

"Just don't go lookin' for trouble." Harold waved good-bye. "There's safety in numbers, but goin' on as you are, without me, I pray you'll be havin' a safe journey free of danger."

"Danger? Really, now!" Rose muttered to Tag, so only he would hear. "We have barely stepped outside of Fleetwood. What kind of trouble can we land in way out here in the middle of nowhere?"

4
Extra Ordinary

"This way, my friends!" coaxed Loken. The Sprite launched off from Myron's shoulder, taking to the air once more. "We shall veer off this trail; take a shortcut to make up for lost time."

"You better not get us lost in the process," warned Rose.

Prodding her mare on to follow the others, she did not even glance back to where they had abandoned Myron's friend.

Though feeling thoroughly dejected, it did not stop Harold Murkins from wishing them well. The man continued to enthusiastically wave farewell while his donkey brayed, and then raised its tail, but not in parting salutations. Harold was forced to step aside, allowing the compact balls of dung that fell onto the trail to tumble away, unimpeded.

"Did you hear me, Loken?" asked Rose.

"Worry not, my lady. I have flown through this forest more times than I care to remember. I know it like the back of my hand."

"Well, in my humble opinion, that does not instil any level of confidence, especially as your hands are so tiny. By your very words, it just means that there is not much to remember in the first place."

"It was a figure of speech, my lady, but as I said before, I will not get you lost, not even in the darkness of night." Loken hovered for a moment as he pointed up through the trees toward the cobalt sky. "The stars are constant, shining brightly on this eve. They will serve as reliable guides along the way. We merely travel a straight course than to keep to this meandering trail."

"Myron and I trust you, Loken. Lead the way. We shall follow, and so will she, lest the Princess be left behind to find her own way," said Tag.

"Yes, make haste," urged Myron, waving him on. "Time is of the essence."

In a surprising burst of energy, the Sprite glowed brightly as his wings pushed him through the night air. In a bid to set a straight course, Loken dipped beneath low-hanging boughs and swerved around tree trunks only where necessary. His golden aura shone like a beacon for the others to follow the route he set before them. One in front of the other, the horses trailed behind the tiny being.

Other than the dull thud of hooves pounding the soft earth, all was quiet. A ghostly mist rolled across the forest floor, enveloping all in an unnatural hush. There was barely a breath of wind and not even the mournful cries of owls could be heard on this night. On this eve, their only company was the full Harvest Moon. This great orb cast its cold light upon the lands; silvery beams penetrating the tree canopy to illuminate the ground here and there while setting dew-laden leaves and spider webs glistening as though adorned with tiny, diamond beads.

The trio of horses intuitively trusted the Sprite to guide them, galloping to keep up with Loken as he zipped through the air.

Myron suddenly gasped in surprise. His breath snagged in the back of his throat as he was pitched forward against his horse's neck. Simultaneously, his stallion squealed in fright, lunging forward as solid ground abruptly gave way beneath its hooves. With a resounding splash, Myron's mount landed belly-deep in a boggy swamp that was hidden beneath the thin miasma hugging the forest floor.

Before he could warn the others to halt, Myron gasped once more. This time, from the shock as a spray of icy water splashed across his back. Chilling fingers of water trickled down his neck and filled his boots as Tag's mount, following too close behind to stop, landed next to Myron's stallion.

Rose shrieked in fright as her mare instinctively followed her stable mates. It ended up in the quagmire, nose-to-rump against Tag's gelding. All three horses began to splash about, struggling frantically to be free of the mucky bottom of this swamp.

"Good gracious!" cried Loken.

He doubled back upon hearing Rose's scream. It was loud enough to effectively mute the explosion of colourful expletives erupting from Tag's mouth as the horses splashed about, whinnying loudly as they became thoroughly stuck. As Loken neared, the glow of his aura shed light on this calamity.

"What happened?"

"What does it look like just happened?" snapped Rose. She quickly slipped her boots from the stirrups. In the most unladylike fashion, she held onto the saddle and reins as she hoisted her legs up high in a desperate bid to keep the stagnant water from filling her riding boots. "You led us directly into this swamp!"

"I swear, I did not know it was here!" declared Loken, his hand over heart in solemn promise. "If I had, I would have led you around the swamp, not straight into this mess."

"Enough, Princess! It was this growing mist," stated Tag. He shivered involuntarily as the water slowly crept up to his thighs and began to fill his boots as his horse wallowed in the swamp. "Loken was flying. He had no way of knowing it was here."

"But Myron's odd friend had already cautioned us of the potential for this to happen! He warned of the dangers that lurk in this forest," reminded Rose.

"The man said no such thing," argued Tag. "He merely mentioned last week's rainfall."

"And *this* is the result of *that* rainfall," snapped Rose. Her eyes narrowed in contempt as she scrutinized their watery surroundings.

"Keep calm, my friends," urged Myron. "There is no need to panic just yet."

"Speak for yourself! There is plenty to panic about at this very moment," insisted Rose. She attempted to coax her mare to back out of the swamp, but her mount merely splashed about, whinnying in protest.

"If this were quicksand, then that would certainly be worth panicking over, but this is just a swamp, a small pond really, we've landed in," said Tag. He patted his gelding's neck to calm the beast as it snorted in discontent.

All three horses were tiring rapidly from their first attempt to be free of this thick, chilling water. They squealed; great jets of steam gushing from their flaring nostrils as they struggled once again. Though they could not move forward or back, the only consolation was that they sank no further.

"Quicksand or not, I find little comfort in your words," grumbled Rose. "At this moment, we can perish in this death-trap that holds us captive now."

"Worry not, my lady. Tag is quite correct," assured Myron, as he assessed their predicament.

"He is?"

"Indeed! Quicksand is quite different from this swamp we are wallowing in. If we had landed in quicksand, these horses would be sinking, and doing so quickly with all their struggling, until they, and we along with them, are swallowed up. In this case, their hooves are merely stuck in the soft mud and decaying vegetation."

"So, it should be easy enough to escape from here?"

"I never said that, my lady," replied Myron.

"Then I have every right to panic!" The metal pieces of her mare's bridle rattled as her grasp tightened on the reins.

"There is a way out of this mess," insisted Tag. "We just need a plan to be free of here."

"Well, if this plan includes having me dismount into that disgusting quagmire of rotting plant matter and muck to swim to freedom, then you can forget about that!" Rose grimaced in repulsion at the very thought of this.

"Just hush for a moment!" snapped Tag. "Let's think on the best way to get free."

Rose reluctantly pursed her lips together, resisting the urge to lash out at her friend as the Sprite zipped about.

With all the splashing by the horses when they had landed in this swamp, the surrounding mist had dissipated, rolling away in the wake of their frantic movements. Loken flitted around, searching for solid ground along the edge of the swamp.

"Princess Rose, should you decide to dismount, it will be a short swim to solid ground, but I promise you, you will be thoroughly soaked and bitterly cold," warned Loken.

"How about one of you swim to shore with me on your back?" suggested Rose. With hope shining in her eyes, she glanced over to Myron, and then Tag, doing her best to look the part of a damsel-in-distress.

"There is no bloody way I'm going to swim with you on my back," grunted Tag. "I'd be tempting fate in the worst possible way."

"Are you saying I am too heavy? I will drown you in the process?"

"I am saying that you will drown me out of spite, Princess," grumbled Tag.

"I am no fool! If that were to be my intention, I'd wait until you delivered me to dry land first, and then I'd toss you back in to drown for getting me into this mess to begin with."

"Enough talk!" snapped Myron. "Our horses will be sapped of all their strength and the will to live, the longer they are forced to linger in these freezing waters. We must take action, immediately."

"I would not recommend taking a swim, if you can help it," advised Loken, as he hovered before Myron's worried face. "Instead, perhaps I can be of some assistance."

"Unless you are offering to transform into a great seal, swimming with me atop your back to deliver me to safety, I do not want to hear about it," dismissed Rose.

"Say again!" Loken frowned upon hearing her words.

"As you are now, I would drown you with the weight of my pinkie finger alone."

"Even if I did morph into a seal just to spare you a chilling swim, it would not get your horse, or the others, out of this predicament," reasoned Loken.

"Can you change into a creature that is strong enough to lift the horses, rider and all, from this quagmire?" asked Tag.

"Now that is a brilliant idea!" praised Rose.

"The only animal to immediately come to mind that can accomplish such a feat is a dragon," answered Loken. "I'd have to transform into one very large dragon to do so, of course, but it can be done."

Myron raised his hand, motioning Loken to stop. "It is a brilliant idea, my friend, but I fear these horses will be scared to death, quite literally. If they do not die of fright, then they will thrash about in terror, causing self-inflicted injuries in the process. Where we will know the creature is you, our horses will only see a very big, terrifying dragon; a great predator to be feared."

"Very true." Loken nodded in agreement.

"So, now what?" grumbled Rose, feeling the mare starting to shiver.

Her question was answered by a raucous call rumbling through the forest.

"Good gracious!" muttered Rose, as she glanced over her shoulder. "Now what?"

"Salvation, I do believe!" answered Myron.

Loken darted off. He headed straight for the approaching shadows rushing their way.

"Master Murkins!" announced Loken, hovering before the man's grimy, sweat-beaded face.

"That's me, all - all right, but you - you can just call me Har - Harry!" He huffed and puffed as he took a moment to catch his breath. "I came a-runnin' as fast as I could when I heard a great commotion comin' from this way. Figured you folks met up with some kinda trouble."

"How right you are, sir! Please follow me, if you will," urged Loken, waving the mortal on. "Perhaps you can be of assistance to us."

"Always willin' to be of service, little Sprite. Go on! Show me the way."

Harold tugged at his donkey's reins, urging her to come along. Following the golden glow that was Loken, as the Sprite escorted him through the otherwise dark forest, Harold hurried to keep up. His surly beast of burden snorted, braying in protest at being forced to trot along to keep up with her master.

Man and donkey came to a stop at the edge of a swamp as Harold stared in wide-eyed surprise at the sight illuminated by Loken's aura and augmented by moonlight. "Hello, my friends! What's goin' on?"

"We decided to go for an evening swim, you dolt! What do you think is going on here?" snapped Rose. She was hoping it'd be a chivalrous, handsome knight, even a helpful farmer coming to their rescue, not the Village Idiot of Cadboll to inflame her already testy disposition.

"Tut, tut! No need to get riled up, my lady," said Harold, shaking an admonishing finger in her direction. "And I hardly think a swamp is the proper place for a swim when there's a pristine lake not far from here. Besides, it looks to be your horses are doin' the swimmin', not you good folks."

"Never mind her," urged Tag, raising a hand in greeting as he welcomed the man.

"How very fortuitous! You are a sight for sore eyes, Harold," declared Myron.

"Oh, my! Did some of that nasty swamp water touch your eyeballs?" Harold's face screwed up in disgust.

"No," answered Myron. "Nor did I swallow any by accident."

"Good! It's even worse if you get it in your mouth. You'd be as sick as a dog with the worst bellyache ever, if you had."

"Nothing like that has happened yet, but we are good and stuck in here," said Tag. He twisted about in his saddle to address Myron's friend pacing along the fringes of the swamp.

"I'd say there's nothin' good at all about bein' stuck in there, young master!"

"And while you are there and we are here, can you make yourself useful?" asked Rose.

"Absolutely, my lady! What would you be wantin' from me?"

"I wish to be back on dry land. Make it so!"

"Ain't that good a swimmer, but I've been told I'm shaped like a barrel, so maybe I can float like one, too. If that be the case, I suppose I can just float over to your horse, grab a hold of you, and then bob over to dry land somehow."

"Yes! Be a good man and do that, will you? And be quick about it, before I get this disgusting water in my boots or worse yet, against my delicate skin."

"Wait, my lady! There is a better way to do this," said Myron, as he removed a coil of rope from his saddle.

"There is?" Both Rose and Harold spoke simultaneously.

The Princess cringed inwardly. These shared words made her think she had more in common with this fool than she thought was possible.

Myron merely nodded his response as he issued a request, "Loken, please guide Harold safely around the edge of this swamp until he is on the other side, opposite to me and my horse."

"Methinks it's a shorter swim from this side than that," assessed Harold. He scratched his chin in thought as he stared across the body of water now darkened by the churned up sediment.

"No need to swim, my friend. If you come around to the other side, I can toss you the end of this rope. I shall tie one end around my horse's neck while you tie the opposite end to your ass."

"You mean my donkey, right?"

"Of course, your donkey," answered Myron, as he stared with raised eyebrows at Harold.

"Just makin' sure!"

Rose slapped a gloved hand over her mouth as she began to giggle.

"Now, what?" grunted Tag.

"He so reminds me of Myron when he was a little..." Rose's index finger twirled beside her head. "You know? Brain-addled."

Tag shook his head in disapproval while Myron chose to ignore her words. He set to work, looping, and then knotting one end of the rope around his stallion's neck.

When he was done, Myron proceeded to knot the opposite end of the rope, thereby providing it with more weight to clear the distance to reach his friend.

After tying this sizeable knot, Myron hefted it in his right hand, feeling its weight. Satisfied, he began to swing the knotted rope in large circles. He yelled out to Harold, "Get ready to catch!"

Harold's hulking form stood at the ready; his hands extended in preparation to grab the rope. His face was illuminated by Loken's aura, glowing brightly for Myron to see his mark. While Harold smiled, eager to help, Sassy snorted, stomping the soft, moist earth. She was clearly annoyed she had been finagled into this situation, facing the murky swamp at her master's side.

"Ready?" called out Myron. The rope continued to rotate in large circles as he prepared to throw the line to Harold. "One...Two...Three!"

The knotted rope sailed from Myron's grasp to bounce off Harold's momentarily stunned face before plopping into his outstretched hands. Coiling up the slack, he tied the end around Sassy's neck. Looping and knotting the rope securely, Harold prepared to pull his friend out of the quagmire.

Turning the donkey about so her rump was to Myron's stallion, the petulant little beast dug her hooves into the squishy earth as she pulled. The slack rope between her and the stallion grew taut. Sassy strained, pulling with all of her might as Harold coaxed her on. Grabbing a hold of the rope, he helped the donkey to haul the struggling duo on to solid ground.

Instead, the harder Sassy pulled, the deeper her hooves sank into the earth, as the rope dug into her neck. All the while the stallion and his passenger remained stuck. They barely budged from that deepest spot in the swamp.

"It is not working," determined Myron.

As the stallion struggled, he could hear the sloppy, sucking sounds bubbling up each time his horse pulled a hoof from the muck, only to sink down once more.

"There's no traction in all this mess," called Tag. "That's the problem."

"Then I'll make it so there is," said Harold, as an idea popped into his mind.

"*You* have a solution?" responded Rose, with a doubtful frown.

"I think I know how to get you and them horses out," he answered, grabbing an axe from one of the packs Sassy was carrying. "Just wait right there!"

"Where would we go?" muttered Rose. The frustration in her voice was evident as she struggled to keep her legs above the stagnant waters creeping steadily closer.

Harold quickly scrutinized the surrounding trees, searching for the right one that was the perfect height with a slim, flexible trunk and plenty of branches to provide the traction the horses needed to gain a better footing against the muddy bottom of the swamp.

Selecting a young cedar tree, Harold proceeded to hack at the trunk like a deranged, starving beaver. With each blow, he sent wood chips flying. When it appeared this tree was ready to topple over, Harold tossed his axe onto the ground. He took a moment to catch his breath before positioning his hands against the cedar. With little left to keep the tree upright, it yielded to his pressure, tipping over. Tapered at the top with slender, flattened branches covered with rough, scale-like needles, the cedar tree splashed as it hit the water, the tips of the branches just grazing Myron's horse.

The cedar rested on the water, most of it staying afloat thanks to the buoyancy of the foliage and numerous branches. Harold placed his boot on the trunk, pressing down to force it beneath the surface. The water quickly swallowed up the tree as Harold's weight forced it to sink to the muddy bottom. As the submerged boughs brushed by the horse's legs, the stallion instinctively raised its hooves, allowing these branches to settle under foot and over the mud.

"Let's try again!" called out Harold. Taking up the slack rope, he gave Sassy a smack on her rump to motivate her.

Tapping his heels against the stallion's flanks, Myron prompted his mount forward. Combined with Harold and his donkey's efforts, the horse plucked each hoof from the bottom of this swamp.

Taking tentative steps onto the submerged boughs, the stallion quickly realized that its hooves were no longer being sucked back into the mud. With eager, lunging movements, the horse clambered onto the tangle of submerged branches. Wanting nothing more than to be free of this water's chilling embrace, the stallion staggered on to solid land.

Dripping wet, the steed shivered as a cool breeze whispered through the trees. Like a dog shaking off after a swim, from the tips of its ears to the end of its tail, the stallion shook off the excess water from its coat.

"Sit tight, my friends! We'll have you out in no time," promised Myron, as he hopped off his horse. Removing the rope from around the stallion's neck, Myron adjusted the loop. He spun this circle of rope and once he gained just the right momentum, he tossed it, lassoing Tag's gelding by its neck on his first try.

Holding tight to the reins and a fistful of the gelding's mane, Tag's heels rapped again his mount's flanks to urge it on while Myron, Harold and his little donkey pulled them free. Once the gelding's hooves made contact with the submerged cedar boughs, the horse easily clambered ashore.

Myron removed the loop of rope from the gelding's neck and with the same level of precision, he tossed the rope, hoping to snare Rose's mare.

Because this horse had landed in the swamp directly behind Tag's, Myron's intended target was farther by an entire horse-length. The greater distance caused the loop to narrow just as it reached the mare. This noose landed repeatedly on the mare's head, snagging an ear or two, but the rope, now weighed down by water, would not open up wide enough to lasso the mare by her neck.

With his umpteenth try, the horse no longer snorted or blinked in response when the rope landed on or near her. Myron's weary arms tossed the circle of rope out again. It sailed through the air and landed directly onto Rose's right leg that she was holding upright to prevent her boots and leather pants from being soiled by the water.

"Really?" exclaimed Rose. Her brows furrowed as she scowled in agitation. It was becoming obvious bad luck and fickle fate were conspiring against her.

"Sorry, my lady," apologized Myron, as he pulled the rope in, hand-over-fist.

"This is ridiculous! You have no idea how exhausting it is to maintain this position," groaned Rose, fighting to keep her booted feet above the murky water.

"I'll toss the rope to you," said Myron, "and then you'll have to loop it over the mare's neck."

"I'll have to touch that filthy thing?" gasped Rose.

"If you want to get out of that swamp, you will," said Tag. "Surely you can manage that? If you do, all you'll need to do is sit back. We'll pull you and your horse free."

"Fine!" grumbled Rose. "I suppose if I can throw as well as I do, then surely I can catch just as easily."

Myron tossed the rope in her direction. It landed with a splash by her horse. Before it could sink out of reach, she snagged the loop on the toe of her boot, making every effort not to get the fine leather wetter than necessary. With awkward, but careful, manoeuvring Rose reached down, snatching up the rope. Widening the loop Myron had created, she tossed it over the mare's head.

"There you go!" announced Rose. "The rope is in place!"

"Ready, Princess Rose?" hollered Harold, as he took up the donkey's reins.

"Yes, yes! Get on with it! I want out of here! The sooner, the better!"

"All right!" called out Harold, as his comrades wrapped the rope around their hands. "Hold on and sit tight!"

"Just do not – " Before Rose could finish her sentence, with a resounding splash, she landed in the swamp.

Between their combined efforts to drag her mare closer to the downed cedar tree and the mare's desperation to be free, as soon as its hooves felt the submerged branches compacted into the muck, the mare lunged forward. With better traction, the horse scrambled on to dry ground. With a final pull the mare came free, but its hindquarters slipped, stumbling to find solid footing.

This sudden movement jarred Rose, jerking her backwards. To the astonishment of all, they watched as her legs flew up. Unseated from her saddle, she tumbled head over heels.

The icy water stole away her breath and the words of profanity perched on the tip of her tongue. She splashed about, fighting to keep her face out of the swamp. Her coattails floated up behind her as the mare stood on dry ground. Briskly shaking the excess water from its coat, Tag was splattered as he grabbed the reins while Myron removed the noose from about the mare's neck.

Before either of her friends dashed to her aid, Harold immediately waded in to her rescue. He thrust out his large, calloused hand as he held on with the other to a branch of the cedar tree he had pushed into the water.

Rose needed no prompting to grab hold. She lunged forward, almost pulling Harold into the water as her freezing hands seized his. With his assistance, she clambered ashore. Standing soaking wet in the chilling night air, her teeth chattered so violently she could not even vent her rage as Tag struggled to keep from laughing aloud.

"How do you fare, my lady?" asked Myron, as he rifled through her saddle pack to find her wool cloak.

"Fr- free- freezing!" Rose wheezed out this word. She shivered as her clothes clung to her skin, leaching the warmth from her body as she stood there.

Myron turned to Tag. "Gather some wood for a fire. Be quick about it!"

With his boots full of water and the bottom half of his trousers soaking wet, Tag required no prompting. Before the cold could seep into his bones, he dashed off while Myron opened up the dry cloak, holding it before Rose to form a screen. "Doff your clothes, all of it, my lady!"

"Are you mad? I'll freeze to death!" gasped Rose, wrapping her arms around her shivering body.

"You'll freeze if you continue wearing those wet clothes. Now, quickly! Remove them, and then wrap this cloak about you. We shall dry out your boots and apparel before a fire."

"Is there nothing in my saddle pack that remained dry other than this scratchy, wool cloak?"

"This cloak was at the top, as were some socks, but everything else beneath these items are damp, if not utterly wet when you made your little splash."

"Even dry stockings are better than nothing," said Rose, through chattering teeth.

Knowing she was right, Myron snatched up a pair, passing them on to her.

Rose's smile of gratitude abruptly faded into a disgruntled frown as she growled in displeasure. "Wool! These damned socks are wool, not silk! Evelyn is in big trouble when I return to the palace."

"Count yourself lucky on this night, my lady," said Myron. "Wet or dry, these wool socks will keep your feet much warmer than those silk stockings you wear now."

"So you say!" snorted Rose.

"I know it to be so. Now quickly, before you catch a nasty cold." Myron unfurled the cloak, holding it forth once more to allow her to disrobe with some level of privacy.

Rose glanced about.

Tag had disappeared from sight on a wood gathering mission while

Harold Murkins was busy removing the wet saddles before drying off the horses.

"I understand your need to maintain your modesty, my lady, but trust me when I say none shall steal a peek, especially Tag, if that is what concerns you."

"Are you saying I'm not peek-worthy, not even to Tag?" sputtered Rose. Her cheeks burned red. They were the only parts of her frigid body to warm as she flushed with anger.

Myron sighed as he responded, "I am saying, the young man is busy gathering wood to build a fire, so you can get warm. Now, quickly! Disrobe before you are unable to do so on your own once those fingers grow too numb to function."

He politely averted his eyes, even though the cloak effectively shielded her from his sight. Instead, Rose balked; she stood there, shivering. Her pouting lips took on a sickly pallor of blue as the cold seeped into her muscles. She now felt colder than when she was bobbing in the filthy water.

"I can hear your knees a-knockin' and your teeth a-chatterin' from where I stand, Princess. Will you be needin' some help?" asked Harold. He stopped wiping down the horses with dried leaves. "Buttons can be very tricky to undo when your hands are shakin' badly with cold, but even with my fat, sausage fingers, I'd probably fare better than you right now."

"Stay right where you are, sir!" demanded Rose, as she peeled off her leather gloves. "I can manage just fine on my own, thank you very much!"

Kicking off her boots and peeling off the soggy, silk stockings first, she quickly shed the rest of her clothes, dropping them to the ground. Snatching the cloak from Myron's hands, she wasted no time in wrapping the dry fabric around her body. Ignoring the itchiness of the wool against her skin, she was just grateful to find some warmth on this first night of autumn. Grabbing from the ground the balled pair of socks Myron delivered to her, she glanced about, searching for a suitable place to sit and don these socks so she wouldn't feel quite so naked beneath this cloak.

"I'll have a fire going here in no time," promised Tag.

In a small clearing near to where the horses were tethered to a tree, he dropped an armload of wood that included kindling-sized sticks and twigs. Using his hands, he scraped away the layer of dried pine needles and leaves until bare ground was exposed. Emptying his pockets of the dried moss and lichen to use as tinder he had gathered along the way, Tag heaped it together in a loose pile before arranging the pieces of kindling over top.

Fishing through his pockets, he found a piece of flint. Using the blade of his dagger, Tag held the flint close to the sticks and twigs. As the metal struck against it to create a brilliant flash of sparks, Tag required several attempts until a small spark fell between the sticks to land on the tinder. At first, there was only a wisp of smoke, but just as Tag knelt down to breathe life into the dying ember, it ignited. This single flame swelled. Soon, amber tongues lapped at the sticks and twigs as the dried moss and lichen curled, burning with the heat.

Carefully, Tag placed more wood onto the growing flames. He waited until he was confident the fire wouldn't burn out before leaving to gather more fuel.

"This way, my lady," said Myron. He steered her to the inviting glow of the campfire as Tag dashed off once more to resume his task.

"Here you go," offered Harold. He doffed his bearskin cloak to remove the vest he was wearing beneath it. Placing this apparel on the ground before the fire, he motioned for her to sit. "It'll be much warmer than sittin' on the cold earth."

"Th- Thank you," said Rose. She tried to speak through still chattering teeth, as Harold tossed his cloak back over his broad shoulders. "It is very kind of you to do so."

"My pleasure, Princess Rose!" Harold bowed in respect. "It's not every day an ordinary bloke like me can say he had a royal bum sittin' on his vest, so I'm the one feelin' truly honoured!"

Too chilled to respond to this strange man's equally strange words, with forced affability, Rose managed a weak smile as she nodded in response. She was sure somewhere in there, Harold meant to pay her a compliment.

Having finished wiping down the horses so they could dry off faster, Harold plopped down on the ground next to Rose. Removing his boots, he proceeded to shake out the water that had seeped in when he rescued her.

"That's better!" Harold sighed as he rested with his feet turned toward the toasty warm flames. His big toes wiggled about. Armed with jagged nails that undoubtedly sliced through his well-worn socks, they protruded like nuggets of baby potatoes escaping from an overstuffed burlap bag. "There's nothin' worse than wet feet on a frosty night, or any night, for that matter."

He and Rose turned to hear the splashing of water. They watched as Myron wrung out what he could from the apparel. Shaking out her clothes to hang up, they still dripped.

"Even with a roaring fire, it will take some time to dry out these pieces," said Myron.

Harold hopped up onto his feet, dashing over to his donkey. Rummaging through one of his packs, he removed a large square of fabric. With a flick of his wrist, he snapped it open, spreading it flat on the ground.

"Give 'em to me, my friend. I can get rid of most of the water without wringin' those pieces out like that."

Curious to see what Harold had in mind, Myron handed over the armload of still-dripping clothes. He watched with interest as his friend dumped these items in a heap into the centre of the square.

He and Rose observed as Harold gathered up the four corners of the fabric. At first, they thought he was going to squeeze the excess water from her apparel by rolling them tightly within the square, allowing this material to absorb the excess water. Instead, Harold did something quite unexpected.

Grasping the corners of this fabric into his right hand, Harold proceeded to spin the bundle about. Using his wrist, rather than his whole arm, much like the way Rose would spin her sling about for maximum velocity before releasing her ammunition, he set this bundle in motion.

To their surprise, the force created by this spinning action caused most of the water to come flying out in a fine spray. As he tired, Harold said, "Time to switch arms, then these things should be ready to be hung up for dryin'."

Taking it up in his left hand, Harold set the bundle spinning once more. A finer spray of water was expelled until there was nothing more.

"Here you go," said Harold, opening up the square.

Myron reached in, and sure enough, the articles of clothing were now damp instead of sopping wet.

"Brilliant! These should dry out in no time," exclaimed Myron. He arranged each item on the overhanging branches to finish drying out by the heat of the campfire. "Thank you, my friend."

"No problem!"

"That was very clever of you, Harold!" praised Rose, nodding her thanks to the odd man with the simple, but ingenious, idea.

"Clever? Been called many things in my lifetime, my lady, but I've never been called that before!" He blushed like a teenaged girl receiving her first compliment from a handsome, young suitor.

"Well, I would never have thought about doing what you just did," admitted Rose.

"Comin' from a genuine princess that probably knows everythin' about everythin', then I suppose it was pretty clever of me. Mind you, isn't this what everybody does before hangin' up their wet laundry?" questioned Harold.

"I do not do laundry, or any type of menial task for that matter, so I would not know," confided Rose. She turned her woolly toes to warm before the fire, enjoying the way these socks seemed to soak up the heat and drive away the chill that had gripped her to the bones. "But even so, I do not recall ever seeing my domestic staff undertake this chore in the same manner as you had. I shall have to recommend to them your ingenious method of removing the excess water before hanging up freshly laundered items. The faster they dry, the sooner I have access to clean, fresh clothing."

"Well, as clever as you thought it was and as much as I'd like to take credit for it, I'd be lyin' to you, if I did. Can't rightly remember who taught me that little trick, but it works, so it just stuck in my noggin to do that."

"Thank you, nevertheless," said Rose. "And thank you for being the one to come to my rescue, fishing me out of that disgusting swamp while my so-called *friends* stood by, watching the spectacle that was me, rather than coming to my aid."

"Was nothin' to it, Princess, and your friends had their hands full at the time, gettin' your mare to dry land and makin' sure she didn't bolt. I just happened to be the closest to you, otherwise, I'm sure your young man friend here would have dove in to save you."

"I'd like to believe that to be true where Tag is concerned, but on this night, you were the hero! You were the one to rescue this princess-in-distress." Rose bowed her head in gratitude. "You showed exceptional courage in doing what you did. You, sir, *are* extraordinary!"

"You mean to say extra ordinary," corrected Harold, his head lowering in humility. "In fact, I'm as ordinary as they come, my lady."

"I beg to differ!" said Rose. "And, as a show of my gratitude, allow me to reward you."

"You jest!" gasped Harold.

"Whatever you wish, I shall make it so."

"I mean no disrespect to you, my lady, but are you foolin' with me? 'Cause people have been known to do that, you know?"

"Make no mistake, sir, I am not mere *people*. I am royalty. Furthermore, I am no fool, nor do I make it a habit of fooling others. I wish to reward you for doing a good deed."

Overhearing this conversation, Tag dumped his armload of wood next to the campfire. He tapped Harold on his shoulder as he whispered, "If you accept, Harold, you better take her up on the offer before she changes her mind! Some pieces of silver is fair compensation for putting up with her silliness."

"If Tag is telling you I shall change my mind, I am not the type to make promises lightly. A promise is a promise! If I promise to reward you, then mark my words, you will be rewarded."

"A reward, you say?" Harold mulled over her words as the gravity of this offer gradually seeped into his simple mind.

"Remember, my friend, make it a good one if you plan on making any deals with her," Tag whispered once more.

He plopped down next to Harold. Yanking off his riding boots, Tag peeled off his socks. He wrung them out, carefully hanging the pair on the end of a forked stick to dry before the fire.

"I can ask for *anythin'*?" questioned Harold. His spiny, porcupine headpiece shifted about as though the dead animal had been resurrected as his fingers reached beneath the tanned pelt to scratch at his scalp.

"Within reason, of course," answered Rose.

"What do you mean, *within reason*, my lady?"

"If it is something silly, like requesting my hand in marriage, then that would be deemed well beyond reasonable. But a piece of gold, or some silver, as a token payment or even a medal of bravery is appropriate, if you grasp the gist of it? These are what I would consider reasonable requests."

"Well then, I'll have to have think on this. It's not everyday a man like me gets whatever he wants."

"Well, Master Murkins, this is your lucky day!" exclaimed Rose.

"Please, just call me Harry, Princess."

"Hairy Princess?" gasped Rose. She frowned in confusion while Tag snorted in mirth, attempting to stifle his laughter upon hearing this exchange. "Hairy or not, I am the real princess here, not you!"

"I mean to say, just *Harry* will do, my lady."

For a moment, Rose paused. Her index finger tapped her chin as she considered this man's words.

"Harry Murkins? No, that particular name is too common for my liking. We shall stick with Harold."

"That's fine, too. Sounds a little hoity-toity to me, but I suppose if it was good enough for my momma, then surely, it's good enough for a royal like you."

"So, what will it be, Harold?" asked Rose. "If not gold or a medal of bravery, how about a fancy, powdered wig; one fit for royalty, so you can do away with wearing dead animals on your head?"

"Sounds very temptin' indeed, my lady, and I mean no disrespect, but you can't tell me a regular wig, no matter how fancy, can do double-duty like this fine piece does!"

He plucked a small crab apple that was impaled upon one of the porcupine quills. The fruit had fallen from a tree he was foraging beneath for mushrooms and had managed to stay put, alongside the several acorns that had become lodged, on his unusual headpiece.

"True enough, but it was only a suggestion, in case you were lacking ideas." She watched in disgust as the man popped the tart, little apple into his mouth, munching on it, core, pips and all.

"And a lovely suggestion it was, but truth be told, my mind is racin' with a hundred and one ideas," admitted Harold. His index fingers twirled by the sides of his head to represent the jumble of thoughts jockeying for position in the forefront of his mind. "Don't even know where to begin."

"I am looking to compensate you with *one* reward, not one-hundred of them," reminded Rose. "Surely, it cannot be that hard to come up with an idea."

"Decidin' on a single idea or a wish, even for a simple man like me, can be quite the dauntin' task, my lady. Only person to ever give me anythin' for nothin' has been my good friend, Cankles – I'm meanin' to say, Myron Kendall. You're askin' me to wish for one thing I truly desire when I've never had this opportunity before. It's mind-bogglin', to say the least!" He wrung his hands in woe as he thought on the possibilities.

"No need to be hasty about this, Harold," cautioned Myron, motioning him to calm down. "It is better to walk away with no reward at all, other than the sense you did a good turn, than to be the recipient of a poorly conceived one that will vex you for the remains of your days."

"Huh?" responded Harold. He frowned in bewilderment upon hearing his friend's warning.

"Trust us when we say she knows all about this messy business of wishing on poorly conceived ideas and the like," stated Tag, with a judicious nod of his head.

"This is not about me," insisted Rose, dismissing Tag and Myron's warning with a wave of her hand. "This is about you, Harold, and what *I* can do for *you* in allowing me to reward you accordingly for a good deed done."

"Same difference," muttered Tag. His eyes rolled in frustration.

"I have no idea what you are talking about," snipped Rose, her tone indignant.

"Right… Now you're the one trying to play the part of the good Fairy, granting wishes," grumbled Tag, "only this is much worse!"

"How can this be worse?"

"When you trapped the Queen of the Tooth Fairies, trying to bribe her for wishes in return for the *'good deed'* of setting her free, she gave you more than what you had ever bargained for by arranging that little meeting with the Dream Merchant. Not only did it get you banished from Pepperton Palace, but here we are on another quest, no thanks to you! I just cannot believe you can even think of granting a wish, knowing how badly things turned out for you!"

"In hindsight, I suppose you have a point," conceded Rose, "but all I wish to do is recognize this man for his heroism. There is nothing wrong with that!"

"I believe a heartfelt thank you will suffice, Princess," suggested Myron.

"It would be adequate, had I been a commoner, but I am a princess! I am expected to do more than what others would consider to be *adequate*. If this man is going to boast to others about his reward I gifted to him, as I know he will, it should be a proper one that reflects my status. I hardly need to hear back from my subjects that I, a member of a royal house no less, found fit to give him a measly *'thank you'* for saving my precious life."

"It hardly was an act of derrin'-do, my lady. I merely waded into the swamp to get you out of the water," reminded Harold.

"You are being too modest, sir! Do me the honour of rewarding you in a manner you are deserving of."

Myron unleashed a disheartened sigh as he considered the most tactful way to address Rose on this delicate matter.

"No point in arguing with her," grumbled Tag, raising a hand to Myron in a gesture to yield to her whim. "Why settle for a genuine *'thank you'* when you can receive something that is tangible?"

Myron sat back, knowing Tag was right in this case. Even though the young man's words were tinged with cynicism, he knew it was sarcasm that would go ignored by Princess Rose, if she even detected it at all. It was apparent she was determined to do what she deemed right in her skewed perception of the world.

"Woe is me!" moaned Harold. He frowned, pinching the bridge of his nose as he listened to the trio of friends argue. "There's so much to consider. Suppose I ask for one thing, only to change my mind later on?"

"You cannot go around changing your mind on a whim just because you suddenly decided you want something different," warned Rose. "It would be tantamount to going to the baker, buying a loaf of bread, eating it, and then returning a handful of crumbs; demanding a refund because you suddenly decided a pie was more to your liking."

"So, no changin' my mind?" ascertained Harold.

"That is correct."

"Like that is something you've never done before, Princess," muttered Tag.

"Hush!" scolded Rose. Reaching over, she smacked her friend's arm in retaliation, only to have Tag shrug off this assault. "Can you not see this man has an important decision to make?"

Harold issued a troubled sigh as he mulled over her words of caution.

"All the more reason not to rush into making a rash decision, my friend," urged Tag.

"I suppose that makes sense, young master." Harold nodded in agreement.

"Sense or not, time is of the essence," reminded Myron.

"It is?" said Harold.

"We must be on our way as soon as Princess Rose is able to don her dried apparel," answered Myron.

"Yes!" She nodded in agreement. "So before we move on, you must make up your mind or forego this offer, for I cannot wait forever, you know?"

"What to do, my friends?" The large man whined as his brows furrowed into a frown of confusion and woe. "What to do?"

"If not monetary compensation, how about a memento to commemorate this most fortuitous and wonderful meeting with me?" offered Rose.

"A memento, you say?"

"Yes! Perhaps a perfumed handkerchief, if I can find it, or how about several strands of my lovely, golden tresses to remember me by."

Tag stifled his laughter as he asked, "And just what is this man to do with strands of your hair?"

"He can do what he wants with it, but if he's smart, he will treasure it always as a cherished token of this meeting and how he saved the life of a fair princess. He will have proof of this event when he boasts to others about this heroic deed."

"I'm thinkin' a true hero has no need to boast about his deeds," said Harold.

"Well, that is just a whole bunch of malarkey! Who told you this rubbish?" queried Rose.

"He did!" Harold smiled as he glanced over to Myron. "And I don't think it is any kind of malarkey at all. Bein' a knight of legend, I figured Sir Myron Kendall was right in his thinkin'. If I had done somethin' truly heroic, I needn't be the one to crow about it, for others would be the ones to do that, if it was truly a worthy deed."

"And saving my life is as worthy a deed as they come," assured Rose. "So, if a medal of bravery does not suit you, perhaps strands of my golden hair will do."

"If you gave me a handful of your hair, I can probably braid the strands together to make a fine fishin' line that trout couldn't spot in the water," said Harold. "That would be good *and* practical."

"Fishing line?" sputtered Rose, her eyes wide in dismay. "My lovely locks are much too precious for catching smelly, old fish!"

A fleeting sting on her scalp caused Rose to jump to her feet. She spun about to face Tag, scowling in anger at the young man.

"You're right, Princess!" He held up the several strands he plucked from her head. "Your *precious* hair is much too brittle, even to weave into a coarse rope!"

"You are still not funny," sniffed Rose.

Tag's lips twisted into a smirk of a grin. He discarded the golden strands over his shoulder before rummaging through his pack to share some cheese and bread with his comrades.

"I don't relish the idea of ruinin' that perfect head of hair, my lady," said Harold. With a polite nod of gratitude, he graciously accepted the serving of bread and the scrapings of cheese Tag served to him.

"That is very considerate of you, good sir!" Rose nodded in approval. "But if not the precious memento of my tresses that is as valuable as gold and even more rare, then what will this reward be?"

"Well, gold is good, my lady, 'til it's all used up. And mementoes are wonderful, if one's got a great memory to remember what the memento was for in the first place," reasoned Harold, "but I believe I can ask for one thing, and it won't be costin' you any hair, or money, for that matter."

"Marvellous! So, what will it be, then?" asked Rose. She watched Harold cram the chunk of bread and cheese into his mouth. "Whatever it is, I will make it so!"

The man raised one hand, gesturing for a moment as the other hand shielded his mouth from her view, so she would not be subjected to seeing him madly masticating this mouthful of food. At least before royalty, he wanted to exhibit some sense of decorum and in doing so, he'd be able to talk while sparing her from being spewed on by stray crumbs of chewed food.

"This should prove interesting," noted Tag. He served up some food to the Princess and to Myron before sitting back to hear what this man was about to propose to her.

With a loud swallow to force down this austere supper, Harold wiped his mouth using the back of his hand. He was finally ready to make his request known.

"I wish to be rewarded with the chance to join you fine folks on this quest!"

Flabbergasted, Rose's mouth fell agape. The piece of bread and cheese she was about to eat dropped from her hand onto her lap, as she stared in stunned disbelief at Myron's friend.

"Say again!" She gasped when she was finally able to speak. "*You* wish to join *us*?"

"On this very quest you're on now!" Harold's eyes gleamed with excitement on thinking up this fine idea while Myron and Tag's backs straightened as the ramifications of this man's words began to sink in.

"Dragon fodder! That is what you will become, if you undertake this task!" warned Rose, shaking an admonishing finger at Harold. "Mind you, that might not be such a bad thing, especially if you can provide a distraction should we need to escape, but have you taken leave of your senses? You'd have to be mad to make such a request!"

"I am?"

"Dragon fodder, I tell you! Not even *I* want to be party to this quest," declared Rose.

"I've no desire to become fodder for any dragon, my lady, but I'd be rightly honoured to come along for this little adventure."

"She is quite right, Harold. This *is* madness!" Myron shook his head as he cautioned his friend. "You are better off, and far safer, too, to ask for monetary compensation or even her whole head of hair, than to accompany us."

"It'd be madness if I hadn't given it serious thought before makin' this request," countered Harold. "This is somethin' I've always dreamed of doin', but never had the chance to be a part of! Now, my dream is about to come true! I can die a happy man."

"I hate to be the bearer of bad tidings, Harold Murkins, but that can well be your fate, if you are ill prepared for any quest, great or small," responded Myron.

"We are not even sure of what we will be up against," added Tag. "The necromancer, Parru St. Mime Dragonite, could well be behind the deadly blight to stricken those in the Woodland Glade."

"Brilliant!" exclaimed Harold, his beady, little eyes shining with excitement.

"Brilliant?" repeated Tag. His brows furrowed in confusion. "How can this affliction be brilliant?"

"I wasn't speakin' of this sickness, I was speakin' of those in the Enchanted Forest. And I don't know about any necromancer, but you're off to see the Elves! That's what I'm talkin' about. I've never met an Elf before! That would be another wish come true!" Harold's large hands clapped together in glee. "Now I know where you're off to on this little adventure, it's an absolute must!"

"Listen up, you hasty-witted bugbear! We do not do *little adventures*, we only undertake monumental, death-defying quests," corrected Rose, hoping to dissuade the man so she would not be subjected to his company.

"But you said I could ask for whatever I wanted… You told me that you'd make it so, and that you never make promises lightly," reminded Harold. He stared with pleading eyes at her. "You're not tellin' me that you lied, are you, my lady? You did say a promise is a promise!"

"She did say just that, did she not, Myron?" Tag nodded in confirmation.

"So she did," replied the knight.

"Huzzah!" shouted Harold. He jumped to his feet. In an undignified, unadulterated display of joy, the large man proceeded to do a victory jig before them.

"You must really want to die," grunted Rose. Her eyes rolled skyward as her palm smacked her forehead in frustration.

"We all die, sooner or later, Princess Rose, but I've been told it's better to live with no regrets than to die with regrets a-plenty."

"Lovely! So you are striving for quality of life, not for longevity."

"A long life means nothin' unless that life is lived to its fullest, Princess. I'd rather live a short life that means somethin' than waste away in old age livin' in regret, given the choice."

"Let me guess," muttered Rose, staring with raised eyebrows at Myron. "It was this noble knight to tell you this, was it not?"

Harold nodded enthusiastically.

"Sir Myron Kendall is the wisest and most noble knight there is! Mind you, I've only ever known one personally in my whole life. But even when I knew him as Cankles Mayron, he always instilled the belief of doin' what one can, so you can pass from this realm with no regrets."

"Wise words, indeed," sniffed Rose. "But what happens if you pass from this world during this quest? What if there is a great calamity that leaves you regretting this decision? What then? Will you hold me to blame?"

"Oh no, my lady! And I'd regret more never venturin' on this mission in the first place, when I have a chance to do so! I'd die a happy man, if that should be my fate."

"Nobody dies happy," argued Rose, her words cynical.

"Nobody is happy to die, but some do die happy. There's a big difference, my lady. I'm speakin' of livin' a happy, meaningful life up to that very moment. Now, that would be somethin' indeed!"

"Very true!" Tag was quick to agree.

"Would you not be happier staying put, here in the safety and comfort of familiar surroundings?" questioned Rose, choosing to ignore Tag's comment.

"Bein' comfortable and happy are two different things, too," stated Harold. "And happiness just doesn't happen sittin' around waitin' for it to come along, one must take the initiative, makin' one's own happiness."

"If this is your idea of happiness, you are more daft than I care to believe," denounced Rose.

"We all have differin' ideas of what makes us happy, my lady. As much as venturin' on this grand quest would make me happy, if you're more concerned about how practical this request is, then know that I can also be of great service to you!"

"Service? To me?" sputtered Rose. With a frown of contempt, she snapped as she waved an admonishing finger at Harold. "I am in awe of your ridiculousity, sir! By your very words, I am wrought with indignaciousness by this very suggestion."

"And I am appalled by the lack of your understanding of our vocabulary!" Tag snorted loudly, almost falling to the ground in a fit of laughter. He knew her attempts to intimidate the man by lambasting him with large words were doomed to fail. "There is no such word as *ridiculousity*."

"And neither is *indignaciousness* a recognized word," added Myron. The knight managed to remain relatively composed, doing a much better job of stifling his laughter than Tag.

"Well, these words should be recognized, as far as I am concerned! And what would you know? Are you two now the self-appointed King and Knave of Words?"

"No, but at least we have a better grasp of the common speech than you do," snorted Tag.

"So you say, but I am genuine royalty."

"So?" grumbled Tag.

"I shall pass an edict proclaiming these new words to be real, and therefore, to be added to that big book of words."

"Dictionary, Princess Rose, I do believe the word you are looking for is *dictionary*," said Myron.

"Until then, we refuse to recognize these words, therefore, *we* do not understand what *you* just said," added Tag. His smug grin caused

Rose's face to redden in annoyance as he continued on. "If anything, you are speaking fluent *gibberish*, the universal language of idiots!"

"To the contrary, my friends! What Princess Rose means to say in her fancy way is that I'm bein' ridiculous and my offer's either an insult or an assault to her dignity," explained Harold.

"Both, to speak the truth, but yes! There you go!" sniffed Rose. She nodded in approval to Harold before casting a baleful stare of reproach at Myron and Tag.

"I do declare... I am both stunned and impressed!" Tag's eyes were wide open in astonishment.

"How so?" questioned Rose.

"It is apparent you and Harold are like-minded! You both speak the same language."

"Hush, you boiled-brain miscreant! Let us remain on course with the subject at hand." Her tone was incredulous as she turned away from Tag to address this simpleton of a man. "And just what can *you* do for *me,* Harold?"

"If I be so bold to say, Princess Rose, though I'm far from handy with the sword or bow like Sir Kendall or your suitor –"

"Let me make this perfectly clear, Harold Murkins!" Rose's index finger poked the large man in his barrel-chest as she jabbed the thumb of her other hand over her shoulder at Tag. "This buffoon is *not* my suitor!"

"If you say so, Princess."

"Oh, I *do* say so!" A disgruntled huff snorted from her flaring nostrils as she spoke.

"Well, before I forget what I was goin' to say to plead my case, I can still be of help to you three along the way. I might even rescue you again, my lady."

"Look here, Harold. I understand your intentions are honest, but the weight of this burden I bear can well be the death of me this time," lamented Rose. The back of her hand pressed lightly against her forehead in woe. "I wish not to be encumbered by the weight of greater responsibility should another soul come along. You can potentially endanger your life, and this will be too great a burden for me to bear."

"With all due respect, my lady, you got that wrong."

"What do I have wrong?"

"It's not the burden that can kill you; it's more like how you carry it," insisted Harold.

"What a bunch of malarkey, I say!" argued Rose.

"The size of the burden, whether you're tryin' to move a small hill or a great mountain, it can be done if you do it one stone at a time. I can help you with these stones. Puttin' it bluntly, I can help you with this burden; lighten up your load a bit in my own way."

"He does have a good point," said Myron, smiling in admiration at Harold.

"You only say that because Harold views you as his wise mentor!" Rose smacked the knight on his arm as she scolded him. "Do not encourage him!"

"I am merely stating the obvious, my lady," replied Myron, with a shrug of his shoulders.

"And it is obvious to us that you had made this man a promise," reminded Tag; wiping his hands clean of crumbs as he finished his meal. "Unless you wish to prove me wrong about how you tend to renege on your promises, you best act on it."

"And allow this man to potentially endanger his life on my account?" gasped Rose. "I think not!"

"And yet, you have no qualms about the two of us endangering our lives on your behalf," noted Tag.

"Well, you two are different, and this fellow is just... *different*," insisted Rose. "You have both been raised and trained for the rigours and dangers of a gruelling quest, while this man is better prepared for foraging about for his food, not to mention hunting, and then skinning dead animals to wear."

"Though that be true, my lady, I can still be of help in other ways," said Harold.

"Explain yourself, sir!" demanded Rose. Thoroughly agitated by his persistence and positive nature, she heaved a disgruntled sigh. "For this, I must hear."

"I can care for the animals you're travellin' with. I can saddle 'em up and unsaddle 'em at night. And while you three are busy with questy things, I can water and groom these horses, too. It'll be just like takin' care of my donkey, 'cept they're much bigger than Sassy."

"Sassy, my ass!" Rose grunted as she rolled her eyes in utter frustration.

"Sassy's *my* ass, but I'd prefer if you called her a donkey. And it won't be much different than carin' for horses. I'm thinkin' they're basically the same kind of animal, but one is much bigger than the other. Kinda like you and me, Princess Rose."

"We are *nothing* at all alike! Other than being of the mortal persuasion, I am still uncertain of your species."

"Thing bein', my lady, I can take some of the load off of those puny, royal shoulders of yours by carin' for your horses along the way. It'd be one less thing you'd have to worry about."

"Well, you do seem to have a way with animals," noted Rose, remembering how the man took the time to wipe down their cold, wet horses with dried leaves without even being asked to do so.

"I'm not half bad at startin' fires, too, with or without a flint, and I can also gather wood at day's end, so we'll have a roarin' campfire to keep warm by. It can also help keep dangerous animals at bay," added Harold, using a stick to prod the glowing embers before them.

"Anything else?" queried Rose.

She seriously considered his offer, appreciating the sense of security provided by a campfire, while relishing the thought that this man would be the one relegated to the menial task of collecting the wood, and not to forget, starting the fire. It was a chore she detested after her first attempt almost cost her beautiful crown of hair when Tag challenged her to undertake the task of starting a campfire while he hunted for food to cook over it.

Harold pointed proudly to the porcupine pelt 'wig' adorning his round head. "And I'm pretty darned good at this, too, my lady!"

"Good gracious! I much prefer a tiara crowning my head, than a dead animal." Rose grimaced in disgust at the thought. "We have no need for animal pelt wigs!"

"Oh, you wouldn't be sayin' that, if you were goin' bald and the winds of winter should come blowin' in," insisted Harold. He wrapped his thick, meaty arms around his equally meaty body, pretending to shiver with cold. "But I wasn't speakin' about wigs, my lady. I meant to say, I'm good at catchin' all sorts of critters, includin' rabbits, squirrels and grouse that are good for eatin', especially roasted over an open fire... that *I* can make and tend to. I can free you up from all these tasks so you three can focus on the business of the quest while I cheer you on."

A smile crept across Rose's face as Tag and Myron flushed with embarrassment, knowing that she was recalling how they had failed miserably in downing a couple of game birds perched in the boughs of a spruce tree. Where they failed, she, with her deadly accurate aim, had no difficulty in dislodging the two, roosting grouse with a single, well-aimed stone.

"You, Harold Murkins, are an unexpected boon to us!" praised Rose, her eyes twinkling with the prospects.

Myron and Tag exchanged quizzical glances upon hearing this sudden change of heart.

"I am?" Harold's pudgy face beamed with delight as he listened to her words of commendation.

"Indeed! I can see now how beneficial it will be to have you accompany us on this adventure," declared Rose. She nodded approvingly to Harold. "So, I shall grant you your wish! You are coming with us."

"Yes!" The man whooped, his clenched fists pumping the air as he dropped to his knees in an unabashed show of elation.

"Are you sure about this, Harold?" questioned Tag. "There is no shame in changing your mind, you know?"

"Tag is correct, my friend, it is not too late to reconsider," added Myron. "Perhaps it is better for you to be homeward bound."

"Balderdash!" countered Rose. "And just why are you two trying to change his mind now, after pressing the fact that I should do my utmost to keep my promise?"

"As you said before, my lady, Tag and I are suited for the rigours of a quest," reminded Myron. "Harold is not."

"So what? Nor were you when we first met," argued Rose. "Even with an addled brain, you insisted on coming with us, and in the end, look how well it turned out for you! You are you again!"

"True, but at great sacrifice," reminded Myron, his hand absentmindedly rubbing the nasty scar hidden beneath his thick, brown thatch of hair.

"The same can happen to this man in the course of our adventure! He can become the man he once was, and it might happen without the same level of trauma you had endured," reasoned Rose.

"But I've always been the way I am," insisted Harold. "Whatever it is you make of me, I'm just me. I'm a simple man with a simple dream; one that's about to come true!"

"So, you have always been this… *extraordinary*?" asked Rose, selecting this adjective carefully lest she incite the wrath of her comrades for insulting the man.

"*Extra* ordinary, my lady, but I'm sayin' this quest can test my mettle, maybe make me do somethin' real special, extraordinary even, for once in my life."

Tag was thinking that Harold was tempted to accompany them more to quell his loneliness, than to indulge in a lifelong dream. Having missed his friend's company since Cankles' return as Sir Myron Kendall, this knight now spent more time at the palace than at his humble cottage. Resuming his responsibilities, it afforded him less time to play host to Harold, as the pair once frequently travelled around Cadboll in the County of Wren, taking on odd jobs and setting traps for rabbits and other small animals for fur and meat. Just as Myron felt inclined to find a suitable home for his pets due to his prolonged periods of absence, his friendship with Harold suffered, too, in accepting his sworn duties to king and country.

"Are you positive about this?" asked Tag, as he searched this man's eyes for the truth.

"Absolutely! I am positively sure, young master! Once I put my boots back on my feet, I'll be ready to go! In fact, I've never been so ready for anythin' in my entire life!"

Like an exuberant child, Harold jumped up and down with giddy excitement.

"Just keep in mind, my friend, there are rules to be followed, if you wish to be party to this mission," cautioned Myron. He raised his hands to gesture for calm as the horses stomped about nervously while Harold's donkey brayed in agitation upon witnessing his master's abrupt and lively display.

Upon hearing Myron's words delivered in a serious tone, Harold suddenly snapped to attention like a disciplined soldier waiting for orders from his captain. His chest puffed out in pride as he saluted to Myron Kendall.

"Rules are good, my friend! I can follow rules, as good as the best of 'em, whatever these rules be!"

"Very good, Harold! We shall discuss them as we make ready," said Myron. He turned his gaze skyward, waving at Loken, now in the form of an owl, to come down from his lookout perch high in the overhead tree.

The Sprite's aura flashed brightly against the dark canvas of night as Loken morphed back to his typical form before floating down to join his comrades. "We are leaving now?"

Before he answered the Sprite, Myron reached up, testing the dryness of the Princess' riding attire. The pieces were sufficiently dry to his touch, toasty warm even.

"Yes, as soon as Princess Rose dons her apparel," answered Myron. He removed the items he had draped on the overhead branches. "Ready our horses, Harold!"

5
A Repeat Engagement

"So what I heard turned out to be true," determined Loken.

He hovered before Harold's excited face as the mortal fumbled about, undertaking his task with enthusiasm. His plump fingers struggled to unknot the reins as he eagerly untethered his donkey after helping Tag and Myron saddle the horses.

"You heard us talkin' from way up there?" questioned Harold. Amazed, he gazed to the treetop where the Sprite had been perched during their impromptu break.

"While I kept watch from that high vantage point, I had adopted the form of an owl so I would pass unnoticed by potential enemies. It also allowed me to watch and listen with the sharp eyes and the exceptionally keen ears of this bird of prey."

"Brilliant! I sure wish I had this power to change my appearance at will." Harold tugged at his donkey's reins to make Sassy follow. "It must be a wonderful thing!"

"One should always be careful of what one wishes for," cautioned Loken. "My power is a wonderful blessing, but it can also be a terrible curse."

Harold frowned as he mulled over these words. "Don't rightly know how somethin' can be both a blessin' and a curse, but I suppose I'll take your word for it."

"Trust me, I speak the truth. My friends can vouch for me," called Loken. He glanced over at Rose and the others before circling over this mortal's head. With a flick of his wings, he flew off to escort this procession through what remained of the night.

"I'll take up the rear," volunteered Harold, "just in case somethin' evil comes up from behind to take us by surprise."

"Good plan!" agreed Rose. She coaxed her mare forward to take the position between Myron and Tag, secure in the thought that if indeed this should happen, it will be *his behind* surprised by something evil, not hers. "I now feel doubly safe."

"As you should, Princess!" said Harold.

Tag twisted about in his saddle, glancing behind to address their new travel companion. "Will there be a problem in keeping up with us, Harold?"

"Shouldn't be, young master. If my little Sassy should start to lag behind, I'll pick her up and carry her. Though she's small, she's as strong and tough as they come, but her stumpy, little legs can tire her out if she's made to trot for too long."

"You can lift that animal?" Rose's brows arched up in surprise.

"I've done it on more than one occasion, my lady."

"Oh, my! You must be as strong as an ox!" She scrutinized his large frame and broad, rounded shoulders. She was not sure of the muscle to fat ratio, but she determined there had to be an abundance of muscles hidden somewhere beneath that insulating layer of blubber, if Harold was as strong as he claimed.

"Some say so, then again, some have called me as dumb as an ox, too. I'm thinkin' I must have some qualities that are kinda ox-ish for people to make such a comparison, but I'm choosin' to believe in the better qualities of this animal, bein' that they can be strong and reliable when there's work to be done."

"Well, bully for you!" praised Rose.

"More oxy than bully," quipped Harold. "But should my little Sassy tire, I'll just carry her 'til she catches her second wind."

"I was not asking about your donkey, Harold. I was speaking about you," corrected Tag. "Will *you* be able to keep up?"

"Oh, I'll be fine, young sir!" assured Harold. "These stout legs of mine were made for travellin' long distances, so don't you fret. And if you find a need to gallop on ahead, you just go on and do that. I'll follow the hoof prints 'til I catch up to you."

"Are you sure?"

"Absolutely! Though some think I'm rather rotund and not in the best of shape, I'm actually quite robust. I might not have great speed, but what I lack in speed, I make up for with great stamina."

"Very well then," said Tag, his heels tapping at his mount's flanks to prod the horse on to follow the others. "Let's be on our way."

❦ ❦ ❦

"I can see it now! We are almost at the Fairy's Vale," announced Loken, pointing through the stand of trees. He was elated to see his home, the glow of his aura intensifying as they neared.

Gliding on a whisper of a breeze, the Sprite escorted his comrades to a large meadow. Emerging one by one from the edge of the forest, they paused, waiting for Harold and his donkey to catch up to them.

As he and Sassy trundled along, coming up beside Tag, Harold's loud huffing and puffing became a gasp of awe as a wondrous sight beheld his eyes. Radiant beams of moonlight streamed through the tree canopy of a massive oak tree to set a-glistening the silvery beads of dew bejewelling the leaves and blades of grass. It was an ethereal vision to behold.

"This is it?" whispered Harold.

"Yes," answered Loken.

"If this is the Fairy's Vale, then where are all the Fairies?" Harold glanced about, scrutinizing their tranquil surroundings. "I thought there'd be Fairies a-plenty in the Vale, hence the name."

"Look up!" said Myron, pointing to the high branches as he, Tag and Rose dismounted.

Harold watched as Loken spiralled skyward as a visual cue to make his presence known to the others. Pinpoints of faint light Harold had thought were nothing more than distant stars started to glow brightly. Golden orbs began to illuminate the surrounding trees in this meadow and above their heads.

"Fireflies?" asked Harold, enchanted by this sight.

"Fairies," corrected Rose, her hands nervously resting over the pieces of jewellery she wore.

"Incredible," whispered Harold, his eyes widening in wonder as he marvelled at this display of light. "I'm speechless."

"Then why are you still talking?" grumbled Rose.

Too captivated by this spectacle to take notice of her terse words, Harold's eyes followed the luminous spheres as they floated on an invisible breeze. Their glow intensified as they drifted toward the ring of red-capped toadstools.

The orbs of light began to bob up and down, swaying side to side in a rhythmic dance to celebrate the autumn equinox. They pranced about, a dazzling show of light moving in synchrony to the tune they sang. In a grand finale, the glowing orbs darted and twirled in the air, leaving trails of shimmering light in their wake.

Harold's head began to spin, unable to keep track of this stunning display of light and aerial precision. His eyes darted to and fro, following the spheres in graceful flight. In awe, he could no longer resist. Harold began inching closer to the ring of toadstools as another group of Fairies floated down to join in dance.

"No!" Rose cried out. Realizing what was about to happen, her eyes widened in alarm. "Stop, Harold!"

This magical sight mesmerized him. Rose's words went unheeded as Harold could only think of getting closer for a better look.

Recalling what happened the first time she had happened upon a Fairy's Ring, Rose was not about to relive the horrors. There was no way she was going to be stripped of her jewels again, not if she could help it.

Seizing him by the arm, Rose yanked as hard as she could. Harold was jerked back, jolted out of his trance. He seemed momentarily stupefied. Blinking hard, he stared down to the toadstools Rose was pointing to.

"You do not want to step on those," warned Rose, pulling Harold away. "Trust me on this."

"Why?" Harold asked, his brows furrowing in confusion as he took a cautious step back. "It's not like those toadstools won't grow back, if I had."

"Bad things happen when you step on a Fairy's Ring. I had the misfortune of stepping on one before. All my jewels were stolen by these little scoundrels!"

The thought then dawned on her that the Fairies might not need a reason to abscond with her jewellery. Perhaps they already had an affinity for shiny objects and now, she was only tempting fate. Rose's hands flew up to her neck. She hastily removed all of her fine pieces. Stuffing them into her pockets, she wrapped her wool cloak tightly around her body.

Harold's shoulders drooped as he apologized, "I didn't mean any harm."

"Just be careful where you tread," cautioned Rose. "The Fairies are tiny, but when they swarm, they are a force to reckon with."

"I'll keep that in mind," promised Harold.

"Good!" she responded. "Now, stay close."

Scrutinizing the meadow, Harold's brows furrowed in confusion as his eyes darted about, searching for signs of the great palace that Loken had spoken of as they journeyed on to get here. There was no palace, not even a modest castle in the middle of this meadow. There was only the most massive oak tree he had ever seen, growing in the very centre of this clearing.

Amongst the twisting branches reaching skyward the golden orbs began to congregate for a better look at the visitors as Loken guided these mortals toward this oak tree.

"Nothing to see, good people, nothing to see!" shouted Loken, as he waved off the curious crowd that gathered. "Return to your business, as we shall return to ours."

With these words, the golden swarms dispersed into the velvety night sky. Some floated off to join in dance around the Fairy's Ring under the light of the Harvest Moon while others engaged in an energetic game of tag. This aerial pursuit lit up the night sky as one Fairy gave chase while the others scattered, dodging and darting amongst the high branches of the oak tree.

"Awww!" Harold groaned, frowning in disappointment to see the tiny beings depart. His eyes followed the delightful, golden spheres in graceful flight. "That was so magical…"

"If you say so, but we should hurry," urged Loken. "Leave your steeds here and follow me."

"Shouldn't we tie these animals up, so they don't wander off?" asked Harold. He glanced about, searching for a suitable tree to act as a hitching post for the night.

"That will not be necessary," assured Loken. "These horses and your donkey will be safe in the Vale. The Fairies will watch over them to make sure they do not stray."

"You're soundin' mighty confident, Master Loken. I'll trust you on this matter," said Harold, with a judicious nod of his porcupine-crowned head. He moved the knotted reins over his donkey's head, resting it on Sassy's withers so they wouldn't dangle on the ground to be trod upon, thereby possibly injuring the animal.

"We shall unsaddle them for the night, Harold." Tag tugged at the cinch of his horse's saddle, loosening the wide strap from the buckle to remove it and the saddle blanket to rest both at the base of a large tree.

Myron followed suit as Harold removed the tack from Rose's mare before removing the assorted bundles from his donkey's back.

"Come with me," urged Loken. He waved the four mortals on now that they were done and the animals were grazing peacefully on the sweet grasses and clover. "It is well beyond the midnight hour. Queen Pancecelia should be back by now."

Following Loken as he floated across the meadow, they strolled toward the grand old oak tree rising proudly from the centre of this tranquil, bucolic setting. With the chilling breath of autumn, the golding of the leaves cast the foliage in a dazzling shade of yellow, some taking on an auburn hue. And now, in the moonlight, the dew-kissed leaves glowed, as though burnished in gold.

They watched as Loken floated upward, disappearing into a large knothole in the trunk of the tree. All they could see was the glow of his aura lighting up the interior.

"What's in there?" questioned Harold.

"The royal residence," answered Myron.

"You jest! It's in there? A grand palace?" The large man tittered, giddy with excitement. "Truly?"

"Yes," answered Rose, as she motioned for Harold to calm down.

"Take a look for yourself," invited Tag. "For something so small, it is still quite spectacular, and even more so when you are the size of a Fairy."

Being head and shoulders taller than Myron, there was no need for Harold to stand up on the tips of his toes to look inside. He peered into the hole in the trunk of the oak tree, the light of Loken's aura reflecting against his astonished face.

"This is incredible!" Harold's eyes followed the courtyard leading up to the steps of the pearly white palace. A smaller knothole higher up in the tree trunk allowed a single beam of moonlight to shine down like a spotlight upon this fine, dentine edifice that was illuminated by the glow of fireflies acting as living light sconces. "I've never seen anything quite like this in my entire life."

"Nor is there another place like it in the world. Its existence and locale are unknown to the vast majority of mortals and we prefer to keep it that way, if you get my meaning?" said Loken, as he hovered before this man's awe-struck face.

"And a secret it'll remain, Master Loken," vowed Harold. With his left hand resting over his heart in solemn promise, he used the right to pretend he was locking his lips, tossing away the imaginary key over his shoulder to solidify this pledge.

"I shall hold you to your promise, good sir. Though none may enter without a formal invitation from the Queen of the Tooth Fairies, it is wise to keep her royal residence a secret, nonetheless. There are some unscrupulous souls in this world, those who would think nothing of committing an act of thievery or worse. They would be eager to plunder from the royal vaults, if they knew where to look."

"That is too odd," said Rose, her tone cynical. "Why would anyone want to steal teeth, even if they were not rotten?"

"I was speaking of the ones filled with *gold*," explained Loken, giving the Princess a knowing smile, "usually mined from the mouths of the wealthy dead."

"I never thought of that," responded Rose, as she considered the potential wealth of such a find.

"There is much you do not think of, Princess," teased Tag.

"The point being, with the advent of dentistry advancing beyond that of teeth extractions, though gold teeth are rare, the Fairies do find the odd one from time to time," said Loken.

"Well, I won't be tellin' no one about what we *weren't* just talkin' about," promised Harold. He winked as his index finger tapped the side of his nose. "But you were sayin' to enter the palace was by invitation only?"

"Indeed." Loken nodded in confirmation.

"I can't speak for my friends, but I sure as heck don't have an invitation." Harold turned out the pockets of his trousers to show they were empty. "But no worries! I suppose I can spend the night out here with the horses and my donkey. I'll keep a watchful eye on them while my friends go on inside."

"Nonsense!" said Rose. "Exclude you from an audience with the Queen of the Tooth Fairies? I think not! It promises to be quite the adventure unto itself."

"Well, that's lovely of you to say so, Princess Rose," said Harold. He pulled his head away from the hole in the tree trunk to address her. "But unless you know of some magic, there's no way we can go inside. I can barely fit my big, old noggin in there, and that's even if I were to remove this special headpiece I'm wearin'."

"A special magic is required to enter, but I am not the one to dispense it," responded Rose.

Harold suddenly backed away from the entrance to this tiny, but ornate royal residence as a brilliant show of light swelled before him.

"Who are you?" asked Harold. He stared through narrowed, suspicious eyes as Loken bowed his head in respectful greeting to the tiny being to appear on the steps of the palace.

"I am Pancecelia Feldspar, Queen of the Tooth Fairies." Flying to the knothole, she hovered before this mortal's face. Sensing he posed no threat, as Loken seemed unmoved by his presence, she alighted upon the grounds of the courtyard. Her wand remained poised in her hand, should she be forced to defend the hollow and those inside her royal residence. "And just who are you, stranger?"

"I swear I'm no stranger than most other folks, Your Majesty. I'm here with these fine people you know as your friends!"

Harold pointed with one hand over his shoulder toward his comrades, as the other reached up to his prickly headpiece. He removed one of the trapped acorns from between the quills. This nut disappeared in his clenched fist. With a quick squeeze, the shell cracked open, allowing easy access to the nut within. Politely bowing his head, Harold placed the acorn before the Queen.

"I come bearin' a simple gift, Your Majesty, a nut from this autumn's first harvest!"

"A nut, indeed!" muttered Rose, with a dismal shake of her head.

"Your gift is appreciated, sir," said Pance. "It shall make for a fine meal to feed many, but first, proper introductions are in order."

Harold nodded in understanding, removing his big, round face from the entranceway to make room for her to pass through.

Taking to the air, Pancecelia glowed brightly as she exited the tree hollow. Loken followed.

"Welcome, my friends! Loken told me to expect your arrival on this night, if you were to answer his call. It fills my heart with hope to see you."

"Greetings, Your Majesty!" said the mortals.

While Rose curtsied politely, Myron and Tag dropped down upon one knee, bowing in respect to this high Fairy.

Harold's eyes bulged and his mouth drooped open in stunned amazement. "Oh, my! Seeing you out in the open now, than against your magnificent palace, you really are a tiny, little thing! You're even smaller than I imagined."

Myron tugged on the leg of Harold's trousers, gesturing him to kneel before royalty, no matter how small. Harold fell on both his knees, looking more like a grovelling man seeking mercy, instead of one showing his respect.

"No doubt, in your eyes, I appear tiny." Pance bowed her head in agreement.

"I mean no disrespect, but I just figured that bein' a powerful queen and all, you'd be much larger, even by Fairy standards," explained Harold.

"If that were so, it will make the task of discreetly harvesting teeth much more difficult. Would you not agree?"

"You're probably right, but I'm thinkin' in my friends' eyes, too, you're pretty puny, Your Majesty!" Harold squinted once more as Pancecelia glowed brightly, her aura flaring as she hovered before him.

"How about now?"

Harold gasped in surprise as the Queen, in a resplendent show of light, transformed before the mortal. This time, she was towering above him as he knelt down before her.

"Oh, my!" Harold's eyes were wide as he fell back with a start, taking in her full, regal size.

Scrambling onto his feet, this mortal found himself standing face-to-face with a being of legend while Rose abruptly darted behind Tag. As beautiful as Pancecelia was, the Princess recalled how this tiny being transmogrified into this larger than life-sized version upon their first, ill-fated encounter. Once more, this Fairy was as intimidating as she was stunning, but even more so in this grand size.

Harold smiled in wonder as he basked in the warm glow of Pancecelia Feldspar's aura. Like a great beacon, her luminescence served to push back against the shadows of the night to light up the meadow.

"Brilliant! I wasn't expectin' this!" Harold gasped in delight.

"Neither was I!" squeaked Rose, as she peered over Tag's shoulder.

Myron and Tag bowed once more, leaving the cowering Princess exposed. Rose lost no time in following their action. She joined them in respectful greeting, ignoring protocol by curtsying as she bowed her head lower than a princess needed to before fellow royalty. In this larger form, even with iridescent, gossamer wings that glittered in the moonlight, this Fairy was a being Rose now respected *and* dreaded, especially after crossing her the first time.

"Do you fear me, Princess Rose?"

"Just overwhelmed by your magnificence, Your Majesty," lied Rose, now feeling as though she was the one who was as small as the smallest Fairy.

"Me, too! This is truly remarkable!" praised Harold. He was absolutely awestruck by her size and beauty. Standing once more, they stood there, eye-to-eye.

"My Queen can appear in this human-sized form, if she wills it," explained Loken, smiling with pride as he gazed upon his lady-love.

"Can you do that, too, Master Loken?" questioned Harold. "Become big, that is?"

"She is a high Fairy, one of royal blood, while I am merely a shape-shifting Sprite," answered Loken.

"Oh, yes! I keep forgettin' you're a Pooka!"

"Yes, but I prefer to be called a Sprite, if you will?"

"I will!" said Harold, nodding in apology. "So you can change and become big, too?"

"I can make myself appear as large as I wish and I can certainly become as big as you are, if I do this!" In a great flash of light, he instantly transformed.

Harold's eyes were as wide open as his gaping mouth. In awe, he stared at his doppelganger. Loken had adopted this human's form; his spitting image right down to the tatty, bearskin cloak and the porcupine headpiece Harold wore with pride.

"Smack me in my gob and call me Harry! Are you... me!" The man used his index finger to poke his likeness in the chest to make sure he was not imagining this.

"I am merely a remarkable likeness of you. Other than my physical appearance, I am still very much the Sprite you know."

"Well, thank goodness for that!" said Rose. "I cannot imagine trying to deal with two Harold Murkins at one time."

"As you can see, I can appear as a full-sized human being, but it is only if I adopt the form of a mortal, such as yourself. I cannot simply appear as a Sprite in this larger size, though it would have come in handy at times."

"Interestin'... Say, can you change into food, too, or only into living people and creatures?" asked Harold.

"Inanimate objects are out of the question, but food, you say? Are you asking because you are hungry?"

"A wee bit peckish after our travels, but don't go worryin' about me, Master Loken. I'm sure I can scrounge up somethin' to eat," insisted Harold. He studied the image standing before him. It was like staring at his reflection in a mirror, but better! Harold stood with his hands on his hips, chest thrust out, as he mimicked his likeness that possessed much better posture than he ever had.

"If you are a friend of Sir Myron Kendall, then consider yourself a friend of mine, too, good sir. You will be afforded the same hospitality and amenities as your comrades," said Pancecelia, smiling kindly at the large mortal. "And, as the four of you are my guests on this night, of course there is food awaiting you!"

"That's mighty kind of you, but I certainly don't want to impose on your kindness, Queen Pancecelia," said Harold. He removed his unusual headpiece to bow his head in gratitude without poking her with one of the many protruding quills.

"We are amongst friends. There is no need for such formality! Please, just call me Pance. And it is no imposition at all, Master...?" She stared quizzically at this stranger as she waited for a name.

"Murkins, but you can just call me Harry."

"Harold, it is! Now, let us reconvene inside. We shall share in a meal and a drink before getting you settled for some sleep before sunrise."

"Sounds wonderful and mighty invitin', Your Majesty, but how do we get as small as a Fairy, tiny enough to fit inside?" questioned Harold, as he scratched his stubbly chin.

"Magic, I tell you!" chirped up Rose, peering over Tag's shoulder again. "But first, you should consider how we get up there into the tree hollow once we shrink down in size."

"If we're made puny, I can tell you now, it'll promise to be quite the climb," assessed Harold, his hand patting the deeply fissured bark of the oak tree. "Not impossible, but a hard climb nonetheless, I'm sure."

"We can use the same mode of transportation we did the first time we were here," suggested Myron. "It will make for a quick and easy ride."

"A ride?" asked Harold, his eyes opening wide in wonder as he considered the possibilities. "A ride on what? For I know of not one horse that's tiny and nimble enough to climb straight up."

"Just know it was quick, indeed, but easy? It was more frightening than anything else," stated Rose.

"So tell me! What will we ride?" Harold asked once more.

"The last time we came we had a wild ride on a dormouse, of all things," answered Tag. He smiled inwardly, recalling how he and Myron whooped in excitement while Rose screamed in terror, almost squeezing the life from his body with her arms as she held on to him. "It was quite exhilarating!"

"Are you mad or was your brain addled during that *exhilarating* rodent ride? It was terrifying!" countered Rose. "I had no problem with being reduced to the size of a Fairy, and I'm sure I would have made for an excellent one had I possessed wings, but think again if you believe for an instant that I am going to go for another death-defying ride on the back of a flea-bitten rodent."

"Fleas or not, dormouses are – "

"Dormice." Rose corrected Harold.

"Yes! Dormice are so adorable, with them big, dark eyes," continued Harold. Like a giant squirrel nibbling on an invisible nut, he fluttered his lashes, as his eyes grew misty. They became like deep, limpid pools as he tried to look like one of these rodents.

"Nice try, but you look nothing like a dormouse," grunted Rose.

"I'm supposin' I'm way too big and just not furry enough," said Harold.

"The point being, it will not be a pleasant little jaunt to get from here to there," warned Rose, pointing at the ground, and then to the large knothole. "The ride is almost a sheer, vertical climb up this tree trunk."

"Oh, my!" exclaimed Harold, his hands slapping together in glee. "Now that *does* sound exhilaratin'! I can't wait!"

Rose rolled her eyes, exhaling loudly in response as she pointed to the edge of the meadow, "Look! There it goes!"

"What?" asked Harold, spinning about on his heels to see what she was pointing at. "There what goes?"

"Your mind! Obviously, you've lost it!"

"Worry not, Princess Rose," said Pance. "I have a better way, if you are not up to riding our resident dormouse."

"Anything is better than rodent-riding," averred Rose.

"We should hurry," suggested Loken. "The sun will be on the rise sooner than we think."

With a flash of her hand, the Queen showered her guests with a sprinkling of iridescent Fairy dust.

"Close your eyes. Breathe it in," urged Pancecelia. "Relax and let its power perform its magic on you."

All four mortals did as they were told, but it was Harold doing so with utmost zeal. He squeezed his eyes shut. Breathing loudly, almost snorting, he inhaled as much of the dust floating around him as he could while he wrung his hands to contain his excitement.

When he felt no different after several heartbeats, Harold opened one eye, checking to see if the magic had worked on his friends, but not on him. Before Harold stood the Queen while Loken hovered just above her right shoulder, but the large man groaned in disappointment, for Rose, Tag and Myron were nowhere to be seen.

"Hey... Where did everybody go?"

"Your friends are right beside you," answered Loken. "Just be careful where you tread."

"They're invisible?"

"Not quite," said Pance. "They have shrunk, but being larger than the others, it is just taking a little more Fairy dust and additional time for the magic to work on you."

Before the Queen could dispense more of her Fairy dust, Harold squealed in fright. Staring down at the ground, his vision blurred as the earth rushed up toward him. Or was he rushing down to meet the earth? Whatever the case, Harold felt as though he had stepped off the edge of a cliff. It was that same frightening rush of falling, even though he could still feel the ground planted firmly beneath his feet.

Instinctively, his eyes squeezed shut. Harold threw his arms up to protect his face as the growing blades of grasses thrashed at him as he shrank.

Harold's heart thundered in his chest. His stomach lurched, churning as a dizzying sensation threatened to overwhelm him.

"Look out!" shouted Tag. He lunged forward, pushing Harold out of the way.

In a daze, Harold staggered back. He opened his eyes just as a monstrous carrion beetle trundled by. It was as large as Sassy! With pincer-like jaws snapping in annoyance, the ebony beast ambled by him. With single-minded determination, this insect was in search of a meal.

Six sturdy, jointed legs effortlessly carried the creature even though it looked weighed down enormously by its hefty, armour-like, ink-black carapace. With short antennae waving about and the unblinking stare of two large, compound eyes, the beetle barely glanced in the mortal's direction. Sensing there was no food to be had here, as the enticing scent of decaying flesh was nowhere to be smelled on these living beings jumping out of its way, the beetle was not even mildly interested in them.

"Oh, my! This is incredible!" Harold exclaimed as he regained his composure. With the great beetle disappearing from his sight, he stared up at the towering forest comprised of grasses, dandelions and clovers that leaned over them to form a dense jungle canopy.

"Incredible? Have you taken leave of your senses again?" snapped Rose. She struggled to remove Tag's sword from its scabbard, just in case the beetle returned to attack. "That monster of a bug is even more disgusting than when it was small!"

"That might be true, but it meant us no harm," insisted Tag. He pushed her hands away, firmly grasping his weapon and twisting his body away from Rose and her reach. "Now, should you mortally wound yourself trying to handle this blade, then that carrion beetle will certainly be interested in devouring your corpse."

"So you say, but the longer we stand in this jungle, the greater the chance a ferocious praying mantis or another predatory creature will attack," countered Rose.

"Prayin', as in?" Harold clasped his hands together in silent prayer. "Or did you mean preyin', as in?" He then snarled; bearing his yellowed teeth as his fingers curled into claws while his face adopted the crazed look of a demented soul waiting to attack.

Recalling his last encounter with a vicious mantis that tried to devour Myron when he was Cankles, Tag decided to draw his sword as a precaution. "The Princess was referring to the mantis that preys on pretty much anything that it deems edible."

"Fear not, Princess, I'll help to keep you safe," offered Harold. He spun about on his heels. His eyes narrowed into menacing slits as he searched about for potential danger.

"How do you intend to do that? You do not even own a sword, nor would you know how to use one, if you did."

The man waved his grimy, calloused hands before her face, wriggling his fingers about as he spoke, "I've got these eye-gougers, Princess! And I'll willingly wrestle down any overgrown insect, if I must, to keep you safe from harm."

"Good luck with that!" groaned Rose. She suddenly cowered, ducking behind Harold as a great shadow blotted out the moon and the stars above.

Pancecelia Feldspar knelt down. Lowering an opened hand, she presented it before the mortals. "I shall lift you up into the tree hollow, if you will?"

Without hesitation Myron hopped up, climbing aboard first. He offered his hand to Rose while Tag gave her a leg up. As the Princess settled down in the middle of Pancecelia's palm, Tag and Myron each offered a hand to Harold, pulling him up to join them.

Before he could be safely seated alongside his comrades, Harold grunted as he took a tumble. With the force of this now gigantic Fairy quickly elevating them to new heights, he landed on his backside next to Rose. Harold's eyes opened wide in wonder as he lay on his back, staring up to the night sky. Through the branches of the great oak tree the multitude of stars seemed to rush toward them in a dazzling blur of silvery light, as the Queen stood upright, lifting these four up and through the entrance of the tree hollow. Her hand came to rest in the courtyard for her passengers to disembark.

"Allow me," offered Loken, extending his hands to Princess Rose to help her down.

Taking his hands into hers, Rose hopped off her ride.

"I do not think I will ever get used to this," admitted Rose, staring up at the Sprite's face.

"Get used to what, Princess? Shrinking down to our size?" questioned Loken.

"Yes! That, and having to look up at you for a change," answered Rose. Now standing shorter than the Sprite, she was taken aback by the sparkle of Loken's sapphire eyes shining in the glow of his aura. It was a far more fetching appearance than when these eyes were a menacing shade of amber, shining of malice and spite when Parru St. Mime Dragonite had cursed him.

"It can be especially difficult for the Princess," quipped Tag, "especially when she is so used to looking *down* on everybody else."

"Not so, young master!" insisted Harold, sensing a slight taint of condescension in Tag's voice. "Princess Rose is an absolute lamb! She's been nothin' but gracious to me, since invitin' me on this quest."

"Bask in the revelry of this feeling, for it will not last, my friend, for often, her good intentions are motivated by self-serving reasons," cautioned Tag. He patted Harold on his shoulder as he gave the man a sympathetic smile.

"And it will serve you well to stop wagging that tongue of yours!" Rose punctuated her annoyance by simply balling up her fist, punching Tag's arm in retaliation.

"Ha! I knew it!" In absolute glee, Harold winked as he grinned, nudging Rose with his elbow. "You *do* like the young sir!"

"What I'd like to do is punch him again, and you, too, if you keep up with this foolishness!" Rose shook her clenched fist before Harold's beaming face.

"Manners, my friends, I need a show of good manners! We are on official business, after all!" Myron clapped his hands to garner his comrades' attention. "I recommend displaying the proper decorum appropriate for this situation and present, regal company."

"Don't have any proper decorations to speak of, but I do have other headpieces more appropriate for events as grand as this! In fact, I've got the perfect skunk one. It's an elegant piece; black with a dazzlin' white stripe runnin' down the centre; suitable for the most formal of occasions."

Rose's face screwed up in disgust as she took a deliberate step away from the man. "Tell me it is not so!"

"It is *soooo* so, indeed, Princess! Had I known I'd be personally invited into the palace of the Queen of the Tooth Fairies, I would've dressed for this special event, had I thought of it in the first place."

"You look fine, Harold," said Myron. He stepped aside, making room as Pancecelia Feldspar, now in her typical size, floated inside to join her guests in the courtyard.

"Welcome, one and all," greeted Pance, slipping her hand into the crook of Loken's elbow that he presented to her. "Please, walk this way."

Before Tag could follow behind Myron, Harold seized the young man by his shoulders, stopping him from proceeding. Bending Tag's right arm just so, he went on to thrust Rose's unwilling hand into the crook of his elbow.

"What are you doing?" snapped Rose.

"You heard Her Majesty!" Harold's tone was matter-of-fact. "She said, *'Walk this way'*, so that's what you're doin'!"

"She did not mean we have to proceed exactly as she does," explained Tag. "She merely meant for us to follow her into the palace."

"Tut, tut!" scolded the man. His large, paddle-like hands stayed Tag's arm as he pressed Rose's hand firmly in place, making sure she did not let go and neither could Tag pull away. "The Queen is settin' an example and a proper, young lady should have an escort, so you best follow suit."

"This is mental!" denounced Rose, struggling to free her trapped hand from his grasp.

"If you prefer, I'm sure Harold would have no problem escorting you inside," offered Tag.

"I'd be honoured!" Harold smiled. His round face became as round as the moon with this affable grin, as he offered his arm to her.

Rose heaved a disgruntled sigh, "Never mind! Inside, we go."

"Great!" exclaimed Harold. Taking up the rear, he followed behind the young couple. He stared in awe at the palace constructed primarily of human teeth. "This is so excitin'! I'll bet it'll be like steppin' into someone's mouth, but much nicer I'm sure!"

"You'll see in a moment," said Tag, as he escorted Rose up the stairway. "Now, come along! Keep up, Harold."

As Pance and Loken glided up the stairs into the keep, Myron and his comrades stepped up the white, teeth-cobbled steps. Harold nodded in gratitude as the attending guards stationed to protect the palace opened the great, double doors, holding them wide for all to enter.

"I've never been in a palace before, Fairy or mortal, but I imagine this is as grand as it gets!" Harold stopped in his tracks to admire the ornately carved pillars comprised of neatly stacked, polished molars of uniform size and the perfect, white lower incisors shed by youngsters that framed the archways in the main hall. "Spectacular! Absolutely beautiful!"

"Thank you!" said Pance.

"But what do you do with all the rotten teeth?" questioned Harold. "I know there's got to be lots, 'cause I've given up more than a few rotters."

"The finest quality teeth are used to construct the front exterior of this palace and its watchtowers, plus the public areas such as this main hall, dining room and my libraries, as well as the private bedchambers. Those of lesser quality are used to build and repair the service areas while the teeth riddled with cavities serve to line our dungeons, as there is no need to impress any unfortunate soul detained down there."

"You have a dungeon?" asked Harold, genuinely surprised by this bit of information.

"Every castle or palace I know of, great or small, has a dungeon," replied Loken.

"Don't rightly know about that, but I'll take your word for it, Master Loken," said Harold. "Just didn't think there'd be a need for one, 'cause all Fairies are good, aren't they?"

"Most are, but sadly, our kind is not exempt from having our share of the immoral and unscrupulous," disclosed Loken. "We know this from personal experience."

"Come along, Harold! There is no time to dawdle," urged Rose, waving him on to follow. "Time is wasting and I really can use some beauty sleep, if I am to meet the day looking my best."

"You prefer to retire for the night, than to join us in imbibing in some honeydew and a light meal before you rest?" asked Pance.

"Thank you for your kind hospitality, unfortunately my need for sleep far exceeds my need for drink or food at the moment." Rose's hand came up to her mouth to stifle a yawn.

"Understandably so." With a clap of her hands, one of the handmaidens glided into the main hall.

"Yes, Your Majesty?" The Fairy bowed her head in respectful greeting to the Queen and those in her company.

"Please escort Princess Rose to our finest guest chamber, and then help her ready for the night."

"Of course, Your Majesty." The Fairy maiden nodded in understanding.

"Thank you," said Rose, smiling in gratitude. "I will see you in the morning."

"Yes, and please, Princess Rose, do refrain from making impromptu wishes while you are a guest in my palace," urged Pance.

"I would never think of it!" Rose curtsied, pretending she didn't know it was a personal jibe at her for when she demanded an immediate audience, wishing the Queen away from her nightly teeth gathering foray to attend to her demands during their first visit. "Besides, it is something I could not do, even if I wanted to."

"Yes... well, that might be for the better." Pance sighed in relief. "I had forgotten the Sorcerer had stolen away with your Dreamstone during your last ill-fated mission."

"I would like to sleep, not be plagued by nightmares, so let us not dwell on it," said Rose, retreating upstairs to avoid a possible scolding. "Good night to all! Sleep well."

"I will make sure you are roused and made ready before the sun rises," assured the Queen, calling to Rose as she followed the Fairy maiden up the grand staircase. "Until then, pleasant dreams."

"Why wake so early?" asked Harold, as Tag steered him on to follow their host and hostess.

"The powers of the Fairy dust will be no more with the coming of the sun," answered Loken. "It begins to wear off with the approach of dawn, but as soon as the sun's light touches you, you will be instantly transformed back to your original size."

"Oh... So, you're sayin' we'll be big again?"

"Yes, and for that reason, you must evacuate the palace before sunrise," added Pance, leading her guests to lounge in the comfort and privacy of the grand library as Fairies darted in and out with trays of dainty, delicate biscuits made of flower pollen and delectable libations to be shared amongst friends.

"That makes sense." Harold nodded in understanding.

"Yes, we wouldn't want to get stuck in here," said Myron. "That would be disastrous on many levels."

"Plus, we'd be good and stuck," determined Harold. He remained standing while Myron and Tag sat down, making themselves comfortable on the thistledown stuffed furniture.

"Please, join us!" Pance motioned the man to sit. "Make yourself at home."

"Thank you, Your Majesty. Was just waitin' for you to be seated first, and then a proper invitation to do so, before I made myself homely," explained Harold, as he sat on a cushioned chair.

Pance smiled at this man's efforts to be courteous, offering him a floret filled with honeydew, her people's favourite beverage. This delicacy, secreted from the posterior end of aphids, was harvested and then distilled to create this sweet ambrosia that was now perfectly aged.

"Well, if my eyes don't deceive me now, I'd say this is a lilac flower." Harold graciously accepted this unusual goblet from Pance.

"Yes, not only are the lilac florets the perfect size for us to use as drinking vessels, but the flower's own nectar enhances the flavour of this honeydew," said Loken, passing a floret to Pance, Myron and Tag, before serving himself.

"Honeydew?" repeated Harold, holding this drinking vessel to his nose to inhale the floral bouquet. "Sounds and smells delicious! What's it made of?"

"Don't ask, just enjoy," urged Tag, raising his goblet to honour his respected company.

Harold frowned in confusion, then his meaty, rounded shoulders shrugged off his concern. The floral bouquet emanating from the amber elixir seduced his senses. The delicate fragrance of lilac wafted to his nostrils as his taste buds tingled with the sweet cordial teasing his palate.

"Oh, my! This is sweet, but with a kick!" Harold's foot playfully flew out before him to emphasize just how spirited this concoction was.

"I recommend sipping this beverage than gulping it down like a cheap ale," said Myron. He smiled to see the expression of surprise and delight on his friend's face.

"No guzzlin' here, I'll be savourin' this one." Harold nursed his flower goblet to make sure the drink would last him for the duration of this night.

"Yes, it is wise to do so." Loken nodded in agreement as he sipped. "For the uninitiated, the delectable flavour can be quite deceiving, masking how truly potent the alcohol can be in this spirited beverage."

Myron raised his goblet once more to the Queen as he spoke, "Thank you for your generosity and for extending such kind hospitality to us once again, Your Majesty."

Pance smiled as she nodded in acknowledgement.

"So, you really have been here before?" questioned Harold, glancing over to Tag and Myron as they imbibed.

"Consider this a repeat engagement for your friends," said Pance, placing her goblet back onto the drink stand.

"Yes, but under very different circumstances," explained Tag. "The last time we were here, we were trying to help Princess Rose find something she lost."

"What did the poor Princess lose?" asked Harold.

"Her moral compass... Her sound judgment... Probably a good chunk of her sanity..."

"You are such a jokester, young master! I was bein' serious!" Harold motioned for Tag to stop kidding with him.

"So was I!" Tag responded with a quirk of a grin on his face.

"The young sir means to say, we were on a quest to help the Princess break a curse," explained Myron.

"Yes, one that she foolishly invoked on her own when she decided to test my patience," added Pance.

"Astounding! So just what did she do to invoke this curse?"

"Princess Rose never told you?" asked Pance, as she cast a stare rife with doubt in Harold's direction.

"The young master and Sir Kendall made mention about the Princess and an ill-conceived plan to be granted wishes from you, but I've yet been told all the details. Didn't think it was my place to pry, but if you're willin' to share in this story, as it has to do with you, I'd love to hear it."

"I think of it as more of a morality tale than a simple story," said Pance.

"Well then, that's even better! I always sleep soundly after a well-told story, especially when there's a lesson to be learned. Just know that if I don't hear it now, there'll be no sleepin' tonight. I'm dyin' of curiosity now."

Pance glanced over to Tag and Myron, searching their eyes for approval to reveal the details of the curse Rose had set into motion.

"Better that Harold hears it from you than us," said Tag. "That way, he won't be fed some cockamamie version the Princess is likely to cook up to downplay her role in all of it, nor can she accuse us of embellishing or exaggerating the truth."

"For pity's sake, do tell! Someone! Anyone!" Harold leaned forward, eager to hear more. "I'll gladly listen to the details from any person willin' to share it with me."

"Very well then, my good man. Do get comfortable," invited Pance. "Even the abridged version is a daunting tale to tell of that fateful night when I first encountered Princess Rose. Allow me to begin now, so you will still have time to rest before the coming of dawn."

"Good gracious! What is taking the Princess so bloody long?" Tag wondered aloud. He paced the length of the courtyard where Myron and Harold sat patiently on the lowest step of the stairs leading into the palace. Loken joined them, along with Pance, as she was eager to see her guests off before the coming of the sun.

"Apparently, she was exhausted after her long day of travel, so much so that when my personal handmaiden went to wake her so she can join us to break fast, Princess Rose declined," explained Pance. "She asked, instead, to sleep just a little longer, promising to rise and make ready very soon."

"I hear the songbirds calling. They herald the dawn." Myron cupped a hand to his ear, listening as wrens warbled in the boughs of this great oak tree. "The sun will be on the rise soon."

"Perhaps I should pound on her door? Make sure she is getting ready and not sleeping in," offered Tag.

"Fret not, young man," said Pance. "Even as we speak, one of my handmaidens is with Princess Rose, seeing to her preparations."

"Please, my lady, do get up!"

Rose's eyes remained closed. Her actions were rote, her hand wiping the trail of drool drying at the corner of her mouth as she slept.

"Already the hour grows late and the sun is rising!" The Fairy gave up with the gentle prodding to rouse this mortal. Instead, she resorted to briskly shaking the Princess by her shoulders.

Rose managed to crack open her weary eyes as she muttered in protest, "Too early... Still dark outside."

"I woke you later, as you had requested, but it is now close to sunrise. You must get up *now*, Princess."

"Tell the others there is no need to wait for me to break their fast. I will join them as soon as I am dressed and ready."

"There will be barely enough time to get dressed, and for you, there will be no time to eat breakfast. Now hurry!"

"What are you talking about?" grumbled Rose. She rubbed the sleep from her eyes as she lifted her head off the soft, perfumed pillow.

"You heard me, my lady. The time to leave draws ever closer, if you wish to leave this palace at all, you must get up *now*!"

"Why did you not say so?" Rose gasped, bolting upright.

Staring beyond the dew bejewelled spider web curtains adorning the window, she could make out the morning sky as the impending sun leached away the darkness of night.

"I did, many times! You demanded to be left to sleep, but the time for sleep has come to pass! You must leave, if you do not wish to be stuck here forever."

"Damn! Damn! Damn!" cursed Rose. She threw back the counterpane. "My clothes! My boots! Where are they?"

"This is not the time for the Princess to be fashionably late," groaned Tag. "I better go get her; drag her from that bed, if I must."

"The three of you should make ready for your exit," suggested Loken, pointing the mortals toward the entrance of the tree hollow. "Go select a suitable leaf to buffer and control your descent. I shall make sure Princess Rose is awake and ready to leave."

"Are you sure?" asked Tag.

"Absolutely! It is no bother at all, my friend. Make ready for your departure, explain to Harold the intricacies of leaf gliding and I shall retrieve Princess Rose so she can do so, too."

Loken's wings thrummed as he took to the air. Leaving Pancecelia to see their guests off, he darted inside the palace and up the flight of stairs.

As he flew down the corridor, Loken called out, "Princess Rose, it is time to leave!"

"Coming! I am coming!" She hollered through the closed door as she shoved her feet into her boots.

"Be quick about it!" urged Loken. Just as he was about to rap on the door, it flew open. There stood Rose, snatching up her leather coat from the peg on the back of the door. "There is no time to lose!"

"Tell Tag and the others to go ahead, if they are so eager to leave this tree hollow."

"It is not a matter of them being eager to leave," said Loken, ushering Rose down the hallway. "They are eager not to get *stuck* in here, as you will, if you do not pick up your pace."

"But we still have some time."

"You, my dear Princess, have none to spare! Unless you suddenly sprout wings to fly down this flight of stairs and out this palace, you are cutting it dangerously close!"

"I shall do the next best thing."

As they reached the top of the stairs, Rose threw her leg over to straddle the handrail. As Loken flew down the winding staircase, the Princess slid down the polished rail. As her quick ride came to an abrupt end, Rose landed on the floor, tumbling head over heels across the main hall to land at the double doors. She arrived just in time to see the last of her comrades make the leap. Tag was the first to depart, followed by Harold. Myron, with a large oak leaf firmly in his grip, jumped from the tree hollow.

Scrambling to her feet, Rose cried out, "Wait for me!"

"There is no waiting, Princess! You must leave now!" demanded Loken.

"But I'm not ready!" cried Rose, as she dashed to the exit.

"Ready or not, you have no choice," said Loken, waving her on across the courtyard toward Pancecelia, as she stood there, a suitable leaf at the ready for the Princess to use.

Just as the first wan rays of sunlight peered over the horizon, Rose was forced to act. Snatching the leaf from Pancecelia's hands, the Princess wavered, teetering to and fro on the very edge of the knothole. Her heart jumped to the back of her throat. She spied upon Myron as he prepared to land, only to be swallowed up by the jungle of grass below.

Rose froze where she stood, the leaf rattling in her quaking hands as she stared down.

Just as the first rays of sunlight heralded the start of a new day, Loken shouted, "Jump, now!"

"Quickly, Princess, you must go!" urged Pancecelia, as she waved her on.

Instead, Rose just stood there. The second time around was no less frightening than the first time she was forced to make this leap.

Aside from the involuntary shaking, Rose was paralyzed with fear. With no other option, Loken was forced to act. He shoved her hard, pushing the Princess out the tree hollow and into the world outside.

"NOOO!" cried Rose.

In a panic, she released her hold on the leaf that was intended to gently glide her down. Instead, her hands frantically scrambled to latch onto a solid hold to end this fall. Pushed too far to grab onto the rough tree bark, Rose clawed at the air. She tumbled down as the wind rushed around her, stealing away with her breath and stifling her scream.

6

It's Complicated

"HELP!" shrieked Rose.

With eyes squeezed shut, she plunged down to meet the earth. Rose's heart jumped to the back of her throat as this fall came to a jerking halt.

"I've got you!" said Loken. His wings thrummed, working hard to support this additional weight as he snagged her by the right wrist.

"Don't let go!" cried Rose.

"Then stop thrashing about!" grunted Loken. "I'll lower you down safely, but a little cooperation, please!"

Her frantic struggle came to an abrupt end upon realizing that death had been averted. A gentle breeze buffeted her body as she dangled at Loken's mercy. She held her breath, fighting to remain calm.

As the morning sun bathed her in its warm glow, Rose gasped. A tingling sensation coursed throughout her body as the golden light broke the spell; undoing the magic of the Fairy dust. Loken was forced to release his grip. In a flash of light, the Princess returned to her normal size.

This unsettling sensation rattled her nerves right down to the bones. Landing on her feet, Rose swayed to and fro, her legs finally buckling beneath her.

Before she could fall upon her knees, in a blur of movement, she was bowled over. The force knocked the wind from her lungs as she fell backwards.

Groaning, Rose blinked hard, squinting as the light crept toward her through the grasses. In a great flash of light, she was now standing in the shadows of three figures backlit by the sun's rays. Gazing up, she recognized it was Tag, Myron, and Harold! They, too, had returned to their normal size. Their chests were heaving as they tried to catch their breath.

"What happened to you three?" asked Rose, clambering onto her feet, as she scrutinized the trio.

"We were almost killed!" declared Tag.

Rose spun about, searching for the dangerous culprit. "Who tried to kill you?"

"*You* almost killed us!" snapped Tag.

"I did?"

"You changed back before we did," explained Myron. "We were hidden in the grass at your very feet when you almost crashed down upon us. We were forced to run for our lives!"

"Oh, my…" gasped Rose.

Her eyes narrowed as she stared at the creature Pancecelia Feldspar was hovering by. Scrutinizing the largest ebony wolf she had ever seen, before Rose could arm her sling should this beast attack, there was a brilliant flash of light.

"I am sorry I knocked you aside like that, but I was forced to take drastic action to save your friends," apologized Loken. "I trust everyone is none the worse for wear after that little ordeal."

"That was scary close!" Harold gasped, his chest still heaving. Using the back of his hand, he wiped the beads of perspiration from his forehead.

"Where Princess Rose is concerned, trust me, Harold, when I say that was only one of many close calls you are sure to expect, if you wish to continue on this mission with us," cautioned Tag. "If your luck holds, you won't get killed."

"Killed?" repeated Harold. "Are you sayin' I can die because of Princess Rose?"

"Like a fly to dung, she has a way of attracting danger or being the cause of it," confided Tag.

"*You!*" snapped Rose, her voice curdling with spite. Her index finger jabbed Harold in his broad chest. "Were you in such jeopardy that you are dead now because of what had transpired?"

Harold frowned. After some thought, he sputtered, "Could be… Meanin' that if I'm dead now, I must be a gh- gh- *ghost!*"

"You are an idiot of a buffoon, that is what you are!" growled Rose. With a dismal shake of her head, she smacked his arm in utter annoyance.

"Glory be! So I'm a *dead* idiot of a buffoon?" Harold blanched, the colour draining from his face at the thought of this dramatic turn of events, so early into this quest. "Oh, my… Always believed that if this quest were to be my end, I'd die a more dignified death, not somethin' embarrassin', like bein' crushed by a wee princess! No disrespect to you, my lady."

Rose snorted in frustration as she lashed out again, this time to slap Harold across his startled face. "Tell me now, did you feel that?"

"Oooh! Absolutely!" Harold vigorously rubbed away the lingering, red handprint left upon his burning cheek. "That smarts somethin' fierce."

"Good! Then it is proof enough you are not a ghost! You are not dead, and therefore, you were never in danger, so there!"

She spun on her heels to face Tag and Myron. Pushing up her sleeves, she prepared to make her point to them. "So, who is next? I have a punch and a kick to spare, if you'll be needing proof my little mishap was far from deadly!"

"No need to get testy, Princess!" Tag muttered; raising his hands in surrender as he cautiously stepped away from Rose and her seething temper.

"I do believe your friends are just saying it could have ended very badly," stated Pance, as Loken nodded in agreement.

"Well, none of this would have happened in the first place, if I had been woken up in a timely manner," grumbled Rose, speaking in her own defence.

"I assure you, Princess Rose, every effort was made to do just that. However, specific orders from *you* to be left alone so you could steal away with more sleep, than to wake early and partake in breakfast with your comrades, were very insistent."

"Well, if I had said such a thing, perhaps I was talking in my sleep, for I do not recall making such a demand." Rose stared sheepishly at Pance. "Whatever the case, it was never my intention to risk my friends' lives while exiting your royal residence in such dramatic style."

"You meant to say, you never intended to risk *your life*, thereby, making us the possible casualties of your *dramatic style*." Tag's words were terse as he corrected her.

Rose glared at him. Her cheeks burned in response to this scolding. Though Tag's words did ring true, she had to wonder if their friendship was worth tolerating the level of humiliation she was now being subjected to, thanks to his impudence.

"She meant no harm, young master," insisted Harold, stepping between Rose and Tag to diffuse the growing animosity as tempers flared. "Heck, I don't remember half the things I say when I'm sleepy. How can she be at fault, if she was just talkin' in her sleep?"

"That is one, big *'if'* where she is concerned!" Tag rolled his eyes.

He was frustrated as much by this man's gullibility and need to see only good in Rose as he was annoyed by her efforts to minimize her actions.

Eager to be on their way and to take advantage of the light of day, Myron joined Harold in pacifying the feuding friends. He raised his hands, motioning for calm.

"I believe we should be grateful none were hurt on this occasion. We cannot undo the past, so just know that the Princess' *inaction* forced Loken to take his own drastic, but necessary, action. We all survived, none were injured, so let us make haste and move on."

"Ah! The voice of reason! This knight is absolutely correct," averred Rose. She wanted nothing more than to deflect this unwanted attention, waving Tag and Harold off to ready their horses. "Time is wasting away with all this needless chatter. We should continue on to the Woodland Glade, and do so with speed, if we mean to come to Lord Silverthorn's aid."

"That would be the prudent thing to do, Princess Rose." Pancecelia nodded in agreement.

"Will you be coming with us?" asked Myron, looking to Pance and Loken as they hovered before him.

"There is little I can do for Lord Silverthorn and his people. At this moment, you seem to offer their best hope," explained the Queen. "For now, my first duty is to see to the safety and well-being of my subjects; tend to matters of my realm. In my stead, Loken will venture forth with you."

"So, you will come with us now?" asked Myron, gazing at the Sprite.

"Not just yet. As I had said last night, I must inspect the borders of the Fairy's Vale; be sure there is nothing untoward I should be aware of before I head off, leaving behind my beloved Celia and her subjects on their own."

"Better safe than sorry, that's for sure!" Harold nodded in approval. He carefully turned his porcupine headpiece inside out so the quills would not pose a danger before putting it away to search in his pack for another pelt to wear that would be more fitting for the occasion, one that spoke of tenacity and reflected his new-found sense of adventure.

"It is merely a precaution and to grant me some peace of mind before I depart, but yes, I intend to make sure all is safe before I leave this place. If there is dark magic at work, whether Dragonite is behind it or not, I want to know, so I can do what I must to ensure the safety of our realm. Once I am confident all is secure, only then shall I join you, my friends. And if that necromancer is about, then I shall be the one to deliver this news to you, but only after I have taken the necessary precautions."

"Excellent plan, but just how do you intend to find us, as we shall be leaving without you?" asked Rose.

"I am familiar with the direction you will be travelling, plus, being a shape-shifter, I am confident I will be in the ideal position to assume a form that will be conducive to hunting you down with relative ease."

I do hope that means you'll be able to find us," said Harold. He plopped onto his head the pelt of a badger before distracting his donkey with a carrot, so the animal would not bray up a storm of protest as he readied her for the trek.

"Between my abilities and that noisy little beast of yours, I hardly think it will be difficult," confided Loken.

Myron placed the wool blanket high on the mare's withers, sliding it down to smooth out the animal's coat before throwing on the saddle. "You best be on your way, Loken. Do what must be done, and if luck and fate conspire in our favour, we shall meet up even before we enter the country of Axalon."

"That is the desired plan," said Loken, with a nod of confirmation to the knight.

"And I shall retire for the day in preparation for another busy night, but before I do, I shall wish you well," bade Pance. "And as I said last night while Princess Rose slept, it is never too late to call upon Silas Agincor. Perhaps it shall require a dire situation to draw him out of retirement."

Rose's heels tapped against the mare's flanks, coaxing it on to keep up with Myron's stallion while Tag steered his mount, following behind her horse. Trailing behind this small procession, Harold followed, trotting along at a steady pace while he led his cranky, little donkey by the reins.

"The nerve of her!" growled Rose.

Thoroughly agitated, she was bristling with resentment as the Fairy's Vale disappeared behind them.

"What nerve?" asked Tag.

He was only vaguely interested in Rose's latest complaint, but felt compelled to ask. Being well acquainted with her, he knew she'd only pester him, if her concerns were not addressed to her liking.

"Since you asked, Pancecelia Feldspar had some nerve to suggest that I call upon the Dream Merchant for his measly help!"

"It's not such a bad idea, Princess," said Tag, with a shrug of his shoulders. "Silas Agincor may find it in his heart to extend a small measure of mercy to you."

"Mercy? From that demented, old Wizard? I think not! Contrary to what your feeble, little mind believes, his help is the cause of so much grief for me. In fact, that miscreant of a magician was so bloody incompetent, incompetence should be his middle name."

"How can incompetence be a name?" Tag wondered aloud.

"Prudence is a name. Temperance is a name. *Incompetence* can be a name, too," explained Rose.

"Oooh, she does have a very good point, young master," said Harold. "It's nowhere near as pretty as Prudence or Temperance, but Princess Rose speaks the truth where names are concerned."

"You're both speaking gibberish again," Tag responded with a dismal shake of his head.

"Well, then," muttered Rose. "If not his name, then incompetence best describes the Wizard's skills! Never mind conjuring up great feats of magic or that wondrous gift of wish-making, that old codger is sorely lacking in both due to all the conditions and restrictions he attaches to those magic crystals."

"Though you are a princess, you're also an idiot." Tag's words were unapologetic. "This so-called incompetence was to keep people like you from running amok, unfettered and unchecked. I shudder to think what would've happened, if you had no rules to abide by!"

"Say what you like. I know firsthand the Wizard we speak of was wanting in his skills to grant wishes. Incompetence of the highest order, I'd say!"

"In truth, I thought it wise Silas Agincor had placed restrictions on that magic crystal and the number of wishes allotted to you each day," countered Tag.

"Overall, there was nothing wrong with working around those restrictions, as far as wishes go, but I was speaking about his stupid rule as it pertains to me. Why am I the only one who can return the Dreamstone to him to put an end to all my woes."

"It was a rule Master Agincor put into place for *all*, royals and commoners alike, wishing to bargain with him. And in your case, it was called acting responsibly on your part in being entrusted with the Dreamstone," said Tag, heaving a disgruntled sigh. "Obviously, it was too much responsibility for you to handle, Princess."

"I am plenty responsible!" Rose twisted about in her saddle to glare over her shoulder at Tag. "If I were not speaking the truth now, then let the powers that be strike me down where I sit!"

Rose yelped in surprise, tumbling from her mare. In a dishevelled heap, she landed before Tag's gelding that had come to an abrupt halt due to the physical obstacle this mortal now posed.

"Owww…" groaned Rose. In a daze, she slowly sat up, rubbing the back of her head.

Abandoning his donkey, Harold rushed by Tag and his mount to help Rose onto her feet. He brushed the dust from her cloak as she shook off the trauma of this spill.

"What happened?" Rose wondered aloud.

"I'd like to say the *powers that be* struck you down, but I'd be lying," confided Tag. He grinned now that he knew Rose was not physically harmed during her little tumble.

"Mind you, the powers that be could've been the ones to orchestrate the placement of that low-hangin' bough," chimed in Harold. "If you think about it, Sir Kendall managed to avoid it, but you rode right smack dab into that branch, my lady."

"Stop thinking, Harold!" snapped Rose. She yanked her arm free of his grasp as she shook a balled fist in Tag's direction. "It was nothing more than an accident, I tell you! I should have been paying attention to where I was going, than to waste my time and endanger my life looking upon that insolent git of an oik, just to speak my mind."

"My sincerest apologies, my lady," called Myron, bowing his head in regret as he reined his stallion in to a complete stop. "I should have warned you about that branch than to have assumed you were paying attention in the first place."

"*Never* assume she is paying attention to anything!" scoffed Tag, laughing at this own joke that came at Rose's expense.

"Good gracious, young sir! And you claim to be a knight-in-trainin'?" Appalled, Harold waggled a condemning finger at Tag. "For shame, Tagius Yairet, for shame!"

"Yes! For shame, indeed!" muttered Rose, sneering in resentment at Tag as she joined Harold in scolding him.

"For pity's sake, what are you two talking about now?" asked Tag, as he hopped off his gelding.

"You, sir, should be a champion to this princess, if you're strivin' to be a real knight like Sir Kendall. And though I've been called a fool by many, even I know a true knight would speak with respect to his royal charge, comin' to her rescue when it's called for."

"So there!" snapped Rose, turning her nose up at Tag.

Tag drew a deep breath as he nodded. "You're right, Harold. A true knight knows better and I would know better had I been permitted to engage in my training. It was planned by my father, but suspended by a *greater power*. So forgive me, if my methods seem unorthodox and unbecoming for one striving to enter the knighthood. Just know that it's not a reflection on Sir Kendall and the level of training he has bestowed upon me, nor was it meant to bring disrespect or disgrace to my father's name and memory.

Just know I was Princess Rose's friend before I was ever called into her service. If she still values our friendship, as I believe she does, she knows my verbal barbs are not spoken out of disrespect, but more to help her maintain a level of humility. It is a quality that even her mother and father understand the importance of, in order to rule a kingdom effectively. So, I do beg your pardon on this matter, Harold. And I ask for your forgiveness, Princess. I shall try harder to be the man my father would have been proud to call his son."

"Well, I can see you've got all the makings of a fine knight, after all; great potential, indeed! No need for apologies, young sir. We'll let bygones be bygones." Harold threw his beefy arms around Tag, lifting him off the ground in a forgiving bear hug.

Tag coughed, wheezing as the air was squeezed from his lungs when this lumbering hulk's arms wrapped around his body in a constricting embrace.

Plunked back onto the ground, Tag wavered on his unsteady feet. He stumbled forward as Harold's plate-sized hand playfully smacked him on his back in jovial approval.

Rose raised her hands, gesturing for Harold to come no closer when he turned his attention to her. "Stand down and back off, you oafish buffoon! I am a princess! Protocol demands that you will *not* hug me without my consent first."

"Oh, I won't be the one huggin' you, Princess." Harold flashed a knowing smile at her.

Before she could protest, Harold thrust her into Tag's arms. "You're the one needin' a hug from him, especially as he's the one needin' your forgiveness."

Rose stumbled. Her hands flew up, bracing herself against the young man's chest as Tag caught her by the shoulders.

Instead of embracing each other in a forgiving hug, Tag immediately propped the Princess back up onto her feet, but still, her hands remained high on his chest, even though she had regained her balance.

Rose was stunned; involuntarily impressed by the firmness of these pectoral muscles she had first noticed when she spied upon Tag while he bathed in a lake during the quest that took them north earlier in the year.

"Well... this is awkward," muttered Tag.

He felt Rose's fingertips against his body. With feathery soft strokes they traced the contours of his muscles, testing their firmness.

"Oh! Um... I..." stammered Rose. Her cheeks burned, becoming as hot as they were red. "I was..."

"You were feeling my muscles, weren't you?"

"*Muscles?* Are you mad?" Rose's hands recoiled from his chest. "What muscles?"

"Oh, come now!" Tag laughed as he teased her. "You were feeling my muscles! Admit it!"

"I admit nothing. The only thing I am willing to admit to is that I was feeling for armour."

"Armour?" repeated Tag, frowning in bewilderment upon hearing this strange confession.

"Yes! It felt like you were wearing armour beneath your clothing."

"Now that is the stupidest thing I've ever heard," scoffed Tag, his eyes rolling in dismay.

"And *you* are the stupidest thing *ever!*" snapped Rose, her hands balling into angry fists.

"Hey, now! Enough! The both of you!" scolded Harold. "Princess Rose just paid you a great compliment, so you best be gracious, young sir! A thank you is in order, methinks!"

"A compliment?" grumbled Tag, shaking his head in doubt. "What compliment?"

"Oh, my! And here, folks tell me that I'm about as smart as a rock!" giggled the large man. "Of course the young lady did just that."

"I did?" Rose's eyes narrowed in suspicion as she glared at Harold.

"Come now, my lady! You told Tag you thought he was donnin' armour beneath his vest and tunic."

"So what?" Rose's tone was incredulous.

"Yes, what about it?" snorted Tag. "All it proves is just how silly this girl is! How many men wear armour *beneath* their apparel?"

Harold playfully thumped Tag on the crown of his head. "Listen up! Give your head a shake, my young friend! What Princess Rose was insinuatin' is that your muscles are hard, *like armour!* Now, how flatterin' is that?"

The large man punctuated this comment with a knowing wink.

Myron's hand ran down his woeful face. He listened to this exchange, knowing how Harold's good nature was only fanning the flames of animosity.

"Hey... You're absolutely right!" exclaimed Tag. He flexed his biceps for her to admire. "She did do just that. And what a compliment, indeed! Mistaking these muscles for forged steel is as good as it gets."

Rose rolled her eyes in exasperation. She grew more disgruntled by the second just listening to Harold and Tag carry on.

"Dream on, you dolt! The only metal that comes close to your flabby muscles would be that of cheap and flimsy tin!" snapped Rose, her cheeks burning bright once more.

Tag puffed out his chest. "Flabby, eh? Well, have a feel now, Princess! If these aren't muscles, then you can call my sword a dagger and Harold's ass a horse."

"Donkey!" corrected Harold. "She prefers bein' called a donkey!"

His hands flapped about, motioning for Tag to quiet down as he glanced over to the little beast of burden, checking to see if she was offended by his words. Instead, Sassy was blissfully unaware of this exchange, hungrily grazing on tufts of grass to care, if indeed she even understood what was being said about her.

Ignoring Harold, Tag brazenly thrust his chest into Rose's astonished face as he antagonized her. "Go on! Feel these muscles now. I dare you!"

"Why do I not punch you in your gut for good measure, to really test the fortitude of these *muscles*?" scoffed Rose. Her fists quivered with as much embarrassment as rage with these taunting words he threw at her.

Myron stepped in between the two bellicose friends. "No feeling! No punching! No more disparaging words!"

"And no name-callin' either, includin' at my little Sassy!" added Harold, wagging an admonishing finger at Tag and Rose.

"Yes, that too!" Myron nodded in agreement. "Before we lose more time and stray from the true purpose of this mission, mount up, people! Let us be on our way."

"I have no problem with that," said Rose. "But first, this rogue of a rapscallion will apologize to me. He will do so now, or I shall refuse to budge from where I stand!"

Knowing that time was indeed wasting away and Rose can be as petulant as any ill-natured donkey, Tag nodded in agreement. Bowing his head in regret, he was quick to make amends. "I am sorry, Princess. I shall be more mindful of my words."

"And you will stop haranguing me over every little thing?" asked Rose.

In a bid for truce, Tag offered her a disarming smile as he teased her. "If I agree to this, will it make you love me more?"

"It will make me hate you less," grunted Rose. She offered the young man a forgiving smile as he gave her a leg up into her saddle.

"Less hate? Coming from you, Princess, I can live with that." Tag shrugged as he turned to gather his mount.

"Oh, my goodness! All this talk of love and hate while bickerin' to and fro between the two of 'em," despaired Harold. He anxiously wrung his hands in woe as he turned to Myron for some clarification. "And you claim they truly are friends?"

"The very best of friends since they were wee children, but it's complicated," confided Myron. "And we are best to stand aside; allow this relationship to run its natural course, wherever it takes them."

"But suppose all their bickerin' causes their friendship to run afoul? Then what?"

"True friendship can endure far more than just a little 'bickering'," assured Myron. He then leaned in close, whispering to Harold, "Trust me when I say that the Princess would have done away with Tag from the start, if she saw little value in his words and in securing his confidence. And Tag is a headstrong, young man. He would have walked away long ago, if he did not believe she had any redeeming qualities, nor found true value in her friendship."

"Hmph! It's complicated, indeed..." Harold drew a deep breath as he mulled over Myron's words. "Well, bein' that you know them better than I do, I'll trust you on this matter, my friend."

"I have high hopes. Besides, even a cat and a dog can learn to live in peace, if they don't kill each other first," responded Myron, giving Harold a wry smile.

"Yes, I suppose."

Harold thought back on Myron's pets and how his once-feral cat and overly friendly hound learned to tolerate each other's company within the close confines of his humble cottage.

With Rose seated upon her mare and Tag reclaiming his horse, Myron steered Harold back to his donkey. "Let us be on our way, my friend. If our luck holds, perhaps Loken will catch up to us before we enter King Maxmillian's domain."

With sturdy mounts and Harold's surprising stamina that was now bordering on legendary for a man of his proportions, the four companions had journeyed far since leaving the Fairy's Vale. There was no fear of getting lost, having been set on the proper course by Loken. And having come by this way before, they wasted little time, venturing straight on through the once-bustling town of Towgem.

All was quiet as the citizens went about their daily business, barely acknowledging the travellers' presence as they made their way down the main road through the centre of this gem mining settlement.

Spotting the large sign aged by the elements that had drawn her attention the first time they came by this way, Rose made a suggestion, "What say you to a rest stop and a hot meal at The Radical Rose Ruby Public Drinking House?"

"No!" snapped Tag.

"Absolutely not!" declared Myron. "We must ride straight through this town, and quickly."

Rose's request had been immediately and soundly quashed. Tag and Myron were so adamant about moving on, she knew there was no point in arguing with them.

At first, she believed it was to take advantage of their momentum while the light of day held, until she spied upon the old biddy and local town trollop, Gertie.

There she was, in all her aging glory, leaning against the doorway to the pub where they had first encountered her. She was like a living, albeit decaying, monument symbolizing Towgem during its heyday half a century ago. With thickly pancaked make-up plied onto her face by unsteady hands, eyes painted as gaudily as a bright peacock and a decrepit, generously plump body squeezed into that same ill-fitting, low-cut dress several sizes too small to accommodate her upside-down, pear-shaped figure, Gertie was hardly a comely or welcoming sight to behold.

Myron and Tag were the first to spot the old girl and they had no desire to be reacquainted with the lecherous hag. And seeing that she was inebriated even more so than during their first encounter, Rose decided it was better to give this woman a wide berth. There was no point in chancing that the town harlot's ale-addled mind might recall her and how the two almost got into a catfight while in her brother's pub.

Rose quickly and discreetly dissuaded Harold from responding to Gertie's lewd advances as the old woman used her arms to squeeze her sagging breasts together, giving the illusion of an ample pair of bosoms on prominent display. The Princess demanded that he not even cast an innocent glance of acknowledgement in Gertie's direction as they neared; for it was obvious her glassy eyes had singled out this behemoth of a man from their small group. The old woman tried to seduce Harold with her best *come hither* look that was encapsulated in those glazed, half-closed eyes and the crusty trails of saliva that had dried at the corners of her gummy, upside down smile that was smeared with an eye-catching red lip paint.

When Gertie's provocative stare failed to entice any one of them, thinking she had gone unnoticed, she began to wave with wild abandon to flag these travellers down. The loose flap of withered muscle, weighed down by gelatinous fat, and sheathed in wrinkled skin that drooped from her triceps started to wobble to and fro. The more frantic her actions, the more animated this flesh hanging from her upper arm became, flapping about like she was trying to catch the wind in order to launch an aerial assault.

When this waving went ignored, drunken words were slurred as she shouted, "So what's a girl gotta do ta get a drink 'round here? Come on, gents, a tankard of ale fer some quality company! That's a fair trade!"

"Look away, Harold. Do not encourage her," whispered Rose. "Do not smile or even hazard an innocent glance at that pickled trout of a hussy."

Rose kept her eyes focused on the road ahead, staring beyond the pub where Gertie stood, holding up the doorway, than to dare make eye contact with this lady-of-the-night who had now brazenly taken to plying her trade during the light of day. And in the harsh and unforgiving illumination of this afternoon sun, it only served to accentuate every wrinkle that creased and webbed her face while deepening each fold of her well-wattled neck.

Harold frowned in confusion upon hearing Rose's anxious tone and the derogatory words she dispensed to describe this hospitable stranger. With great effort, he fought the urge to gaze in her direction when he heard the aging temptress try to whistle them down.

Gertie's pasty tongue emerged like a sickly slug, protruding from between what was left of her rows of yellowed, decaying teeth. It slid over her cracked, painted lips before letting the ale-tainted saliva spew forth as she whistled to summon their attention.

"Look away!" demanded Rose.

"But she's so friendly, like my lovin' granny, rest her soul. It seems to me like that nice, old lady is just lookin' to make some new friends. She just wants to share in some pleasantries."

"Are you mad?" whispered Rose. "Just keep moving! I promise you, what she has to share will be far from pleasant."

Harold tried to obey Rose's demand. Attempting to remain focused, he struggled to keep his eyes fixed on the road, than to steal a peek at Towgem's self-appointed, one-woman welcoming committee.

"But I think she's just bein' the friendly type," insisted Harold.

Tag set his heels to the gelding's flanks, coaxing his mount on to pick up its pace as they rode right by Gertie. He grimaced in disgust as a sideway glance happened to catch the old woman as she hitched up the hem of her dress to seduce the men with a peek at her legs. Pale, goosy flesh bulged out like lumps of cottage cheese wherever there were tears and runs in her tightly stretched black stockings.

Tag averted his eyes from this less than enticing vision as Gertie shared in her womanly charms. "That old biddy is too friendly, if you get my meaning?"

"Not really, but there's nothin' wrong with bein' friendly," stated Harold, pulling his donkey along to keep up with the others as they hastened away.

"Trust us, Harold, there is plenty wrong when she charges you money or ale in exchange for her *friendship*," disclosed Myron. He shuddered involuntarily as the memory of almost being smothered against that woman's breasts came flooding back to haunt him.

"Oooh… so she's like a mercenary of sorts, chargin' a fee in exchange for her friendship, like the way a soldier would sell his skills with shield and sword to a lord or king," determined Harold.

"Sort of, but not quite," replied Tag, with a dismal shake of his head. "Keep riding, Harold, for I'm sure whatever skills she has, it could well be the death of you. Just know she promises to deliver a lingering, more agonizing death than what would be dispensed even by the edge of a dull and rusted sword wielded by a true mercenary."

"Like killin' me with kindness?"

"Yes, the old crone's brand of *kindness* will kill you, and then some," muttered Rose. She snorted in dismay; both frustrated and astonished at how gullible this man truly was, even though he looked old enough to be her father.

The old woman's calls of seduction eroded into words of profanity hurled in their direction as she watched potential customers ride away.

Rose prodded her mare on. She could only hope Harold would follow suit, in case the painted harlot decided to give chase. And the only thing worse than being chased down by this old woman is if she were to catch up to them.

"Can I at least wave farewell to her?" asked Harold.

"No harm in that, I suppose," answered Myron, as he urged his stallion on. "As long as you don't stop to engage her, then we should all be fine."

"Well, I see nothing has changed since we last stood before this very landmark." Tag's tone was cynical as he searched for any amendments to signify better tidings to those wishing to enter this country. "It is as welcoming as ever!"

Harold frowned, struggling to read this prominent sign only the blind can possibly miss. It established that from this point forward the lands, and all within, were to be subjected to King Maxmillian's royal decree as per noted on this sign. This declaration had long ago been defaced and modified by disgruntled citizens and travellers alike, wishing to enter or leave this country, but not without first paying a litany of fees or outstanding taxes to do so.

"The King means to tax to death his subjects and all those wishing to travel through his country," complained Myron.

"Don't see nothin' welcomin' at all about bein' asked to pay so much in the way of taxes, when all we're plannin' on doin' is to travel through these parts."

"Hence the altered name, my friend." Myron pointed to the capital *'T'* added to the front of Axalon and the modified *'n'* that had been carved out to form the letter *'t'*. "Tax-a-lot says it all, but King Maxmillian is too miserly to replace this atrocity of a sign."

"There's no point, especially if the part about all the taxes remains the same, or worse yet, if they were increased," stated Tag, with a disgruntled shake of his head. "It'd only be defaced or reduced to a pile of cinder by angry citizens and spiteful travellers as soon as they can safely get at it without fear of reprisal."

"King Maxmillian is being more practical than miserly," insisted Rose. "You cannot even begin to imagine the amount of manpower required to create a new sign, not to forget the cost of hiring the men to remove this old one before installing the new. In my way of thinking, the King knows all too well the expense that will be incurred in doing this. It is money that is better spent elsewhere."

"Or to keep locked in his coffers should his *loyal* subjects decide to abandon their homes, re-establishing themselves in new and less costly realms, thereby causing King Maxmillian's tax revenues to shrink accordingly," said Tag.

"So you say," grunted Rose. "But the citizens of Taxalot, I mean to say, *Axalon,* know there is a price to pay for the protection of a monarch and his great armies, not to mention all costs incurred in creating and maintaining the multitude of amenities that keep the country running as it should."

"Grant you that," Tag nodded in agreement, "but even you must admit it is rather selfish to place taxes upon taxes, especially when revenues collected go to support his decadent lifestyle. As far as I could tell while detained at his palace, there was little I've seen that was beneficial to those being taxed to death."

Harold began to giggle.

"What now?" asked Rose.

"The King's name…" chortled Harold, "it should be Max-*million.* Like *million,* as in lots of money."

The only response he solicited from Rose was a roll of her eyes as she thought on how much Harold reminded her of Myron when he was his former, simple self.

"Taxes or not, this is the path we must travel to reach Lord Silverthorn's domain," reminded Myron.

"Then go, we must!" Harold stared at the roadway stretching out beyond this royal signage. "If we're made to pay along the way, I've got some fine pelts I was goin' to fashion into headpieces. I can barter 'em for passage through these lands, if necessary."

Rose huffed, her words gushing out in an air of frustration, "Trust me, King Maxmillian will *not* be interested in those disgusting animal pelts."

"But I've got beavair," stated Harold. "And they're nicely cured so they don't stink, not even a little bit of castor oil."

"I know of castor oil, but what the heck is a *beavair?*" Tag frowned in bewilderment. "I've never heard of such an exotic creature."

"It's just my fancy way of sayin' beaver," explained Harold, with a shrug of his shoulders.

"What?" asked Tag.

"It just sounds much more extravagant if you say that word with flare, givin' it an air of richness… Bea-*vair!* Now, did that not sound fancier than sayin' just plain, old beaver, even though I'm speakin' of the same critter?"

Tag and Myron shook their heads while Rose nodded in complete understanding. "It does sound so much more elegant when the word rolls off your tongue just so… bea-*vair.*"

"Focus, people!" Myron clapped his gloved hands, signalling for order. "We have come this way before. We know what we can expect from this monarch. I recommend you be prepared to loosen your purse strings, even cough up a ring or two, or perhaps those earrings you are wearing, Princess."

"I will not part with these fine pieces of jewellery unless it is absolutely necessary," declared Rose. "In my way of thinking, King Maxmillian will be gracious, welcoming even, should he discover we are here. I can pretty much guarantee he will forego any fees to be collected from us, especially after we had acted as intermediaries in ensuring delivery of his precious supply of Troll-crafted goat cheese through Lord Silverthorn's forest."

"I pray you are right," said Myron.

"Come now, we all remember how fickle his *eminence* was upon our first meeting," reminded Tag, with a dismal shake of his head. "I can hardly see him changing."

"So we'll be meetin' with more royalty? One of greater standin' than even our own Princess Rose?" gasped Harold.

"Greater in title *and* in overall size, my friend," promised Tag. He forced his stomach out like a great paunch, and then pretended to pat a rotund jelly of a belly. "But if we are lucky, we will be able to avoid King Maxmillian altogether, journeying on without interruption or interference on his part."

"Even if we did have an audience with the King, I assure you, he will welcome us like returning heroes," insisted Rose.

"I highly doubt that, but we can always hope," said Myron. "If his delivery of cheese remains unimpeded since we negotiated the lifting of that infamous embargo, King Maxmillian will be too busy enjoying his precious cheese to pay us any attention."

"Oh my! It must be a very special cheese," determined Harold.

"It reeks of dead goat, but is considered to be a true delicacy, if one has a taste for rare and exotic cheeses," said Rose.

"Some of the best things in life have a foul odour or unusual flavour, but promise great things, if one can overlook these qualities," stated Harold.

"In all fairness, Princess Rose doesn't reek that badly and she does hold promise of great things when she isn't being so snooty and pretentious," teased Tag.

With a disapproving shake of her head, Rose glared at Tag. "I will not dignify your words with an angry retort."

"By these very words, you just did!" mocked Tag.

Ignoring this hostile exchange, Myron glanced over his shoulder in the direction that brought them to the border of this kingdom.

"Are you searching for Loken?" asked Tag.

"Yes, but I see no sign of him."

"Perhaps we should wait for the little fellow to catch up?" Harold stood on his toes, craning his short, thick neck to see beyond the trees and above the shrubs.

"No... I am confident that in due time, Loken will catch up to us," replied Myron. With a gentle prod of his heels against his stallion's flanks, he urged his mount on. "Let us proceed and make the mandatory stop at King Maxmillian's travesty of a Visitors' Centre; be done with the onerous task of paying any fees his tax collector will deem fit to wring from us."

"You sound so negative. I anticipate my purse shall remain

unopened and our funds, untouched." Rose smiled, optimistic about
the outcome. "And neither will that miserable tax collector abscond
with any of my jewels on this day."

"I hope you are right." Tag sounded as doubtful as she was confident
about the possibilities. "I suppose we shall find out soon enough."

Following behind Myron's stallion, the horses proceeded at an easy
pace as Harold took up the rear, coaxing his donkey along to keep up
with the others. Not even a quarter of a league from the border, on a
major crossroads, the four comrades came upon a small building that
was constructed smack dab in the centre of the roadway.

To Harold, the placement of this structure seemed mighty peculiar,
but his companions knew it was strategically and deliberately built
here. It was so none could use the excuse they didn't see it, and
therefore, could not pay the outstanding fees and taxes, as it applied to
all travelling this major thoroughfare into and out of Axalon.

Myron hopped off his steed, ordering the others to dismount and tie
their animals to the hitching post just outside the entrance to this small
structure no bigger than a large woodshed. A sign with a prominent 'V'
to signify that this was indeed the official Visitors' Centre was really
nothing more than the tax collector's workplace than a conveniently
located station to gather information on local tourist destinations,
popular inns and public drinking houses, as well as farmers' markets
and annual events hosted by this tax-stressed country.

"Should I stay here? Keep an eye on our animals to make sure a
band of brigands don't make off with them?" asked Harold. He tugged
on Sassy's reins as the cranky little beast bore its yellowed teeth to
nip at the rump of Rose's mare when it got too close for her miserable
disposition.

"All are required to report inside for an official head count," said
Myron, jabbing a thumb over his shoulder toward the small building.
"And the animals will be quite safe, for on the other side of this
building are two guards, armed to the teeth."

"They're here to guard against theft?" asked Harold.

"Yes," said Tag, with a cynical grin, "theft against the Crown by
those attempting to sneak by this checkpoint without paying what
King Maxmillian declares is owed to him."

"Well then... methinks I should head on inside with the rest of you
good folks," said Harold, securing the knot of Sassy's reins as the
donkey began gnawing on the hitching post.

Tag led the way, holding the door open to allow Rose, Myron and
Harold to enter first. Glancing about, other than the addition of several
cobwebs in the rafters and the removal of the 'most wanted' poster that

featured Rose's likeness, and Tag's as her accomplice, nothing much had changed. Even the lanky, old bean counter tending the ledgers was the same. There he was, dressed in the same dreary, threadbare, moth-eaten suit and looking as judgmental and miserly as the first time.

The tax collector peered up from his leather-bound, dusty, old accounting records when the door hinges creaked to announce the arrival of these visitors. Before even taking the time to greet them, he pursed his thin lips. His brows furrowed and the narrow bridge of his long, pinched nose wrinkled in non-verbal judgment as he mentally assessed how much he could potentially squeeze from these travellers' pockets based upon the richness of the apparel they wore.

"Good day!" Rose politely greeted the man as she approached the tall counter.

The tax collector's wiry brows suddenly arched up in surprise upon recognizing Princess Rose and her manservant, Tag.

"Well, well, well! I remember the two of you!" His eyes scrutinized the young couple, and then glanced over to where a poster of their likeness once hung. "What brings you back to the fair country of Axalon, Princess Rose? Is it a matter of commerce? Doing some business here on behalf of King William to help spur our local economy, I do hope?"

"No, not on this day," answered Rose. "We are here on matters of great importance, nonetheless."

"Matters concerning the noble King Maxmillian, I take it?" His gaunt face was shadowed with worry. The chair he sat on creaked as his back straightened upon hearing this news.

"We are merely passing through King Maxmillian's domain on our way to see the Elves in the Enchanted Forest," explained Tag. He nudged Rose aside to address the tax collector.

"I see." The rickety old man pushed his chair away from the desk. His joints and bones creaked as loudly as this sad piece of furniture did as he stood up, making his way to the counter. "So, will you be using some of our fine amenities as you pass through this realm?"

"Amenities?" repeated Harold.

"Yes, my good man! The head tax per person is reduced, and can be reduced greatly, depending upon what amenities: inns, pubs, and shops you plan to frequent, as well as the public roads you plan to use as you travel through our great realm."

Harold's pudgy fingers reached under his badger headpiece as he scratched his head in thought. "Don't rightly know what you mean by all this head tax and amenities business, but I'm guessin' you'll be wantin' some money."

Rose unleashed a sigh of exasperation as Myron stepped forward, leaning across the counter to address the tax collector.

"So, what will you be requiring from us this time?" questioned Myron.

"First thing first, my good fellow. I take it, the four of you are travelling together?"

"What of it?" questioned Harold.

"If so, I can offer you a generous discount," replied the man, dipping the nib of his quill into a pot of ink to begin his calculations on a piece of parchment.

"Indeed, we are travelling together." Myron nodded in confirmation.

"Very good! And if you've been here before, it qualifies you for a further discount for returning to Axalon, thereby helping to stimulate our economy. Also consider it extra incentive to come back again."

"The three of us, with the exception of this man," Myron jabbed his thumb over his shoulder, pointing to Harold, "were here earlier this year."

The old man's eyes narrowed as he studied the knight's face. "I have a keen memory, sir. I know I've never seen this ox of a man before. I do recognize these young folks, but you, sir… I have no recollection of ever seeing you prior to this day."

"But I was here… with them!" insisted Myron, pointing to Rose and Tag.

The tax collector scrutinized the man standing before him. By Myron's apparel that included the hefty sword at his side and by his well-muscled frame, he knew this stranger had to be a knight, perhaps even Princess Rose's personal bodyguard.

"Well, had you been here in disguise, then a very clever disguise it was! You cannot tell me you are the same rake-thin, stick of a fool that had accompanied these two during their first visitation to this country."

Myron drew a deep breath as he confessed, "Yes, I am that *fool* you speak of. We are one and the same."

The old man's brows furrowed in doubt. His aging eyes narrowed, scrutinizing the knight's solemn face. "No… I hardly think so!"

"He speaks the truth," said Rose. "Much has changed since we last came by this way, so yes, this is Sir Myron Cankles –"

"Kendall," corrected Myron.

"Yes, yes!" said Rose, waving the knight off. "He is the same fellow who travelled with us when we last came by this way."

"Well, my lady, if nothing else, this fellow's face is vaguely familiar to me. As I am predisposed to believing in the words of a princess, the three of you shall be entitled to the *Returning Patron Loyalty*

Discount, but that big fellow will not, unless he has the papers, namely dated receipts, to prove he had been by this way in the past two years."

"I've no such papers, nor have I ever been to this country before today," confessed Harold. "So, if I've got to pay, then pay I must."

Rose raised her hand before Harold's face, gesturing him to stop talking for the moment. With this motion, the large man stepped away from the counter to make room for her, allowing the Princess to speak her mind.

"As we are here on business, I do believe King Maxmillian will see fit to waive these fees and taxes on this occasion," said Rose.

"If you were here to conduct business with King Maxmillian, not Lord Silverthorn, that would be the case. As you are not, I highly doubt you will be exempt from the applicable fees and taxes that are sure to apply to you and your procession, Princess."

"Ah, but if we are detained and must contend with the ramifications of time wasted here while you calculate and recalculate what is owed, it may well indeed become King Maxmillian's business, and in not a good way either," warned Tag, as he wagged a stern finger at the tax collector.

"Was that meant as a threat, young sir?" The old man stopped writing to glare at him.

"Only if you find the truth to be threatening," answered Tag, his words smug.

Myron was quick to intervene. "What this young man means to say is King Maxmillian will not be pleased if you have a hand, even inadvertently, in circumventing the delivery of his prized cheese."

The tax collector rested the writing quill onto the parchment as he considered this warning. "Believe me, Sir Kendall, if King Maxmillian's regularly scheduled, monthly delivery of Troll-crafted cheese was even slightly delayed, the entire kingdom will be wise to it."

"I mean to say we are here, on our way to the Enchanted Forest, to ensure that there will be no such delay in the days to come," corrected Myron.

"You don't say!" snorted the old man. His gnarled hand picked up a brass bell, clanging it loudly.

"We do!" insisted Rose. "If you detain us, you will have much to answer for."

"I answer only to King Maxmillian and I am certainly in no position to detain you. However, on my King's authority these men are."

The four comrades turned with a start. Two soldiers stormed inside, turning the point of their respective pike at them.

"Oh, no!" cried Rose, as she ducked behind Harold.

"Oh, yes!" said the tax collector, issuing orders to the guards. "Gentlemen, seize their horses, confiscate their property, and then deliver them to King Maxmillian."

"Bloody hell!" groaned Tag. He raised his hands in surrender, staring down the length of the weapon pointed at his face. "Not again."

7
An Unbreakable Vow

"Enter!" King Maxmillian's booming tenor resonated through the tapestry-lined chamber. "Stand before me!"

He licked the cracker crumbs and the oily traces of cheese from the pads of his fingers and thumbs before wiping them on a linen napkin. Satisfied for now, Maxmillian was ready to receive his reluctant audience.

With a snap of his fingers the three servants standing attentively to one side hastened into action, coming to the aid of their liege. Scampering by the two knights posted at the foot of the dais, the trio promptly stepped upon this raised platform where the throne rested.

It was plain to see the King had outgrown the ancestral throne of his forebears, even more so than before. His corpulent form, replete with generous rolls of fat, was firmly wedged between the armrests of this great, gilded chair.

Before Harold was able to make an innocent observation that could potentially result in grave consequences for all, Rose was forced to intervene. She reached over, squeezing his arm. Harold glanced down to see an index finger pressed to her lips, gesturing for his silence.

Rose pretended it was not a case of the King's morbidly obese physique becoming too ample to comfortably fit on this throne. Instead, she selected her words carefully; electing to give the impression this piece of furniture had mysteriously shrunk during their absence.

"I see the royal throne has gotten too small to accommodate one with a stature as imposing as yours, Your Highness." Rose curtsied politely as she addressed him.

Maxmillian merely grunted in agreement as he momentarily floundered about.

One servant hastily removed the small, silver tray wielding the soiled napkin that was tossed carelessly over an empty plate and the drained wine goblet. This tray had been resting on the King's bulging belly that doubled as a portable table for his many and frequent between-meal snacks. Desiring only the very best life has to offer, his ever-expanding girth was fast becoming a testament to his gluttony and opulent lifestyle.

Struggling to sit upright upon this throne in order to properly address his audience, and to do so with an air of dignity, a cascade of crumbs caught in Maxmillian's beard tumbled down his body, dusting the front of his apparel. These crumbs came to rest on the rounded apex of his belly, gathering on the richly embroidered vest that was stretched so tightly across his chest and stomach that the ornate, brass buttons were stressed to the point of popping. With the aid of two manservants, one grabbing each hefty arm, they helped to prop him upright.

The clawed feet of this heavy throne were permanently fixed to the dais. They remained firmly planted while this resplendent, but aging chair squeaked, groaning under the strain of this sizeable man's shifting weight. As Maxmillian wriggled about, settling against the padded backrest, his plump outer thighs bulged through the gaps between the cushioned seat and the bottom of each armrest.

Staring down through beady eyes that seemed much too small for his plump, moon of a face, he scrutinized the four that had been ushered into the throne room for this impromptu meeting.

King Maxmillian's meaty jowls continued wobbling about even after he issued a loud '*harrumph*' to clear his throat before addressing present company.

"Well, we meet again, Princess Rose. I see you have returned with a *larger* and more able-bodied contingent than the first time."

"I fail to understand, Your Highness." Rose stared in confusion at the King of Axalon as she went on to explain. "With the exception of this freakishly large man wearing the unusual headpiece, these are the same two fellows to accompany me the first time I was hauled into your throne room to be thoroughly interrogated by you."

The ample rolls of fat creating permanent creases on the King's forehead grew deeper as he scrutinized them.

"Impossible!" declared Maxmillian. Failing to recognize Myron and Tag, his pudgy hands waved off Rose's claim. "If what you say is true, then the scarecrow of a fool has packed on muscles galore while the boy has returned as a young man."

"Sir Kendall has done just that, plus he has grown a brain, so to speak, but the *boy* returning as a *man?*" snorted Rose. With a roll of her eyes, she giggled, "Do not let his physical appearance fool you, Your Highness. Tag Yairet still possesses the mind and maturity of a boy."

Before Rose could expand on her disparaging remarks, Myron and Tag unleashed a collective, disheartened sigh as they stepped forward to speak in their own defence. Each dropped down onto his left knee as they bowed respectfully before addressing the King's scepticism.

"Princess Rose speaks the truth, Your Highness," said Myron. "I return not as the fool I once was, but as the knight I truly am and was always destined to be; the former first officer to King William's army and the second-in-command to Tag's father, the late Captain Yairet."

"Hmph! It was not some bizarre cock and bull story to filter back to me, after all." Maxmillian scratched his bearded chin in contemplation as he studied this transformed man. "So the rumours were true. You are indeed Sir Myron Kendall, returned from the dead."

"As you can see, I am far from dead, Your Highness. I was just... a different man back then."

"Different in body and mind, I understand," noted Maxmillian, his generous jowls wobbling as he nodded in agreement.

"And if you recall, this young man is Captain Yairet's son. Since we were last in your esteemed company, Tag has been under my strict and constant tutelage, learning everything he can about the knighthood. He has taken to the rigours of training with great enthusiasm, proving to be an apt pupil."

"Apt, indeed!" Maxmillian nodded. "Even by this young man's poise alone I can see he has taken to his training with zeal. It has obviously served to boost his confidence in such a way that he is definitely not the same lad I recall from our first meeting."

"Thank you, Your Highness." Tag bowed in respect. "And contrary to Princess Rose's personal attacks directed at my abilities or where my character is concerned, my training in the knighthood, thanks to Sir Kendall, has helped immensely in honing my skills with the sword. He has also helped to prepare my mind for the uncertainties of battle. So, I stand before you now as a servant to my liege, King William."

"We were appointed to keep Princess Rose safe during our travels," added Myron.

"So gentlemen, here you are, the fabled Sir Myron Kendall and the progeny of the late, great Captain Yairet! And both had been relegated to the post of glorified babysitters to this rabble-rouser of a princess!" Maxmillian's haughty tone was mocking as he teased Myron and Tag for their ill fortune.

"It is a task we accepted with honour," said Myron.

"So you say! In my opinion, I do not know whether you should be commended or pitied for undertaking this *honourable* task. However, what I do know for sure is that I do not envy your plight."

"I will have you know, these two buffoons felt truly privileged when my father appointed them to this dangerous mission!" snapped Rose.

Maxmillian merely responded to her ranting by raising a single hand, motioning Rose for silence as he addressed the hulk of a man towering next to her. "And what of you, sir? Correct me if I am wrong, but I had been informed that you come with a cantankerous donkey, instead of a noble steed. And that badger pelt, rather than a mighty steel helm upon your head, implies you are hardly the knightly sort."

Harold timidly stepped forward. Having observed Myron and Tag kneel prior to addressing the King, he dropped down upon his left knee before speaking.

"Me? Oh, good gracious, no! I'm no knight, or sir of any kind for that matter, Your Highness. My name is Harry Murkins and in all honesty, I'm just an ordinary man. Some will even tell you I'm even less than ordinary."

"You are not lying to me, are you?"

"No..." Harold answered in a meek voice. Intimidated by this royal, with a loud gulp, he forced down that ever-rising tide of fear that knotted into a lump at the back of his throat. "I wouldn't dream of lyin' to you."

"If you are, I will have your ass; roast it over an open fire, and then feed it to my hounds!"

"No, Your Highness! Please don't hurt my little Sassy! I'm speakin' the truth!"

Maxmillian sputtered as he snorted in laughter at this simpleton of a man. "It may indeed look sassy to some, but I'd hardly call it *little*."

The King's comment drew a confused, yet horrified expression from Harold. He frowned in bewilderment upon being the recipient of this monarch's threat that was delivered with a great belly laugh that caused his well-cushioned body to wobble and quiver to no end.

"This has nothing to do with that little donkey of yours, you dolt," whispered Rose. "King Maxmillian was being quite literal."

"You jest!" gasped Harold. He blanched. His heart raced in panic as he imagined the King carrying out this threat that would leave him permanently disfigured.

"King Maxmillian will carve off your backside and serve it up on a silver platter to his royal pets, if he believes you are lying to him," warned Rose.

"But I'm not... and how am I to walk, if he doesn't believe me? I need my bum to sit on, if nothin' else!" Harold's large hands protectively cupped his buttocks as he spoke.

"Worry not, my friend," urged Myron. "Just speak your mind and speak your truth."

"So, just what is your *truth*, Master Murkins?" queried Maxmillian, staring with scrutinizing eyes at the anxious man standing before him. "A twit of a fool in the company of a princess, a noble knight and a knight-in-training seems hardly a likely pairing. What is your part in all of this?"

"My part's quite small in the big scheme of things, Your Highness. I'm just here lendin' my friends a helpin' hand on this quest. I've been tasked with takin' care of their horses and such along the way."

Harold hastily removed the furry headpiece, clutching it in his hands as he bowed his head in humility, hoping this gesture would lend strength to his words.

"A quest you say?" Intrigued, Maxmillian struggled to lean forward on his throne to learn more from this odd fellow.

"My friend is being truthful," said Myron.

"My trusty tax collector had mentioned this quest, too, when he had you four brought before me. He was rather vague with the details in his haste to return to his post, but he did say something about this quest affecting the import of my precious cheese. Is this so?"

"That is certainly a possibility where your cheese is concerned," answered Myron. "But we are here to circumvent such an event, if we can."

"I take it, those giant hasty-witted, canker-blossoms – "

"Hasty canker what?" questioned Harold, bewildered by these odd, derogatory words spewed forth by the irate King.

"Trolls, my good man! I am speaking of those behemoths in the Land of Small! I am betting those fool Trolls allowed their goat herds to run amok in the Enchanted Forest again," groaned Maxmillian. He ran a sweaty hand down his woeful face. "Undoubtedly, Lord Silverthorn and his people are up in arms once more because of this."

"If that were only so," sighed Rose, with a dismal shake of her head. "It is much worse than that, Your Highness."

"What can be worse than those damned Elves imposing another embargo on the shipment of my precious cheese?" snapped Maxmillian. Beads of sweat dotted his furrowed brows as he contemplated the worst possible outcome: to be deprived of his favourite delicacy.

"Forget the cheese!" snapped Myron. "Lord Silverthorn's people are dying as we speak!"

"The Elves are under attack?"

"That was our first assumption, but no," disclosed Tag, "The Elves are stricken by some strange and deadly malady."

"Strange, indeed!" surmised Maxmillian, as he used a silk handkerchief to blot his forehead. "However, it is my understanding the Elves, throughout their long history in this realm, are not prone to the ills that plague mankind. If what you say is true, how can this be so?"

"It is a mystery, but whether it is a new malady to strike the Elves down or the conjuring of dark magic to afflict them, Lord Silverthorn is in dire need of our help," said Myron.

"So, in truth, this can potentially have little or no impact on my cheese supply." Maxmillian peered over tented fingers at the four.

"True enough," admitted Myron. "But consider this, Your Highness; whether this indeed is dark magic at work or a deadly illness, would you not want it stopped before it spreads like a terrible plague into your kingdom?"

"Oh, yes! Doin' nothin' gets you nothin', except grief," added Harold, shaking his head with all certainty. "There'll be no need for cheese, or anythin' else for that matter, if you're dead!"

"So tell me, just how did you four become embroiled in matters concerning the Elves?" questioned Maxmillian.

"They are our friends and allies," explained Tag. "They came to our aid during our bleakest moment. For this very reason we cannot turn our backs on them during their hour of need."

"But what can four mortals do for those allegedly considered to be immortal, at least up until now?"

"Our hope is to deliver a tincture, Your Highness, some medicine that can potentially be just the thing to remedy this deadly fever," disclosed Myron.

"But how do you know it will work? It is a long way to travel for something that may not have any affect on the Elves and can prove potentially lethal, if you, too, become afflicted by whatever ails the Elfkind."

"It is a risk we are willing to take," said Rose.

Maxmillian's brows knitted into a frown as he stared in wonder at Rose. "Is that so, Princess? Even you are willing to risk your life for those arrogant beings that are the very embodiment of flawless, physical perfection personified? With their lovely, golden tresses and those pearly white teeth that can blind you should they smile in your direction, if the sun's light is just so?"

"Well, I am indebted to them," she answered. "I suppose it is the right and proper thing to do."

"Of course it is the proper thing to do," averred Tag.

"Well, it is a noble gesture, if nothing else," commended Maxmillian. "As long as my cheese shipments are not trifled with, I suppose there is no reason for me to stand in your way."

"This must be some very special kind of cheese for you to make such a big deal about it, Your Highness," determined Harold.

"Where I am concerned, it is *all* about the cheese!" insisted Maxmillian. "To the average man with a taste for the ordinary, this cheese is considered too robust. It is a delicacy appreciated by only those with the most discriminating taste! And for the Trolls creating it, this cheese is their only source of meaningful income."

"It is?" responded Harold.

"Yes, indeed! Anyone, anywhere, can raise a goat, but few have the knowledge or skill to craft this delectable cheese. And heaven forbid should those giants be forced to make a living that would require them to seek employment outside their domain! An encroachment into our lands by those behemoths can prove catastrophic on many levels!"

"So, cheese means money?" asked Harold.

"Cheese *is* money! And being that I am the sole and official distributor of this special, Troll-crafted delicacy to lands beyond Axalon, the royal coffers shall be severely depleted, if there is even a temporary shortage, never mind an out-and-out embargo on delivery to my realm."

"With all due respect, Your Highness, commerce is vital for the well-being of any kingdom, but at this moment, the survival of the Elfkind has far greater precedence," reminded Myron.

Maxmillian frowned as he thought back on when this chivalrous knight first appeared before him as a simpleton of a village idiot. Back then, as Cankles Mayron, this man's intentions were still noble, but his ability to prioritize issues that truly mattered could be called into question. This was no longer the case.

"I prefer the former you," decided Maxmillian. The corners of his thick lips drooped in disapproval as he mulled over Myron's words.

"To keep it in proper perspective, Your Highness, the fall of the Elfkind can lead to the doom of yours," stated Tag. "If dark magic is at the root of the mysterious deaths plaguing those in the Enchanted Forest, then not even you and your sorely taxed subjects will be safe."

Maxmillian was silent as he contemplated this stern warning.

"Being a royal, I understand the importance of commerce," said Rose. "My friends do not speak in jest. More than riches, more than that stinking cheese you love so much, we are speaking of very real dangers that can threaten our existence as we know it, if we do not take action and do so with utmost haste!"

"So you say, Princess. Your words paint a grim picture, indeed! But take a moment to consider this: Suppose there is nothing evil at work here? Perhaps the long-lived Elves are not as resilient as we all believed them to be? Maybe an ill wind, one that carried with it a disease the Elves are susceptible to, is at work here and not some dark magic?"

"Are you willing to chance it? Potentially place your kingdom in jeopardy on a supposition?" questioned Tag.

"At this point, what else am I to do, but speculate?" asked Maxmillian, his rounded shoulders rolling in a shrug. "There is always the possibility it is not as dire as you all claim the situation to be."

"We considered *all* the possibilities, Your Highness," assured Myron. "It is not just the Elves that are dying; their forest, too, has been afflicted. An ill tide washes over the Woodland Glade and we fear it will spread beyond the Enchanted Forest, should it go unchecked."

Maxmillian shifted uneasily on his throne as he contemplated this new information. "The forest is dying, too?"

"From what we have heard thus far, there is something not right about the Enchanted Forest and it has *nothing* to do with the change of seasons," answered Tag.

"I've never been there myself, but I've heard it's not so *enchantin'* these days, if you be gettin' my drift, Your Highness?" added Harold.

"So you say, but if you had not seen it for yourself, then just who was the bearer of this ill news?" queried Maxmillian. "Was it Lord Silverthorn to deliver word of this to you?"

"No, he remains by his wife's side, for she, too, is stricken by this fever," answered Rose. "We heard the news first from Loken, personal advisor and consort to Pancecelia Feldspar, Queen of the Tooth Fairies."

"That infamous, shape-shifting Pooka?" gasped Maxmillian. "Parru St. Mime Dragonite's personal minion, you mean to say!"

"Yes, but – "

"But nothing, Princess Rose! That little miscreant is notorious for the ease with which he can fabricate lies. It is a well-known fact that wretched being does so as easily as he can change his form!"

"Loken has changed, not just in the physical sense," insisted Myron, "but in his heart and mind, too. With free will restored, he is no longer the Sorcerer's minion."

"How very convenient for that demented little troublemaker!" Maxmillian grunted as he shook his head in disapproval. "I will tell you now, the more you reveal, the less I am inclined to believe you and your cohorts, Sir Kendall."

"With all due respect, Your Highness, you were not there during our last confrontation with the Sorcerer," said Tag, as he came to Myron's defence. "Loken was by our side! That Sprite you hold in such contempt was almost killed by Dragonite when he tried to save us from the Sorcerer's wrath."

"Save you? I hardly think so! If that Pooka did, it was either by accident or he had an ulterior motive in doing so," said Maxmillian, with a dismissive wave of his hand.

"Yes, he did," confided Rose. "Loken did have his reasons!"

"Ha! I knew it!" Maxmillian's meaty hand slapped down upon the armrest, punctuating his agitated words.

"What you did not know was that Loken never intended to aid and abet with that necromancer," explained Myron.

"Oh, so now you will tell me that little bugger was under an evil spell; made to act on the Sorcerer's every whim?"

"You are almost correct, Your Highness," replied Myron. "Dragonite had manipulated Loken. The Sorcerer had cursed the Sprite, casting a terrible enchantment upon his ladylove. It was potent enough to force his Queen to spurn him after he was falsely accused of murdering his family. It drove Loken to do the unthinkable in a bid to spare her life and to clear his name."

"Bah! What a bunch of malarkey! This is sounding more like a joint fabrication of a wild tale concocted by you four, rather than a true story founded on facts!" With a dismissive grunt Maxmillian rejected Myron's claim.

"We cannot force you to believe in our words of warning, as it is clear you question our source," said Rose, "but tell me this, great king. Are you willing to chance it? Are you willing to risk endangering your people, and heaven forbid, jeopardize your shipment of cheese delivered through the Elves' forest on the possibility we are indeed speaking the truth?"

King Maxmillian silently pondered her words.

"Remember, if the Elves die, their forest is threatened to perish, never to recover," reminded Tag, his words matter-of-fact. "No forest, no cheese, for the Trolls avoid direct contact with the sun's light whenever possible, requiring the shade provided by the Elves' great trees to make their deliveries, as they are reluctant to travel during the darkness of night."

"Those big babies!" snapped Maxmillian. His brows furrowed with genuine concern as he contemplated the ramifications, if he were to guess wrong.

"You know most, if not all, fear the darkness, hence the blue mud they smear on their sensitive skin to prevent burning in the sun so they may travel by the light of day," reminded Myron. "If the Enchanted Forest dies, they will cease shipment of cheese to Axalon."

"I never considered that," admitted Maxmillian.

"Well, you should!" snapped Rose. "So, for pity's sake, time is truly of the essence! Let us pay whatever you want and allow us to be on our way!"

Harold nodded in agreement while Myron and Tag exchanged quizzical glances. They knew the Princess was prepared to pay the prescribed fees and taxes, but they never believed she'd be so eager to do so, without questioning the amount first. They were expecting her to haggle, negotiating some kind of discount.

"What is the meaning of this?" Maxmillian's eyes narrowed in suspicion. "No bargaining? From what I know of your reputation, this is highly irregular of you, Princess Rose. So it begs the question: Just what are you four up to, truly?"

"We are in a hurry! I do not wish to waste your time, or ours, for that matter."

Maxmillian drew a deep breath as he made his position clear. "As I hold no trust in the words delivered by Dragonite's former minion, I shall rue the day should that maligned little being pull the wool over my eyes. And as you are all so intent on acting on *his* words, I can only pray that the demented Pooka has not deceived you in the process. With this in mind, I have but one option that will be to my satisfaction, as well as yours, Princess."

"If we both stand to find satisfaction in this option you propose, do tell! What do you have in mind, Your Highness?" asked Rose.

"I require adequate insurance you are on a legitimate quest. It must be a mission that sees you curtailing this mysterious affliction that can potentially affect my cheese shipments, if it is even true, rather than some covert business venture you have undertaken on your father's behalf, all in a bid to avoid paying taxes to move goods secretly through my kingdom."

"Why would I do that?" snapped Rose. With utmost indignation, she scowled at him.

"Because King William is not only a wise ruler, he is also a shrewd businessman while you, if rumours hold true, are just tight with your purse strings! If there is money to be made, I want assurance that you are being upfront about it, and that I get what is due to me!"

"And what will you have me do to prove to you that I am speaking the truth?"

"I require you to take a solemn oath, a pledge of sorts," demanded Maxmillian. "If your words have any credibility, you will abide by them. If you do, you shall pass through my kingdom, unhampered and with no need to pay the mandatory taxes and fees all others are subject to."

"I can do that! If we take this pledge, you will allow us to be on our way?"

"You have my word, Princess Rose." Maxmillian placed his left hand over his heart as he raised his right hand to make this promise. "And it is *you* alone that must make this pledge to me."

Rose did the same, placing her left hand over her heart while raising her right. "Then you have my solemn promise to uphold this pledge, Your Highness."

"Excellent! Then on your return from the Enchanted Forest you shall stop by my palace as we put our plans into motion."

"Plans?" repeated Rose.

"What plans?" asked Tag. "You said you wanted the Princess to honour a pledge, not make plans with you."

"And she *will* uphold this pledge, young sir, but the plans are not about me!"

"I'm confused," muttered Harold, as he scratched in his head in thought.

"Not as confused as I am," admitted Rose. "I thought I was making a pledge promising I was not dealing in a covert business; to keep my word on this."

"You will indeed keep your promise, but it is pledge to marry my one and only son, the heir apparent to the throne of Axalon!"

Absolutely gobsmacked, Rose's mouth drooped open as her eyes bulged in surprise. The realization she had foolishly acted in haste overwhelmed her, now knowing she had sealed her fate in making this promise.

"A weddin'!" exclaimed Harold, clapping his hands in delight. "A royal weddin' at that! I love weddin' celebrations, not that I've ever been to one!"

"Whoa! Hold on here!" snapped Tag, as he motioned Harold to contain his excitement. "What is the meaning of this? Nothing was said of a wedding! Nothing at all!"

"Princess Rose made no such pledge to marry your son," reiterated Myron. He gently pushed up on Rose's lower jaw to close her gaping mouth as her mind continued to reel with this revelation.

"Princess Rose eagerly *and* willingly made this pledge, vowing to keep her promise. It is not my fault she did not bother to take the time to ask for precise details as to what exactly this pledge pertained to."

"So, you resorted to deceit, tricking her into this sham of a betrothal," said Tag, shaking his head in disgust.

"A pledge can take on many forms, from a promise to pay outstanding debts to accepting a pledge of betrothal. There was no trickery or coercion on my part," insisted Maxmillian, raising his hands as though to show he had nothing hidden up his sleeves. "There was only the lack of due diligence on hers, in failing to ask the vital question of what this pledge involved, before swearing to honour it."

"Then consider this pledge null and void due to her ignorance," urged Tag.

"It is not complicated. A pledge made between those of royalty is an unbreakable vow. Can you imagine the chaos if every man pleaded ignorance each time something did not go his way? This pledge Princess Rose made cannot be undone! By her very words she promised to uphold this formal agreement to wed my son. As it is now, my loyal servants stand as my witnesses. They will declare before all wishing to dispute this that Princess Rose had indeed pledged her troth to my son!"

Tag snapped, "In all fairness to your son, why would you want him paired with Princess Rose! Do you wish to punish him?"

"Punish my son? How so?"

"No disrespect to the Princess, but I speak from experience, having known her since we were small children," confided Tag. "She is not the easiest person to live with."

"Name one female that is, young sir! Besides, it is my insurance I will stand to gain from whatever you four are up to. Such an alliance will ultimately prove mutually beneficial both to me and to those in Fleetwood! This is something I know Princess Rose's parents will not dispute, and will wholeheartedly agree to, once they can be convinced of how mutually beneficial it can be for both our realms!"

"With all due respect, Your Highness, what do you know of this matter where the King and Queen of Fleetwood are concerned?" asked Tag. "Had they suggested such a pairing in the past?"

"No, but I know that when all of high society had converged on Pepperton Palace for the sixteenth birthday gala Princess Rose did not see fit to attend herself, Queen Beatrice and King William made it known to all in attendance of their intentions to find an eligible suitor for her, if she did not return from her quest with a young man in mind."

"So what?" replied Tag. "The mission we were on was foremost on her mind; not finding a husband along the way!"

"And just how many months have passed since her birthday gala?" queried Maxmillian. "I have yet to receive word that Princess Rose has been promised to another. And did she return from her quest with a fitting suitor? I think not! Therefore, I am taking advantage of this golden opportunity."

"Well, officially we are still undertaking that same quest, in a round about way," explained Tag. "That being said, Princess Rose has yet to declare her intended suitor for betrothal, and she certainly has not voiced interest in *your* son!"

"So you say, young man, but the more time you stand here arguing your case, the more I am coming to doubt your motives to be true for travelling through my lands."

"Honestly, we are on our way to aid the Elves during their time of need," swore Myron, his hand over heart in solemn promise.

"In truth, this is the only reason we came by this way," stated Tag. "It is to travel to the Enchanted Forest to reach them."

"*Honestly... In truth...*" muttered Maxmillian, as his eyes rolled in doubt. He raised a hand, motioning both for silence. "Listen to what you are saying! The last time a fool used these very words on me, it was because he was lying! And do you know what happens to those who do me the discourtesy of lying, especially to my face?"

The four watched in dismay as his plump index finger slowly and deliberately dragged across his thick neck. The tip of this digit became buried beneath a layer of fat as it slid from ear to ear as Maxmillian made a guttural, slicing sound for added drama.

Rose's back stiffened as she drew a deep breath to compose herself. While her friends believed she was too stunned to speak her mind, the Princess was deep in thought. Struggling to find a way to back out of this pledge, the thought of marrying a younger version of King Maxmillian was just too much to bear. She envisioned a young man, with a flushed face and a rotund, porcine body that forced him to waddle along like an overstuffed duck, huffing and puffing to keep up with her. How was she, the fairest princess in all the lands, to wed a prince that did not complement her in every way? The very idea unto itself was absolutely ludicrous and appalling!

"I'd rather not deal with the whole messy business of a public execution," said Maxmillian. "However, it will not sit well with my subjects to believe their ruler is becoming soft and easily manipulated."

"Well, meanin' no offence, but you are lookin' a good deal squishy around the midriff, Your Highness," noted Harold, as he forced his belly out to form a great paunch. He then decided to hold his tongue when the King shot a baleful glance in his direction.

"There will be no public executions!" declared Rose. "My friends meant well. They should not be punished for speaking out in my best interest."

"So, in *your* best interest, I am to stand before *my* subjects, looking like a fool because you plan to break this pledge you had made?" snorted Maxmillian.

"I did not say that!"

"Do you resist because you feel my son is not worthy of your hand in marriage? For if you have reservations, I will have you know that my wealth matches, if not exceeds, that of King William's."

"It is not that," said Rose. She struggled to find the words that would not land her and her friends in even greater trouble, but there was just no way to politely decline this proposal without further insulting King Maxmillian or his son.

"Well then, what is it? Speak up, Princess Rose, for I do not have all day and neither do you, if you claim to be in the hurry that you are! I demand your answer now, before you become an undesirable spinster that even my cherished son will be repulsed to wed!"

"*He* would be repulsed to marry *me*?" Rose gasped. Insulted by Maxmillian's words, she stomped her feet like a spoiled child having a fit. "How dare you?"

"I am only speaking the truth, Princess. Not only are you a rake-thin waif of a young woman with barely enough meat on her bones to stand upright in a stiff breeze, but with your advancing years, in no time at all you will be twenty. At that ripe old age, no man, royal or commoner, will see fit to marry you, not even for a grand dowry containing all the riches of Fleetwood."

"Say again!" snapped Rose. Unable to believe her ears, her cheeks burned a fiery red as her resentment swelled.

"It is a well-known fact that a woman passes her prime much faster, and with far less grace, than any man; human, Elf or Dwarf. And though my son deserves only the best, suffice it to say, he will bend to my will, if I deem it a marriage of convenience, one that can prove to be mutually beneficial for all concerned. It will be a marriage that I am positive your parents will readily approve of."

Again, Rose stood before him, stunned into silence for she knew in her heart that in her parents' present state of mind, they would likely abide for the riches to be gained in such an pairing.

"Do not look so surprised, my dear. Just mark my words, Princess Rose, I am doing *you* a great favour!"

"I think not!" she protested.

"Believe it, young lady! Even with royal blood coursing through your veins, it is no magical elixir! You have no power to stave the ravages of time. If you put it off for too much longer, you will have great difficulty in securing a husband, regardless of his title and status, or yours for that matter."

"I am shocked! Shocked and appalled by your words!" cried Rose.

"That may be so, but keep in mind, Princess, once a flower begins to wilt and fade, passing from its fleeting moment of glory, a selective man with even a modicum of taste and scruples will move on to a fresh blossom, than to cling to one that will wither and droop as the sun continues to climb. Soon, you will be known as the royal *Spinster* of Fleetwood, not the fair princess of your father's realm."

"This is madness!" declared Tag. "You cannot expect her to fulfil this sham of pledge she was tricked into making with you."

"Careful, young sir!" cautioned Maxmillian, his eyes narrowing in contempt as he scowled at Tag. "Be mindful of your words. I will not execute Princess Rose for breaking her pledge, but I have no qualms about seeing your head, not to mention those of your friends, rolling about my courtyard for maligning my good name and besmirching my reputation as a no-nonsense ruler."

"Stop!" cried Rose. "Enough with these threats! I will do it! If my parents approve of this marriage, then I will do it."

"Excellent! Then I shall send word to them immediately!" declared Maxmillian. Giddy with excitement, he struggled to sit upright upon his throne.

"I only ask that you *do not* send word until I return from our mission," demanded Rose. "I will not be tricked again. I want to inspect this message; read each and every word so I understand all the terms and conditions, as I will have conditions, too, before it is delivered."

"Really?" grunted Maxmillian.

"I believe you called it *'due diligence'*, Your Highness," responded Rose.

"Fair enough!" He conceded with a nod of approval. "I can agree to this."

"What are you doing, my lady?" Myron whispered into her ear.

"I am trying to save your necks while getting us out of here as quickly as possible." Rose spoke in a hushed tone. "Plus, I shall see to it that my parents decline this proposal."

"Is there a problem, Princess Rose?" Maxmillian's brows furrowed with concern upon snatching words here and there of this muted exchange.

"No, Your Highness," answered Rose, as she raised her hand to Tag and Myron for their silence. "No problem at all."

"Very good then! Perhaps it is time for you to meet your future husband!"

With a clap of his hands the two men standing at attention as they guarded the door to the great throne room suddenly trumpeted their horns to summon the royal progeny.

From the main hall, the mournful creak and echoing thud of an opening door from the upper chambers of the castle sent a great draft swirling through the throne room. This chilling breeze set the flames guttering in its wake, light and shadow dancing against the high walls with the approach of King Maxmillian's heir.

Before this royal made his grand appearance, his great shadow stretched into the throne room, growing ever larger against the far wall to herald his coming.

It was just as Rose had feared! If this prince's shadowy form was any indication, the young man was the corpulent replica of his father; a large, bag-throated, fat toad that was as round as he was tall!

Just as he entered the throne room, his father announced, "I present to you the heir apparent to the throne of Axalon, my beloved son, Prince Percival Augustus Chadwick!"

Rose's eyes widened in shock as she took in the image that had cast such a great and imposing shadow.

'He cannot be kin! He must be adopted,' she thought. Her jaw dropped in astonishment as she revelled in this vision of beauty that was Prince Percival.

His golden locks, silken and shining in the glow of the torches burning in the throne room, rivalled hers. The delicate waves gracing the crown of his head swayed like ripened wheat in the autumn breeze with each step as the Prince sashayed into the throne room. This perfect mane served to frame the chiselled features of his face. In her eyes, it was like that of an exquisite statue carved of the finest marble come to life. He was utterly flawless!

Rather than unruly and unkempt like his father's, Prince Percival's eyebrows were impeccably groomed, sitting atop a subtle brow ridge that spoke of intelligence rather than a young man possessing the brutish qualities of the working class.

Rose was immediately drawn to his piercing blue-grey eyes. If he did see her, the Prince said nothing.

Ensconced in a heavily embroidered vest worn over a fine silk shirt that 'swished' with the swing of his arms as he strutted before all, to Rose, he cut a dashing figure. There was a regal air about him as the crimson velvet cloak that sat atop his squared shoulders billowed behind him.

The cloak made him appear greater in size, while the fitted vest accentuated a slender, yet well-muscled form that was pleasing to her eyes. As she fawned over his presence, all Tag could see was a gaudy rooster parading before them.

With his shoulders pulled back, his head held high, and haughty steps that were measured but light, Prince Percival commanded attention from all in the room. He meandered over to one of the guards appointed to the foot of the dais. Standing in a full suit of armour, the polished steel of the breastplate provided a near-flawless reflection. Before taking his place on this raised platform so he could stand above all those in the room, but still below the majesty of his father, the Prince tilted his head, stealing an admiring glance of his reflection. Flashing an adoring smile at his likeness, he pushed the stray golden strands in place. Licking the pad of his thumb, he smoothed his already perfect eyebrows. Unable to resist, he gave his image a quick wink of admiration prior to taking his place before King Maxmillian.

"Oh, my goodness! This *is* the perfect match!" gasped Tag, as he addressed Rose. "He is the male version of you!"

8

Providence

Prince Percival had marched right by Rose and her comrades. Even though their presence was obvious, for it was nigh on impossible not to notice a physical presence as large as Harold's, this royal chose not to acknowledge them. With head held high, he did not even afford these strangers a modicum of courtesy by means of a simple nod of acknowledgment.

"You summoned, Father?"

"Yes, my son!"

"This better be good! I'll have you know I had my nose buried in a rollicking good tale of adventure written by a wily old Wizard. This latest story is so satisfying, I was reluctant to answer your call." The sulking Prince's handsome face suddenly scowled in annoyance.

"It is very good, indeed! I have a special introduction to make to you." Maxmillian waved his son forward to approach him so he would not be forced from his seat to address the young man. "It is an introduction that is worthy of your time and attention."

"I will be the judge of that, Father. Now, whom do you wish to honour with my presence?" The young noble glanced over his shoulder and down his regal nose at the four gathered at the foot of the dais. "For I see none in your present company worthy of this great privilege."

Tag cringed inwardly. At first glance, as much as King Maxmillian's son was like Rose in the manner of his pretentious choice of apparel so all would know he was a member of nobility, by Prince Percival's very words and hubris demeanour, he had a personality to match Rose's on her worst day when she felt compelled to take advantage of her royal status, to the mortification and misery of all!

"You speak with haste, my son, for in this very room you are graced with the presence of the lovely and *eligible* Princess Rose of

Fleetwood! Your future bride to be exact, if I get my way."

Percy spun about on his heels, scrutinizing the only female in the room. "You are *the* Princess Rose-alyn of Fleetwood?"

"I am, my lord."

These four, small words were spoken in a tone that was so sickly sweet it made Tag gag in response. He shuddered as he watched Rose smile demurely, curtsying in the most ladylike manner before this strikingly handsome young man.

"Princess Rose, allow me to introduce you to this captivating noble, a royal beyond reproach! Feel free to bow down in the magnificence that is my son, Prince Percival, the sole and legal heir to the throne of my fair kingdom!"

Percival bowed graciously, taking Rose's right hand into his.

Tag frowned with concern, for it was at this very moment he could have sworn he heard the hiss of a snake as Prince Percival planted a whisper of a kiss upon the back of Rose's hand as a charming smile curled his lips. It was one of those mesmerizing smiles: perfect lips framing a flawless set of pearly-white teeth. It was the kind of smile that'd make even the most frozen of hearts melt at a single glance, yet it was an unsettling smile, one that left Tag feeling ill at ease in this royal's presence.

Tag stood to one side, rolling his eyes in disgust, knowing that at this very moment he and his comrades no longer existed in her world. In fact, they were being completely ignored by both of these starry-eyed royals.

Like a young girl besotted by love, Rose blushed upon receiving this kiss. Her heart palpitated, fluttering with delight. It felt as though a thousand butterflies were about to burst from her chest as she admired this young man. Her eyes twinkled with adoration as she giggled in response, curtsying once more upon being the recipient of this intimate greeting.

"I am delighted to make your acquaintance," said Rose.

"Most feel honoured *and* privileged to meet me, even awe-struck when standing in the presence of my great bearing, and yet, there is something so quaint that you are *'delighted'* to be in my presence."

"Forgive me." Her eyes were sincere as she peered up adoringly at his face. "Of course I feel both honoured and privileged. To be in awe does not do justice to how I feel at this very moment!"

Percival scrutinized her face to judge its symmetry, and if indeed it was as perfect as his. "Oh, my! You have such enchanting, purple eyes, the likes of which I have never seen before on any living creature, human or animal!"

"Amethyst." Tag muttered beneath his breath.

The Prince glanced over with a resentful sneer. "Did you say something?"

Before Tag could respond, Rose answered on his behalf. "He said my eyes are the colour of the precious gemstone, amethyst."

"*Semi-precious*, and as I said before, *purple* better describes the colour of your eyes because I say so." Giving her a knowing wink, he smiled once more in a deliberate bid to dampen Tag's contribution to their conversation while maintaining her undivided attention.

"Who am I to argue," conceded Rose. With a smile and a lilt in her voice, her heart skipped a beat, melting a little more under his enchanting spell.

"I must say, you hardly seem the wilful, headstrong young lady your parents lamented about during your birthday gala, of which you were so conspicuously absent, my lady."

"Please, just call me Rose, Prince Percival."

"I prefer to call you Rose-alyn. It is not so common a name as just *Rose*. As for you, you must call me Prince Percy."

"Percy, it is."

"*Prince* Percy will do for now, after all, I am higher on the rungs of the monarchy than a mere princess. I demand to be addressed with the appropriate level of respect, even by you, Rose-alyn. Do I make myself clear?"

"Yes, Prince Percy!" She nodded eagerly. "It is perfectly clear. And I am truly sorry I was not at my birthday gala to greet you in person, and to spare you from the insipid tales and blatant rumours my parents have a habit of concocting of late."

Though she was momentarily taken aback by his order that she was to address him rather formally, she was happy and relieved he was not a gluttonous, obese, younger version of his father, as she had initially feared. No doubt, the young man was graced with his late mother's finer physical attributes and delicate facial features. In Rose's mind, on the scale she used to judge the characteristics of all young men worthy of a second glance, and using Tag as her measuring stick, for she knew him the best, she conducted a mental inventory, comparing the qualities of the two.

This marvellous specimen of a prince towered a whole hand-span taller than Tag. This admirable height difference was further enhanced by his perfect posture and lean physique, one sculpted by many hours of lifting a book than brandishing a sword.

Prince Percy was gifted with the most exquisite features, like those found on the finest marble statues honouring the heroes of old to be crafted by the most talented artists known to man or Elf. Those steely, blue-grey eyes, that perfectly formed nose that had never violently clashed against a clenched fist and the strong jawline punctuated by a cleft chin to compliment his dimples all worked to accentuate those high cheekbones when he smiled at her. These were the physical qualities she admired and had only seen rarely amongst the mortals, but were most prevalent amongst the Elves; a race deemed as the most perfect in the world.

These fine attributes, combined with the added confidence he exuded that came from believing he was created by the higher hands of divine powers, served to captivate Rose's heart and mind.

In comparison, Tag possessed rugged good looks and a physique honed and designed for the rigours of battle for a fellow of his age; physical features she knew many young women found attractive. As for the Prince of Axalon, it was more than just the refined good looks bestowed upon Percy that made him stand out against this knight-in-training. This charismatic royal was downright dashing in every respect of the word! Even when he spoke, he was so eloquently articulate it sent a shiver of scintillating delight down her spine.

There was also a profound difference in their deportment, both in carriage and manner.

In Rose's opinionated opinion, lately, it seemed that Tag lived with one hand always on the hilt of his sword. He prickled with an undercurrent of brooding angst, like he was willing to pick a fight with anything or anyone that dared to cross swords with him or even looked cross-eyed in his direction. On the other hand, Percy had a majestic air about him, a regal, serene quality of kingly proportions. Rose sensed this member of royalty would never lower himself to do something so menial and crass as to fight, especially in a bare-knuckled brawl. Instead, this prince would see fit to appoint others to do the fighting on his behalf.

"As far as I am concerned, parents, whether royal or not, do tend to exaggerate where their offspring are concerned. Nonetheless, it was disconcerting that you did not see fit to attend a celebration that was in your honour."

"In hindsight, I regret I was not there, now knowing you had made the effort to attend. But let us start a-fresh, for it is a great honour and an absolute privilege to finally make your acquaintance, Prince Percy," said Rose, her cheeks blushing once more as she spoke. "I am truly delighted to be in your presence!"

"Of course you are! Who wouldn't be?" averred Percy. He thrust his shoulders back, rising to his full height. Holding his head on high, it was as though it was to allow her to better admire his regal stature. He then stared down his nose at her as he performed a cursory inspection. "Do you always dress like this?"

"Like what?" asked Rose. She glanced down at the humble raiment she wore.

"Like a man, and worse yet, a *common* man!" Percy's nose wrinkled in disgust as he scrutinized her.

Rose shrank beneath his scathing and critical gaze. "This is not my normal manner of dress. I am in the midst of quest, therefore, I am dressed accordingly."

"I suppose that is plausible," sniffed Percy, grimacing in disdain. "I pray this is a rare occasion, one that will not be repeated, for this apparel you don now does nothing for you. It is hardly flattering, doing nothing for your complexion, your womanly form, if indeed you have one under those rags, nor your tresses. To put it bluntly, it is not becoming at all!"

The more Percy spoke, the more irate Tag became, fidgeting about as he fought to bite his tongue than to dispense words to verbally dismiss this inane ranting.

"You may have the title of a genuine princess, but surely you do not expect me to be seen in public with you, dressed in these slovenly threads, especially during social functions, do you?

"Hey! Watch your mouth! Contrary to what you just said, I think Princess Rose looks absolutely fetching, in her own weird way!" snapped Tag, unable to hold back any longer.

"Hush!" ordered Rose. She ignored Tag's kind words of support, for she was anxious to win back Percy's heart. "Had I known I was to be presented to you on this day, I would have dressed appropriately, in one of my formal gowns and only the finest pieces of crown jewels, not these dowdy, run-of-the-mill ones I wear now. However, as I am undertaking an important mission, the nature of the quest and the promise of the inclement weather to come, forced me to dress as you see me now. Other than that, I dress as a proper princess should, in only the finest silk brocades and the most sumptuous velvets."

"Well, that is a relief!" Percy nodded in approval. "There is no point in being a princess if you cannot look the part, and in our circles, appearance is everything. Would you not agree, my dear Rose-alyn?"

"Definitely," answered Rose, as she pretended she didn't hear Tag's disgruntled sigh. "But this quest – "

Percy raised a hand, gesturing her for silence. "Does this quest concern me?"

"It concerns the Elfkind."

"*Borrr-ing!* I am not interested in this petty mission you have undertaken with your servants."

"Of course not, because it has nothing to do with you," muttered Tag. With a dismal shake of his head, he unleashed another dreary sigh of discontent. "And we are *not* her servants!"

"You don't say!" Percy's eyes flashed with resentment as he glared at Tag. "So tell me then, just who are you? And with the way you are huffing and puffing, do you have some kind of breathing malady afflicting you?"

"My name is Tagius Yairet. I am the son of Captain Oliver Yairet, formerly of King William's army and I am also Princess Rose's closest friend."

"Oh, yes! Your father is the *dead* captain, the one killed in battle to the east about a decade ago."

"Yes." Tag nodded his head in confirmation.

"Though I was only a child, perhaps a year or two older than you were when this tragic event unfolded, if I recall my history lessons correctly, that was a calamity if ever there was one! It was a foolish idea to take on the Sorcerer and his mercenaries! It was doubly foolish to confront that necromancer when Captain Yairet and his men were so outnumbered from the start."

"In the defence of my deceased captain, though we were greatly outnumbered at the outset, had we not acted when we did, many innocent lives would have been lost on that fateful day," countered Myron. "In the end, we rose victorious, and this is what matters the most."

"And just who are you?" queried Percy, as he stared at this knight, scrutinizing him from head to toe.

"I am Sir Myron Kendall, my lord. I was the first officer to Captain Yairet during that historic battle."

"No!" gasped Percy. His perfect brows arched up in surprise. "*The* Sir Myron Kendall?"

"Yes, my lord." Myron bowed in respect.

"Well, if this is true, according to history, you are supposed to be dead – dead and long gone, if not completely and utterly forgotten in the annals of history!"

"Then history must be rewritten, for clearly, I am *not* dead, my lord."

King Maxmillian motioned to one of his servants to deliver another tray of cheese and crackers, so he may listen to this lively exchange while dining from the comfort of his throne. He observed as his son took command of the throne room, staring judiciously at Myron and Tag as he determined his next course of action.

Percy's index finger tapped against his lower lip as he pensively considered the large man with the badger pelt clutched in his hands. Harold was fidgeting nervously behind Rose while the Prince stared him up and down, trying to make sense of his presence.

"I can understand Princess Rose-alyn being in the company of a knight or two, but where you are concerned, sir, I am afraid to even ask."

"Then don't!" snapped Tag, his arms crossing his chest in defiance as this arrogant tone continued to grate his nerves raw.

Percy sneered, glaring with mounting disapproval at this knight-in-training. Shaking an admonishing finger at Tag's agitated face, he snarled, "Your show of insolence could well be your end, Yairet!"

"What now? Are you going to threaten us with a public execution, too?"

"Ah! So you raised my father's ire, too, did you?" responded Percy, a cruel smirk of a grin twisting his lips. With a tone rife with condemnation, he addressed Rose, "Really, my dear, this fellow claims to be your friend, and yet, I sense the quality of the company you keep is due to misfortune or providence, and not so much that of choice."

"*Providence?*" snapped Tag, his hands balling into clenched fists. "I should deliver a healthy dose of providence to the backside of your fat head!"

Myron seized him by his shoulder. Squeezing it as a non-verbal order to stop, he pre-empted Tag's efforts to strike back with physical retaliation.

Percy stood before Tag, nose to nose, as he growled, "Your impudence is testing my patience!"

"And I lack the patience to deal with someone as petty and shallow as you!"

Appalled, Percy gasped, "You dare speak with such disrespect to a member of royalty? The heir apparent to the throne of Axalon, no less?"

"I just did! No daring required," grunted Tag.

Snapping his fingers, one of Maxmillian's servants stepped forth. With a nod of Percy's head, tilting it toward his new rival, the servant acted on the Prince's behalf. The man removed his white gloves, using them to slap Tag across his face.

Percy nodded in approval to the servant for accosting the young man, as he would have seen fit to do so himself while Rose, Myron and Harold watched in stunned silence.

"Take that, you impudent lout!" snorted Percy.

"Take what? I didn't feel a thing!"

"Perhaps a sound beating is more to your liking," growled Percy, his eyes glancing over to the servants waiting for further instructions.

Before Tag could answer this threat with his fists, Harold and Myron held tight to him. Rose stepped in between the two adversaries as their animosity grew by leaps and bounds, hurtling toward an exchange of blows, if she did not intervene immediately.

"Stop it!" ordered Rose.

Knowing Tag was the scrappy type and knowing now that Percy was much too dignified to engage in fisticuffs of any kind, she was compelled to act. It was done more so to preserve her future husband's perfect features from being ravaged by a severe fist pummelling delivered by her agitated friend than to spare Tag from a beating. Any level of physical abuse Tag could potentially be subjected to, should Percy choose to retaliate on his own, would undoubtedly leave her precious man more bruised in his efforts than his intended victim.

"Stop it right now! This is no way for civilized men to behave," admonished Rose.

"Yes, slap on a muzzle and tighten the leash on that mongrel cur of yours, Rose-alyn!" demanded Percy. He waved off Tag like he was no better than a stray mutt that found its way into his castle. "It would serve him well to learn some manners in dealing with those of greater pedigree and a higher station in life."

"I have plenty of manners! I just choose to use them on those more deserving!"

Before Tag could further fan the flames of contempt, Rose abruptly raised her hand, motioning him for silence.

"Steady on, Tag," whispered Myron, as he and Harold struggled to restrain him. "We need to leave this place, and soon! We cannot afford to be locked up in a dungeon because you allowed this prince to get the better of you. If nothing else, think of Lord Silverthorn and his people. They need our help, and quickly. We must make haste!"

The pinpoints of fire burning in Tag's eyes were extinguished as he unleashed a deep breath to quell his anger.

"Temper! Temper!" chided Percy, waving a finger before Tag's disgruntled face. "You'd be wise to hold that belligerent tongue of yours, or I shall ask my manservant to cut it out, so it will flap no more."

"He did not mean it, my lord," said Rose. Her hand slapped over Tag's mouth, stifling an insult or threat that was sure to land him in a dungeon, or worse.

"I believe that loathsome cur meant every word that spewed forth from that mealy mouth of his," grumbled Percy, staring with utmost disdain at Tag. "And where is your sense of dignity, my lady? This pitiful excuse of a *friend* is a sorry reflection on you. It speaks resoundingly of your inability to surround yourself with quality people."

"Quality people?" Rose frowned.

"Yes, the kind to shower you with adoration and respect, as a proper princess is due."

"I believe you misunderstand," she protested.

"If this is the sorry and sordid quality of the company you elect to keep, I'd be a fool to allow this nonsense to continue, if you are indeed destined to be my bride."

"I think you are –"

"You either think too much, or not enough, Princess Rose-alyn," grunted Percy, with a disapproving shake of his head. "It is better to leave the thinking for those with the true capacity to do so."

"Say again!" gasped Rose.

"There is no point in taxing that pretty, little head of yours, my dear! Better to focus on beauty and silence, and the marrying of the two. If you can do that, you may prove to be a worthy bride after all!"

Percy's insulting comment left her and her comrades momentarily dumbfounded.

"Hey! I will have you know, Princess Rose is perfectly capable of thinking and speaking for herself!" snapped Tag, struggling to be free of Myron and Harold's hold.

"Obviously the girl can think and speak," muttered Percy, his tone cynical. "But being her superior in every way, she will learn to speak when she is spoken to, and she will share in her thoughts when I ask for them."

"Princess Rose is not some inanimate object, like a trinket for you to wear on your arm to be admired by all," argued Tag.

Percy looked Rose up and down, inspecting her like she was nothing more than a filly he was selecting to add to his stable. "Once properly dressed, she has the potential to be a fitting *accessory*. We can even have matching crowns made, but of course, mine will be larger and appropriately festooned with larger, more precious jewels!"

"Unbelievable!" snorted Tag. His eyes rolled in frustration as he jabbed Rose's arm with his elbow. "Are you going to let him speak to you like that, Princess?"

Percy pressed an index finger to his lips, gesturing Rose for silence as he gave Tag a malevolent, *hold-your-tongue-or-I-shall-tear-it-out* look of reproach. "As my intended bride, if she knows what is good for her and the monarchy, she will be a good little princess and do what is expected of her. She will come to treat me with utmost respect and behave with unquestioning obedience, if she hopes to one day become my consort."

Rose's look of adoration suddenly vacillated, conflicted by feelings of adulation and resentment as she considered Percy's condescending tone and words. None, not even her parents, spoke to her like this, and yet, there was something so commanding, seductive even, about his imposing demeanour and noble air, especially when he said the words *'my consort'* before all to hear.

Sensing his son was beginning to rankle her friends' nerves, enough that they can possibly dissuade her from honouring her vow, Maxmillian was forced to act. He was not about to let Percy undermine his plans to secure greater wealth and power. He struggled to sit upright once more as he raised his hands for silence.

"This introduction has now come to a close," announced Maxmillian. "There will be time enough to become better acquainted before the royal wedding. For now, it is time for Princess Rose to be on her way so she may tend to a previous engagement."

"Brilliant! An excellent idea, Your Highness," agreed Myron. Raising his hand to Tag, he motioned his friend to say no more or instigate any kind of trouble to prevent their safe and immediate departure from the castle.

"Oh, yes… that little *quest* of yours," grumbled Percy, his tone snide. With a charming smile meant only for Rose, he took her by the right hand, planting a kiss upon it once more. "Consider this a parting token of our first meeting; a small memento for you to cherish and remember me by, until we meet again."

Any negative thoughts creeping into the back of Rose's mind were instantly vanquished as she blushed, her heart sent all a-flutter again from this simple act of adoration bestowed upon her.

"Would you care to join us on this quest?" asked Rose.

Tag's jaw dropped open as his mind floundered, searching for the adequate words to squelch this offer without landing them in the bowels of the castle keep.

Percy's nose wrinkled in disgust. "If I do, will it guarantee me fame or fortune? And at minimal risk to my life, of course?"

"No, it will not!" Myron hastened to answer. "However, there is the greatest chance you will meet a nasty end or succumb to whatever it is the Elfkind are plagued by."

"Ewww!" Percy grimaced in repulsion. "Being the heir apparent to the throne of Axalon I am not about to chance that, not unless the reward greatly outweighs the risk!"

"The greatest reward will come in saving some lives," responded Tag, his tone was decidedly smug as he addressed the royal.

"Well, as there is no guarantee you will even accomplish that, my time is better spent on finishing that rollicking good tale of a quest that is sure to conclude in a manner to my liking," decided Percy, waving off this impromptu invitation to adventure.

"Now that is a brilliant plan," agreed Myron. He hustled, steering Rose to the great double doors to make their exit. "It is better for you to remain within the protection of these mighty walls."

"And heaven forbid should something happen to you on our watch!" added Tag, following close behind them. "We wouldn't want that to happen."

"Fare thee well, my love, until we meet again!" called Percy, demonstrating his best royal wave as she departed.

"Farewell, my prince!" Rose called over her shoulder as she was ushered away. She stared dreamily at Percy as Tag and Myron rushed her out of the throne room before Maxmillian found reason to detain them once again.

Percy gave her another one of his charming smiles, blowing her a kiss while Maxmillian hollered, his booming tenor echoing through the great corridor. His parting words chased behind them, "Farewell for now, Princess Rose! We shall meet again upon your return! Remember, you *must* uphold your pledge or there will be dire consequences!"

"Quickly!" ordered Myron, hurrying Rose out the castle and down the stairs of the keep. "Time is a precious commodity not to be wasted."

Harold lumbered along close on their heels, following his friends into the courtyard where a servant and two stable boys tended to their mounts.

"We are free to leave," announced Myron, shooing away King Maxmillian's staff as he snatched his steed's reins from the servant. "We'll be off now!"

With a curt nod, the servant motioned the stable boys to return to their duties as he withdrew into the castle.

As Rose inserted the toe of her left boot into the stirrup to mount her mare, she gushed with pride, "Was Percy not the very definition of charming?"

"I agree wholeheartedly! Prince *Prissy* was *not* charming at all," grumbled Tag. In his annoyance and eagerness to leave, he almost hoisted Rose up and over her mare as he gave her a leg up into the saddle.

So taken by this chance encounter with destiny, Rose was not about to let Tag dampen her cheerful mood. Instead, she chose to ignore his agitated tone. She revelled in this newfound adoration for the handsome, young man that held great potential as the husband of her dreams.

"If you ask me, he is an egomaniacal, arrogant prig, if ever there was one," snorted Tag. He threw himself onto his mount, pulling hard on the reins to wheel his steed about to follow Myron's.

"I believe you are mistaking his unabashed confidence for arrogance," countered Rose. "It is an easy mistake to make, if it is a quality one is lacking in."

"Are you saying I lack confidence?"

"Are you saying you do?" responded Rose, glaring through narrowed eyes at Tag.

"Of course not! But I get the sense that is what you are implying, where I'm concerned."

"If the shoe fits…" snipped Rose.

"Look here! If you ask me, I'd rather be short on confidence than to be a miserable sod that oozes arrogance."

With a carefree smile, Rose tossed back her golden tresses. She giggled, teasing her friend, "I did not ask you, but by your very tone and words, if I did not know better, I would say you are just jealous!"

"Jealous of that uppity snob? I think not!" Tag dismissed her remark with an irreverent wave of his hand. "In fact, I found that loathsome git of a pompous prince to be downright sanctimonious. I'm just grateful I am *nothing* like him!"

"Nothing like him, indeed!" Rose said with a nod. "Prince Percy is a *royal* prince. It is like comparing a purebred stallion to a lowly donkey of questionable pedigree."

"Ain't nothin' wrong with donkeys," stated Harold, as he patted Sassy's withers.

"The point being, Tag is merely a knight-in-the-making. And should my father ever knight him, he will be a captain at best. Tag will never be a prince, not even a duke or a baron!"

"Better a humble knight with integrity than an arrogant sod of a royal, any day!" retorted Tag, his heels prodding the gelding on.

Sensing another acrimonious quarrel was about to erupt to an all-new level of nastiness between the pair, Harold tugged at Sassy's reins, manoeuvring the donkey to place them between the feuding friends.

"We should move, be on our way," urged Harold. Creating a physical buffer, he wanted nothing more than to make it difficult for the two to keep bickering.

"Yes," Myron called over his shoulder as he led the way from the castle's courtyard. "We must make up for lost time. Pick up your pace, my friends."

"But what about Harold?" asked Tag.

Myron brought his horse to a stop. Wheeling his stallion about, he faced Harold. "Time truly is of the essence, my friend. We must part ways."

"But I'm part of this quest! I'm here to help." Harold's heart dropped to the pit of his stomach upon hearing Myron's decision.

"And you would have proven very helpful, I'm sure. However, we have lost precious time we will never get back. From this point forward, we must guide our horses on at top speed. You will never be able to keep up with us."

"But – but – " stammered Harold, wringing his hands in woe upon hearing the finality with which these words were delivered.

Feeling pity for him, Rose spoke up. "I promised you a quest, Harold Murkins. Alas, fate has intervened, but not on your behalf. We must move with speed while the light of day holds. I pray you understand our need to depart."

"But if you plan to ride only while there's daylight, then suppose I manage to catch up to you sometime durin' the night? Then what?" asked Harold. "Can I still be a part of this quest, if I do?"

"That is highly unlikely," answered Myron. "But if you attempt this, we will be taking this main road that will deliver us northward. At the speed we intend to travel, if we have no further delays, it should take us just beyond the boundaries of this country, and then on toward Lord Silverthorn's domain at dawn."

"Yes, we'll probably only make it that far, setting up camp for the night on the outskirts of Axalon," added Tag.

"Well then," said Harold, heaving a decisive sigh of determination, "I, too, shall take to this main road. Me and my little Sassy will venture on, and if the fates decree it, we'll meet up again."

"You're going to attempt it?" questioned Rose.

"Of course! My momma didn't raise a quitter! Don't know when I'll meet up with you again, but I'm determined to do my best!"

"The road is long. Won't you get lonely?" asked Rose.

"No fear of that happenin', my lady! I've got Sassy to talk to. And the best thing of all, she don't talk back, no matter what," Harold gave her a smile and a wink. "You three ride on ahead, I'll catch up to you when I can."

"Are you sure you want to do this, Harold?" asked Tag.

"Got nothin' better to do with my time. Just don't any of you worry about my Sassy and me. We'll be fine. We'll get there when we get there. Wherever *there* happens to find you three."

"Then, we'll be off," said Myron. Prodding his stallion's flanks with the heel of his boots, he urged his steed on.

Tag and Rose followed. They prompted their mounts on, pressing their steeds into a full gallop to keep up with Myron's steed as it charged through the courtyard.

Rose glanced over her shoulder to see Harold and his donkey standing alone. The large man was waving farewell as he shrank from her sight.

Myron raised his left hand, motioning for Tag and Rose to slow down. He guided the horses off the diminishing roadway to a small clearing bordered by trees.

"Are we stopping for the night?" asked Tag. He glanced up to the deepening, twilight sky.

"Yes," answered Myron.

"But the light will hold for a little while longer," said Tag. "We can venture into the Enchanted Forest before the night steals away with all that remains of the day."

"True enough," said Myron, as he hopped down from his stallion. "However, I fear the forest will be a far more treacherous place than an enchanting one. It will not be the same as when we first ventured into the Elves' domain. It is better to go forth in the full light of day and with our wits about us. For now, it is time for us to find some rest."

"Yes, no point in taking unnecessary risks," agreed Rose, stumbling as she dismounted from her mare. "This is as good a place as any to rest for the night. And if Harold is indeed on his way, it will be easy enough for him to find our camp, should we overnight here."

"I hardly believe he'll catch up at this point, but yes, if he does, we'll be hard to miss," said Tag, taking Rose's mare to tie with his to a tree where the grasses still grew lush in its shade.

"It is a pity Harold is not here as we speak," lamented Rose.

Tag frowned, baffled by her seemingly heartfelt words. "Are you saying you actually miss the big man?"

"In his own odd way, he is rather unforgettable, so I suppose I do. But I was also thinking that if Harold were here now, he'd be busy this very moment; helping to set up camp, finding some food, getting a roaring campfire underway and so on."

Tag's eyes rolled in frustration as he removed her mare's saddle. "Worry not, Princess, just make yourself comfortable. Myron and I will get a fire going as soon as these horses are readied for the night."

Placing the saddle on a log so it'd maintain its shape, Rose immediately claimed it. Plopping down as though it was a chair, she wouldn't be made to sit on the damp ground.

With a blazing fire hungrily devouring the wood Tag had placed within the ring of carefully positioned stones, he joined Rose.

Tag sat on the ground, stretching out his stiff legs to get comfortable before the fire. He rested his back against a sturdy log adjacent to Rose. Tilting his head back, he relaxed, staring up to the dark, velvety sky. Searching for constellations familiar to him, his weary mind drifted as he closed his eyes, enjoying this momentary reprieve.

Myron surveyed their surroundings as he seated himself beside Tag. His eyes strained to see into the darkness as he attempted to filter out the crackling and popping of burning wood that melded harmoniously with the ambient sounds of the night. With no sign of either Loken or Harold, Myron sighed in resignation, knowing that to fret would do nothing to expedite their reunion.

Gazing up, Rose watched as the deep cobalt sky glistened with pinpricks of twinkling lights. She relaxed, closing her eyes to soak in the tranquillity of the night.

The steady beating of wings filled the air, growing louder. Frowning, Rose peeled her drowsy eyes open to discover what was disturbing this moment of serenity. Dark forms flitted about, blocking the light of the stars with their erratic movements.

One such creature swooped into the light cast by the fire. Hunting a moth attracted to the glow of the flames, the little bat dove down, capturing the insect in mid-flight.

This frenetic flapping of wings compounded Rose's restlessness. With her chance for sleep thoroughly disrupted by these pesky, nocturnal creatures, Rose reached to her side, her fingers wrapping around the thongs of her sling. She decided now was just as good a time as any to hone her skills, and these bats were the perfect moving targets.

Her fingers reached into the suede pouch dangling from her belt. Retrieving one of the steel balls nestled inside; Rose peeked in, checking the contents. She was pleased to see another magically replace the ball she had removed, bringing the total number back to seven.

Glancing up to the night sky, her eyes singled out a little brown bat. It flew lower than the others, circling closer toward the light and heat of the inviting fire.

Standing up, Rose positioned the steel ball onto the sling's cradle. She began to rotate her wrist, quickly gaining speed in an effort to generate greater power upon releasing the metal sphere. Keeping her eyes focused on the tiny bat winging about, her sling continued to rotate ever faster.

Hearing the *'whirrr'* of the sling slicing through the air, Tag pried his eyes open to gaze upon Rose. Squinting in the light of their campfire, Tag was quick to notice the weapon, as well as the unwitting target she was intent on striking down.

Just as she was about to release the steel ball, Tag's hand shot out, seizing Rose by her arm. The sphere flew from its cradle, propelled on an errant course to send it over a shrub, disappearing into the shadows of the night.

Before she could unleash her wrath upon Tag, a little bat swooped down, grazing her head. Shuddering in disgust, Rose ducked as she grunted, "Repulsive vermin!"

Reaching for another steel ball, this time she meant to meet her mark. Before removing the projectile from her pouch, a dazzling flash of light momentarily blinded the group.

"Damn you!" cursed Rose. Squinting from the glare, she shook a clenched fist at the blur of a Sprite. "What is wrong with you, you fool? Why must you keep popping up like that? And of all things, as a disgusting, little bat!"

"It is night." Loken shrugged as he fluttered about, looking for a safe place to rest. "What other creature would I take the form of that is better suited to travel effortlessly through the darkness?"

"So you say, but how about turning into an owl instead the next time you feel a need to fly during the night?"

"Why? So I'd make for a larger target for you to strike down with your sling?"

Rose's arms crossed her chest as she snapped, "You need not be bigger for that to happen, you imp! Owls are not as detestable as those flying rodents!"

Myron raised his hands, motioning for calm. "Enough with this animosity, the both of you! Loken is here now. That is the most important thing."

"Indeed!" said the Sprite, as he buzzed around Rose's head to agitate her further.

"So what happened to you?" asked Tag, presenting his hand to Loken. "We were starting to worry that something bad had happened."

Loken alighted upon the palm of Tag's hand. Doubled over, for a moment the Sprite clutched his side as he gulped down great breaths of air, composing himself before delving into the explanation of his longer than anticipated absence.

"Something bad did happen! Didn't it?" assessed Rose, as she tucked away her weapon. "Do tell!"

Still hunched over trying to catch his second wind, Loken raised an index finger. He motioned for her to stop talking and give him a moment's respite before bringing them up to speed with the latest news.

Rose conceded, reclaiming her makeshift chair as she waited for the Sprite to explain himself.

Finding at his foot an acorn cap devoid of its nut, Myron picked it up. He blew the dry dust from it before filling this tiny vessel with water from his flask. Holding it carefully between his finger and thumb, he presented it to Loken.

"You must be thirsty, my friend. Calm your heart. Catch your breath. Quench your thirst before you speak."

Loken accepted the offering, nodding graciously to the knight as he took a deep draught that really amounted to less than a single drop of water, but was more than a mouthful for a being his size.

"Better?" asked Rose.

"Much!"

"Good! Now start talking," she insisted.

The Sprite took another deep breath, wiping his mouth with the back of his hand as he gathered his thoughts.

"So, what happened to you?" queried Tag, watching as Loken sat down, making himself comfortable in the middle of his slightly cupped hand. "We thought you would have caught up to us at the borders of Axalon, if not sooner."

"That was the plan. It was never my intention to be so greatly delayed."

"And just what caused this delay?" questioned Myron, leaning in closer to listen to the Sprite.

"Through no fault of my own, I was vexed by ill luck. I had fallen to grave misfortune soon after we parted company."

"Get to the point!" urged Rose. Crouched before him, she waved at Loken to carry on. "What misfortune do you speak of?"

"The Sorcerer is back!" declared Loken.

"No…" Rose gasped, dropping to her knees as these words seized her heart with fear.

"You saw Dragonite?" asked Tag. "That necromancer is not dead?"

"It was what we had hoped, but consider this hope to be effectively dashed," answered Loken. He watched as a look of panic washed over Rose's ashen face.

"Details, Loken!" demanded Myron. "Precise details of this encounter, if you please! What exactly happened? Do you know for sure that it was indeed Dragonite?"

"In my mind, I have no doubt."

"So tell us, what makes you so sure it was the crazy Sorcerer to begin with?" asked Tag.

"When we parted company, I did as I had told you I would. I was inspecting the borders of the Fairy's Vale to make sure they were secure. I wanted to be certain there was nothing evil lurking about to potentially jeopardize the lives of my Queen and her subjects."

"And?" said Rose, her eyes growing as large as her impatience. "How did you happen across the Sorcerer?"

"I am getting to that!" snapped Loken. "While inspecting the northeast reaches of the Vale, I came across some ominous signs."

"What signs?" asked Tag.

"At first, it was not so much what I saw, it was what I felt. As I flew through a great stand of oak trees, I was overcome by the strangest of sensations."

"A strong sense of foreboding?" assumed Myron.

"It was not even that at first. It was more of an odd sensation; that strange inkling of knowing one was being watched in secret. As I made my inspection, from the corner of my eye, I saw him! At first, it was nothing more than a fleeting blur of shadow and light darting behind a tree, as though to escape my sight. So quick he was, it made me wonder if it was nothing more than a trick of the mind."

"But it wasn't," determined Tag, listening intently to Loken's every word.

"For a moment, I hovered there, in absolute silence. I waited and watched for the culprit to show himself."

"And then?" asked Rose. Apprehension filled her heart, but she needed to know.

"And then, nothing. All was quiet… unnaturally so. There was not even the song of a sparrow or the cry of a raven to be heard. It was deathly silent, as though the forest was smothered by something evil. I flew toward the tree in question, never taking my eyes from it as I approached. Taking to the high branches, I peered down on whomever it was I had initially spied upon."

"And that's when you saw him?" asked Rose.

"When I looked, there was nothing, and no one! It was as though he had magically vanished!"

"But you said you saw a shadow dart behind the tree, that you never took your eyes from it," reminded Myron.

"Indeed, I did! Upon closer examination, the bark of the tree trunk was still warm to the touch where he had been leaning against it to hide from my eyes. Then again, I saw him! A dark, hooded figure disappeared behind a nearby tree. By his size, that distinct, loping gait and his manner of dress, I knew it had to be Dragonite. I wasted no time! I immediately morphed into a dragon of such great size, should he attack me with a sword, he'd nary place a scratch on my scales."

"So you squashed him!" said Rose. "You killed that vile necromancer!"

"Just as I was about to make my move, plunging my dragon head down through the tree top to snatch him up between my teeth, I was blinded by a brilliant flash of light! I felt a searing pain strike my open mouth to burn my throat."

"And then?" gulped Rose.

"I remember writhing in agony as I crashed to the ground."

"And you crushed the Sorcerer while you were at it," hoped Rose, her balled fist grinding into the palm of her hand. "You destroyed that maniac!"

"If that were only so," lamented Loken, with a dreary sigh. "The next thing I remembered was my dear Celia hovering over me, tending to my wounds when I finally opened my eyes. I know not how long I was unconscious, but the scoundrel had fled. Dragonite was long gone."

"You were wounded in the assault?" asked Myron, staring with concern at the Sprite.

"Never mind him!" Rose admonished Myron before turning her attention back to Loken. "More importantly, did you hurt the Sorcerer, at least a little bit?"

Myron and Tag frowned at Rose; their annoyance was obvious enough to force her into silence for the time being.

"Had I not adopted the form of a very large dragon in the first place, most definitely I'd be dead; gone in a puff of smoke, I'm sure! Whatever dark powers the Sorcerer had unleashed on me, Celia's powerful magic healed me, acting as quickly as she had. If anything, it was the nasty knock on my head when I hit the earth that delayed me. Other than that, I'm none the worse for wear."

"Thank goodness you are so resilient for one of your size!" exclaimed Myron. "But what happened next? You said the Sorcerer had escaped."

"While I endured an unnatural slumber, Celia was wise enough to know that I would *not* have morphed into a gargantuan dragon, especially while in the Fairy's Vale, unless I had good reason to. In her infinite wisdom, she and her subjects employed their magic to safeguard their domain should the Sorcerer return. If he should reappear in my absence, they will do everything in their powers to repel him until I return."

"I ask again," said Tag. "Did you see his face? Do you know without a shadow of a doubt he was indeed Parru St. Mime Dragonite?"

Loken grew silent. His hand rubbed his chin as his eyes narrowed in pensive thought.

"You did see his face, did you not?" probed Rose.

"In truth, I did not actually *see* his face, but everything about him; his manner of dress, his gait, his powers, that black crystal... Everything I noted at that very moment warned me it could be no one else, but the Sorcerer!"

"Are you positive?" asked Myron.

"As positive as I can be." Loken nodded in confirmation. "And if it was not the Sorcerer, then you tell me who else could have done what he did, disappearing as he had. And that black crystal..."

Loken launched into the air as Tag's hands suddenly palmed his face. He shook his head in woe while Rose sank back, blinking hard as she forced herself to accept this terrible possibility.

"Good gracious!" muttered Myron, as he sat upright. "This certainly does not bode well for any of us."

"True enough," agreed Loken. He hovered before the knight's distraught face. "At least we have one thing in our favour."

"What – what are you talking about?" sputtered Rose. "You claimed the Sorcerer is alive! Alive and no doubt seeking revenge! Nothing is in our favour! Nothing, I tell you!"

"Yes, the situation is dire," admitted Loken, "but at least we now know what, or in this case, whom we are up against."

"Hey..." said Tag, peering up from his hands to gaze at Rose and Myron, "there is nothing to say that the Sorcerer knows that *we* know."

"We could have the element of surprise on our side." Myron nodded in agreement.

"What are you talking about?" snapped Rose.

"If that was indeed the Sorcerer on the prowl, he undoubtedly believes he killed our little friend when he attacked. Otherwise, Dragonite would have made doubly sure Loken was dead, finishing the deed than to risk him forewarning others," answered Myron.

"Plus, unless Dragonite has suddenly developed the power of divination or the gift of foresight, he wouldn't know that we are working with Loken," said Tag.

"Do you think this is even possible?" Rose's eyes brightened with a glint of hope.

"Why not?" answered Tag.

"I say it's better to have some hope, no matter how small, than to wallow in a quagmire of despair, surrendering to defeat before the end," added Myron.

Rose drew a deep breath, buoyed by her comrades' sense of optimism. "I suppose we are not yet defeated."

"Far from it!" averred Tag.

"Speaking of being defeated," said Loken, as he glanced about. "Where is your large friend? Did Master Murkins abandon this quest?"

"We were forced to leave Harold behind," explained Myron. "Unfortunately, we lost precious time when we were delayed."

"More like *detained*, if not taken as temporary prisoners," corrected Tag. He glared at Rose as though it was her fault.

"By the King of Axalon?" questioned Loken.

"You guessed right," answered Tag.

"I take it, that miserly bugger was putting the screws to you for more funds in order to pass through his domain."

"So we thought," answered Myron.

"Hmph!" grunted Loken, his index finger tapping his chin as he carefully considered the knight's words. "I sense a *'but'* in there."

"A big *but,* as big as it gets!" grunted Tag.

"I'm confused! Are you saying King Maxmillian continues to hold Harold hostage until you return?" asked Loken.

"Oh, if it were only that simple," muttered Tag.

"Now I am truly curious! This is sounding absolutely dreadful. Do tell!"

Rose waved off Loken's concern. "It is not dreadful at all, nor is Harold being held prisoner by King Maxmillian. We were forced to leave the fellow behind to make up for lost time."

The Sprite glanced over to see Myron and Tag's woeful faces and downcast eyes, but it was the young man's bitter tone that drew Loken's concern. "You say one thing, but your friends' shared expression of trepidation betrays you, Princess Rose. Exactly what did transpire at Maxmillian's castle during my absence?"

Rose rolled her eyes in frustration. "These two are making something out of nothing! If anything, it is good news all around."

"How can an impromptu betrothal to an oaf of a prince you know nothing about be good news?" gasped Tag.

"Whoa! A royal wedding? Harold is being detained to insure Princess Rose weds the Prince of Axalon?"

"Are you deaf? I said Harold is fine," stated Rose. "And contrary to Tag's comment, I believe this is a grand pairing, if ever there was one!"

"So, you agreed to this?" Loken frowned in confusion.

"Of course I did!"

"Take no offence, my lady, but I am more than a little surprised. In my humble opinion, Prince Percival is the very epitome of conceit. He is quite the narrow-minded, arrogant snob of a mortal. Why would you want to marry a sod like that?"

Tag burst out laughing. He slapped his thigh as he guffawed, "Ha!

So I am not the only one with less than glowing sentiments where that royal prig is concerned!"

"Your opinion does not count," snapped Rose, waving an admonishing finger at Tag, and then at Loken, "and neither does yours!"

"So, you are not being coerced into this marriage?" questioned Loken, his eyes blinking rapidly in disbelief.

"Of course not!" Rose's words were terse as she scowled at the Sprite. "Why? What's it to you?"

"It all seems very... sudden," replied Loken.

"To be honest, even I was a bit surprised at first, but I found Prince Percy to be very charismatic and charming! If anything, he embodies everything I desire in a prince: tall, handsome, eloquent and well-groomed for starters."

"I see," responded Loken. "And what of his character?"

"What about it? I already told you Prince Percy is charismatic and charming."

"You do know that throughout history some of the most notorious leaders were also some of the most charismatic, charming men to bring about the ruin of their very kingdom?" queried Loken. "They tend to hide behind a public veneer to shield from all their true greedy, grasping, even cruel nature."

"I will have you know, my Prince Percy is not like that, not in the least!" argued Rose.

"You are quite right." Tag nodded in agreement.

"I am?" Rose frowned in response to this sudden change of heart.

"Yes! Instead, that arrogant sod of a prince is a blow-hard! He is a crass, snobbish know-it-all," declared Tag. His hands flew up in frustration, thoroughly agitated that Rose could still not see what was obvious to everyone else in her company.

"Just because he is smart and confident, it does not make him an arrogant know-it-all! And be mindful of what you say, Tagius Oliver Yairet, for Prince Percy is my intended husband! Your show of disrespect to him is no different than being disrespectful to me."

"Do take care, Tag," cautioned Myron, raising a hand to the young man in a bid to curb his spiteful words. "Princess Rose is quite right. You are in her service, therefore, it is not your place to speak your mind, no matter how honest or well intended your words are meant to be."

"True, I am in her service, but I am speaking as her friend, first and foremost."

"And if you are truly my friend, you would be happy for my good fortune, not spouting utter rubbish about my husband-to-be!"

"You are correct, Princess. It is *not* my place to speak!" Tag bowed mockingly before her. "Heaven forbid should I force you to see the obvious! It was foolish of me to believe I could make the blind see and the deaf hear when there is no desire for either of these senses to come into play."

"What is done, is done," stated Myron. "We have more important things to worry about than these royal nuptials."

"What can be more important than my impending wedding to undoubtedly the most sought after bachelor in all the known realms of the free world?" grunted Rose.

Myron sighed as he answered, "I was speaking of the Sorcerer! That foul being is back, lest you forget!"

"And let us not forget about Lord Silverthorn and his people," reminded Tag.

"These matters are more pressing," admitted Rose, "but not necessarily more important than my wedding and all it entails when it comes to the future of Fleetwood and Axalon."

"If the Sorcerer has his way, there will be no future, not for you or your combined kingdoms," reminded Myron.

"Yes, and never mind the rest of us!" snapped Tag.

Rose slumped down as she digested these words.

"Fine! I suppose if that wretched Sorcerer is behind all this, it is up to us to fix it." Rose's words were spoken with purpose.

"Us? You mean to say *you!*" said Tag, his arms crossing his chest in utter defiance.

"Me?"

"Yes, *you*, Princess! If Loken is right about this, the only way the Sorcerer could have assaulted him as he did was to use the powers of the Dreamstone. And need I remind you just who was responsible for that magic crystal landing in Dragonite's hands in the first place?"

"You?" Rose answered with a shrug of her shoulders.

"Me? Now how was *I* responsible for that happening?" grumbled Tag, his eyes narrowing in resentment as he scrutinized her.

"Well, I suppose it could be the Dream Merchant's fault for even tempting me with the crystal in the first place. Mind you, all three of you had a crack at trying to kill the Sorcerer, but you all failed. Perhaps we can all share equal blame for that tragic turn of events," decided Rose.

"Incredible!" snapped Tag.

"No need for compliments," said Rose, waving off his words. "After all, it is only right to share the blame in all of this."

"Yes, there's plenty of that to go around," muttered Loken, with a dismal shake of his head.

"Look here, allow cooler heads to prevail," demanded Myron. "This day has been exceedingly long for all of us. What say you that we call it a night; find some rest before angry words are spoken needlessly?"

"Already done, Sir Kendall, already done!" Rose grunted with an indignant huff. "Sleep is a far better option than to hear more lies about my future husband."

"Yes, you go off and dream of your Prince Prissy," teased Tag.

"That, I will do! And while I am at it, I shall dream up of how I will demand my father to relieve you of your duties in his service and as my personal bodyguard, you belligerent dolt!"

"At this point, you'd be doing me a great favour!" snapped Tag. "Though your parents had earlier requested I be the voice of reason because they had serious doubts as to your ability to select a proper suitor, I will gladly relinquish this role of royal matchmaker, too!"

"Huzzah!" cheered Rose. "Now that is a brilliant plan, for it is obvious to me your ability to reason is greatly impaired where my choice of husband is concerned."

Before Tag could toss more fuel onto the already raging, proverbial fire, Myron stood up, motioning the young man to retrieve the bedrolls as he gestured to the Princess for silence. Rose complied, biting her tongue as she watched Tag stomp off, marching right by their supplies and horses.

"Where do you think you are going?" called Rose.

"If it's fine by you, *my lady*, I'm going to take a piss first, before I deliver your bedroll to you," muttered Tag, as he disappeared into a thicket. At this point, he wanted nothing more than a moment of privacy before settling down for a night.

"I will allow it!" hollered Rose, pretending she still had total control over Tag, even his bodily functions, as she waved him off.

"Nature calls. I hardly think you could have stopped him," noted Loken, as he settled on Myron's shoulder. "Besides, the young sir is in a downright *pissy* mood, that's for sure!"

"My dear fool of a friend is just jealous!" snipped Rose, dismissing Tag's foul mood and Loken's comment.

"He is a fool because he is your friend, or in spite of it?" questioned Loken, staring with raised eyebrows at the irate Princess.

Rose scowled in response, glaring at the Sprite.

"For once, you could be right, my lady," whispered Myron. "Whatever you choose to believe, just know that Tag speaks out because he feels you deserve better."

"Better than Prince Percival Augustus Chadwick of Axalon? I think not!" retorted Rose, with a dismissive wave of her hand. "In my mind, there is not a single prince that even remotely comes close to being more handsome and more charming than *my* prince!"

"Perhaps you are right, but Tag is most concerned of the Prince's questionable treatment of you."

"How so? For I have not the vaguest idea what you mean by this."

"Did you not notice how Tag's nerves were set on edge when the Prince spoke of you like you were nothing more than chattel, an extension of the dowry he hopes to receive in marrying you?" questioned Myron.

"My dowry promises to be priceless," stated Rose. "Prince Percy thinks of me as a finely crafted jewel to be hoisted upon a pedestal for all to admire, and for him to treasure until the end of his days."

"I pray you are not being gullible, my lady," said Myron.

"I hardly think so!"

"Consider this," offered Myron, "should you wed, do you truly believe in the years to come you will be satisfied standing in Prince Percival's formidable shadow? I hardly think you will relish being treated as insignificant, more than a commoner, but less of a royal than he is, for he will eventually stand in your stead as the ruler of Fleetwood, should you wed him and your Father meets with ill fortune, passing away before you are of appropriate age to assume the throne?"

"Then my mother will step in as the Queen Regent until that time."

"Not if you are married to Prince Percival. He will automatically ascend to the throne, thereby making both you and your mother *his* subjects."

"You worry all for naught! That will never happen," insisted Rose. She discreetly blotted away the tears raised by Tag's harsh words and Myron's unyielding candour in broaching this sensitive subject matter she really had no desire to discuss. "And I am a princess, a beautiful one at that, so of course Prince Percy would be proud to show me off to the world!"

"I know it is not my place to say, my lady, but I do believe Tag worries for all the right reasons," stated Myron.

"You are correct. It is *not* your place to say." Rose watched as Loken abruptly launched off from Myron's shoulder.

The knight jumped to his feet, brandishing his sword while the Sprite transformed in a great show of light.

Rose gasped in surprise as their horses whinnied, squealing in fright. She tumbled from her seat as Loken appeared before her as a massive brown bear. Towering before her, his shaggy, immense body blocked her view as his new form reared up. Balanced on his sturdy hind legs, Loken peered beyond the row of shrubs surrounding their camp. His rounded ears twitched about, his nostrils flaring as they vigorously sniffed the air. Though the campfire provided some light, it was not enough for Myron to see beyond their illuminated circle into the growing darkness beyond.

"What is it?" whispered Rose. As she darted behind Myron for safety's sake, she snatched up her Elven longbow.

"I'm not sure," answered Myron.

His grip tightened on the hilt of his sword. His eyes narrowed as he stared into the deepening night. Standing on his toes, Myron craned his neck for a better look.

"What do you see?" asked Rose.

"Hush!" growled Loken. In this form his eyesight was poor, especially in this darkness, but his keen sense of hearing and smell more than compensated for this. "Someone comes!"

"Perhaps it is only Tag," offered Rose.

"Tag headed off that way," whispered Myron, jabbing his thumb over his shoulder in the opposite direction. "Why would he be returning from over there?"

"Oh, I don't know! Maybe because he is an idiot? Or perhaps he is trying to scare us to teach me some silly lesson," muttered Rose, as she peered around Myron.

"Quiet!" growled Loken.

His ears flicked forward. The faintest of sounds, like the snapping of a dried twig underfoot that went unnoticed by his mortal comrades was alarmingly obvious to the Sprite. It caused him to drop on all fours.

With a loud snort and a tremendous roar, Loken charged. His hulking form barrelled toward the stand of shrubs that rustled ever so slightly.

Loken skidded to a stop at the edge of the clearing, rising up to his full height. Hoisting a huge paw, the long, lethal claws slashed through the leaves and branches to expose the interloper. A shrill scream startled him, stopping Loken in his tracks.

"It *is* Tag!" cried out Rose, as she motioned for the Sprite to stop his attack.

"Since when do I sound like a screaming girl?" grumbled Tag. He dashed out from where he had disappeared to moments before, still tightening the belt of his trousers as he ran.

Myron turned with a start. Glancing over at Tag, and then toward the intruder Loken had frightened. "If Tag is here…"

"Then who is that?" asked Rose.

"What's going on?" Tag scratched his head in confusion as he watched his comrades. "I came running when I heard you scream."

"It wasn't me!" snapped Rose.

Loken's snout pushed through the undergrowth. Using his large fangs, he snagged the cloak worn by the mysterious culprit that had curled down in a trembling ball before him. With a loud snort, he lifted his quarry up and over the wall of shrubs, dumping the intruder onto the ground before the trio.

"Don't hurt me, please!" The hooded figure cowered, huddling close to the ground. "I mean no harm!"

Myron hoisted his sword, the tip of his blade pointed dangerously at this stranger. "A show of hands! Prove you are not armed!"

The leather bag the quaking figure carried slipped to the ground, falling with a heavy thud. Two empty hands shot up into the air to show they bore no weapons.

Rose armed her bow, aiming her arrow as she asked, "Who are you? What are you doing here?"

Tag dared to step closer. His hand flashed out, yanking back on the hood to reveal the stranger's face.

"I know you!" He gasped as their eyes met.

9
The Disenchanted Forest

"What are you doing here?" Tag stared in amazement.

"Tag Yairet?"

"Yes, but what brings you here? You're so very far from home." He smiled at this familiar face softly illuminated by the silvery light of the ascending moon.

"I knew you were heading this way, but I didn't know just how close you actually were! When I heard voices, I proceeded with caution, in case you were a band of murderous thieves making camp for the night."

"Worry not," assured Tag. "You're safe now."

The grizzled fur on the apex of Loken's mountainous shoulders stood on end to make him appear even more imposing. His powerful claws raked the earth as a visible show of his might, should things suddenly take a turn for the worst.

"You know this person?" growled the Sprite.

"Yes! We shared a kiss not so long ago…" Tag grinned as he fondly remembered their first meeting.

"Oh, my!" These words rumbled forth from Loken just as he morphed back into his Sprite form. "I never would have thought of you as being… you know?"

"A man's man?" teased Rose.

She stared suspiciously into the darkness at this person with the soft voice. Even with the hood of the cloak pulled back, in this poor light, she could only make out the ebony hair that was either shorn close to the scalp or was tied back and away from this downcast face.

"I'm not a man, Princess Rose!" insisted the stranger, snapping in annoyance as Tag hoisted her onto her feet.

"How do you know me?" Rose's eyes narrowed in suspicion.

"How can I not?"

Rose cringed, her beautiful face scowling in contempt when this irate voice from the past seemed to smack her soundly across the face. The sense of recognition almost bowled her over in unpleasant surprise.

"It's you!" shouted Rose. She raised the tip of her arrow once more, only to have Myron redirect it, so none would get hurt should she mistakenly unleash this projectile.

"Who is this person?" Loken demanded to know. He buzzed about like an agitated bee, zipping in closer for a better look.

"It is *Ugly*, the fortune-teller!" groaned Rose. Her arms flew up in the air; utterly frustrated she was prevented from using her weapon. She was angered by the unexpected presence of this dark-haired minx and all her womanly charms Tag was so beguiled by.

"An ugly fortune-teller? I think not!" Loken stared in confusion as he hovered before this stranger's face. "You are sorely mistaken, Princess! I'd say she is quite beautiful by mortal standards."

"The Princess actually meant to say *Agly,* the fortune-teller," explained Tag, correcting the Sprite's confusion.

Tag smiled warmly at their unexpected guest, graciously offering the crook of his elbow to her. The lone traveller eagerly wrapped her hands around his arm.

"And I am inclined to agree with you, Loken," said Tag, as he guided her to the warmth of their campfire. "Agly is truly beautiful!"

"Hush!" She pressed an index finger to her rosebud lips that Tag so admired. "Thank you for your kind words, but please, never speak that name again! I now answer to Isabella, Bella to my friends."

"Why? Because *ugly* was too close to the truth?" snipped Rose, watching in resentment as Tag seated the young lady on the log before their campfire.

"No, because I mean to travel in secret. Bella sounds not even remotely like my former name." Her words were terse as she addressed Rose. "I now go by Isabella Marjorie Telling, but Bella will suffice."

"Clever!" Myron flashed her a knowing smile and a wink. "*I. M. Telling* speaks nothing of your vocation as a fortune-teller."

"If you are being sarcastic, sir, I will tell you now, the average person is not clever enough to figure it out. I am what I am, therefore, I can never totally escape or ignore my true calling."

"Well, I think Bella is a lovely name," said Tag, nodding in approval. "It suits you perfectly!"

"I once had a female dog named Bella," snipped Rose. "Actually, I used to call her Isabella because it was much more dignified, but nonetheless, she was still a *bitch* no matter the name."

"Meee---owww!" hissed Loken, pretending to be a cat bearing his claws in preparation for a fight. "I see the Princess is already acquainted with this young lady."

"Just ignore her," urged Tag, turning his back on Rose to address the beautiful, young lady. "What happened? Why this change of name? And what brings you to these parts?"

"I came by this way to seek you out! I sensed you were in the vicinity, but I did not know exactly how close you really were until now."

"You were searching for me?" asked Tag. He was visibly surprised, but inwardly pleased by these words. "Why?"

Bella pressed an index finger to his lips as she spoke in a hushed tone, "We must be very careful! You never know what demented soul is lurking in the shadows."

"You don't say," grunted Rose, glaring in contempt at this interloper.

Seeing Bella sidle closer to her friend, and then casually place a hand on Tag's knee, Rose was forced to make her move. She nudged Tag over to squeeze between him and this girl. Using her hips to wriggle onto the log, Rose became a physical barrier between the two, just in case they decided to get too familiar again.

"So why all the secrecy?" questioned Tag, as he motioned for Rose to be silent and allow Bella to speak.

"There is danger, grave danger, awaiting you. You are already aware of the evil that has befallen the Elves of the Woodland Glade, yes?"

"Yes," answered Tag. "That is why I'm here with my friends. We are off to give Lord Silverthorn and his people whatever aid we can provide."

"Ah, yes! The medicine!"

"How do you know about this?" asked Rose, as she shot a baleful glance at Bella. "Were you spying on us? Listening to our every word?"

"I believe it is called the gift of foresight. You did say she is a fortune-teller, after all," Loken reminded Rose.

"I am, indeed, and this danger I speak of was foretold by my crystal," disclosed Bella; patting the bulky bag Myron had set at her feet as he joined them by the campfire.

"Yes! Yes! So you say," muttered Rose, dismissing the Sprite's comment and Bella's prediction. "We already know the Elves are in danger. So what? Help is on the way, so you can go now. You are free to go on your merry, little way. Leave us to tend to our business as we see fit."

"I meant to say, *you are all* placing yourselves in great peril by aiding Lord Silverthorn and his people."

"Are you saying that we are heading directly into some kind of trap?" questioned Myron.

Upon hearing his voice Bella frowned at the knight, and then a knowing smile crept across her face as recognition set in that this man was indeed Cankles Mayron.

"It is you! You have changed! Or perhaps, it is better to say, you are the person you were meant to be from the start… Sir Myron Kendall!"

"How right you are! But how did you know?" asked Myron, as he sat across from them, watching as Rose squirmed about to make more room by insinuating herself well and good between Bella and Tag.

"I am a seer of the future, remember? And I can see much has transpired since we last met. You had come to face your greatest fears with the courage of a true knight. " She offered Myron a knowing smile. "Well done, Sir Kendall!"

"How can I forget?" said Myron. "Your ability to predict the future was nothing short of amazing, once one took the time to delve into the true meaning of your readings."

"So, you are indeed a fortune-teller," determined Loken, as he alighted upon Myron's shoulder. He bowed in polite greeting to Bella, "And as my friends failed to properly introduce us, I am – "

"You are Loken, the consort and senior advisor to Queen Pancecelia Feldspar," concluded Bella, offering the Sprite a congenial smile and respectful nod of acknowledgement.

"Yes, I am! And your skills are evident to me, young lady!"

"What do you know?" Rose muttered as she dismissed Loken's words of praise. "How good she is at this whole business of divination is up for debate, no thanks to that stupid crystal she uses!"

"How so?" questioned Bella. "Did not the things I had cautioned you about on your quest come to fruition as I had predicted?"

"Oh, yes! Everything you had warned us about, especially the dragons, came to pass," said Tag.

"As well as the location of the Sorcerer's lair that was hidden away, shielded from our eyes behind the Devil's Tears," added Myron.

"And just as I had predicted, you found the Sprite you were looking for," said Bella, as she smiled at Loken.

"Oh, whoop-de-doo!" snapped Rose. Her tone was incredulous as her eyes rolled in utter exasperation. "I was speaking of the first and last time we saw this so-called fortune-teller! Her final prediction spoke of Tag, and how he was destined to die; that he would never survive the quest we had embarked on!"

"I said no such thing! If I remember correctly, I warned this handsome, young man that he'd not be coming back this way, passing by my humble abode again, on his return home. So, unless you used magic to cloak your presence as you passed by my cottage, what I said was true! You *did* take a different route to journey back to Fleetwood."

Rose's palm smacked her forehead as she groaned, "Oh! So that's what you meant... I suppose misunderstandings will happen when you speak in riddles."

"Well, as far as I am concerned, you were spot on with your prediction, young lady!" noted Myron. "We called on a bit of magic to expedite our return to Fleetwood."

Tag turned his head, giving Rose his best I-told-you-so look of reproach. The only reaction he garnered was the Princess sticking out her tongue in derisive response.

"This is fascinating!" remarked Loken, his wings rattling with excitement. "You must be known, far and wide, for your powers of divination."

"Not really," said Bella. She smiled with modesty at the tiny being.

"I agree! She is quite bad at it!" Rose nullified the Sprite's kind remark with a derogatory one of her own. "With her flawed crystal, I'd say it was more like lucky guesswork than anything else!"

"Flawed?" repeated Loken, frowning in curiosity as he listened to Rose's agitated words. "How is her crystal flawed?"

Before the Princess could exaggerate the truth, the fortune-teller answered, "Long ago, my crystal was extracted from the mountains far to the north. Passed down through the generations, it came to be mine. Let me just say it has seen better days, having endured abuse mostly from those who were not happy to see what was in store for their future. Plus, I admit I had dropped the crystal on an occasion or two, being that it is awkward to handle in terms of its cumbersome size and weight."

"So, your crystal is broken," determined Loken.

"More slightly damaged than utterly broken."

"Yes, so much so, it requires a degree of creative licence and a vivid imagination in order to interpret those flashes of ever-changing images," grunted Rose, with a dismal shake of her head.

"It takes great skill and years of practice to master the abilities to properly interpret what is revealed," countered Bella.

"Yes, even more so now, thanks to your clumsiness," muttered Rose.

"The point being," interrupted Myron, steering the conversation back on course, "you sought Tag out because you have ill news pertaining to this mission we've embarked on."

"Ill news, indeed!" Bella nodded in confirmation as she gathered her thoughts. She turned the palms of her hands toward the fire to warm them as a chill trickled down her spine.

"Go on, my lady," urged Tag. "What is this danger you alluded to?"

"Please, just call me Bella!" She insisted while smiling demurely at Tag.

"Then continue on, Bella. Tell us of this danger," invited Tag.

"I had abandoned my home to the north; left all I knew and owned to begin my search for you, when my crystal revealed dark omens of things to come."

"Did one of those dark omens include running into *you* again?" muttered Rose, her eyes rolling in cynicism.

"You keep up with that and I predict those eyes of yours will roll right out of your head!" snapped Bella. "As I said before, I knew Tag was in the general vicinity, and it is not necessarily an evil portent of the future, now that I'm here to warn you that the destiny of all is in your collective hands!"

"Warn us of what? Tell us something we do not already know," urged Rose, nudging away Bella's arm just as she reached out to clasp Tag's hand.

"If it is to warn us the Sorcerer has returned and seeks revenge, we already know this," said Myron. "Our little friend had a near fatal encounter with Dragonite in the Fairy's Vale the other day."

"If indeed it was the Sorcerer, his powers have somehow been restored and now grows," revealed Bella.

"So, the necromancer must employ the magic of the Dreamstone to regenerate his powers to exact his revenge," determined Tag.

"With this in mind, all shall be subjected to truly dangerous times, if his powers grow, unchecked and unfettered," cautioned Bella.

"How dangerous?" questioned Rose.

"If my skills of divination continue to hold true, the necromancer's revenge will be far-reaching; devastating beyond belief. Be warned though, it is *not* about gaining untold power in a bid for world domination."

"But for Dragonite, it has always been about world domination," said Myron.

"This time, it is personal. The perpetrator of this dark magic is motivated purely by hate, greed and a need for revenge. It was an emotion so powerful, I felt it emanating through my crystal, like a terrible dark force swelling from within."

"Well, I do suppose the demented soul is rather incensed as we were more than a little irksome during our last confrontation," confessed Rose.

"Irksome? Have you lost your mind, Princess? We nearly did away with that fiend! We almost killed him," reminded Tag.

"Almost, but not quite," said Myron.

"And there lies the problem, for it was better had he met a hasty end," said Loken. "I am well acquainted with the Sorcerer, enough to know the level of suffering we managed to subject him to would be equivalent to repeatedly poking a wounded bear."

"And that is not a good thing…" determined Rose.

"Not good at all," confirmed Loken.

"Yes, and what makes it worse is that the Sorcerer managed to spirit away with the magic crystal," added Tag.

"Fine!" snapped Rose. "So we know it is the Sorcerer. We know he uses the Dreamstone to imbue himself with greater powers. Perhaps we should take this fortune-teller's advice. We should play it safe and just head on home."

"I said no such thing!" responded Bella.

"The advice we should heed is this: Knowledge is power, power we can use to our advantage, Princess Rose," said Myron. "This young lady came to forewarn us, so we may use this information to better prepare for this quest."

"Oh, yes… that element of surprise you and Tag are always so keen on employing," grumbled Rose.

"It is indeed a tactical advantage," assured Bella. "Take what you will, but I had a need to warn you, all of you, so you'd have a chance to take the appropriate actions to do what you must to curtail this evil."

"Well, too bad you were not able to predict how useless this trek would be for you! You ventured all this way to warn us of what we pretty much already know! It is all very redundant, and so are you!" scoffed Rose. "You are best to move on at this point. Go ply that less than reliable trade of yours on the gullible, for I am on to you!"

"I am here to warn you that if this fiend is not put to a stop, tragedy will strike!" declared Bella. "All of you will be in grave danger."

"I said it before, I will say it again: Tell me something new! And when is the danger *not* grave?" With a flippant wave of her hand, Rose dismissed Bella's dire prediction. "I do believe you have other motives in being *here*, of all the places in this big, wide world."

"You don't say!" snapped Bella.

"Yes! In fact, I predict you are here for the sole purpose of distracting *my friend* from his sworn duty to keep *me* safe in our bid to see an end to this madness that is the Sorcerer!"

"You are a fool for dreaming up such a silly assumption! Why would I do something as infantile and as selfish as that?"

"Because you are a brazen hussy, a trolloppy trollop if ever there was one! I know you have designs on Tag! You see him as nothing more than a means to better your standing in life, if only you can set your claws into him and trick Tag into becoming your betrothed!"

"Oh! You mean like that sham of a marriage you're planning with that hoity-toity Prince of Axalon?" snorted Bella.

"It is not a sham, I tell you!" shrieked Rose. Her eyes narrowed in suspicion as her back stiffened upon hearing these accusing words. "And how did you know about my engagement to Prince Percival?"

"Remember what you said? I'm a lousy fortune-teller with a *'flawed'* crystal! And yet, somehow I was privy to this news that not even your parents are aware of at this moment!"

"Oooh! She *is* good!" praised Loken, nodding in delight.

"And further more, I have no intention of marrying your *friend*, as tempting and as scrumptious as he is! Tag is destined for another, someone special; a young lady who is truly deserving of his love and knows the true measure of his worth."

"Oh! And let me guess who that might be!" Rose snorted in utter contempt as she envisioned her handmaiden happily wed to Tag. "For I see nothing but a lowly scullery maid in his future!"

"Love knows no bounds," responded Bella, her tone matter-of-fact. "I can only say that the one to win his hand in marriage will be truly blessed, for in his heart, there is none more noble, more gallant and honest than this knight-in-training!"

"And what would you know about that?" sniffed Rose, dismissing Bella's claim.

"Hey… Are you saying I possess none of these qualities?" grumbled Tag, glaring in annoyance at Rose.

"Enough! We digress yet again," shouted Myron. "Focus, people! Allow this young lady to finish."

Bella nodded, drawing in a deep breath as she gathered her thoughts. "The words I share now are shadows of what will be, if you fail to take action and control the outcome of the future, Sir Kendall."

"Fine! Keep talking!" urged Rose. "Elaborate on those fuzzy *images* of yours, if you can?"

"As you journey to the realm of the Elfkind, the dark power that continues to smother the Enchanted Forest will only grow. Do what you can to aid Lord Silverthorn's people, but be mindful that in doing so, the perpetrator of this magic will summon all in his powers to stop you, lashing out in retaliation."

"What's new? So we keep a watchful eye out for the Sorcerer's mimely minions," dismissed Rose. "They are hard to miss and they are never too far from their demented master."

Bella stared at the Princess as she warned her of what was yet to come: "From the images presented to me, there was no army of mimes to contend with. Instead, there is something far more nefarious at work here."

"Tell us more," urged Tag.

"Come now!" muttered Rose, shuddering at the mere thought of encountering these performers Dragonite held in such high regard. "What can be more nefarious than deploying those detestable mimes?"

"In its current condition, my poor crystal could not reveal with absolute clarity all there was to see. However, if you fail in your bid to help the Elves, based on the carnage I was witness to, of seeing the Woodland Glade in rout and ruin… Giants shall fall… Mountains shall crumble. It was far more devastating than anything a worthless army of mimes is capable of."

Myron sat upright as he pondered Bella's prediction. "Then I can only think that Dragonite has resorted to recruiting trained and seasoned mercenaries as he did before, when he first tried to grapple control in the east."

"Bloodthirsty mercenaries like the ones he used in the battle that killed my father?" asked Tag.

He swallowed hard, forcing down the lump in the back of his throat. Tag finally realized the enormity of the situation. If this was indeed the case, especially now that Lord Silverthorn and his highly skilled legion of warriors were incapacitated by this mystery illness, they were truly heading into certain peril.

"It does make sense," responded Myron. "Those mimes were utterly useless as fighters when we were engaged in battle, and in the past, Dragonite almost won the war waged with professional soldiers, until Captain Yairet's reinforcements arrived to tip the scales in our favour."

"As much as I detested those mimes, somehow, they are sounding to be much less of a threat than even a small battalion of ruthless assassins," gulped Rose, her slight shoulders drooping with the weight of this news.

"I think Myron is right," said Tag. "The Sorcerer would be a complete and utter fool if he believed an army of mimes would prove to be any better this time around."

"In all honesty, I cannot tell you if it will be trained mercenaries being called upon to serve him," admitted Bella. "Just know that mimes will be the least of your concerns this time!"

"And you know without a shadow of a doubt that Dragonite is behind all of this?" questioned Loken.

"Who else could it be?" responded Bella. "Though the images were fleeting, all I was witness to gave me the overwhelming impression it had to be a powerful Sorcerer engaged in the forbidden arts."

"So, as in Loken's case, I take it the culprit's face was not revealed in full to you?" asked Rose.

"His face was shielded by the shadow of his hood," answered Bella. "And that obsidian crystal? There was no mistaking that."

"By his apparel and manner of movement, it was indicative of the necromancer, was it not?" asked Loken.

"Yes, that is why I came to this conclusion." Bella nodded in confirmation.

"As did I," said the Sprite.

"So, we are yet to positively identify this scoundrel," determined Myron, unleashing a weary sigh.

"It has to be Dragonite," insisted Tag.

"Yes... but for all we know, it could be another Sorcerer at work here," said Rose.

"Another necromancer in these parts? One that dresses and moves like Dragonite while bearing a black crystal? Even targeting those who had aided us in the past when it came to capturing that madman?" asked Tag. "I highly doubt that!"

"Fine!" snapped Rose. "But suppose it is another Sorcerer just as demented as Dragonite?"

"True, this could be the work of another rogue Wizard, but think on this, Princess: Is there another out there you had the ill fortune of driving mad, too?" questioned Tag.

"When I think about it, no. However, consider this piece of information: Suppose it is Silas Agincor behind this?"

"Say again!" gasped Loken. The Sprite fluttered before her face. "You cannot be serious! The Dream Merchant?"

"Hey, even Dragonite started out as a benevolent Wizard, before he went all crazy in his head over those mimes to become a malevolent Sorcerer," reminded Rose, her index finger twirling next to her head.

"That is just crazy talk!" grunted Tag, waving off her comment.

"Why?" asked Rose. "Since our last ill-fated quest, there is nothing to say the crazy old Wizard really did go off to become some fool writer, embellishing on our tales of adventure and no doubt twisting them so he comes across as the hero. There is a real chance he is behind this."

"Now you're the one who is 'crazy' in the head!" snorted Tag.

"Unless Silas Agincor has taken leave of his senses, why would he be behind this, going as far as killing Lord Silverthorn's people?"

questioned Myron. "This hardly makes sense, especially where the Dream Merchant is concerned. He is not a cold-blooded murderer and you know it!"

"And suppose the old Wizard is mad, as in crazy?" asked Rose. "What if he needs more fodder for his stories? Suppose he is setting us up for this quest so he would have something to write about?"

Tag groaned in utter frustration. "You should be the writer! You're the one with the runaway imagination, not the Wizard."

"I admit I have a fecund imagination, but maybe that wily old Agincor found out he is lacking in this department? Perhaps he is resorting to this madness to seed his own feeble imagination, so he has new material to complete his latest story," insisted Rose.

"Look here, my lady, we do not even know if Silas Agincor did pursue this writing career he spoke of," reminded Myron.

"I heard he uses a pen name," interjected Loken.

"Though we all know he had a fondness for telling tales, I suppose there is nothing to say he is any good at writing them or even possesses the imagination to create his own material," continued Myron.

"When you think about it, what sensible person would want to become an author?" asked Tag. "It's a thankless job that pays next to nothing, if at all. Very few are celebrated and most are ignored, forgotten or both! And even if the population was highly literate, many would prefer to watch actors perform a play based on the story than to exercise the mind and imagination with a good read!"

"Yes! Readers, fans of the written words, are becoming rare and a truly treasured commodity coveted by every writer," Loken said with a nod of agreement.

"All the more reason for Agincor to abandon his dreams of becoming a writer," stated Rose. "Instead, he has turned to dark magic in retaliation."

Myron's eyes rolled in frustration. "I highly doubt that."

"And if Silas Agincor did?" Rose wondered aloud as she searched Myron's face. "Personally, as much as I love reading a great book from time to time, there must be something daft in the mind of a person able to conjure up such wild imaginings to write about! I've never met any authors myself, but I've heard they are an odd and superstitious lot, some taking to strange rituals just to get their creative juices flowing so they can set word to parchment."

"Are you saying writers are insane?" asked Bella, frowning upon hearing Rose's comment.

"Yes, but probably no more so than fortune-tellers." Rose's words were terse.

"That was rude," scolded Tag.

"That was the truth," corrected Rose. "Suppose that washed-up Wizard is making mischief on a grand scale, just so he would have fresh material to draw on. Suppose, at this very moment, he is spying on us? Jotting down what he sees and hears, than to use his own imagination."

"While the Wizard may be lacking in imagination, I do believe yours is the one that is running amok!" teased Tag. "Master Agincor is hardly the type to resort to murder, and the act of murder can hardly be categorized as *'mischief'*!"

Rose turned to the fortune-teller in hopes of gaining her support, if not Tag's. "What do you think about all of this, Ugly? Is there a possibility my words hold true?"

"The name is *Bella* and I need not call upon my crystal for this. Of course it is possible… but from what I know of the Dream Merchant, it is highly unlikely."

Before Rose could launch into a verbal or physical altercation with Bella for not backing her claim, Myron was quick to speak up, "Do you honestly think Silas Agincor would resort to such deadly measures just for some fresh story ideas, Princess Rose?"

"Hey, if some writers think nothing of blatantly stealing the ideas of other authors, what's to say that crazy, old fool is doing this, and worse!" answered Rose. "And remember, when we last saw Silas Agincor, he said he was no longer the purveyor of dreams, wishing for nothing more than to retire from this whole, sordid business. Perhaps he found the whole business of story writing much harder than he had first anticipated. And rather than admitting defeat and returning to his former vocation, he has resorted to underhanded means, bolstered by his powers, to create stories where there are none."

Tag scoffed, chortling at Rose's suggestion.

"You laugh now, but suppose I am correct? There is nothing to say what I warned you of is not true. I just find it mighty odd that both Loken and Bella were so quick to cast the blame on Dragonite, especially as both did not see this culprit's face! In all likelihood that miscreant is dead and Agincor is the demented one running amok."

"Your ideas are far-fetched, to say the least, but really?" Tag's brows furrowed. "The Dream Merchant becoming evil? I think not!"

Rose glared at her friends as she tried to convince them once more, "It can well be the Dream Merchant has gone bad, and not just *bad*, but the evil, maniacal kind of bad. As I said before, even Dragonite was a somewhat respected Wizard before he went crazy. Suppose Agincor follows in his footsteps?"

"You are serious..." determined Tag, as he scrutinized her grim expression.

"Would I bother wasting my precious breath, if I were not?" Rose's arms crossed her chest in defiance.

"Well, I, for one, am willing to give your words serious consideration," offered Myron, not because he truly believed her, but more so to pacify the Princess and to keep the peace. "I recommend we all keep an open mind on this subject."

"That is all I am asking for," said Rose, nodding in gratitude to the knight.

"I suppose odder things have happened," conceded Tag. He was still as sceptical as ever, but understood Myron's approach to dealing with this princess.

"You, being the oddest of them all, Tag," snipped Rose. "I just don't want to be taken by surprise!"

"Plus, you prefer to believe the Sorcerer is dead," reminded Loken.

"That, too!" admitted Rose. "Just know that Dragonite had 'evil' down to a fine art, so even if Agincor decided to take a step into the dark side, he'd have to take a quick trip to crazy-town first to achieve the Sorcerer's level of evil to become such a threat to us."

"Well, whatever is in store for us as we enter the Enchanted Forest, we shall be sure to keep our wits about us," promised Myron.

"For this to happen, I recommend a fitful night of sleep," said Loken, as he took to the air. In a show of light, he morphed into a Great Horned Owl before perching on a high branch. "Sleep now, and I shall take the first watch."

"Now that is an excellent idea!" exclaimed Tag. He stood up to gather their bedrolls.

Tossing one to Myron and the other to Rose, Tag took his bedroll, unfurling it before the campfire as he extended an invitation to Bella. "And you can sleep in this one."

"Alone, of course!" Rose wanted to put the kibosh on any idea Bella may have had on getting reacquainted with Tag.

"Thank you for the offer, but I really should move on," said Bella.

"Then you should do exactly that," prompted Rose, waving the fortune-teller off.

"It is not safe for a young lady to be out in the middle of the night," cautioned Tag, ignoring Rose's words as he moved the bedroll closer to the flames.

"But what about you?" asked Bella.

"I shall keep watch with Loken for now, and as far as I'm concerned, it is far too dangerous for you to be on your own in the darkness, so humour me. Say you will stay the night."

"You do not give this girl enough credit, Tag," muttered Rose. "She made it all the way here in one piece! Surely she will be fine to continue on."

Hearing these testy words, Bella made her decision. "I suppose one night in the company of friends will do no harm."

"Of course!" Tag flashed her a congenial smile. "You must be exhausted from your long journey."

"I am, but I must be on my way at dawn." Bella smiled back at the young man.

"I will be sure to wake you, if you are not already gone by first light," offered Rose, giving the fortune-teller a snide grin.

"No need for that," responded Bella, as she nestled down into Tag's warm bedroll. "Rest assured, I will be gone long before you even wake, Princess!"

"Another one of your predictions?" grumbled Rose, as she tried to get comfortable on the hard ground.

"No, it is more like common sense. You seem to attract trouble wherever you go, so it is far safer for me to be as far away from you as humanly possible. Just know, the closer you get to your destination, the greater the danger."

"Really?" snapped Rose, her tone indignant.

"Good night, my friends! Find some rest," urged Myron, as he hunkered down in his bedroll. "There will be time enough for more acrimonious words in the morning, so get some sleep while you can."

As the pale light of the morning sun leached away the darkness, Rose's eyes fluttered open. The metallic clatter of stirrups rankled her nerves, waking her from a slumber plagued by dreams of a meddlesome fortune-teller attempting to insinuate herself within the Princess' inner circle of friends. Rubbing her bleary eyes, Rose realized it was nothing more than a pesky nightmare. She yawned, stretching her stiff, aching muscles to see Myron and Tag ready their horses for another day of travel.

Bolting upright, Rose glanced over to where she last saw Bella, sleeping across from her near the now cold campfire. The bedroll was empty; neatly rolled up and tied into a tight bundle while the beautiful fortune-teller was nowhere to be seen.

"Hey... Where is that ugly *Agly* girl?" asked Rose, huddling down deeper into her bedroll to absorb the warmth before forcing herself to join her comrades.

"You mean to say *Bella*," corrected Tag, as he adjusted the saddle on her mare's back.

"And you know exactly whom I was referring to!" Rose grunted in a dismissive tone. "Please tell me she is making herself useful by preparing some breakfast for us!"

"Dream on, Princess!" muttered Tag. "You will be happy to know Bella is gone."

"Gone? As in she left us?" Rose slowly sat up as a small smile curled her lips.

"Long gone, my lady," answered Loken, as he floated down from an overhanging tree branch.

"Huzzah!" cheered Rose, kicking off the bedroll to leap onto her feet. She felt energized and ready to meet the new day, as early as it was. "It is my lucky day! I can feel it!"

"Because the young lady chose to be on her way long before you had a chance to exchange nasty words with her again?" questioned Loken.

"I never said that," replied Rose.

She merrily skipped over to her saddlebag to scrounge up some provisions suitable to consume as a morning meal.

"You need not say a word," grumbled Tag. "Your actions betray you."

"What actions?" Her perfect brows arched up in surprise as a sweet smile creased her beaming face. Rose tried her best to look genuinely bewildered and innocent of any wicked deeds or thoughts. "I am just pleased that girl is gone, considering how fearful she was that something evil would befall her, the longer she chose to stay in our presence."

"Come now, Princess! You are more than a little pleased Bella chose to leave," responded Tag.

"I am pleased she lived up to her promise of departing at dawn, but you act as though I hated that girl," said Rose, as her hands hunted about her saddlebag.

"Hate is such a strong word, but you definitely loathed her. You always did," reminded Tag. He checked the fit of the mare's saddle once more, adjusting the cinch before joining Rose for a meal.

"I *loathed* that homely wench? I think not! I admit I pitied her desperation and how she threw herself at you the first time! And equally pitiful was how you were so easily beguiled by that tramp when she kissed you!"

"Well then, it's a bloody good thing you were not witness to her early morning departure," quipped Loken, as he alighted upon Tag's shoulder.

"Why? What happened?" Rose's eyes narrowed as she glared at Loken, and then at Tag.

"Nothing happened." Tag was quick to respond as his cheeks burned a telltale red.

"Look whose actions are betraying whom, now!" snapped Rose.

"What are you talking about?" Tag's shoulders rolled with a shrug of indifference. "I did nothing."

"Really? Are you actually blushing? Or did an invisible hand magically smack those burning cheeks of yours?" interrogated Rose. "It is as though your face is on fire!"

"I don't blush!"

Loken abandoned his perch on Tag's shoulder, launching into the air once more when the young man jumped to his feet. Tag pretended to leave her company for the sole purpose of retrieving their water flasks as his cheeks glowed a deeper shade of red with Rose's accusing words.

"Oooh! That trollop made an inappropriate move on you! She kissed you again!" exclaimed Rose.

"So what if she did?" Tag answered sheepishly, drawing a deep breath in a bid to calm his nerves.

"You better not have kissed her back!"

Seeing that this was a sore point with the Princess, Loken decided he was better to keep his mouth shut. He alighted upon a branch, out of the line of fire of this verbal volley.

"If she had, what business is it of yours, if I kissed her back?" snapped Tag, thoroughly incensed by Rose's damning tone. "Are you jealous or something?"

"Something, yes! Jealous, no! For pity's sake, what do I have to be jealous about? After all, I have a handsome, charming prince awaiting my return!"

"If not jealousy, then you must be angry because you cannot control me as you once did when we were children! I can kiss whomever I please," declared Tag, thrusting Rose's water flask into her startled face.

"You can kiss an ugly, warty toad, for all I care!" sputtered Rose, jamming her hands deep into the saddlebag as she felt about. "I just do not need you being distracted on this mission! Is that not so, Myron?"

The knight finished saddling his stallion as he turned to address her upon hearing his name. "I was busy, my lady. Did you say something?"

Rose's shoulders slumped in disappointment. She realized Myron was either utterly distracted by other matters or he was only pretending to be, so he wouldn't be drawn into this argument. She waved him off, dismissing his lack of contribution for her benefit. "Never mind!"

She turned her attention back to Tag, as she snapped, "The point being, you need to remain focused! Your duty is not to kiss strange girls, it is to keep me safe!"

"When have I *not* kept you safe, Princess? Aside from failing to steer you away from the clutches of Prince Prissy, I have done well keeping you safe from harm."

"You are an idiot! And it is Prince Percival to you!"

"I know his name!" snapped Tag.

"As you should! But as I was saying, you are an idiot, a well-intentioned idiot, but an idiot nonetheless. I have been exposed to more danger than you can shake a stick at since we embarked on the quest to break the curse and reclaim the magic crystal."

"Yes, you were exposed to danger, but it was danger instigated by *you*, while Myron and I are the ones to keep you safe!"

"My friends!" Myron sat down next to Tag as Loken settled on the knight's shoulder. "I am sure there will be more danger as we proceed, and more chances for Tag to prove his worth! Before our comradeship is torn asunder by unnecessary feelings of animosity, let us stay the course. We shall remain focused; put a stop to the Sorcerer before his dark magic becomes far-reaching and irreversible."

"That is a brilliant idea," said Tag, with a judicious nod.

"Brilliant, indeed!" agreed Loken, growing weary of this verbal sniping between friends.

"Excellent!" said Myron, not even waiting for Rose to chime in. "Let us break our fast with a hasty meal, then be on our way."

Realizing her travelling companions would only side against her if she chose to pursue the matter, Rose decided to fight the urge to squeeze in the last word on this subject. Her hands searched about the depth of her saddlebag to serve up some hard cheese and the half-eaten loaf of bread buried with her personal belongings.

Tag observed as her brows arched up in surprise, only to scrunch down in a scowl of anger. "What now? Did a rat sneak in and steal all the cheese?"

"A rat, indeed!" cried Rose. "That pilfering tramp stole from me as I slept!"

"What?" queried Tag.

"She made off with my purse, the pouch containing all of my coins! Unbelievable! I take that back! It is totally believable she is capable of such thievery!"

"Consider it fair compensation for making this dangerous trek to share in her predictions," said Tag, waving off Rose's concern. "And remember, she left everything of her former life behind in order to seek us out."

"Easy for you to say," grumbled Rose, as she tossed the stale bread to Tag. "I could have used that money to buy us some fresh provisions!"

"We have adequate supplies to last us on our trip to the Elf realm and remember, your future father-in-law has granted us free passage to and from his domain. If anything, Bella is in greater need of this money as she flees to the south."

"She flees? Why bother?" grumbled Rose. "It is not as though she is putting herself in any danger, not like we are."

"I beg to differ," responded Myron. He tore off of some bread as he waited for Tag to carve off a chunk of cheese. "By sharing in what she knew, if indeed it is the Sorcerer we are up against, she has only added her name to his ever-growing list of enemies he shall vent his wrath upon, for aiding us in the first place."

"Are you sure?" questioned Rose, as she nudged Tag over to make room on the log for her to sit.

"Well, I do not know about the rest of you, but I tend to agree with Sir Kendall. I am darned sure of the young lady's fate, should Dragonite catch wind of her involvement," stated Loken, as he hovered before her. "Based on what we know thus far, that is exactly what that madman will do. He will exact his revenge, if he is not stopped."

"Well then, I suppose I cannot blame her for fleeing as she did, but really, to do something as pathetic as to steal from *me*, a princess no less? It was despicable, when all she needed to do was to ask for it."

"Right… and had Bella asked, with that generous heart of yours, you would have handed her your purse, no questions asked?" Tag's words were sceptical. "I highly doubt that!"

"I do have a generous heart, but I am no fool! Of course I would not just hand it over to her!"

"Well, there you go then! She probably predicted that was what you'd do, so she helped herself to what she was entitled to," reasoned Tag, indifferent to Rose's plight.

"Oh, and should we encounter thieves demanding an exchange of our lives for what little I have left of my riches, these thieves will be merely *'helping themselves'*, too?" questioned Rose.

"I never said that," muttered Tag.

"Well, you seem mighty pleased that your little fortune-teller friend can now add *thief* to her growing list of unscrupulous skills! And had she asked me, I would have given her fair compensation for her useless, but well-intentioned deed. I would have owed her exactly what she was entitled to, based on what little she shared against what we already know."

"Generous, indeed," noted Loken. With a disgruntled sigh, he flew to a blade of grass, scooping up some water to drink from a bead of dew.

"Here is a generous helping of cheese," said Myron, as he passed the food on to the Princess. "Eat quickly, for we must be on our way."

"We are not going to wait for Harold?" asked Rose.

"If he had travelled through the night, he would have caught up to us by now, I'm pretty sure of that," responded Myron, washing down a mouthful of food with a swig of water. "In all likelihood, Harold has wisely chosen to return to the safety of Fleetwood."

Other than the droning thrum of Loken's wings and the steady plodding of hooves on the trail, there was neither the song of wrens nor the alarmed chatter of squirrels to be heard. There was barely a whispering of wind rustling through the trees.

The silence was unnatural.

As they trekked deeper into the Enchanted Forest, that foreboding sense of doom gnawing at the back of their minds continued to grow. Not a word was spoken as they studied their surroundings. This was definitely not the forest they had ventured through on their first quest.

The towering trees cast deep shadows looming ominously over the path they travelled. Leaning over Rose and her companions, the interlocking canopy felt as though the forest was closing in on them, as if to scrutinize those who dared to enter this domain. The negative energy throbbing through the forest was as palpable as the beating of their hearts. There was no welcome here.

Venturing on, dead leaves began to litter the forest floor, crunching beneath the horses' hooves. As Myron urged his stallion on at a canter, the drying foliage was kicked up, swirling like miniature cyclones in their wake.

High overhead, the sunlight danced through the tree canopy still festooned with leaves yet to surrender to autumn's chilled breath. In a riffle of wind the leaves cast in hues of golden yellow, russet-orange and brilliant red shimmered, backlit against the sun to cast a strange glow on the forest floor.

The sun penetrated the thick cover to create small patches of light that pooled on gnarled roots, clumps of emerald green moss and crowns of sword ferns growing here and there. The dappled sunlight filled the travellers with a sense of hope that not all was lost in the growing darkness, but this light was fickle, dancing on the forest floor, and then vanishing as the leaves swayed at the mercy of the invisible wind. It was when these leaves shifted, blocking out what sun there was did the horses snort, shaking their manes in agitation as though something sinister was in the air.

"There is evil at work here," stated Loken. He landed on Rose's shoulder as he surveyed their surroundings. "I cannot see it, but I can sense it."

"This is feeling more and more like the *disenchanted* forest," whispered Rose. A cold shiver ran down her spine as the north wind suddenly whispered around them, gathering dead leaves to send them swirling and tumbling along the ground.

"This place is definitely not the same," said Tag. His eyes darted about as he glanced up to the treetops, searching for signs of potential danger. There was nothing, only the crowns of the towering trees leaning menacingly over them as they passed beneath. "There is something truly unsettling about this place, even by the light of day."

"I did warn you that the forest was not the same these days," reminded Loken. He launched off of Rose's shoulder, darting ahead of Tag to take the lead before Myron's steed. "Evil dwells here; like a curse has taken hold of the very heart of this forest."

"I can sense it, too," said Myron, his words spoken in a whisper. "It is as though there is a sickness in the air."

"Whatever it is you sense, just make sure you do not do something silly," cautioned Rose. She glanced over, directing this warning to Tag.

"Like what?" asked Tag.

"Like empty your bladder against one of these trees, that's what! If the forest is feeling unsettled now for whatever reason, I can only imagine how these trees will react, if you did that again."

"I'm not stupid!"

"Yes, you are, but I am hoping you are not *that* stupid," remarked Rose.

"I promise you, I won't be making that same mistake twice."

The terrifying moment when Tag was attacked by a grand old willow he had urinated against replayed in his mind. The tree came alive, hoisting him clear off the ground. In an act of vengeance, it almost strangled him, attempting to tear him apart with those slithering, snake-like branches and tenacious tendrils of roots that wrapped around his neck, ankles, and wrists.

"Then consider this a harmless reminder of what *not* to do," responded Rose.

"It is not as though I landed on my head when that willow tree attacked. Of course I will be more mindful as we venture deeper into this forest!"

"Hush!" ordered Myron. He raised a hand, motioning for Rose and Tag to be silent.

"You, hush!" Rose snapped at the knight. "It is not like I am shouting at Tag."

"Indeed, but with this unnatural silence that shrouds the forest, your voice carries far," warned Myron.

"We do not want to tip off the Sorcerer that we are near," reminded Tag, his words now spoken in barely a whisper.

"If there is dark magic at work here, let us keep our wits about us. I recommend disengaging your mouths. Keep your eyes and ears open for potential danger," recommended Myron, watching as the Sprite nervously circled about.

"Travel on ahead," urged Loken.

"Where are you going?" asked Rose. "Are you planning to abandon us?"

"Not at this very moment." Loken pointed overhead. "I am going to fly up there, above the trees so I can survey the lands from a greater vantage point. If there is danger lurking about, there is a chance I will see it, before the danger has the opportunity to know we are here."

"That makes good sense to me," said Tag. He watched Loken move with the speed of a dragonfly as the Sprite propelled his tiny body skyward.

"We shall wait for you here," called Myron. "It will give us a chance to rest our horses."

"Very well," said Loken. "I shall not be long."

Dismounting, the trio led their mounts to drink at the edge of a brook.

"Here! Take this," ordered Rose, passing her reins on to Tag.

He accepted, allowing the gelding and mare to drink side by side. "And where do you think you are going?"

"Nowhere," answered Rose. Her words were indifferent, as she followed the coursing waters. "I just want to take this moment to stretch. My muscles feel stiff from sitting in the saddle for so long. A walk will do me good."

"Fine," said Tag. He tugged on the horses' reins to make room at the water's edge for Myron's stallion to quench its thirst.

"Do not stray too far, my lady," warned Myron. "Loken will return soon."

"Worry not," Rose called over her shoulder as she ducked beneath the vine-like branches of an elegant willow tree, its slender leaves already turning a golden yellow under the first sun of autumn. "I will not wander far."

"You better not," warned Tag, watching as she disappeared behind a shower of gilded leaves. They floated down as she parted these willow branches, slipping between them.

Rose shrugged off her friend's words. The tenseness of her muscles melted away with each step she took on the soft carpet of moss cushioning her feet. She drew a deep, cleansing breath, enjoying this momentary freedom from the hard saddle as the sounds of the water playfully gurgling and splashing over rocks served to calm her nerves. It was like an enchanting song calling to her, luring her on to follow.

As a breeze sent dried leaves scattering before her feet, Rose glanced down. She gasped in surprise as the footprints in the layer of moss where she had trod upon browned and curled. This primitive plant shrivelled as though the weight of her steps were like poison to this layer of vegetation. With each step, the ground-hugging moss died.

"This is odd!" called Rose, venturing on to test her steps.

"What is odd?" Myron asked, holding tight to his steed's reins as the stallion's head suddenly jerked up from the brook it was drinking from.

"Whoa! Calm down," urged Tag. The horses left in his charge began to strain at their reins to get away from this rushing body of water.

Myron and Tag gasped; watching in dismay as a dark substance seeped up from the rock and pebble-strewn bottom of the brook to turn the water as black as ink.

"Good gracious!" Myron did not need to urge his mount to get away from the water's edge as the agitated stallion backed off.

"What is this stuff?" asked Tag. He struggled to hold onto the anxious horses as the animals pranced about, nervously stomping and pawing at the earth.

"Whatever it is, it is not good!" answered Myron, watching as the blackness grew, spreading downstream. "We should leave immediately!"

Tag nodded in agreement, turning his gaze skyward. "Loken! Come back!"

Loken had only now burst through the tree canopy when he heard his name and this request to return echoing through the forest. Sensing the urgency in Tag's voice, Loken quickly glanced about, searching for potential danger.

"Oh, no!"

His eyes were fixed to the east, struggling to see as the forest seemed to come alive, rippling apart like a sea of tall grasses in the wake of a great serpent slithering forward.

"I must warn the others!"

Loken took to the air, stealing a final glance at the impending peril. Diving down through the tangle of leaves and branches, he yelped in surprise. He flew into a near-invisible barrier.

"What the…" Loken gasped as his eyes snapped open.

His heart raced in panic. He was thoroughly trapped, stuck to the silk strands of a massive spider web that spanned across the branches of two neighbouring trees. It was so large, the usual assortment of moths, flies, and mosquitoes normally caught on a web were able to fly straight through, easily avoiding the sticky strands. Instead, the Sprite could make out the mummified forms of thrushes, wrens and bats that had fallen victim to this tensile snare. Spooled in a cocoon of resilient silk strands a dying raven struggled weakly. The venom worked to slowly paralyze the bird. Rather than outright kill the raven, the toxin kept its prey alive, so it'd be fresh for when the spider was ready to feed.

As Loken struggled against these gummy strands, he felt a slight tremor rippling through the web, vibrating toward him. His eyes followed the length of this silken cord radiating from the centre of this huge trap to terminate at the mouth of a large knothole in a tree trunk. The Sprite's jaw dropped open in horror. From the depth of this dark hole he caught sight of two large, black, shiny eyes surrounded by six smaller ones, each staring with deadly intent. This creature lingered in the shadow of its lair. Gingerly placing the tip of its front foot onto this line, it tested this strand for signs of fresh food caught in its trap.

From the placement of those eyes and the size of that foot, the Sprite knew it had to be a gargantuan arachnid. And the more he struggled, the more likely he was going to make for a tasty snack for this spider. Loken's heart thundered in his chest to resound in his ears, blocking out the commotion down below as he struggled to be free. Even if he were to scream for help now, none would hear his cry.

"Princess!" hollered Tag. He fought to maintain control over the horses as he and Myron waited for Rose to return. "Get back here, now!"

"Hey… Do you feel that?" questioned Myron. He glanced down as the earth beneath their feet began to tremble.

Just as Tag detected this sensation, a feeling of foreboding seized his heart. The horses squealed in fright. Wheeling about, they yanked free of their masters' hold. With a whinny and a snort, Myron's steed led the charge. Leaping over the blackened water, the stallion guided the mare and gelding westward, away from the approaching danger.

"What is that?" asked Tag. He and Myron spun about on their heels. They stared to the east, searching through the forest as the earth trembled beneath them and a sound, like the steady roll of thunder, grew louder.

Myron's eyes flew open in surprise as he hollered, *"RUN!"*

Rose had rushed back to join her comrades only to be accosted by this order.

"Run? From what?" she asked.

"UNICORNS!" shouted the knight. He frantically gestured to Tag and Rose to run like their lives depended on it. *"STAMPEDING UNICORNS!"*

Rose stood there. Momentarily confused, she was unsure if Myron was playing a cruel trick on her, or if he really did mean they were about to be trampled to death by a rampaging herd.

Stepping off the dying carpet of moss, she suddenly felt the tremors rising from the earth, rattling up her body and through her bones to send her teeth chattering. The thunder of hundreds of hooves crashing through the forest and careering toward them overwhelmed her with utter fear.

"MOVE!" Myron shouted above the growing din. He dashed off, believing Tag and Rose would automatically follow.

Seeing the Princess panic, frozen where she stood, Tag darted back, seizing her hand. His touch instantly broke her fear-filled trance as he yanked hard, pulling her along.

Tag glanced behind them. He spied upon the first of many spiral horns as a large, snowy white stallion leading the stampede burst through the stand of trees and surrounding shrubs.

"Quickly, Princess!" urged Tag.

Holding tight to her hand as they sprinted away, the pair trailed behind Myron as the knight crashed through the forest to clear the way for his friends. Behind them, he can hear the clatter and splash of hooves ploughing straight through the blackened water as the unicorns surged ahead, quickly gaining on them.

"Faster!" hollered Tag. "Run faster!"

Myron yelped in surprise as he skidded to a stop. The tips of his toes leaned dangerously over the edge of a deep ravine as his arms frantically flapped about, fighting for his balance as he teetered on the brink of this chasm.

Tag snagged Myron. Grabbing him by the shoulder, he yanked him back to safety.

"What do we do now?" asked Rose.

Peering down, the chance of landing safely in the river coursing through the ravine was highly unlikely. If they did survive the plunge, it would not be without breaking numerous bones upon dashing their bodies on the rocks and boulders below. As far as she was concerned, there was about as good a chance of surviving a fall as there was avoiding a terrible death delivered by the pounding hooves of what felt like hundreds of unicorns stampeding through the forest, heading straight this way.

"Climb!" ordered Tag. "Into the trees!"

With no need of prompting, Rose abandoned her comrades. She dashed away, claiming the closest tree. Myron and Tag ran off in opposite directions, leaping up to pull themselves into the sturdy tree branches. They held on tight as the ground quaked beneath them. As frightened as Rose was as she clung to the shaking tree trunk, she watched in awe as the stallion led the herd to the edge of the ravine. The mares and their foals followed close on the stallion's hooves. Pushing off, each unicorn easily cleared this chasm. Bounding effortlessly with the grace of a fleet-footed deer, the herd leaped over the ravine in the haze of a multi-coloured rainbow to disappear deep into the forest on the other side.

Myron and Tag listened for a moment. They could hear the steady drumming of hooves fading away, heading to the west. To the east, there were no unicorns straggling behind to surprise them. All was strangely quiet once more.

"Oh, my!" gasped Myron. "That was close!"

"Too close!" agreed Rose.

Myron shielded his eyes against the glow of the sun as he peered up at Rose. To his surprise, she had climbed much higher than he thought possible without the aid of another to help her along. And more surprising was the selection of tree she chose to escape in. This spindly, old pine tree she was clinging to was quite dead! Not only was it dead, what remained of its bug-infested trunk was rotten and leaning slightly to one side.

"It's safe to come down now, Princess," said Tag. He lowered himself from the tree he had taken refuge in.

"Are you sure?" asked Rose, as she clung to the moss and lichen encrusted tree trunk. Doubting Tag's judgement, she turned to Myron for his reassurance. "We are not going to be taken by surprise by another herd taking up the rear, are we?"

"At this moment, you are much safer on the ground than up there in that insect-riddled toothpick," answered Myron, as he made his way down.

Before he could reach the forest floor to help the Princess from her high perch, Rose screamed. The tree's gnarled network of roots, loosened by the reverberation of the hooves pounding the earth, sprang from the ground as the tree lurched, and then leaned dangerously. In a mad panic, Rose scrambled to climb down. Her frantic movements caused the tree to uproot completely. Myron and Tag were forced to the ground, dropping on their hands and knees as clots of earth were sent flying in an explosive spray, pelting them with rocks and soil.

Another scream resounded through the forest as the tree creaked. It toppled over the ravine, taking Rose with it.

10

A Magic Most Vile

"HELP!" screamed Rose.

The dried, gnarled crown of the dead tree crashed down on the other side of the ravine. The jolting impact knocked the Princess free of the trunk she clung to. With hands thrashing wildly, Rose snagged a branch. Her breath hitched in the back of her throat. With her heart thundering in her chest, she fought to hold on.

Forcing her eyes open, Rose dared to peek. It was just as she feared. She now dangled over the very chasm she was trying to avoid that forced her to unwittingly climb into this tree in the first place. Below, the moss and fern strewn floor of the narrow ravine was carved out by rushing waters. Deep, dark swirling eddies pocked by submerged rocks and huge boulders waited to catch her body, should she fall.

Her eyes opened wide in terror. The branch she clung to crackled as the rotting trunk moaned in protest. It began to sag from her weight, lowering Rose deeper into the ravine.

With a loud *'craaack'* this branch snapped. Her scream of fright was gagged as a powerful hand dove down, snagging her by the scruff of the neck.

Dangling helplessly over the gaping maw of this deep gorge, Rose shouted at her rescuer, "For pity's sake, pull me up! Get me out of here!"

"Stop squirmin', Princess! Just wantin' to get a better grip on you first."

Upon hearing this familiar voice, Rose glanced up to see a hefty figure backlit by the glare of the westering sun. The sight of a grimacing raccoon staring with empty eyes momentarily startled her, but recognition immediately set in. It was merely a raccoon pelt worn on a man's head, not a vicious creature waiting to attack her face.

"Harold!" exclaimed Rose. She reached up with both hands in hopes of latching onto his arm. She was never so happy to see his ugly face than at this very moment as death prepared to make its claim. "You made it!"

"Don't know what you think I made, my lady, but I'm here, and it's a bloody good thing, especially bein' in the fix that you're in right now!"

Harold easily hoisted Rose onto the tree trunk he now straddled. It continued to bow under their combined weight.

"Quickly, Harold!" shouted Myron. Yanking the dirt-showered Tag onto his feet, both dashed to the downed tree. "Before that trunk breaks, get back onto solid ground, the both of you!"

"Hurry, Princess!" ordered Harold, as he crawled backward along the length of the horizontal tree. "Follow me!"

Face-to-face with Harold, Rose glowered in agitation as she snapped at her rescuer, "I can only move as quickly as you do, so get going!"

"I'm tryin'," said Harold.

"Try harder," urged Rose.

Like a giant, bloated caterpillar inching along the length of the tree trunk, Harold made his way as fast as his hulking body could move, grunting with exertion as he picked up his pace.

Rose felt every tremor as the tree quaked, reverberating with Harold's less than graceful movements. Terror seized her heart. The realization this tree could suddenly pitch, rolling to one side or the other, leaving them both clinging to its underside filled her with fear.

"Almost there!" called Tag. Urging them on, he and Myron waited at the base of the uprooted tree, attempting to brace it. "Just be careful!"

"Don't look down, Princess!" hollered Myron, growing anxious as the tree suddenly shifted. "Just follow Harold, but be quick about it."

"I am going as fast as I can!" snapped Rose. "And I've already looked down! Trust me when I say I'm highly motivated! I have no desire to have my body dashed upon the rocks below."

"More crawling, less talking," ordered Tag, as he and Myron leaned against the tree to stabilize it.

As Harold crawled toward their voices, Myron instructed him, "Just reach down with your foot. You're over solid ground now."

The large man cautiously leaned over to his right, the toe of his boot blindly straining to touch the earth. He unleashed an audible sigh of relief, feeling solid ground beneath him once more. With far less grace than a blubbery seal rolling off a floating log, Harold slid down, landing on the ground with a hearty '*thud*' and a groan.

Rose shimmied her way along the length of the trunk. Throwing her legs over the tree, she plopped down onto Harold's belly, bouncing off to land on her feet as Tag steadied her.

"Thank goodness, you're safe!" exclaimed Tag.

"Yes!" Rose's words were brusque as she wiped the dirt and dust from her hands. "No thanks to you!"

"What are you complaining about now?"

"Was it not *your* brilliant idea to climb into the trees?" questioned Rose. Her index finger accusingly jabbed Tag on his chest as she addressed him.

"True, but it wasn't my fault you chose to climb the most rotten, decrepit tree in the entire forest." Responding with a shrug, he stepped back from her condemning digit. "In fact, you practically shoved us aside to scramble up that rotter!"

"Fret not, Princess Rose!" Myron was quick to interject, hoping these words would help to pacify the Princess by pointing out her good fortune. "Thankfully, the tree was strong enough to endure this fall and, lucky for you, you were light enough for it to bear your weight."

Just as the knight spoke these comforting words a delicate sparrow alighted upon the tree bridging the gap. The four friends took a moment to delight in the bird's cheerful song. It hopped along the trunk when the earth on both sides of the ravine collapsed, sending dirt, rocks and the downed tree tumbling into the chasm. The startled bird took to the air once more.

"Oh, my!" gasped Myron.

They watched as a plume of dirt and dust swirled high into the air as the tree crashed down with a great cascade of earth.

"Phew! That could've been tragic!" exclaimed Harold. Removing his raccoon pelt headpiece, he used its ringed tail to wipe away the beads of sweat from his forehead. "I'm thinkin' that's more than enough adventure in one day for you, Princess!"

"I agree!" Rose peered over the edge to see the tree shatter in half, sending splintered bark and shards of rotting wood exploding in all directions upon striking the boulders below.

Myron sighed in relief as he and Harold clasped wrists in warm salutations, "It is wonderful to see you, my friend! You saved the day, yet again!"

"More importantly, he saved *my life* once more," reminded Rose, nodding in approval to the large man. "You have an impeccable sense of timing, Harold! I was never more glad to see your face."

"We thought you had turned back," said Tag, patting Harold's shoulder in gratitude. "How did you ever find us all the way out here?"

"Oh, I'm no quitter, young sir! I was determined to catch up!"

"But how?" queried Myron.

"I left that windin' main road, took shortcuts wherever I could, cuttin' through fields and farmlands to travel the straightest route to get me out of Axalon. I found where you folks had spent the night, and I just followed from there, trackin' you down as best I could. So, here I am!"

"You tracked us down?" questioned Rose. "Like common animals?"

"Oh, you're far from common, my lady! But if I can track down one of these clever critters," said Harold, pointing to the furry raccoon pelt adorning his head, "then trust me when I say it wasn't that hard to follow your horses into this forest."

"That makes sense," responded Myron.

In all the years he had known this fellow, Harold was always a simple man of simple means. He managed to scrape out a living hunting and trapping, for he possessed obvious skills. And when it came to tracking animals, whatever the size or shape, Harold was most successful, even putting his skills to good use by helping the local villagers locate their lost children or livestock that had strayed away from their properties.

"Perfect or not, happenstance or not, your timing was spot on, my good man!" praised Rose, with a grateful nod. "My thanks and gratitude are in order, but keep in mind, another wish will *not* be granted to you."

"That's fine by me and you're welcome, my lady, but it was nothin' really. I just happened to be at the right place at the right time when a unicorn herd went thunderin' by. Knew somethin' had to be up, so I left my Sassy behind. Came a-runnin' over... and there you were, danglin' like a sausage ready to fall off the roastin' stick into the fire, or a deep gully in this case."

"I'd say luck and fate conspired to deliver you here, my friend!" stated Tag, nodding in approval. "We're glad you are safe."

"Fate, or not, it was my runnin' that delivered me to this very place. And how lucky for me, for it was quite the sight to behold!" declared Harold, as he beamed with excitement. "In all my life, I've never seen a real unicorn. And to see a whole herd, albeit, stampedin' by? It was nothin' short of spectacular!"

"Perhaps from where you stood," grunted Rose. "But it does not take a fool to know it is always better to be *behind* a stampeding herd, than to be in *front* of it!"

"True enough, Princess, but from where I stood, it was truly magical! I've always heard tales about this, but you never know for sure 'til you see it with your own eyes. It was a magnificent, colourful sight to behold!"

"From the trees, we saw nothing. What was there to behold?"

questioned Tag, frowning in confusion.

"Did you not see it?" Harold's eyes grew wide with wonder once more as he thought back on the spectacle he had the good fortune of witnessing firsthand.

"See what?" asked Rose. "How you came to my rescue *again*, while these two buffoons were busy mucking about?"

"I was speakin' of that beautiful rainbow that formed as those unicorns were leapin' to the other side of the ravine."

Tag scratched his head in bewilderment upon hearing this strange claim. "A rainbow? As the unicorns bounded over?"

"Yes!" Harold nodded excitedly.

"Oh, come now!" chortled Rose. With a wave of her hand she dismissed Harold's claim. "Even I know that is nothing but a bunch of phoo-phaw!"

"Phoo-phaw?" repeated Harold. His brows furrowed in bewilderment upon hearing these unfamiliar words. "What's that supposed to mean?"

"It is her *fancy* way of saying that it was nothing but a myth perpetuated by those who claim to be well acquainted with these elusive creatures," explained Myron.

"In other words, it is nothing but a bunch of malarkey, if that suits you better," added Rose.

"I beg to differ, my lady!"

The four mortals turned with a start. Before them stood the captain to Lord Silverthorn's military might.

"Captain Ironwood!" greeted Tag, as he and Myron bowed their heads in respect.

"Salutations! And contrary to what you believe, my friends, that large fellow spoke the truth about the unicorns and the rainbow which is nothing more than their multi-coloured flatulence," explained Halen.

"A *rainbow*! Really?" Rose's words were tainted with doubt. "How is it even possible, Captain Ironwood? There is an abundance of sun, but there is no rain to speak of, not even a drop, if these elements are what comes into play for such a display to be possible!"

"The unicorns in this forest are delicate creatures compared to their equine cousins you ride, Princess Rose. When they graze on certain plants, especially if they consume too many dandelions, the bitter stems and stalks can be difficult to digest, wreaking havoc on their sensitive digestive system."

"So, eating dandelions causes them to become flatulent," determined Myron.

"Gaseous to the extreme!" The Elf nodded in confirmation.

"So basically, the entire herd broke wind, simultaneously," said Tag. "Still, it doesn't explain that rainbow Harold claimed to have seen."

"The phenomenon is usually fleeting. It depends upon the position of the sun, wind conditions and from the angle it is viewed," explained the captain. "If the unicorns are stressed and subjected to extreme physical exertion, they will indeed *break wind*, as you had so eloquently put it."

"I knew it was true!" exclaimed Harold, slapping his thigh in glee. "Unicorns *do* fart rainbows!"

"Depending upon the amount they exude, they unleash a vapour, like a fine mist. These barely visible droplets, if they catch the sun's rays just so, appear to form a beautiful rainbow."

"Right…" Rose's voice was tinged with doubt as she sniffed the air for a lingering odour reminiscent of the stink expelled by their horses from time to time. "If that was so, then how come they left no foul reek in the wake of that supposed *rainbow*?"

"We are speaking of unicorns, my lady," said Halen.

"Meaning?"

"Let me just say it is like comparing this bodily function between an Elf and a human being. Where a mortal can be heard and smelled, easily clearing a room with the foul air emitted from his posterior, on the rare occasion an Elf must *release* internal pressure, we are far more discreet. I can only compare the scent to the light fragrance of lilacs on a spring morning."

"Being a princess, I am never so vulgar, but to smell of sweet lilacs? That would not be so bad."

Captain Ironwood shrugged his broad shoulders as he addressed her. "Indeed! And it is one of the things that makes these creatures so magical."

"I suppose you will now tell us that their dung turns to glittering heaps of gold when it hits the ground?" grunted Rose.

"Now, *that* is ridiculous! However, to a farmer, no doubt a wagonload of unicorn manure can prove to be as priceless as gold. When ploughed into the fields before planting their crops, I understand it makes for outstanding fertilizer! Vegetables and grains growing from these enriched soils can yield a bumper crop when harvesting time rolls around."

"Rainbows and unicorn dung aside, it is a surprise to see you here, Captain Ironwood." Myron bowed his head in courteous greeting to the Elf.

"This is the Enchanted Forest. Where else would I be? Which brings

to mind, I recognize Princess Rose and Tagius Yairet, but you, sir…
your voice is familiar, but I cannot place the face and body attached
to it."

"Myron Kendall is the name. No doubt you'd remember me as
Cankles Mayron when we were last in your company months ago."

Halen's perfect brows arched up in surprised as he stepped forward,
extending his hand in greeting. "So, it is true! You did find your true
self once more; mind, soul *and* body! I never would have recognized
you had you not introduced yourself, my friend."

"Understandably so! Much has changed since we last met. I've
been busy reclaiming my former life." Myron's hand clasped Halen's
wrist in a gesture of warm salutation.

"If you fill out that frame anymore and magically added to your
height, you'd easily be mistaken for one of us! Perhaps not quite as
perfect as an Elf with our golden tresses and sublime beauty, but you
are definitely not the scarecrow of a man I remember!"

"Whoaaa!" Harold suddenly gasped. His eyes opened wide
in wonder as he rushed up to Halen Ironwood to better inspect the
enigmatic being. "Are you really an Elf?"

Halen tugged on his left ear as he spoke, "Do you know of any
other race existing in this realm with such exquisite ears? And let us
not forget the gift of grace combined with a body and face that is the
envy of every mortal alive."

"This is so excitin'! I've never met a real Elf before!"

"That is odd… Are you saying you have met mortal beings
pretending to be Elves?" questioned Halen, staring suspiciously at the
human being that stood as tall as the tallest Elf.

"Can't say I have, but what I am sayin' is that you're the first
genuine Elf I've ever had the pleasure of meetin'!" exclaimed Harold.
He snatched the raccoon pelt from his balding head before bowing
deeply in respect to Captain Ironwood. "You look so… beautiful!"

"Our women are divinely beautiful! Our menfolk, by mortal
standards, are unbearably handsome. For some, to gaze upon us with
eyes that linger can be too much! It is like staring into the brilliant
face of the sun for too long. Mind you, Lord Rainus Silverthorn is
considered to be beautiful, when I think about it. But you shall see for
yourself in good time."

"Well, it's a pleasure to meet you, Master Elf!" He bowed graciously
before him. "My name is Harold Murkins."

"The pleasure is mine! My name is Halen Ironwood, captain to
Lord Silverthorn's army. And welcome, all of you, to our woodland
realm." The Elf bowed in polite greeting.

"Introductions and pleasantries aside, what dark magic has encroached upon your lands, Captain Ironwood?" asked Rose.

"Yes, the waters are tainted… the forest feels sick," added Tag.

"Not to forget that unicorn herd that came by this way," said Myron. "Something caused those creatures to stampede, almost trampling us in the process."

"Those creatures were what brought me to these parts in the first place," revealed Halen, "but I had no idea you four were in a deadly race at the front of the herd."

"I wasn't at the front, Captain Ironwood." Harold was quick to interject. "I was just followin' them animals for a better look and, as luck would have it, I happened upon my friends quite by chance."

"And a good thing you did!" Rose nodded in gratitude. "This forest has become a dangerous place."

"These are strange times, my friends. A dark magic grips our domain." Halen unleashed a troubled sigh. "Lord Silverthorn will inform you of all you need to know, based on what little we have discovered thus far."

"Brilliant!" exclaimed Myron.

"Then follow me." Halen turned eastward.

"An excellent plan, Captain Ironwood. Please lead the way," urged Rose. She was eager to spend the night in the safety of four strong walls and a sturdy roof than to tempt fate by spending a night in this cursed forest.

"Hey… Where is Loken?" asked Tag. He glanced about, searching for their comrade.

"The Sprite travels with you?" queried Halen.

"Yes, but I am betting that little bugger abandoned us when those unicorns suddenly appeared," said Rose. She shielded her eyes from the glare of the sun to peer into the treetops to see if Loken was spying on them. "Or better yet, I bet that Sprite was the one to spook those unicorns into stampeding."

"Why would Loken do that?" grumbled Tag, dismissing her accusing words.

"You know Loken is notorious for being a little prankster! I would not be surprised if he was *the* unicorn that led the stampede."

"Now that is just crazy talk, Princess!" disputed Tag. "I think something happened to Loken and I do believe you have a serious issue when it comes to trust!"

"Trust issues? *Me?* Now you are the one talking crazy," snorted Rose, her eyes narrowing in suspicion as she scowled at him.

"Take my hand," ordered Tag.

"Why? So you can shove me into the ravine?"

Tag's eyes rolled in dismay, extending his hand to her once more. "Just come away from the ledge. It's probably very unstable now. We don't need you falling in after Harold went through the trouble of rescuing you."

"My mistake!" said Rose. Her cheeks reddened with embarrassment as she accepted Tag's hand.

"As usual," muttered Tag. He promptly led her away from the edge of the ravine that continued to crumble away.

"I thought you were contemplating some kind of revenge on me."

"I'm not the vengeful type," stated Tag. "You are."

"I am? Well, we shall just see about that!"

Myron raised his hands for a moment of silence as he spoke, "We digress, yet again, my friends! Was not the subject of concern focused on the mysterious disappearance of Loken?"

"Did the little fella catch up to you three?" questioned Harold. His worried eyes glanced about. "For I haven't seen hide nor hair of that little Sprite since we left the Fairy's Vale, not even durin' my lone travels through Axalon."

"Something bad must have happened to him," determined Myron.

"Where did you last see the little imp?" asked Halen.

"We were by a brook over yonder, watering our horses as we waited for him," said Tag, pointing the way.

"The last we saw, Loken was flying up toward the tree canopy," added Myron. "He wanted a higher vantage point to look out for danger."

"Perhaps he is still there," said Halen.

"I do hope so. Follow me!" urged Myron, waving his comrades on to retrace their steps.

"What fresh hell is this?" gasped Loken.

His heart raced, horrified to feel the web he was trapped on vibrate, trembling under his body as a gargantuan spider cautiously leaned out of its lair to test the lines once more.

Two large, coal black eyes surrounded by six smaller ones stared hungrily, fixing their unblinking gaze upon fresh prey. Emerging from its hiding place, the creature gingerly positioned the tip of each foot of its front-most limbs on to the nearest silken threads radiating from the centre of the web.

With the promise of a meal, the creature eased itself out of the tree hollow using its eight long, spindly legs that tapered down, terminating with sharp hooks designed for climbing and securing its prey. Feeling each and every vibration that resulted from Loken's frantic movements, it was a sure sign a fresh meal required tending to!

The spider's head, fused to become one with the thorax where the legs expanded from, was followed by a large, bulbous abdomen. Emerging from the knothole and onto its expansive web, the true size of this arachnid in all its horrific glory was revealed to Loken.

Rather than bristling with hairs, a feature common to the many garden spiders, this beast possessed an air of elegance about it. The smooth body had a glossy, ebony sheen like polished armour. As the posterior of the abdomen pressed down onto the lip of the knothole to anchor a silken safety line before advancing, Loken spotted a dash of red on the monster's underside. At first, the Sprite thought it was blood from feeding on its prey, but a second glance revealed it to be a marking that was ominously shaped like that of a scarlet skull, complete with two black marks to represent the orbs where eyes would go, if this was a human skull.

A rattling hiss drew Loken's attention as pincer-like jaws gnashed together before retracting to reveal two piercing fangs sheathed behind them. As sharp as needles and as hard as a spearhead, each hollow fang was filled with paralyzing venom that would eventually melt innards and flesh into a soupy mush.

To Loken's horror, the spider's body alone was as large as the biggest serving platter to be used by any human. The immensity of this creature became all the more alarming as its spindly, but powerful legs fanned out to support its body.

The spider began to descend from its lair. Rapidly negotiating the web, it clambered over the tacky spiral strands to traverse the non-sticky lines radiating from the centre of this trap to reach the ensnared prey.

Loken realized struggling was futile; it only served to excite the beast. He ceased his thrashing to lay motionless on the sticky trap as his mind raced, thinking of the best way to escape.

Just as abruptly, the spider stopped. It was momentarily confused by the sudden lack of vibrations rippling through the web to tell it exactly where its prey was trapped. Extending the tip of one of its forelegs, it touched a radial strand of silk. It detected nothing. Plucking at this thread, it sent out a vibration coursing throughout the web. As it reached Loken, quivering through his body, his heart raced. Each beat hammering in his chest was like the lightest touch of a harpist's fingertip strumming a single note, muted but unmistakeable, it was the call to feast.

Glancing about, Loken noted the size of the other creatures that fell victim to this spider. Seeing death looming ever closer as the monster skulked toward him, he acted. In a brilliant flash of white light, Loken transformed.

For a brief moment, the form of Myron Kendall protected in a full stand of armour hung suspended in the webbing that sagged dangerously. Complete with a steel helm and lowered visor to guard his head and face against those nasty fangs, Loken felt relatively safe. Just as he reached across his body to draw his sword to cut himself free, the spider rushed toward him, undaunted by his sudden change in size and appearance.

With the integrity of the massive web severely compromised by the weight of Loken's new form, the silken threads ripped apart.

He tore through the web, leaving the arachnid hissing furiously on the remnants of its tattered trap while its meal disappeared through the thick foliage. The loud clatter and banging of armour as Loken fell, bouncing off boughs and branches, filled the air.

Glancing overhead, Halen immediately nocked an arrow onto his bow.

"Look out!" cried the Elf. Taking aim, the tip of his arrow followed the large shadow dropping toward them. "What the bloody hell is *that* doing in the trees?"

"Wait!" shouted Myron. Recognizing his stand of armour, he pushed down on the tip of the Elf's arrow.

In a brilliant flash, a visibly shaken Sprite appeared. Bouncing off of a twig Loken launched into the air. His wings rattled with nervous energy as he circled high above. Relieved to see his friends and Captain Ironwood waiting on the forest floor, he glided down to join them.

"What happened to you?" questioned Tag. He opened his hand wide for the Sprite to land upon.

"I was up there when I spied upon a herd of rampaging unicorns heading this way," answered Loken, as he pointed above to the tree canopy.

"Well, thanks for *not* warning us!" sniffed Rose. She shook an admonishing finger at the Sprite as he alighted upon the palm of Tag's hand.

"I was attempting to do just that when I flew directly into danger!" snapped Loken.

"A sorry excuse! What can be more dangerous than a crazed herd of stampeding unicorns?" grunted Rose.

"I was trapped! Only now did I survive a harrowing encounter with a hideous spider!"

"A *spider*? Oh, boohoo on you!" Her hands flew up in frustration as she dismissed his words. "Big, hairy deal!"

"Big, indeed, Princess Rose! The beast was huge, but it was not hairy at all!"

"I believe you are exaggerating!"

"Unlike some, I am hardly the type to embellish on the truth, my lady!" Loken's wings rattled with indignation upon being the recipient of this public scolding. "I do not exaggerate when I say the spider was of monstrous proportions!"

Rose and her comrades were suddenly forced to duck. Shielding their heads, they were pelted by an assortment of dead and dying birds and bats. Each creature was mummified in silk. They rained down from the tattered web as the spider tore it down to weave a new one.

"Bloody hell!" groaned Tag, as he pushed Rose out of the way.

He peered up, searching for other falling carcasses to dodge. Shuddering in disgust, he wiped off the sticky strands of silk that clung to his raiment.

"Gross!" yelped Harold.

He flinched as a large object fell, striking him on his left shoulder to bounce off and land on the ground at his feet when he was too slow to avoid the pelting. He picked up a dark, feathered creature thoroughly entombed in silk. Based on its size, shape and the black talons poking through the webbing, it could only be a raven.

"That was rather disgustin'," groaned Harold, as he tossed aside the carcass.

"So you say! But more disturbing than being pelted by these dead creatures, consider the nature of beast that can do something like this," urged Loken, as he pointed overhead. "If you take a moment, you can appreciate the proportions of this spider by the very size of its prey."

"This is definitely not the normal fare for an ordinary spider," stated Halen, nodding in agreement.

"Exactly! Tiny flies and gnats these are not!" reminded Loken. "This alone should give you some indication as to the enormity of the monster I was forced to tangle with, no pun intended!"

"It is a good thing you escaped," said Halen.

"Indeed," Loken nodded to the Elf. "Had I been a regular Sprite, rather than one gifted with the ability to shape-shift, there was no way I would have escaped from that death trap!"

"Tainted waters, a unicorn herd running wild, and now a giant spider of monstrous proportions… What is the meaning of this, Captain Ironwood?" questioned Myron, as he looked to the Elf for some much needed answers. "You spoke of magic, but what kind of magic is capable of all this?"

"I believe you know as well as I do what is at play here... I suspect the forbidden arts have been invoked," answered the Elf, speaking with utmost certainty, "a magic most vile!"

"This forest has become a dangerous place," responded Rose. Fear tugged at her heart as she listened to Halen Ironwood's ominous warning. "We cannot stay here."

"If this dark magic goes unchecked, the whole world will surely become a very dangerous place," cautioned Myron.

"Indeed, my friend! Time is wasting away. Let us make haste to Driven Hill," urged Halen, waving the Sprite and his companions on to follow.

"For an audience with your lord and master?" asked Harold, hoping to see more of the Elf's domain of legend.

"Yes! It is not my place to speak on Lord Silverthorn's behalf. He is the one you and your comrades must confer with, if you seek answers to these questions."

"Driven Hill, you say?" repeated Harold. The pointed snout of the raccoon pelt he wore seemed to spring to life as his brows arched up in curiosity. "What is this place? It sounds a wee bit threatenin' to me."

"It was only *threatening* to the animals that were *driven* away from this hill to make room for the Elves," explained Rose.

"Let me assure you, it is not as bad as Princess Rose makes it sound, my good man. Driven Hill is our secret enclave within this once enchanted forest," explained Halen.

As the Elf led the way, he lifted a tree branch for Rose and her friends to pass beneath.

"Secret enclave, eh? It all sounds very mysterious," said Harold. A nervous grin crept across his round face as he ducked under the raised bough. "I hope that doesn't mean you'll have to kill us once we find out where it's hidden away."

"Your friends have been to Driven Hill before, but that does not exempt them from the threat of death, should they foolishly reveal its exact location to unsavoury characters wanting to invade our solitude."

"Oh!" gulped Harold. "There's nothin' to fear from me, Captain Ironwood. I'm known for bein' quite forgetful, if you get my drift?"

"Worry not, Master Murkins," teased Halen, "unless you have designs on our realm, you have nothing to fear."

"The only things I'm capable of designin' are fancy, critter headpieces, like the one I'm wearin' now." Harold plopped the raccoon pelt back onto his head.

"That is quite the fashion statement, indeed," noted Halen. He smiled; struggling to hide his obvious disgust to pretend he was unmoved by the husk of a dead raccoon perched on this strange mortal's head. "But enough talk for now! Step lively, my friends. Let us retire to the safety of Driven Hill before darkness falls and misfortune follows."

"Thanks for lettin' me retrieve my donkey, Captain Ironwood," said Harold.

He eagerly snatched up Sassy's reins, relieved to find she was exactly where he had abandoned her. The little beast was quite content to be left to rest and graze, than to be forced to frantically gallop to keep up with her master when he dashed off in mad pursuit of the unicorn herd.

"You are welcome," responded the Elf.

"My little Sassy is undoubtedly as grateful as I am to be reunited again."

"Think nothing of it, my good man," said Halen. "We had to travel in this general direction anyway, so it was no bother."

"Oh, I'm thinkin' it's *somethin'*, indeed, Captain. She's a tough, old gal, but Sassy wouldn't fare very well overnight in this strange forest, if I left her on her own."

"On this night, you need not worry. I will make sure she is properly sheltered, fed and watered when we reach Driven Hill."

"Thank you, kind sir!" said Harold.

"That reminds me," said Tag, glancing about as he trudged along behind Rose, "I wonder what became of our horses."

"I take it, they bolted with the approaching unicorn herd?" questioned the Elf. He glanced over his shoulder to see the look of concern on the young mortal's face.

"They escaped when they sensed the herd was coming our way," answered Tag.

"Those crazed beasts did not '*approach*'," corrected Rose. "They rampaged through the forest with every intention of killing us!"

"It would seem so, Princess Rose, but the unicorn, by its very nature, is a shy, retiring creature," insisted Halen. "Those beautiful animals were almost pushed to the brink of extinction due to overhunting by your kind. There were far too many wishing to harvest their horns for the purported medicinal properties, which were absolutely unsubstantiated to begin with! And if not for medicine, to use their horns to make sword and dagger handles, for those with deep pockets and a penchant for rare and exotic objects. Sadly, mankind's insatiable greed had taken its toll on the unicorn population."

"That is why the only existing herd left in this realm sought refuge in the protection of your forest," said Myron.

"Yes, and I know every unicorn in our domain, Sir Kendall. That old stallion, as well as the mares and foals in his herd, would have raced away from, rather than gallop toward a human being," added Halen.

"Then something definitely spooked them, enough to make them stampede," determined Tag.

"Perhaps it was this same thing that created that monstrous spider," offered Myron.

"That is a very real possibility," replied Halen, as he made a mental note of the location of the tattered spider web. "Whatever the case, I shall have my men search the forest for your steeds after they hunt down and kill that treacherous spider. If your horses are about, they will find them."

"That would be greatly appreciated, Captain Ironwood," said Rose, as she hastened her pace, trotting to keep up with the Elf's great strides. "Being made to endure long hours in the saddle is bad, but being made to walk for any duration is worse!"

With dusk melting into the impending night, Rose sighed in relief to see the inviting glow of the many lanterns illuminating the cottages as they approached the community of Driven Hill.

"This way!" Halen directed the small party to the royal residence of Lord and Lady Silverthorn.

Rose could not help but notice the window boxes that once spilled over with a plethora of vibrant flowers were in a sad state. The stems now drooped. No longer was there that riot of colours vying for their eyes' attention. The blossoms were now faded; the petals wilting more from the presence of the dark magic Captain Ironwood had spoken of, than the chill to herald the start of autumn.

Whatever the case, the feeling of dread and gloom that loomed over them as they entered this forest had now permeated deep into the Woodland Glade and into the very heart of Elfdom.

She watched as Captain Ironwood stepped onto the stoop of the small cottage they, with the exception of Harold and Loken, were delivered to on their first official meeting with Lord Rainus Silverthorn. Just as

Halen raised a balled fist to rap upon the door, an Elf maiden pulled it open. Standing before them, she was almost as tall as the captain, but there was no mistaking she was the fairer of the sexes.

Her captivating appearance elicited a loud gasp of surprise and wonder from Harold as his eyes drank in her ethereal beauty – a loveliness he had never before been witness to. It was just as Halen Ironwood had promised; if she was any indication, then the Elf women were indeed as beautiful as he had claimed them to be. Her flowing gown shimmered in the candlelight, sparkling like beads of dew gleaming in the first light of the morning sun. Set against delicate, porcelain skin, her sapphire eyes shone like the brightest stars against the deepest night sky in the dead of winter. Backlit by the glowing candles, the warm light reflecting off the crown of her head shone like a halo of burnished gold to amplify her true loveliness.

"Welcome, Captain Ironwood! I see you bring guests." Arissa's dewy lips curled into a demure smile as she bowed her head in respectful greeting, motioning for all to enter.

"Good evening, my lady," said Myron, bowing his head in salutation. "Is your lordship present?"

"Lord Silverthorn has not left his wife's side since she fell ill to this deadly blight." There was a melancholy in her voice.

"So, Lady Silverthorn lives?" asked Tag, as hope struggled to buoy his troubled heart.

"She lingers. Her condition has worsened with the coming of night."

"Well, it is a good thing we are here now," said Rose. "We bring a special tincture."

"A tincture, you say?" Arissa's delicate brows furrowed with curiosity.

"Yes, a medicine we believe can be beneficial to Lady Silverthorn and the others," explained Tag. "There is a chance it will help to reduce the fever your people are suffering from."

"How did you come to hear about this deadly affliction all the way in Fleetwood?" questioned Arissa, as she motioned the mortals to follow her.

"I was the one to tell them," announced Loken, as he flew in through the open door to settle on the fireplace mantle. "In fact, at the onset on this deadly malady, Lord Silverthorn informed me of this. I shared this dreadful news with my friends, in hopes they would have a remedy for your people."

"That is how we came to be here," added Myron, bowing his head in polite greeting.

He followed Tag and Rose inside while Harold took up the rear.

For a moment, the large man stood at the doorway, waiting until the captain issued a personal invitation for him to enter.

"Do come in," urged Halen, waving him inside.

As Harold stepped through the doorway to peer into this seemingly modest abode, he gasped in surprise. His eyes opened wide in wonder, gazing about the spacious home. He admired the finely crafted furniture, the luxurious tapestries, and the many oil paintings of which the main subject of each composition was Rainus Silverthorn. Glancing about, his eyes settled on the larger-than-life portrait of the Elf Lord. This painting, with its ornately carved, gilded frame, hung over the massive stone fireplace gracing the far wall where Loken was resting on the great mantle.

The snout of Harold's raccoon pelt headpiece dipped down over his furrowed brows. Frowning in confusion, he tried to make sense of how such a small cottage on the outside can possibly contain such a spacious interior with high, vaulted ceilings throughout.

"This home is… huge! It's like a palace on the inside."

In his excitement, Harold rushed by Halen Ironwood to exit what first appeared to be a quaint, little cottage. Once outside, he scrutinized the exterior, and then he ran around the royal residence, taking in the modest home that somehow masked the grand scale of the expansive interior.

"Come in," invited Halen, waving the mortal inside. "Time is wasting away, my friend."

Harold nodded, clearing the three steps onto the stoop of the cottage in one great stride. Standing at the doorway, he was even more confused now than when he first peered inside this home. Harold scrutinized these surroundings once more. He rubbed his eyes in case a strange magic was tricking him into seeing a deceptively large interior.

"How is this even possible?" asked Harold, turning to Halen for answers.

"Nothing is impossible for Elves! We have had an eon to master all the tricks of woodwork when it comes to carpentry and engineering," explained Halen. He motioned for the man to join his comrades as their hostess escorted them into the great dining hall to await an audience with the master of the house.

"I thought you were goin' to say it was some kind of Elf magic," said Harold. He marvelled at the massive, polished beams forming the trusses to support the high ceiling. Each one was meticulously carved with a flourish of ivy, stylized blooms and delicate images of doves and prancing unicorns.

"Ah, yes! That, too! However, in our hands, what seems like magic to mankind, it is our inherent skills; attention to detail that allows us to design what you deem as being *impossible*," added Halen, following behind the mortals as the maiden led the way.

"Please be seated. Remain here," ordered Arissa. "I shall inform Lord Silverthorn of your arrival. In the meantime, take a moment to relax and reflect. I shall have food and drink delivered to you."

"Thank you," said Myron, as he pulled a chair from the great table to seat Rose first.

Nodding in gratitude to the knight, she plopped down, sinking into the plush cushion padding this chair that was elegantly carved and gilded in gold leaf. This was so much better than sitting on a hard saddle for hours on end.

No sooner than Halen had the visitors comfortably seated, Rainus Silverthorn came bounding down the long hallway upon receiving news of their arrival. His great strides, emphasizing the very urgency of the moment, were like those of a dancer leaping across a stage. His steps delivered him quickly to the dining room.

"Welcome, my friends!" greeted Rainus. "Is it true? You come with a miracle cure?"

"Greetings, Lord Silverthorn," said Rose, nodding her head in polite salutation as her male comrades stood and bowed before the harried Elf. "Whether we come with a miracle cure is yet to be seen, but yes, we may have a possible remedy."

Myron removed several bottles from his pack, placing them on the table before Rainus. "We come with a medicinal tincture, one derived from the willow tree. When properly distilled, it becomes a potent medicine to combat fevers and inflammation that afflict humankind."

"It works?" questioned Rainus, immediately recognizing this mortal by his voice and the glint in his world-weary eyes.

"It does," assured Myron.

The Elf raised a cobalt blue bottle to study its contents against the glow of the candles burning in the centre of the table. In this light, his usually perfect face looked haggard. It served to accentuate how dishevelled his platinum blonde hair was and how dull his eyes had become. Normally a dazzling azure with piercing focus, they had lost their sheen.

"If administered in a timely manner, and in the proper dosage, this medicine works for us, this much we know," assured Tag. He pulled out four more bottles he had absconded with from the palace apothecary. "We pray it will do the same for your people."

"I recommend dispensing the medicine immediately to all stricken with this fever," said Myron.

"I shall begin administering this tincture, first to my wife," said Rainus, as he nodded in gratitude.

"Shake the bottle well, one full spoon... No, make it two. This is the dosage I'd recommend," said Myron, after taking into consideration the Elves' greater size. "Do so now, and administer another dose in three hours, and every third hour after that, until the fever breaks."

"Very well," said Rainus. He nodded in understanding as he turned to Halen Ironwood. "Deliver these bottles to the others, my friend. You heard the man, administer this tincture as Sir Kendall had prescribed. Do so now and pray it is not too late for this medicine to work its magic."

"Consider it done," responded Halen. He eagerly gathered up the remaining bottles. Bowing respectfully to Rainus and the mortals in his company, the Elf hastily departed to deliver possible salvation.

"Wait here, my friends," urged Rainus. "I should not be long. I must go to my beloved; care for Valara first, before I make proper time to meet with you."

"No need to explain." Myron waved the Elf off to tend to his wife. They watched as Rainus Silverthorn hastened away with the bottle clutched in his hands; a look of hope gleaming once more in his eyes.

"The poor soul! He is absolutely wrought with despair over Lady Silverthorn's condition," determined Loken, as he alighted upon the table to join his comrades. "So much so, he barely took notice of me, or any of us, for that matter."

Harold respectfully removed the animal pelt from his head. Resting it on his lap so only the ringed raccoon tail appeared over the edge of the table, the large man spoke, "Though a proper introduction would've been nice, for I've never met an Elf lord before, I can't say I blame him for rushin' off as he did."

"I'd be distraught, too, if I were him," agreed Myron, as he nodded in sympathy. "But worry not, my friend, for there will be time enough for proper introductions when Lord Silverthorn is less distracted."

As they watched Rainus duck into the royal bedchamber at the far end of the hall, Arissa returned with a helper. While she carried a serving tray filled with fruits, freshly baked bread and a large wedge of cheese for these guests to dine on, he delivered a silver tray, carefully placing it onto the table between Tag and Princess Rose. Upon this tray were five large, crystal goblets, a tiny silver thimble and the biggest bottle of red wine Harold had ever laid eyes on.

"Are we expectin' giants to join us for refreshments?" asked Harold, staring in amazement at these oversized goblets.

"You'd think," responded Tag. He smiled in understanding. "Let me put it this way, the Elves enjoy their wine and tend to imbibe freely when the occasion calls for it."

"And lucky for the Elfkind, they do not suffer the ravages induced by partaking in too much wine, as we mortals do," added Myron. "They can indulge in much greater quantities before feeling the intoxicating effects of the alcohol."

Harold stared at his friends, taking a moment to digest these words.

"In other words, it takes a lot to get these Elves drunk, hence, the abnormally large goblets to accommodate the large servings they like to consume," explained Tag.

"Amazin'!" commented Harold.

"Indeed! Unlike Tag and Myron, both of whom got stinky drunk the last time we were here," continued Rose, "the Elves can handle their spirits much better than the average man."

"I'm less than average, so I should be fine, but I won't be imbibin' on this night," said Harold. "Not that I don't trust them Elves, but I want to keep my wits about me... Stay alert should I hear Sassy brayin' in the night to warn if danger is lurkin' about."

"Wise decision," said Rose, nodding in approval to Harold. Her eyes narrowed, glaring with an obvious look of reproach at Tag and Myron as she addressed them, "And if our friends are smart, they will think twice before indulging, too."

Just as Arissa was about to pour, Myron motioned her to stop. Holding up two fingers sideways, he indicated the depth of the serving size. "Thank you, and feel free to fill Lord Silverthorn's goblet as you see fit, but this smaller portion for us will be more than adequate."

Arissa nodded in understanding, serving the guests first and topping up the tiny thimble for Loken before filling the final crystal goblet. Just as she placed the bottle and full glass at the head of the table designated for the master of the house, Lord Silverthorn returned. With a morose demeanour brought on by weariness and dread, Rainus entered the dining room, slipping into the great armchair to join his guests. He motioned all to remain seated, than to stand and bow in his presence once more.

"How does Lady Silverthorn fare, my lord?" asked Myron, as he stared into the Elf's worried eyes.

"With some encouragement, Valara managed to down the tincture. Her fever-addled mind caused her some confusion, but for now, she sleeps. I suppose there is nothing more to do than wait." Rainus turned to Arissa before she could leave with her helper, giving her further instructions. "Please tend to my wife. Remain by her side while she rests. Let me know if there is any change in her condition."

Arissa bowed politely before leaving Rainus and his guests, allowing them to converse privately.

As the door to the bedchamber closed behind her, Rainus' normally erect and regal posture seemed to shrink. He slumped in his chair like a defeated man. Heaving a weary sigh, it was as though the woes of the day melted away with that first big gulp of wine.

"It is beneficial for Lady Silverthorn to rest," assured Myron. "We shall find out soon enough if the medicine works."

"I pray it does, my friend," said Rainus, "for at this moment, I have nothing else left to me but my prayers."

"Prayin' is good," said Harold.

"So you say," responded Rainus. "In my mind, prayers are nothing more than the verbalized hopes of the most desperate."

"Just give this medicine time to work," urged Myron.

"It is all I can do, for there is no known power of the Elfkind that can undo this wicked affliction. As far as I am concerned, if this tincture works, then it will truly be a miracle and at this point, I am in dire need of a miracle, large or small."

Rose stared at the great Elf Lord. At this very moment, everything about him spoke of utter defeat. In all the times she had seen him, Rainus Silverthorn was always impeccably and stylishly dressed without a single crease or wrinkle to ruin the illusion of perfection. His flowing, silky tresses that always looked flawlessly groomed by the finest boar-bristle brush, so much so his head of hair had become the object of envy for the Princess, now appeared unkempt.

It was as though this Elf no longer cared about personal grooming. As distressing as it was to see his untidy hair, the dark circles that ringed his eyes were all the more apparent against his fair complexion that had now adopted a sickly pallor. These physical signs were all indicative of his mental and emotional condition; the result of too many sleep-deprived nights fuelled by woe.

Before, Rainus appeared to be the vision of perfection, and not just to mortals, but to his people, too. Now, all signs of regal elegance that was the hallmark of this great Elf had all but disappeared beneath the crushing weight of his worries.

Before taking another sip, Rainus sat upright, hoisting his goblet on high. He offered a toast to his guests. "Here is to your good health. I pray it is long lasting. And here is to the restored health of my wife and my people, if the fates should grant us some measure of mercy."

"Here, here!" said all in his company. Even Loken raised his thimble of wine in good cheer.

"I know it is difficult not to worry under such dire circumstances,

Lord Silverthorn," said Tag. He wiped away the carmine moustache staining his upper lip that formed by drinking from this big bowl of a goblet. "You must have faith, my lord. If all goes well, Lady Silverthorn will recover from whatever it is that ails her now. You must give this medicine a chance to work."

"In my people's long and illustrious history, we *never* required faith to avoid sickness or pestilence, the typical ills that had easily ravaged those of your race through the ages. And now, to be incapacitated as we are now, it is difficult to hold on to faith, young master. I always had confidence that such a thing was not possible, but look at what has become of my dear Valara! And my people, they suffer in the most inhumane way."

"I know you take little comfort in our words," said Myron, "but you must believe your wife will recover, that the medicine will work in due course."

"I shall find comfort once my beloved wife shows signs of recovery."

"I am sure it is most disconcerting to see her in the throes of a fever-fuelled dream," said Tag, "but I am confident the Elves are far more resilient than the human race. Lady Silverthorn will come around and will be as good as new."

"It was more than disconcerting, young sir! Before now, I believed us to be immune to such things, but it was most alarming indeed to witness the ravages of this sickness," said Rainus. He heaved a dreary sigh as his mind replayed the moment the first Elf fell to this sickness and more soon followed. "It was truly disturbing to see the ill suddenly regurgitate their food and water in that most violent and unexpected manner! It was not natural, spewing like that, even purging the fine wine offered to them!"

"That *purging* is called vomiting. Often, when a fever strikes, the body refuses to digest most of what is offered," explained Myron.

"Vomiting…" repeated Rainus, as he turned over in his mind this new word to be added to the Elvish lexicon. "To vomit is a bad thing."

"If one cannot hold down food or water, eventually it can cause the victim of the malady to waste away, making them too weak to recover," said Myron.

"So this vomiting is a very bad thing," assumed Rainus. "To vomit is to die…"

"Sometimes, it is a good thing," insisted Tag.

"How so?"

"Well, in my case, I had once consumed far too much wine in one sitting," answered Tag. "If I had not 'purged' myself of that excessive amount of wine, I probably would have died or suffered the worst hangover ever, that it would've had me wishing for death."

"Yes! For the human race, this *gut-response,* so to say, can occur not just during bouts of sickness, but with excessive drinking, consuming too much food or eating food that is tainted," added Rose. "For my friends, more often than not, vomiting goes hand in hand with their bouts of drinking."

"Oh, my!" gasped Rainus. "Mankind truly is a fragile race."

"Sadly, it would appear that the Elves are becoming just as frail," noted Rose.

"That is what is so disturbing, my lady. Elves *do not* fall to sickness. Until now, we were always regarded as being far more resilient than mere mortal men, hence the reason we refer to your race as being *mortal.*"

"Well, something evil wreaks havoc on your forest and your people, and as your kind have been rendered as helpless as us *mere mortal* types, there is a good chance the medicine will prove to be just as effective, if not more so," said Rose.

"If anything, it is this small glimmer of hope I cling to that helps to ease my foul disposition," admitted Rainus, nodding in gratitude to the Princess.

"Yes, thanks to us," said Rose.

"Indeed, you must be commended for your efforts, for it was no small feat to get here, but it is yet to be seen if your efforts were pure folly."

"Then we must hope for the best," urged Loken, taking a contemplative sip. "I prefer to believe there is no reason to lose hope, not just yet."

"You must have reason to hope for the best," said Harold, nodding in agreement with the Sprite. "If your wife's life means anythin' to you, Lord Silverthorn, you'd be holdin' on to all the hope you can muster. Along with a good dose of that medicine, they can work together to speed her recovery."

"My dear Valara means *everything* to me, good sir! She is my life, the very air I breathe, my sole reason for living." Rainus reclined in his chair as he absorbed this man's words. He stared intently at the large stranger sharing this table. "You speak with much wisdom, my friend. Do you have a name?"

"I can't say I have much in the way of wisdom, my lord, but yes, I do have a name. Don't we all?" answered Harold. He stared nervously at Rainus Silverthorn, trying to determine if this Elf had presented him with a trick question.

"Our friend speaks the truth, Lord Silverthorn," giggled Rose. With a shake of her head, she smiled across the table at Harold. "He has a tendency to speak the honest truth, but wisdom? From him? I mean no disrespect, but this simpleton of a man is many things, selflessly brave even, but he is far from wise."

"Thank you, Princess Rose," said Harold. He beamed with delight, selectively hearing her describe him as being 'selflessly brave'.

"Let the man speak." Rainus raised a hand to Rose, motioning her for silence. "You have a name, so please, share it with me."

Harold bowed in respectful greeting as he introduced himself. "My name is Harold Murkins, my lord, but you can just call me Harry."

Rainus' brows arched up in amusement. "I am inclined to say *Harold* is more becoming. It has a noble ring to it."

"Well, thank you kindly, Lord Silverthorn." This time, bowing his head in humility.

"So, tell me, Harold, how did you come to be in my woodland realm? Are you a good friend or advisor to Princess Rose or is it this bravery she boasted about that sees you here in her company? To keep her safe?"

"I came to her rescue a time or two so far, and even though we met only a few days ago, I'd like to believe we're good friends, but in all honesty, the kind Princess allowed me to come along on their adventure."

Rainus frowned in curiosity. "Princess Rose *allowed* a random stranger to come along?"

"Well, I'm not an out-and-out stranger as I'm good friends with Sir Myron Kendall, but it wasn't so much an outright invitation, my lord. It was more like she granted my wish of goin' on my first quest *ever*. That's why I'm here with them now."

"That is downright perplexing, Harold. You do know that a quest, especially one involving Princess Rose and her brave comrades, entails a great deal of risk and facing some tremendous perils."

"What quest is not without risk, Lord Silverthorn? And is danger not what makes a quest a real adventure?"

"You poor, gullible man!" lamented the Elf. "When I speak of risk, I mean to say you are sure to encounter a good measure of danger to both life and limb in following Princess Rose about as you do. Did she not tell you about the last mission that saw us in the heart of dragon country, deep in the Fire Rim Mountains to the north?"

"I already warned Harold of what dangers lurk on such missions," assured Myron, "but he insisted. Princess Rose granted his wish, and who am I to go against her or to deny this man of his greatest desire?"

Rainus glanced over to Harold. With an equal measure of amazement and suspicion, he eyed this mortal's large frame and the unusual animal pelt headpiece that now rested on his lap.

"And even against the advice of a trusted friend you still insist on accompanying them on a journey that will likely see you smack dab in the middle of peril?"

"Yes, Lord Silverthorn. It was my greatest wish to join them on this quest! I dared to seize this opportunity, a lifelong dream really, to live a life of adventure, at least one great adventure, before I meet my end."

"Well, my good man, you are either brave beyond reason, or you are a fool that cannot be reasoned with," determined the Elf, with a dismal shake of his head. "You do understand that your *end* in this realm can well be hastened by partaking in a misadventure with Princess Rose, do you not?"

"I do! And I've been called worse than a fool in my lifetime, my lord, but is not the purpose of a quest to test one's mettle?" asked Harold, speaking in earnest. "One's true character can't be discovered, if one plays it safe, seekin' the sanctuary of a mundane life! At least, that's what my momma used to always tell me and she's never been known to lie."

"Testing one's bravery is not the same as tempting fate, Harold Murkins," replied Rainus. "Surely, the way has already been marred by misfortune in keeping company not so much with Loken, Master Yairet and Sir Kendall, but certainly with Princess Rose."

"I will have you know, Lord Silverthorn, it is not as though I tricked or lured this man into coming along with us," stated Rose. "Let it be known, I did all I could to dissuade him from joining us on this quest, but he would hear none of it."

"By offering to grant Harold his greatest wish, I'd hardly describe it as '*dissuading*' him!" grunted Tag. With a cynical roll of his eyes directed at Rose, he raised his huge goblet to take a swig of wine to wash away the venomous words rising in his throat.

Rainus sat upright, peering over tented fingers to scrutinize Rose. "Pray tell, Princess, what would ever compel you to offer this man such a wish? Have you taken on the role of the Dream Merchant upon Master Agincor's retirement?"

"Of course not! And it is not as though I said, '*Hey, you with the dead animal on your head! You are coming with us on this dangerous mission that will possibly cost you your life*'! Oh, no! Harold Murkins was the one to broach me with this request, after I promised to reward him for saving my life."

"This man truly saved you from danger? Do tell!" Rainus sat back, raising his glass to encourage Rose to continue with her tale.

"Oh, you exaggerate, my lady!" Harold casually waved her off as he blushed with modesty. "I just got the three of you and your horses unstuck from a great swamp, that's all."

"You are being much too modest, Harold! If it were not for you, we probably would have drowned, along with our horses!" declared Rose, as Myron and Tag simultaneously unleashed a disgruntled sigh.

"So he helped to remove us from that swamp," admitted Tag. "We're thankful for that, but I believe you're exaggerating on the facts!"

"I am a princess! I do not exaggerate! Harold was truly heroic on this day, too, saving me from certain death when a crazed unicorn herd came stampeding through the forest to do us in."

Rainus frowned on hearing this. "This is news to me, Princess Rose. I had sensed the creatures were growing restless, but to stampede? They would run from, not toward, human beings. Care to elaborate?"

"Allow *me* to elaborate without embellishing on the details, Lord Silverthorn," offered Tag.

"By all means, young man!" urged Rainus.

"We had stopped to allow our horses to drink and rest while Loken took to the treetops to survey the lands for possible danger," said Tag, as he glanced over to the Sprite sitting in the centre of the table, nursing his wine-filled thimble.

"Yes, I flew on high," added Loken. "From this great vantage point it was where I first spotted the unicorn herd. They were charging westward, heading straight toward my comrades."

"And you were able to forewarn them of the approaching danger?" queried Rainus.

"No, my lord. I became entangled in a massive spider web. Had I not escaped when I did, I would have most certainly become a tasty morsel for that gargantuan beast."

"Gargantuan by your standards, I take it?" asked the Elf, a look of concern etched upon his face.

"*HUGELY GARGANTUAN*, by even *your* standards, my lord! I'd say with its large body and great, spindly legs, it would easily span across the width of this table I sit on now!"

"You don't say!" gasped Rainus.

"Oh, I do!" insisted Loken, his wings shuddering as he shared in this frightening moment.

"The monster had retreated when we caught up to Loken, so we did not see it with our own eyes," said Tag. "But based on the size of its prey entombed within great bales of sticky silk that pelted down upon us from its tattered web, it was obvious this was no ordinary garden spider Loken confronted!"

"The horrors!" gasped Rainus. His eyes darkened with concern as he pondered this news. "And what of the unicorn herd you spotted, my little friend?"

"Something obviously spooked them, enough to send the entire herd crashing through the forest," answered Loken. "I did not see what it was to cause them such panic, but at that moment, I felt it was most important to warn the others to get out of the way."

"But you became trapped on this great spider web," concluded Rainus, as he struggled for some understanding of what was happening in his realm while he remained by his wife's side.

"Very much so!" Loken nodded in agreement.

"Yes, and just prior to the approach of this stampeding herd, we had noticed something alarming," said Myron.

"Alarming? What do you speak of?" asked Rainus.

"The creek the horses were drinking from became as black as the night while the moss under the Princess' feet withered, dying wherever she stepped."

"Dark omens!" gasped Rainus.

"And it only got darker when we were almost trampled to death," added Rose.

The Elf listened intently as the mortals retold their frightening tale and how they were forced to run when their own horses bolted, and how Harold had come to the rescue, plucking the Princess from the maws of certain death.

"Truly a harrowing tale," said Rainus.

"Harrowing indeed, Lord Silverthorn," responded Myron. "On our way here, Captain Ironwood told us that you would have some answers to share."

Rainus indulged in a lingering sip as he contemplated on the events of the past week and his guests' account of their own adventure upon entering his forest.

"What say you, Lord Silverthorn? We have our suspicions, but we'd like your insight as to whom, or what, you suspect is behind all of this," said Tag.

"If it was just this deadly ailment to consider, I would believe that my race is in decline. The halcyon age of the Elves has come to pass; the powers that be deem it that we are no longer as perfect and as resilient as we once believed. Perhaps we were being punished for some reason."

"To an extent, we all feel invulnerable until we get sick," offered Harold. "Maybe your people are gettin' sick for the first time, so it's just a matter of adjustin' to becomin' more human like us."

"No disrespect to your kind, sir, but there'd be *no* adjusting to becoming like a human being." Rainus shook his head. "But consider this, my friend, there is something insidious at work here. If it was just a matter of falling to some new and strange illness, it does not account for the changes in the forest."

"Like the tainted water and rampaging unicorn herd," said Myron.

"And let us not forget that monster spider," added Loken.

"That, too," said the Elf, brooding as he stared in pensive contemplation at his goblet of wine.

"So?" Rose prompted him to share in his thoughts. "What is on your mind, Lord Silverthorn?"

"I am thoroughly vexed, Princess Rose! Obviously, I'd be a fool to believe it is nothing more than a sickness, one perhaps spread from the human race to my people, but in light of these other events, it is something far more sinister at work here."

"I agree," said Myron. "But what do you think is happening in your forest and to your people?"

"Magic… Vile magic of the worst kind," answered Rainus, as his eyes darkened with dread. "It is the only thing that makes sense at this moment."

"We seem to be in agreement, Lord Silverthorn. Even Captain Ironwood suspected as much," determined Myron. "And we believe we know who is behind the unleashing of this dark magic."

"I have my suspicions, but do tell!" Rainus leaned forward, eager to learn more from this knight. "What do you know of this?"

Myron drew a deep breath. He gathered his thoughts before presenting the facts, glancing over to his comrades for non-verbal cues to speak his mind and to do so candidly.

"Tell him," urged Tag, waving Myron on. "Tell Lord Silverthorn what we know."

"I beseech you, Sir Kendall, speak!" ordered Rainus.

"The Sorcerer has returned," said Myron.

The Elf's face blanched as he fell silent.

11
A Horrible Idea

"Did you not hear what he said, Lord Silverthorn?" asked Rose. Expecting a greater response, she searched the Elf's distraught face.

The pad of Rainus' index finger traced the rim of his crystal goblet. It hummed, droning a single, steady note that caused the carmine liquid to vibrate as his fingertip lightly circled the mouth of the chalice.

"Well?" asked Rose, huffing with impatience as the great Elf sat in silent repose. "What say you, my lord? Do you have any thoughts on this matter?"

When no answer was immediately forthcoming, the palm of her hand slapped down on the table's surface to invoke a response.

"Well… This is news I certainly did not expect," admitted Rainus. "When the first of my people fell to this strange illness, we searched our forest for a possible source of its cause. But when this deadly scourge infected my wife, I dared not leave her side. I remained here, sending Captain Ironwood forth with all my able-bodied warriors to delve into this mystery."

"And they found nothing?" assumed Tag.

"Less than nothing, Master Yairet!" Rainus shook his head. "At least, they have yet to discover anything that would shed some light on the events of late. And certainly nothing to substantiate Sir Kendall's claim that Dragonite was responsible for any of this. But that is neither here nor there at this point!"

"How so, when this *is* the point?" questioned Rose.

"The Dream Merchant, Silas Agincor himself, delivered word to me when we had regrouped at the climax of our last quest. He was the one to reveal to me that the deranged Sorcerer had met his demise, and at your hands, I must add!" reminded the Elf, as he glanced over to Tag. "Agincor claimed the demented soul had vanished upon receiving your death-delivering blow."

"I understand your doubt," said Myron, "but believe me when I say it was nothing more than wishful thinking on our part to be rid of that murderous fiend, once and for all."

"I truly wished it was so, Lord Silverthorn, but it has become painfully obvious to me that I had failed," admitted Tag. "Because I did not kill him, Dragonite wreaks havoc with his restored powers. Now, he is bent on revenge!"

"You speak the truth?" asked Rainus, searching this mortal's eyes for signs of deception. "How can this be possible?"

"From all signs discovered thus far, the Sorcerer was indeed terribly wounded, but he did not die from his injuries as we had hoped," answered Tag. "We suspect he used the forbidden arts, perhaps even manipulated the powers of the Dreamstone, to restore his health."

"This is madness!" declared Rainus.

"If you need proof, Lord Silverthorn, I was attacked in the Fairy's Vale prior to returning to your forest," disclosed Loken.

"By the Sorcerer?" questioned the Elf. "Are you positive?"

"I swear, my lord, I have no doubt it was him," answered Loken. "That madman caught me unawares. He tried to kill me! I survived, unfortunately, the Sorcerer managed to escape after he attacked me at the edge of the Fairy's Vale. His assault left me temporarily incapacitated, unable to mount a pursuit."

Rainus sank back into his chair, an index finger tapping his chin as he mulled over these foreboding words.

"What say you now, Lord Silverthorn?" asked Myron.

"I say my heart wishes you were all wrong. However, my mind warns me to consider all possibilities, Sir Kendall. I was just so sure Master Agincor had spoken the truth when he delivered news of Dragonite's demise."

"The Dream Merchant did speak the truth, as he knew it, at the time," reminded Tag. "However, we were all wrong on this matter. We just wanted to believe the Sorcerer was dead and would no longer pose a threat to us."

"And none wanted to believe this more than me!" insisted Rose. "You'd think that sorry excuse of a Sorcerer would do us the courtesy of dying like the cur that he is."

"I swear, Lord Silverthorn, we have nothing to gain in deceiving you where that Sorcerer is concerned," declared Myron.

Rainus leaned forward, pushing his wine goblet away as he addressed his guests. "I believe you... I wish it were not so, but I do believe you, my friends."

Myron breathed a sigh of relief as he spoke, "By Loken's fleeting glimpse of the culprit as he fled the Fairy's Vale, and by the dark magic unleashed in your very domain, all signs point to Dragonite."

"If the Sorcerer has managed to restore his health and regain his powers, then I have no doubt he will be seeking revenge. However, it begs the question: Why me? Why has he targeted my people and my domain on his crusade for vengeance, when Princess Rose was the one wanting to reclaim the Dreamstone from him while Master Yairet was the one to run his sword through that fiend?"

"We have our suspicions," replied Tag.

"And what are these suspicions, young man?" Rainus' brows furrowed with curiosity.

"We believe Dragonite has instigated a campaign of revenge," answered Tag.

"I agree. But for what reason, other than he is insane, not to mention more than just a little peeved at you four?" asked the Elf, as he glanced over to Harold. "And perhaps even this big fellow in your company?"

"Dragonite seeks revenge on those he holds responsible for destroying his lair to the north," explained Tag. "Undoubtedly, he blames all of us, with the exception of Harold, for sending his legion of useless mimes scattering in defeat, and for rescuing Myron from his clutches when the Sorcerer believed he was about to claim victory over us."

"Yes, and I believe you are being subjected to the Sorcerer's wrath because you had come to our aid during our most dire moment," added Myron.

"So you believe, in the Sorcerer's demented mind, that I am guilty by association?" asked Rainus.

"It is fair to assume that madman believes any person, whether Elf, Wizard or Sprite, willing to come to our aid is a worthy recipient of his vengeance," reasoned Myron.

"Well, whether I came to your aid, or not, I suppose it is common knowledge, far and wide, I never liked that necromancer and his fool army of mimes!" grumbled Rainus, shaking his head in disgust.

"So you do believe Dragonite is behind the misfortune and strange events to befall your forest?" asked Rose.

"Obviously, Princess. In light of what I know now, it is the most logical explanation for the strange happenings in my domain."

"It would certainly explain this deadly affliction that torments your people now," added Myron. "I have no doubt the Sorcerer has unleashed the powers of the forbidden arts to do so. How else would your people fall ill in this manner, when historically, you were never susceptible to illness?"

"I would be a fool to discount all you have presented to me, my friends." Rainus nodded in thoughtful agreement.

"Well! Thank goodness for that!" exclaimed Rose, throwing her arms up in mock glee. "So, what are you going to do about it, Lord Silverthorn?"

The Elf's brows arched up in surprise as he addressed her. "What am *I* going to do about it?"

"Well, yes! It is your domain after all. It is obvious to me that you had antagonized that madman, so much so, you and your people now suffer the full brunt of his retaliation!" Rose's words were matter-of-fact. "Common sense dictates that he vents his wrath on you, rather than me, because he bears a far bigger, deep-seated grudge, where you are concerned! It is clear to me Dragonite views you as a greater threat than I was and will ever be."

Rainus sat upright, peering judiciously over tented fingers at Rose as he considered her words. After some deliberation, he spoke, "I have no doubt I am, by far, a greater threat to the Sorcerer, but did it ever occur to you, Princess, that Dragonite seeks vengeance on me because I chose to do as Master Yairet said?"

"Tag says a lot, even too much at times," said Rose. "Can you be more specific?"

"I am referring to the fact that the Sorcerer's wrath I am subjected to now is because I came to *your* aid during *your* quest to reclaim that cursed magic crystal Dragonite had so desired in the first place!"

"I suppose it is a possibility." Her slight shoulders rolled in a shrug.

Rainus unleashed a dreary sigh of resignation.

"Look here, Princess," said Tag, "you know bloody well Lord Silverthorn and his people were only the first to be dealt Dragonite's wrath. And you know darned well the Sorcerer was about to strike in the Fairy's Vale when Loken intervened, almost getting killed in the process."

"And then you three were almost trampled by rampagin' unicorns," reminded Harold. "Though I'm not the smartest tool in the woodshed, as my momma would say, even I'm seein' a pattern here, my lady. I'm thinkin' it's more than mere coincidence."

"I would agree. The Sorcerer is lashing out at all those who willingly came to your assistance, Princess," stated Rainus. His fingertips impatiently drummed on the table as he addressed her nonchalant attitude. "He started his campaign of revenge against those closest to where he had slunk off to lick his wounds like an injured animal, hidden away from all while he recuperated. Now, he is in a position to strike, lashing out first at those in closest proximity to his lair."

"So the demented soul is exceedingly violent now because of what had happened to him," responded Rose.

"Yes, and it will only be a matter of time before he seeks *you* out to exact the worst of his revenge!" added the Elf.

"Are you saying this is all my fault?" sulked Rose.

"*YES!*" declared Tag, Myron, Loken and Rainus. Their unequivocal answer was simultaneous.

"Wow!" gasped Harold, waving an admonishing finger in her direction. "For shame, Princess Rose, for shame!"

"Are you now siding with them?" Rose's arms crossed her chest in defiance as she glared at Harold.

"No disrespect to you, my lady, but I'm all for common sense risin' above all this craziness. I'd have to say majority rules, and it's lookin' like you've been outnumbered on this matter."

"Aha! You are wiser than you claim to be, my good man!" praised Rainus. "This may well be the defining quality of your character that shall spare your life should you continue this *misadventure* with Princess Rose and her loyal cohorts."

"Never mind him! And even if this was totally my fault, which I don't believe it was," countered Rose, "being that I was so trusting and somewhat ignorant when this whole mess unfolded, I am here now. At least I am trying to set things right!"

"As you should!" snapped Tag. "And pleading ignorance is no excuse!"

"Can't fault her for tryin' to fix this," said Harold, hoping to pacify the irate, young man. "Maybe we should focus on how best to handle the Sorcerer and this vengeful nature of his."

"Good plan," agreed Rainus. "And trust me, Harold Murkins, that necromancer has plenty to be vengeful for."

"Fine! So what do *we* plan to do about that madman?" questioned Rose.

"We?" repeated Tag. He cast an accusing gaze in her direction.

"Yes, we! For you know as well as I do that I cannot take on the Sorcerer on by myself. I need your help! I need help from all of you."

"At last!" exclaimed Tag, slapping his thigh in exuberance. "You have been humbled, enough to admit you need us!"

"Yes, yes!" snapped Rose. "Mock if you like, but what is the plan? There is a plan, right?"

"To put it bluntly, the immediate plan is to hunt the Sorcerer down," replied Myron.

"And then?" asked Harold. Giddy with anticipation, he was eager to learn more now that this quest he had embarked on was taking on a tangible sense of urgency.

"We do away with that necromancer!" declared Tag. He was unwilling to mince his words as he patted the scabbard of his weapon. "This time, Dragonite will die upon my sword."

"And that's the mission?" questioned Harold, scratching his head in thought. "The quest is about *killin'* the Sorcerer? I thought it was about gettin' that Dreamstone back from him to stop all this madness."

"That was always the intention, but in light of the situation and Dragonite's efforts to unleash his dark magic, it is now about killing *him* before he kills *us*," stated Myron.

"And before he steals away with more innocent lives in my forest," added Rainus.

"This is soundin' mighty serious," said Harold.

"Good gracious, you dolt! Of course this mission entails killing that vile soul!" snapped Rose. "We warned you from the start there would be danger; danger you accepted at your own risk! Did you think we were going to corner him? Tie him down? Give the Sorcerer a good tongue-lashing in hopes it will be enough to bring his reign of terror to an end?"

"Well… I was thinkin' – "

"Oh, no! You, my dim-witted friend, were not thinking at all!" scolded Rose. "We plan to give that maniac exactly what he deserves!"

"Death seems rather extreme to me," said Harold, rubbing his chin in thought. "There's no comin' back from dead."

"That is the idea!" said Rose, unsympathetic to the Sorcerer's intended plight. "He must be stopped, no matter the cost!"

"If there was another way, Harold, we would consider it," explained Myron. "However, there is no reasoning with that madman. The Sorcerer will destroy more innocent lives, if we do not take the appropriate measures to stop him! We must do so quickly in hopes of catching him while he is unaware of our presence in this forest."

"And takin' appropriate measures in this case means to kill the Sorcerer?" asked Harold, seeking confirmation as he slowly dragged an index finger across his thick neck.

"Trust me, my friend, killing that necromancer is the only way to stop him now," declared Tag. "Dragonite was never one to be reasoned with before, but now, in light of our past history, he is a true menace."

"Not just to us, but to all of society," added Myron, "you included, Harold."

"All those who stand in his way, whether it is to stop his bid for world domination or to undermine his campaign of revenge, are in imminent danger," warned Rainus.

"If you choose now to abandon this quest, Harold, I shall free you of your duties. You have no obligation to hold to your promise," said Rose.

"I consider it the highest of honours to be bestowed upon me, my lady, to be in your esteemed company. I've no intention of abandonin' my friends, it's just that…" Harold's words faltered.

"It's just what?" questioned Rose, watching as a look of genuine dread crept across his face.

"It's just that I've never killed a man before." Harold wrung his hands in woe.

"Make no mistake, my friend, Parru St. Mime Dragonite is not a *man*. He is a monster!" declared Loken. The Sprite took to the air, hovering before this mortal's distraught face.

"A monster, you say," repeated Harold. He stared intently at Loken.

"I know better than all of you what that madman is truly capable of," continued the tiny being. "He is treacherous and devious, a master manipulator devoid of a conscience. Believe me when I say the world will be a far safer place without that maniac."

"I have no doubt you're speakin' the truth, my puny friend!" said Harold, "but still, I've never taken the life of another."

"And I intend to keep it that way, if you mean to continue on with us, Harold," assured Myron. He sympathized with his friend, knowing that this behemoth of a man would not even lift a finger to defend himself when town drunkards and bullies would regularly pick on him, beating him for sport because he was different.

"Truly?" asked Harold, his eyes opening wide in gratitude.

"There are few men meant to assume the role of a warrior, and you, my gentle friend, are not one of them," answered Myron. "And unless it is to spare your own life or the life of another, you should have no reason to bear arms against this enemy. This is what Tag and I are here for."

"Phew!" Harold unleashed an audible sigh of relief. "That's good to know. I'm more of a fretter than a fighter. I've certainly never wielded a sword before, renderin' me pretty useless, if I'm made to fight."

"Some are destined to serve in the knighthood," explained Myron, glancing at Tag, "while others like you are better served to cater to those trained in the way of the sword and shield."

"Like bein' a squire, but not goin' as far as becomin' a knight."

"Yes," said Tag. "And a worthy knight is nothing without a loyal squire by his side to aid him."

"I can be loyal that way," promised Harold, with a nod. "I can aid you both in this capacity! I'm just not keen on killin' anybody, evil or not, if you get my drift?"

"One must possess a strong constitution to commit such a grave deed, even if it is justified," added Rainus. "It is an action that should never be taken lightly, even if the enemy is deserving of this fate. Your hands are unsullied by the blood of others; better to keep it that way."

"Very true!" Harold nodded in agreement. "And I have every confidence we, or perhaps it's better to say, that all of you will deliver this fate the Sorcerer is deservin' of!"

"You are such an optimist," grumbled Rose, thoroughly agitated by his positive tone and cheerful disposition.

"Well, thank you, my lady!" responded Harold, bowing his head politely to her.

"It was not said as a compliment. It only means that you have no appreciation for the gravity of the situation."

"You're probably right," decided Harold. "Just the same, there's nothin' wrong with hopin' for the best."

"I recommend coming up with a workable plan that will guarantee the capture of the Sorcerer," suggested Rainus.

"By his very nature, he will not be caught out in the open. It will require luring that madman out of hiding and into a trap," said Myron, as he cogitated on a possible strategy.

"I've had a lot of experience huntin' and trappin' all sorts of clever critters," interjected Harold.

"So?" Rose snorted in derision.

"Well, I was just thinkin', most animals have a regular trail they use for foragin' and such, and the Sorcerer might have the same thing. I could use my trackin' skills to find the trail he's been usin' through this forest. If there is one, we could set up a snare, like what I'd use for rabbits."

"That is a stupid idea!" retorted Rose. "You cannot hope to capture a powerful bear using a trap designed for snaring a measly rabbit!"

"I understand where you are coming from Harold," said Myron, raising his hand for Rose's silence. "However, the Sorcerer isn't some animal meant to be tracked, hunted, and skinned like one of your fancy headpieces."

"Ewww!" groaned Harold, as he shuddered in disgust. "I can't imagine wearin' *him* on my head!"

"As I was saying," continued Myron, "the Sorcerer is a malicious soul with a cunning mind. And now, he seems imbued with increased powers, making him even more dangerous than we had at first anticipated. I see the merit in your plan, my friend, but Dragonite is clever enough to be wary of snares and such."

"I suppose you're right," sighed Harold. His heart sank as his hopes to aid his friends were effectively dashed. "But we still need to think up a way to capture the Sorcerer."

"Should we employ a trap, it will require a suitable bait, something that is desperately desired to lure its intended victim," said Tag. His eyes glanced over to Rose as he gave her a knowing smile.

"Hey! Do not look at me like I am a rancid piece of meat to bait your so-called trap! I already said 'no' when that madman demanded I marry him so he may acquire the throne of Fleetwood! I still refuse his proposal, especially now, as I am intended for another!"

"You are?" queried Rainus, momentarily stunned by her words.

"Yes, she is, but don't get her started," cautioned Tag, waving the Elf off to keep everyone focused on the matter at hand. "That is a whole other matter and we have more pressing issues to deal with at the moment."

"The point being," reminded Rose, "I refused that madman's proposal before, and I have even more reason to refuse him again!"

"I hardly think the Sorcerer wants to take your hand in marriage these days, my lady," responded Myron.

"Yes, I'm thinking he'd prefer to have your head... on a pike," Tag's words were matter-of-fact.

"Lovely! Absolutely lovely!" snapped Rose, as she jumped to her feet. "You want to sacrifice *me*, the Princess of Fleetwood? You want me to offer up my life so that demented soul can be captured? This is madness!"

"Do you have a better idea?" grumbled Tag.

"No! But any idea is better than the one you proposed!" Rose plopped back down on her chair. Her arms crossed her chest in stubborn defiance.

"You are the object of Dragonite's wrath, the one to set him on this path of destruction, Princess Rose." Rainus was quick to remind her. "You will make the most suitable *bait* to lure that villain out of hiding."

"So you say, but let me be absolutely clear about this, Lord Silverthorn. It is a horrible idea!"

"Why do you say so, Princess?" asked the Elf.

"Because I no longer possess the Dreamstone, that's why!" Rose raised her opened hands to show they were empty. "I hardly think that madman has any interest in me now, especially when he already possesses the cursed crystal."

"The Sorcerer's interest now is in possessing *you* for the sole purpose of exacting his revenge, for all the misery he believes was instigated by you, my lady," explained Myron. "He'd sooner see you dead than wed, there is no mistaking that."

"I take no comfort in your words, Myron Kendall!" declared Rose.

"Look here, Princess! We can either waste time searching for our elusive foe by following in the wake of his destruction, or we can draw him out, under our terms," reasoned Tag. "We have a chance to capture that demented soul before he does worse."

"Easy for you to say, my impudent friend! Just keep in mind both you and Myron are supposed to be protecting me, not offering me up to be sacrificed!"

"Do you honestly think we'd deliberately put you in harm's way?" grumbled Tag, rolling his eyes in frustration.

"Oh, absolutely! You've done it before. It's evident you'd willingly do it again!"

"I meant to say, we'd never deliberately put you in harm's way, not without having measures in place to keep you safe to begin with," responded Tag.

"Lord Silverthorn!"

All heads turned to spy upon Arissa. With silent steps, she rushed down the corridor toward the dining hall.

Rainus stood up to greet her. "What is it?"

"Come, my lord! It is Lady Silverthorn!"

"Has she taken a turn for the worst?" cried Rainus, as Arissa clasped his hands, urging him to follow.

"To the contrary, my lord! She asked for you!"

"The fever has broken?"

"Come see for yourself! I believe the medicine is working. The fever lingers, but she is not burning as she was before. Lady Silverthorn even has an appetite, requesting a bowl of vegetable broth to slake her thirst and to quell her hunger!"

"A miracle! Or at the very least, a good omen!" declared Rainus. He struggled to contain his excitement, even as the gleam in his eyes returned, as did the feeling of hope in his heart. "A very good omen, indeed! I shall see to her; offer my dear Valara another dose of that magical elixir while you warm some broth."

Rainus turned away, abandoning his company.

Rose and her comrades watched as he gleefully pranced down the corridor, disappearing inside the bedchamber where Valara now recuperated.

As the door latch clicked behind the elated Elf, Princess Rose turned her attention back to those sharing the table.

"Well… that was rude of him!"

"Lord Silverthorn is just eager to see how his wife is farin' now, my lady. You can't blame him, after all they've been through," responded Harold. "You should be happy for him."

"I *am* happy for him! Absolutely ecstatic!" snapped Rose. Her tone was sardonic as she heaved a disheartened sigh.

"You should be happy for yourself, too," added Harold, as he passed the platter of bread and cheese to her.

Rose merely responded by glaring through narrowed eyes levelled in resentment at the large man.

"If it wasn't for you, Loken, the young master and this great knight deliverin' the medicine, there's a chance Lady Silverthorn and the others might be worse off, or even dead now," continued Harold.

"Our friend speaks the truth, Princess Rose!" averred Loken. "This mission to deliver the medicine was not in vain. That is something positive, indeed."

"True enough, I suppose," said Rose. "However, it will all be in vain, if the Sorcerer is not stopped."

"Hence the reason we must devise a worthy plan to capture this wily adversary," reminded Myron.

"I still believe using Princess Rose to lure Dragonite out of hiding will be our best bet," said Tag.

"You must really hate me!" groaned Rose.

"You stand corrected, Princess. I hate some of the things you say and do, but you are not without *some* redeeming qualities," teased Tag.

"Somehow, coming from you, that did not sound like a compliment."

"Aside from it being my sworn duty to keep you safe, Princess, if I did not believe in these redeeming qualities you possess, then I would not be bothered in believing you have the good sense to do what must be done to bring Dragonite down upon his knees."

"I am no sycophant!" admonished Rose. "Flattery will get you nowhere, Tagius Yairet."

"Is that like a sick elephant?" queried Harold, never hearing of this word before. "If it is, you look nothin' like one, my lady."

"A sycophant, in this case, refers to one who can be plied with praise or flattery in order to curry favour or to take advantage of her position of power," answered Myron.

"Methinks I understand," said Harold, with a nod and a shrug.

"You know it is never my intention to ply you and that big ego of yours with false words of flattery, Princess. I just know that somewhere in your heart you know you will do what must be done to put things right," explained Tag.

"You think you know me so well!" grunted Rose.

"I have known you all your life, so yes, I do!"

Harold meekly raised his hand to speak.

"What is it now?" snapped Rose.

"I just wanted to say that even though I haven't known you for all that long, my lady, I'm pretty confident the young sir speaks the truth about you. I'm far from smart, but I'd say I'm still a pretty good judge of character."

"You don't say! And what judgement have you come to where I am concerned, dare I ask?"

"From what I've seen of you so far, I believe you know right from wrong, and bein' the princess you are, you'd always find it in your heart to do what's right 'cause that good nature is already in you."

Rose responded with a cynical roll of her eyes.

"Awww, come now, my lady! You know this young sir wouldn't bother speakin' of these fine qualities, if it weren't so!" insisted Harold. "And I truly believe your friends when they say they'd do everythin' in their powers to keep you safe, if you're willin' to do what you can to help capture the Sorcerer."

"Are you trying to guilt me into taking some kind of action, Harold?"

"I don't believe you're the type of person that can be guilted into takin' any kind of action, my lady. However, I do believe you have it in your heart to do what's right, when so many lives are countin' on you."

Rose's arms crossed her chest as she brooded, mulling over these words dispensed by Cadboll's reigning King of the Village Idiots.

"You mean to test me!"

"Good gracious, no, my lady!" responded Harold. "It isn't my place to test you, or anybody, for that matter! I'm just sayin' that I know you'll do the right thing."

"And that would imply sacrificing my life to capture the crazy Sorcerer."

"You know Tag and I will keep you safe. We would never let that happen, my lady," vowed Myron.

"At least, not deliberately," teased Tag, giving her a knowing wink.

"See, Princess Rose! You have nothin' to fear, if you trust your friends," assured Harold. "I'm not much good with a sword, but that doesn't mean I can't help to keep you safe durin' this quest, too."

"You, Harold Murkins, are far too trusting for your own good," retorted Rose.

"And I mean no disrespect to you, my lady, but it seems you're not trustin' enough. I just know I can trust the words of Myron Kendall and Tagius Yairet. If they say they'll do everythin' in their powers to keep you safe, then I believe, with every fibre of my bein', they'll do just that."

"Really!" Rose sniffed with obvious disdain at Harold's words that were meant to tug at her heart and conscience.

"You can't tell me, in your heart, that you trust neither one of them with your life. If that were so, you'd never have left the safety of Fleetwood to begin with. I'm pretty sure of that, my lady."

"What say you, Princess?" asked Myron.

"I say, let me think on it," answered Rose, intent on not making any immediate or foolhardy promises to her comrades.

"Very well. For now, we shall enjoy this food, quench our thirst, and then retire for the evening," suggested Myron. "After some much needed rest, we can have a fresh start in the morning."

"I agree," said Tag, stifling a yawn with one hand as the other reached for his wine goblet. "With clear minds and a fresh perspective, I am confident we can devise a foolproof plan that will see to the capture of Dragonite. If we can do so at minimal risk to you, is this something you will consider, Princess?"

"Minimal risk? What about at *no risk*?"

"I would be lying if I said that," confessed Tag. "We are all at risk in undertaking this enterprise."

"What we can do is to take measures to minimize the risks to your life, should you accept," said Myron.

"Do you promise to do all, in your combined powers, to keep me safe?" questioned Rose.

"Even I will do what I can to help, my lady," vowed Loken, his hand over heart in solemn promise.

"Come now, Princess! Between the noble Lord Silverthorn, this great knight, this incredible, shape-shifting Sprite and brave Harold to aid us in capturing the Sorcerer, what can go wrong?" asked Tag.

12

Your Logic is Simply Stupid

"Pssst! Pssssst!"

Like the buzz of a pesky mosquito hovering by her left ear, this sound droned in Rose's sleepy mind. Instead of opening her eyes, she rolled over onto her stomach, hoping to steal away with more sleep. Burying her face in the soft, rose-scented pillow, she clamped it firmly over her ears in hopes of smothering this bothersome noise.

"Pssst! Princess Rose, wake up!"

"Go away!" Rose's words were muffled, delivered through the down-filled pillow. "It is much too early for anyone or anything."

"Morning has broken. The sun is on the rise," announced Loken. He jumped up and down on the corner of this pillow, pestering her to get up. "There is much to do, my lady."

"Then why do you not go and wake the others first?"

"The others are up, dressed and ready to meet the new day." The Sprite's voice tightened with annoyance to see that she was unmoved. Bouncing off the pillow and into the air, Loken hovered above her head. His wings thrummed loudly in an obvious bid to make sure this mortal did not fall back to sleep. "In fact, our friends gather in the dining room as we speak, to break their fast in the company of Lord Silverthorn."

"Tell those eager early birds to go ahead; start without me. I will join them when I am good and ready to do so."

Loken unleashed a dreary sigh as he spoke, "So you say, my lady! Just know that the day waits for no one, not even for royalty. If you see fit *not* to partake in breakfast or to share in the planning to capture the dreaded Sorcerer, our friends will be quite happy to make these plans without you."

"Sounds good to me, Loken." Rose answered through a stifled yawn.

"Very well, my lady. I will inform Tag to proceed. He will be more than pleased to elaborate on this scheme he is cooking up!"

Rose's head popped off the pillow. Bolting upright, she glared menacingly at Loken as she growled, "He would not dare!"

"I believe the young man is ready to do just that," argued Loken, with a nod of confirmation. "Your absence, this failure to have a say in the planning when you have an opportunity to do so, speaks volumes of your indifference. This alone is sufficient licence for Tag and the others to scheme away; concocting a plan without you."

Rose flopped over onto her back, squinting as the golden sunlight seeping through the cracks and seams of the window shutters stabbed at her eyes.

"You are being impossible!" groaned Rose.

"I beg to differ, my lady, but worry not. You just rest that weary, little head of yours. I will tell them to proceed without you," offered Loken, as he alighted upon the headboard of her warm, cosy bed to issue this final warning.

"I think not!" snapped Rose. "Tell the others I will not be long. Tell them to go ahead and eat without me, but until I am there to have my say, they are not to utter one word of a plan until I am present to voice my opinion on this matter."

"As you wish," said Loken, as he bowed politely.

Rose watched as the Sprite took flight, launching into the air. Circling above her once, Loken dove down, exiting the bedchamber through the gap between the closed door and the floor.

"Well, good morning to you, Princess!" greeted Tag. "It's about time you saw fit to grace us with your presence!"

He watched as Harold politely excused himself from the table first before coming to Rose's aid. He pulled the unoccupied chair away from the table to seat her next to Rainus Silverthorn.

"It is never a good morning when the first thing I wake to is a menacing little Sprite trying to coerce me from my warm bed, and then I'm subjected to seeing your smug face at the breakfast table," grumbled Rose. She sat upright like a proper, young lady as Harold pushed her chair closer to the table.

"Here you go," offered Rainus. Pouring a tall glass of apple cider, he passed it to her. "This will wake you up. It is a sure cure to clear away those cobwebs, Princess."

"Thank you," said Rose.

Accepting the beverage, she took several large, unladylike gulps to quench her thirst. The sweet orchard apples pulverized and squeezed together with the tart, wild crabapples combined to create a delightful, but not too sweet, beverage. Freshly pressed, it lacked the kick of alcohol usually associated with most ciders.

"This is truly delightful!" exclaimed Rose. She used a linen napkin to daintily blot away the dribble of cider running down her chin.

"Indeed!" said Rainus, topping up her glass. "It is a refreshing way to start the day. Now, drink and eat up!"

He slid a covered serving dish before Rose. Lifting the silver lid, he presented to her some dried, pitted prunes.

Rose's pert, little nose abruptly wrinkled with obvious disdain, becoming as crinkled as the shrivelled skin of the prunes she was gawking at.

Harold placed a bowl of warm porridge before her. "Here you go, my lady. Some of these prunes atop of this mush with a dollop of honey and cream will fill you right up. It'll stick to your ribs; keep you goin' through the mornin' and longer!"

"Fresh plums I can tolerate, but more so when served up in a tasty dessert. However, whether dried or stewed, I *do not* eat prunes," explained Rose, pushing the silver bowl and the serving of porridge away.

"You're not hungry?" asked Harold.

"I am famished! But my delicate constitution prevents me from dining like a peasant, or in this case, like an Elf. I would fare better with two soft-boiled eggs, several thick slices of well-fried bacon or smoked ham served with some lightly buttered toast on the side."

"I am sorry to disappoint you, Princess Rose," apologized the Elf, "but did you forget that my people thrive on what *grows* from the ground than what *walks* on it?"

"I did not forget, my lord. It was just wishful thinking on my part. I thought that perhaps you had some regular food stuffs on hand for occasions such as this."

"Had I known of your coming in advance, I would have made special provisions," answered Rainus. "Unfortunately for you, I was too distracted of late, so please accept my apologies for falling short of your expectations, Princess Rose."

"No need to apologize, Lord Silverthorn," assured Myron. "You have been more than hospitable and accommodating. Princess Rose will graciously dine on this lovely meal that was prepared for us, prunes included."

"No, I will not!" insisted Rose. She arms crossed her chest, turning her nose up like a spoiled child at the bowl of dried fruit she had pushed away.

"Yes, you will!" countered Tag. He slid the serving of prunes back before her. "If you know what's good for you, you'll eat them! And just be grateful Lord Silverthorn saw fit to house and feed us, when he didn't have to."

Rose scowled like a brat on the verge of a tantrum.

"Come now, Princess," urged Tag, his silver spoon tapping the side of the serving dish. "Need I remind you what happened the last time you declared how much you hated prunes after your first encounter with Pancecelia Feldspar?"

"No need for that," sighed Rose.

"Well then, do the mature thing. Prove me wrong," urged Tag. He took up the delicate, silver serving tongs. Plucking up the biggest prune in the dish, he placed this single, dried fruit atop her porridge. "Eat what's good for you."

All watched as Rose grimaced in distaste.

"I fail to see why so many find prunes so detestable," noted Rainus. Holding between his index finger and thumb what looked like a giant raisin, he admired the dried, chewy plum. "These little gems are very tasty and nutritious! Plus, they will help to keep you regular, if you get my meaning?"

"Yes, Lord Silverthorn, I do. My dear mother would sing its praises, too, and with as much zeal." Rose sighed in resignation as she stared at the slovenly fruit crowning her bowl of porridge. "However, can we discuss matters more important than the dietary benefits of eating prunes?"

"Absolutely!" The Elf nodded in agreement. "So, my friends! Have you settled on a plan? One that is sure to stop the Sorcerer in his tracks?"

Tag took a moment to swallow his food, washing down the mouthful with a gulp of apple cider. "We did come up with one plan last night during your absence, Lord Silverthorn, but sadly, it was one not to Princess Rose's liking."

"Who said she had to like it?" questioned Rainus. "As long as it works, no disrespect to Princess Rose, but who really cares?"

"I most certainly do!" declared Rose, jamming her spoon into her bowl like she was stabbing the porridge in case it came to life.

"Of course you do, my dear," acknowledged Rainus, with a polite nod of his head, "but it does not change the fact that the needs of the many greatly outweigh the wants of the few, or in this case, *you*. And besides, are you not reputed for loving your desserts?"

"Who in their right mind does not love sweets?" Rose answered sheepishly as she thought on how many battles had been waged against her mother when Queen Beatrice would cajole, threaten and beg her to eat a proper meal first, rather than indulging in desserts as her main meal at each sitting. "In my way of thinking, dessert is the most important part of every meal, but what does this have to do with anything?"

"Just think of this as receiving a big dollop of *just desserts*, for what was initially instigated by you, Princess."

"Good gracious, Lord Silverthorn! You are sounding rather bitter," noted Rose, inwardly cringing from the sting of his words.

"In truth, I do believe I am sounding *better*, not bitter, thanks to my dear wife now being well on her way to a full recovery." Rainus smiled cheerfully. "For the first time in days, I had a restful night of sleep. My disposition has improved immensely, and does so accordingly as Valara's condition improves."

"Excellent!" said Myron. The knight nodded in approval upon hearing this joyful news. "Trust me when I say we are all relieved and pleased to hear that Lady Silverthorn is on the mend."

"Excellent, indeed!" exclaimed Rose, her hands clapping together in delight. "And knowing that Lady Silverthorn is recovering, thanks to *my* efforts to deliver the lifesaving medicine to her and your ailing people, does this not lessen the burden of blame on me?"

Rainus stared, mulling over her words.

"Well? What say you, my lord?" hoped Rose.

"You and your friends must be commended on your valiant efforts to deliver the medicine, but no, it does not lessen your blame or responsibility, Princess Rose. And, if you had any moral scruples, you would take full responsibility for all that has transpired, no thanks to you!"

"For pity's sake, Lord Silverthorn!" groaned Rose. "For a noble Elf you are rather unforgiving."

"And you, my lady, are being rather selective in terms of your memory. Need I remind you of how many of my people, my courageous warriors, had died all in a bid to aid you in reclaiming that cursed Dreamstone you had so coveted?"

"I'm not going to say *I told you so*," said Tag, offering her a smug grin, "but you must admit, Lord Silverthorn has a valid point, Princess."

"Now, now!" chimed in Harold. "Give her a chance! She'll make things right. That's what real princesses do! Isn't that so, my lady?"

Rose heaved a dreary sigh, her eyes rolling upon hearing Harold's hopeful words.

"You are a real princess, right?" queried Harold, staring earnestly at Rose.

"Of course, I am!"

"See, my friends!" Harold's eyes shone with genuine admiration as he smiled at her. "Princess Rose will put things right! She'll do the noble thing by fixin' this mess she started up."

Tag shook his head as he addressed the gullible, but optimistic man. "I do believe your trust in her is misplaced, Harold."

"Hey…" growled Rose. Her eyes were like daggers as she glared at Tag. "Are you saying I am *not* to be trusted? That I am incapable of taking matters into my own hands to right a wrong?"

Without blinking an eye, Tag responded: "Pretty much!"

"How dare you?" Rose shook a clenched fist at Tag. "I will show you, you rapscallion of a knave!"

"No disrespect to you, Princess, but ultimately, words mean nothing," mocked Tag, pretending his hand was a sock puppet addressing her with mute words. "Your actions, or lack thereof, will speak volumes. Just remember, good intentions mean nothing, if they are not backed by meaningful action."

"Damn you, Tag! I'll show you the meaning of taking appropriate actions!"

Rose rammed her spoon into the bowl of porridge, stuffing the whole prune and a great scoop of oatmeal into her mouth. As though she was drunk on power, she continued her angry tirade, food spewing from her mouth as she made it clear to all, "I will eat this damned prune! I shall devour this damned mush of a meal! And then, we – as in all of us – shall get down to the business of capturing that damned Sorcerer, once and for all!"

"Oh, my! She does mean business!" exclaimed Harold. His eyes shone with admiration, inspired by her fiery nature and take-control attitude.

"Brilliant!" said Tag. Pleased to see this no-nonsense approach Rose had suddenly adopted, he was inwardly surprised to see her devour her meal without another word of complaint.

"Brilliant?" Rose snorted in doubt as she choked down a mouthful. "Well, prove to me how brilliant you are by devising a plan that will see to Dragonite's capture without getting me killed in the process, or so help me, Tag, if I die, I am so going to kill you!"

Harold frowned upon hearing this strange threat, but it was one that did not seem to faze those sharing the breakfast table.

"How do you plan on killin' the young master, if you're already dead, my lady?" questioned Harold. He scratched his head in thought as he pondered her threat. "Seems like an impossible feat, unless you call upon the forbidden arts to do so, and I really wouldn't recommend doin' that!"

Rose unleashed a disgruntled sigh that sent the oatmeal she was in the midst of swallowing to dribble down her chin. She wiped her mouth on the napkin, as she answered, "Of course I cannot kill Tag, if I'm already dead! The point being, he better come up with a plan that *will not* see me killed or there will be dire consequences, one way or the other!"

"Oh! So this is like the *ultimate* threat," determined Harold, nodding in understanding. "Like when someone says, '*I'll give you what for*', but you don't know what that *what for* is, but chances are it'll be really bad."

Loken took to the air, hovering before the large man's round face. "We have gotten used to how Princess Rose speaks. It is apparent to me, you are coming around now, garnering a better understanding of how her mind works."

"Hush, you little imp! And never you mind, Tag! I prefer to hear from one truly capable of effective planning." Rose shoved her empty bowl away, clearing space in front of her so she can have fist-thumping room to punctuate her feisty words, in case she was not taken seriously. Turning to the Elf, she addressed him, "So, Lord Silverthorn, in all your wisdom, have you thought of a foolproof plan?"

Rainus lifted a single finger, motioning her to give him a moment to swallow the sip of cider before addressing her question.

After doing so, the Elf's response was blunt: "No."

"No, as in you have not yet devised a clever plan that will *not* see me killed in the process of capturing Dragonite? Or no, you have no plan, whatsoever? Nothing at all?"

"In my defence, Princess Rose, I was busy tending to my wife. I left the five of you to put your heads together to come up with a workable plan. Remember?"

"Yes, yes! I remember now," muttered Rose, as she turned to Myron for a solution. "So, Sir Kendall, before Tag serves up one of his cockamamie plans that will likely lead to my untimely demise, did you come up with something brilliant?"

"I have a plan, but how brilliant it is may be called into question by some," answered Myron.

"This does not sound promising," responded Rose.

"Let the man speak," urged Loken, his wings rattling loudly in annoyance. "Go on, my friend! What is this plan of yours?"

"Yes, do share, but please refrain, if it includes sacrificing my life," interjected Rose.

"I tossed and turned most of last night," confessed Myron. "I was vexed, searching for a possible solution; a grand and elaborate plan to be deployed with the greatest results at minimal risk not just to you, my lady, but to all concerned."

"Oh, my! This sounds promisin'," said Harold, leaning forward to learn more.

"Hush!" ordered Rose. "Allow him to speak!"

Harold appeared contrite as he pursed his lips together, pressing his plump, sausage finger against them to demonstrate his compliance to her order as he nodded in understanding.

"Yes, do share in this plan," urged Tag, waving Myron on to continue.

"After much thought and deliberation late into the night, Harold's idea of setting a trap repeatedly came to mind," revealed the knight.

"I am not liking the sounds of this," moaned Rose.

"Well, in my humble opinion, I have come to the conclusion that Harold's plan offers us the most promising and practical option," responded Myron.

"This is madness!" gasped Rose. "No offence to your behemoth friend, but how can a simple plan concocted by the mind of an equally simple man be any kind of option, at all?"

"It is logical, my lady, because a simple plan is the last thing that maniac would anticipate from us," explained Myron.

"Your logic is simply stupid," complained Rose.

"You speak in haste, my lady," said Loken, marching across the table to address her concerns. "Over the course of a decade, I have had the ill fortune of becoming well acquainted with that necromancer. This knight is quite correct where Dragonite is concerned."

"How so? Do explain," demanded Rose, forcing herself to listen to the words of this Sprite.

"That madman, being the egomaniac he is, will automatically assume that if a trap were laid out to capture him, it will be something very elaborate! Something he believes worthy of him; requiring great effort to capture a criminal mastermind."

"The Sorcerer is definitely a criminal, but he can hardly be described as a mastermind of any kind," countered Tag.

"I know that, and that is exactly the point," said Loken, taking to the air to hover before Tag's frowning visage. "Parru St. Mime Dragonite is a legend in his own warped mind! He is pompous, arrogant, egotistical, and above all else, he is in dire need of believing he is much smarter than all of us combined."

"Therefore, he will automatically assume a great and elaborate plan is in the works, one so intricate it will become a testament to his self-proclaimed brilliance," said Rainus.

"He will expect nothing less." Loken nodded in agreement.

"I do believe I know what you are all getting at," said Tag, nodding in approval. "And you must admit, Princess, Loken does know the habits of our nemesis better than any of us."

"Good gracious!" groaned Rose, her eyes rolling in frustration as she glanced over at Tag. "It makes sense you would understand this 'simple' plan, but someone, please explain it to me! Obviously, I am much too intelligent to understand it!"

"Think on it, my lady," urged Myron. "If the enemy is expecting his adversaries to engage him in an elaborate game, one that will pit him in a deadly sport to outwit him, especially now, as he lacks the military might to overpower us with physical strength, then would it not serve our purpose to do what he is *not* expecting?"

Rose's index finger tapped her chin as she mulled over these words.

"So, I take it, you are devising a simple plan," determined Rose, "one that is so unpretentious, so unassuming, the Sorcerer is sure to suspect nothing?"

"Exactly!" Myron answered with a confident smile.

"So, this is not a matter of you regressing back to being a simple man liking simple things, simply because you are a simpleton once more?" queried Rose, as she scrutinized with a degree of concern this knight.

"Absolutely not!"

"Then correct me if I am wrong. It is to take advantage of that madman through the element of surprise, catch him unawares, so to speak," said Rose.

"Yes," responded Myron.

"It is brilliant, I tell you! And when has the element of surprise ever failed us?" added Tag, giving her a sly wink as his index finger tapped the side of his nose. "It has served us well before. It shall do so again."

"I will give you that, Tag. But what do we truly know of Dragonite's military might at this point?" questioned Rose. "There is nothing to say his mimes have regrouped under his banner. Worse yet, suppose he has acquired a legion of mercenaries trained in the art of war to reinforce his army of miming rabbles? If this is so, you know, as well as Myron does, this can prove to be most devastating!"

"Allow me to address your concerns, my lady," offered Rainus.

"Please do!"

"In our search for answers to uncover the source of this illness that ravaged my people, Captain Ironwood and my warriors had conducted an intensive search of my domain. They did not uncover one sign of an army, mime nor mercenary, loyal to the Sorcerer."

"That sounds promising, but there is nothing to say Dragonite has not secreted them away, hiding them from our sights, until he is ready to strike," responded Rose.

"I know every inch of my forest," assured Rainus. "My people know this realm. Whether it is an army of bumbling mimes or a legion of seasoned assassins, they would not be able to hide from our eyes."

"You sound so very confident, Lord Silverthorn," said Rose.

"I *am* confident, but if you recall your past misadventures where that necromancer was concerned, in all your experiences, was the presence of his mimes not the precursor to Dragonite making his appearance?"

"Lord Silverthorn does have a legitimate point." Tag nodded in agreement. "Before we ever encountered the Sorcerer, we *always* met up first with one or more of his ridiculous minions."

"You must remember, Princess Rose, Dragonite is not just an evil creature, he is a creature of habit," stated Loken. "More than his loyal mimes were ever an effective army to defend his territory or to fight on his behalf, they were nothing more than a physical barrier or obstacle between us and him; completely disposable."

"So, you are suggesting that the mimes were near to the Sorcerer to forewarn him of our approach?" asked Rose. "To use them as a feeble line of defence or distraction, so he could launch an attack or execute his escape?"

"I'd say it is a fair assessment," answered Rainus, as he nodded to Rose. "Loken can vouch that Dragonite never cared about the body count, even where his army was concerned."

"When we were first made to battle him in the Land of Small, Dragonite didn't hesitate to kill the mimes that failed to act in accordance to his plans," reminded Tag.

"More than those fools were a source of entertainment to him, the Sorcerer merely used those idiots, plus, they never talked back to him," added Loken. "I know with all certainty that more often than not, Dragonite used his *silent* network of mimes to warn him of your presence, my lady. It was the reason why you and your comrades would run into his mimes well before you would encounter him! And you must admit, it has occurred on more than one occasion."

"Think of it as an advance warning system, a way to alert the Sorcerer of our approach, for you know firsthand those mimes were rather useless when it came to actually fighting," said Tag.

"I think I understand, young master," said Harold, giving Tag, and then the Sprite a thoughtful nod.

"You do?" Rose frowned in doubt, even as she spied the flicker of comprehension burning in Harold's eyes.

"Yes, my lady! Those mimes were used like the way farmers use hounds on their property to warn them if a fox comes sniffin' around their chicken coops. The hounds would either chase off, chase down or, at the very least, start barkin' and howlin' to warn the farmer he's about to lose a hen or two, if he doesn't take action."

"That's a simplistic way of saying it, my friend, but yes!" said Rainus.

Harold's eyes grew large in amazement. "Huzzah! I must be gettin' smarter associatin' with intelligent folks like you."

"I hardly think you're getting smarter, Harold. You probably had no reason to even think of such things before now," said Rose, with a dismal shake of her head.

"True enough, my lady." Harold bowed his head in humility. "But I'd like to believe I'm gettin' smarter because your smarts are rubbin' off on me!"

"*Ewww!*" groaned Rose, shuddering at the thought. "Trust me when I say I have no desire to rub *any* of me off on to you!"

Tag rolled his eyes as he grumbled at Rose, "Come now! Be nice for a change. You know Harold meant to pay you a compliment. He believes you are smart, probably even smarter than anyone has ever given you credit for!"

Rose stared at Harold. With an equal measure of contempt and confusion she eyed the man as she assessed Tag's explanation.

"A compliment, you say?"

"Absolutely, my lady, the most sincerest of compliments, not some hollow words to feign flattery," promised Harold.

"Truly?" Rose's perfect brows arched up in surprise to hear the sincerity in his voice.

"I honestly believe a person's character can be defined by the company he keeps!" confided Harold. "In my humble opinion, stupid breeds stupid. I truly believe that bein' in your esteemed company, and bein' in the presence of these brave and noble men here to protect you, it has made me a better person! I suppose I'm bein' forced to use my noggin like never before!"

"Well, when you put it like that, I suppose it is understandable." Rose smiled kindly at Harold. "After all, I've been told I can be very influential, when I want to be."

"I'll tell you now, Princess, I'll have words of flattery to dispense, too, once you help us with this plan Myron speaks of," promised Tag.

"Well then, let us get down to business," urged Rose. "Just what is this '*simple*' plan you have so much faith in?"

Myron pushed aside the dirty dishes as he spoke, "Pretend this area

I cleared is the Enchanted Forest."

"My domain is expansive, Sir Kendall. Which part of the forest do you speak of?" asked Rainus.

Taking the covered serving dish of prunes, Myron placed it before him. "This represents the community of Driven Hill."

Placing his fork and spoon parallel to each other just above this silver bowl, he continued, "To the north of here is a gully, as represented by the cutlery. Now, if we position Princess Rose here…"

Myron reached for what was left of the loaf of bread. Tearing off a small chunk to represent Rose, he placed the piece of crust between the fork and spoon.

"So, I take it, the plan is to use me as bait, after all?"

"As dreadful as it sounds, my lady, you know as well as I do, you are the one sure thing, possibly our best hope, to draw Dragonite out of hiding," reminded Myron.

"Are you daft? Placing me smack dab in the middle of this trap sounds highly dangerous and rather irresponsible of you," insisted Rose. She struggled to remain calm as Myron's plans unfolded before her, but not in the way she had hoped. "I thought you said you had devised a strategy that would have minimal risk to all."

"Allow Myron to finish," urged Tag, motioning to her for silence.

"Fine!" She snapped in annoyance and in ever-growing fear. "Carry on with this plan of yours!"

"This natural depression in the forest, by its very design and placement, is the perfect location to execute our plan," explained Myron, pointing to the sides of the cutlery. "This gully provides the necessary cover, places for us to hide, so that you, my lady, will appear to be alone and defenceless, but that will be far from true. We will be right there, in close proximity to keep you safe."

"That is true," agreed Rainus, with a thoughtful nod. "The natural terrain rising up from this gully will offer a high vantage point. And with the undergrowth and trees for concealment, one can safely and discreetly observe for approaching danger, or in this case, the Sorcerer as he approaches."

"So you say! But when you tell me that you will be '*right there*', you mean to say that you will be right next to me?" hoped Rose. "Within arm's-length, is that not so?"

"We will be close enough to keep you safe, but far enough that the Sorcerer's suspicions will not be roused," answered Myron, tearing off more pieces of bread to represent the Elf, the Sprite, Tag and the final piece to symbolize himself. He strategically placed these pieces near and around the crust representing the Princess.

"That is somewhat reassuring," noted Rose. She reached over, swapping the largest piece representing Tag for hers.

"Why did you do that?" questioned Tag.

"I am a princess, therefore, I should be represented by the largest crust."

"Makes sense," grunted Tag. "By your temperament you are the *crustiest*, after all."

"We digress!" announced Myron, steering the conversation back on course.

"So, when the Sorcerer approaches, the trap will be deployed to capture him?" asked Rose.

"That is exactly what he will expect," said Myron.

"So, you intend to spring the trap before he gets too close?" questioned Rose.

"Yes, and as he will be wary, anticipating a trap as he nears, we shall take added measures," replied Myron.

"What are these measures?" Rose listened intently.

"Not only will we place a snare to trap him when he comes to confront you, but we shall place a trap here… and here."

The knight placed Rose's goblet at one end of the ravine and his at the opposite end to represent the traps.

"By the lay of the land, Dragonite will be forced to advance from either the north or the south. If we set two more traps, as such, we stand to triple our chances than to deploy a single trap where he will most likely suspect one will be set. If done just so, we can capture the fiend before he even becomes aware of them or us."

"We can devise other 'tools' to improve our chances of capturing Dragonite," said Rainus. "This gully is perfectly designed for it."

"But suppose the Sorcerer – " Rose's question was abruptly cut short as Rainus sat upright, raising a hand for silence. His ears pricked up as his eyes glanced toward the door of his royal residence.

"What is it?" asked Tag, twisting about to peer over his shoulder.

"Someone approaches," announced Rainus. His keen ears detected footfalls only an Elf can hear. These footsteps were heading toward his home. By these hurried strides, he sensed the urgency.

Rainus crossed the room, positioning himself behind the door. He placed his hand upon the door handle.

Pausing for a moment to consider the approaching footsteps, Rainus flung the door wide open. To the surprise of all, Halen Ironwood rushed into the room, raising a hand in a gesture of hurried salutations as Rainus waved him on to join them at the table.

"I come with news – " Halen's sentence was cut short by Rose's scolding.

"Thank goodness it is only you, Captain Ironwood!" Rose breathed a sigh of relief, before turning to Rainus to admonish him. "It would serve you well, Lord Silverthorn, not to open doors willy-nilly without knowing who is standing on the other side first! For all we knew, he could have been the crazed Sorcerer standing there!"

"Forgive me for causing you undue stress." Rainus bowed his head apologetically to Rose. "However, I knew the exact identity of Captain Ironwood as he approached my residence."

"Really? And just how is that even possible?"

"In case you have forgotten, we are gifted with exceptional hearing. From the resonance of his footfalls and by the length of his strides I could tell it was one of my kin. In this case, I was expecting Halen's return."

"Fine!" Rose grunted, before turning to the Elf. "What news do you bring, Captain?"

"As I was saying," continued Halen, "I have urgent news to share with all."

"Why else would you be here?" Rose snapped with impatience. "Details, please!"

"Oh, my! You are in a mood most foul." Halen frowned with concern. "Should I ask?"

"Of course I am in a foul mood! My life is being risked once again to capture that crazy Sorcerer! Now, share in this news you spoke of!"

"As you wish, my lady," responded Halen, turning to address Rainus. "I was about to say, my men and I were searching the forest as you had requested, my lord, when we spied upon a cloaked and hooded figure lurking about. We knew not of his identity and when I demanded he reveal his name and business in our forest, the stranger defied my order."

"Did he attack you?" asked Loken, as he hovered before the Elf's face.

"Not at first." Halen shook his head. "The scoundrel dashed away; racing eastward toward the Land of Small. He was determined to evade us, however at one point, we almost had him cornered."

"What happened?" asked Myron.

"That fiend unleashed a fiery ball of light at us! We managed to duck out of the way, but this blast struck an old oak tree. Its very limbs and trunk groaned with pain. The tree was dying before our very eyes. Not only did it burn on contact, its bark blackened, spreading throughout its branches and autumn-hued leaves. As though afflicted with a strange disease, its remaining leaves were abruptly shed, falling upon us like a terrible, black rain."

"What about this mysterious stranger?" asked Myron.

"Yes," added Tag. "It was Dragonite, wasn't it?"

"He made good his escape as we dove for cover. As for his identity, due to his propensity for dangerous magic, I would say, and my men will agree, it had to be Dragonite."

"Are you positive?" questioned Rainus.

"It makes sense." Halen's words were spoken with conviction. "Though the shadow of his hood shielded his face from our eyes, by his very actions, I would say it is a fair assumption, my lord."

"Of course it was the demented Dragonite," insisted Rose. "I cannot think of another being that would dare lurk around as this fiend does! If it sneaks around like the Sorcerer, if it fails to yield to your command; then it can be no one else but the Sorcerer!"

"I'd say it is better to err on the side of caution," suggested Myron. "We are best to proceed with due care; to handle the situation no differently as we had planned. Even if Dragonite is not the guilty culprit, let us keep our wits about us, for we must keep in mind that we are dealing with a murderous villain."

"You do not attack a battalion of armed Elves unless the intention is to kill or be killed," stated Rainus.

"This villain has the way to dispense dark magic," reminded Loken, his wings rattled nervously. "We are safer to proceed as though we are hunting that necromancer, even if we are not."

"For once, I could not agree with you more, Loken," said Rose, nodding in approval to the Sprite.

Rainus stood up from the table as he addressed his company. "Breakfast is over, my friends. It is time to resume the hunt."

"Let us gather our weapons first," said Myron. "We shall meet back here as soon as we are ready."

"Make haste," urged Rainus. "Halen, bring to me my vest of mail, my sword and bow, as well as a full quiver."

"Yes, my lord." Halen bowed in respect before departing to gather these items. "I will not be long."

"You found them!" exclaimed Rose.

She rushed over to greet her mare. Petting its velvety muzzle, Rose was never so glad to see this horse safe, saddled and ready to go, along with Myron and Tag's steeds. Though she was never particularly fond of horses, she despised nothing more than being made to walk.

"Yes, my lady," said Halen, giving her a leg up onto her mount. "We found them late last night, not far from the ravine of yesterday's mishap."

"Bolting away as they did, these poor creatures must have been so nervous. Were they difficult to catch?" she asked, as she eased herself into the saddle.

"No, my lady. With some Elvish words of encouragement to settle their rattled nerves, these horses were easy to corral and capture. They were brought here where my page groomed, fed and watered them before retiring them in our stable. They settled right in with Master Murkins' donkey to keep them company through the night."

"Thank you very much, Captain Ironwood," said Tag, as he hoisted himself onto his gelding's back. "This will help immensely! We can cover far more ground on horseback than on foot."

"You are welcome, young sir," said the Elf, as he collected his mount to join them.

Settling onto his steed's back, Rainus called to his captain, "Halen!"

"Yes, my lord?"

"Show us the way," ordered Rainus, motioning for him to take the lead. "Take us on the most direct path to where you lost sight of the Sorcerer."

Halen Ironwood nodded as he mounted his steed. "Of course! Follow me."

As though the captain's steed read his mind, the horse nickered under the Elf's shifting weight. The horse pranced about, turning eastward with barely a tug of the reins or a prod from the Elf's boots to urge it onward.

Rainus followed directly behind, shadowed by Tag, Myron, Rose, and a dozen Elven warriors armed to the hilt, for an added measure of protection.

"Hey! What about me?" hollered Harold. He watched in disbelief as the Elves and his friends began to ride away, abandoning him. He was left standing there with Sassy's reins held taut in his hands, as he urged the obstinate beast to move.

"You will never keep up, Harold!" Myron shouted over his shoulder as he steered his stallion away. "We have no time to lose! Stay safe! Wait here for our return!"

Loken hovered momentarily before Harold's distraught face. "No worries, my friend. We shouldn't be long."

"But I really want to help!" Harold heaved a disheartened sigh of dejection, watching as the others disappeared into the surrounding forest.

"I understand, but it is not as though you can ride your little donkey, or even run for as long and as fast to keep up with these great horses."

"True enough, but I was thinkin' I would eventually catch up, if I tried really hard. After all, I did it before, I'm sure I can do it again."

"You should be commended for your efforts, Harold, but the Enchanted Forest is not a safe place for you, especially if you attempt to travel alone."

"I know that, but I'm willin' to take the risk!"

"That would be a foolish thing to do."

"But suppose somethin' bad happens and they need my help again? Then what? I'd be feelin' pretty badly, like I had deserted them in their most dire moment, if somethin' tragic should happen."

"Just as our friends would feel as bad, if not worse, should evil befall *you*," explained Loken, his wings thrumming with nervous energy in his eagerness to catch up to the others.

"Well, you just go on without me," insisted the crestfallen mortal. Harold sighed while Sassy brayed with delight when the reins fell slack in his grip, signifying she was not about to be forced to trot along to keep up with her master.

Loken scrutinized the large man. With a disgruntled huff, the Sprite admonished Harold. "You stubborn fool! You have no intention of staying put. Am I correct?"

Harold said nothing in response. He stared at the ground, nervously flicking a stone with the toe of his boot.

"Look me in the eyes, sir," ordered Loken, as he hovered before the mortal's face. "I get the sense you will come chasing after us as soon as I disappear from your sight."

The mortal's face burned with embarrassment as his eyes pulled away from Loken's unyielding stare.

"Fine! Leave the donkey here," snapped Loken. "If you insist on following, then you best keep up with the others. Hop on my back!"

"No offence, but are you mad, Master Loken? I'll crush you like a bug!" gasped Harold. His eyes were large in dismay as he stared at the tiny being. "I don't want to be doin' that!"

"Give me a moment," demanded Loken. In a brilliant flash of light the Sprite transformed!

When the flare of light dimmed, Harold's eyes bulged as he stared at Loken's newly adopted form.

Standing proudly before him was a magnificent, snowy white unicorn that stood at least three hands higher at the withers than the largest horse Harold had ever seen. A gentle breeze sent the flowing, silky white mane and tail rippling in its wake while an exquisite, smoothly polished horn that spiralled from his forehead glistened in the golden sun. Loken's new form pawed at the earth, eager to be on his way.

"Oh, my! Is that really you, Master Loken?" Harold gasped in awe as he admired this splendid specimen of a unicorn.

"Of course! What can be more suitable and more natural than a unicorn galloping through this forest? It was either this, or to morph into a hulking big ox, one large enough to carry your ample weight. Now, hop on and be quick about it!"

"No saddle? No reins?" asked Harold, wondering how he was to get on without the aid of stirrups. "How am I to stay on or steer you?"

"Do you trust me?"

"Of course I trust you."

"Then just get on and hold tight," ordered Loken. His hooves clattered as he pranced about with growing impatience, angling closer to the fence. "Now hurry!"

"If you insist," said Harold.

Hitching Sassy to the fence post so she wouldn't stray in his absence, Harold clambered onto the rails of the fence. Clumsily climbing onto Loken's broad back, he grabbed hold of this thick mane.

Before he could tell Loken he was ready to go, the Sprite's unicorn form reared about, pushing off the earth to bolt away. In a thunderous clatter of hooves, Loken sped off with Harold holding on for dear life.

Taking the most direct route, Loken crashed through the undergrowth, careering through the great stands of trees. With head held high and muzzle held low, the spiral horn on his forehead worked like a wedge to part the vegetation away from his eyes as he forged on. These branches parted as he charged ahead, only to come together in his wake to slap Harold in his face.

With this thrashing by branches smacking his cheeks and forehead, Harold was forced to close his eyes. He leaned low over this unicorn's neck; holding on tight and praying Loken would catch up with the others soon so this harrowing ride can come to an end.

Above the thundering of these powerful hooves, Harold could hear Loken's laboured breaths as jets of spent air gushed from his heaving lungs through his flaring nostrils. With great, galloping strides, he swore he could feel the Sprite's heart hammering through this equine form and straight through his own body.

Harold couldn't tell if he was just more responsive to all these sounds and sensations because his eyes were closed, or if the physical exertion of racing at full speed in this new shape was taking its toll on the Sprite. Perhaps these cues were indicative that Loken's adopted form was about to keel over due to the monumental exertion required to run while carrying such a heavy load.

This thrashing of tree branches ended abruptly. Harold's eyes snapped open when he heard a voice shout out, *"HALT!"*

Loken burst into a clearing, his hooves sinking into the earth. Unable to stop in time, he reared up, twisting about to send his passenger tumbling to the ground.

Harold cried out in surprise. He crashed down to earth, groaning in pain as the wind was forcefully knocked from his lungs. In a daze, he lifted his head, opening his eyes only to spy upon a row of arrows pointed at his face.

13
Trolling for Trolls

"Stop!" cried Harold. With eyes squeezed shut, his hands flew into the air in surrender.

"You fool!" admonished Rose. "You could have been killed!"

Immediately recognizing the large man sprawled out on the ground before the circle of armed Elves, she sighed in relief as Rainus motioned his men to stand down.

Loken spoke on the mortal's behalf, "I did not think I'd catch up to you so quickly. I should have realized something was afoot when I no longer heard your horses galloping ahead of me."

"A unicorn, Loken?" Tag shook his head in dismay. "Really?"

"It made sense to me. A lone unicorn would go by relatively unnoticed by those inhabiting this forest. We had moved unhindered and unmolested until now," explained Loken. His silky mane floated down around his neck after a vigorous shake. "Besides, an ordinary horse would soon become permanently crippled, if made to gallop while bearing a mortal of Harold's great size. And I was not about to transform into an ox or one of those huge, cumbersome draught horses that are powerful, but lack in speed and grace."

"You, Loken, I can understand coming along on this mission, but why is Harold here?" queried Myron. "I gave specific orders for him to stay behind."

"It's not his fault," insisted Harold, accepting Rainus and Tag's hands as they pulled him up onto his feet. "When he realized I was determined to catch up, in case you needed my help again, Loken just wanted to keep me safe. He didn't want me travellin' on my own, which was what I was intendin' to do."

"For pity's sake, Harold Murkins! You are a fool of a fool," scolded Rose, shaking an admonishing finger in his face. "Even I have enough sense to follow Sir Kendall's order to stay put, had he asked me to remain behind."

"Well, more than I was feelin' like a fool or feelin' left out, I was more concerned if somethin' bad were to happen to you again, my lady. I'd be absolutely devastated, if I weren't around to save you again."

Harold felt it necessary to impress upon the fact he had come to her rescue twice since embarking on this adventure, and there was a very real chance he'd be needed again.

"It is a good thing my men have such control over their faculties," said Rainus, motioning for Halen Ironwood and the others to put away their weapons for the time being. "I shudder to think what could have happened if they were mere mortals. Undoubtedly, the results would have been tragic on your part, my good man."

"Yes, well, thank you for not shootin' those arrows at me and Loken," said Harold. "But no harm done, and I'm here now. So… what's goin' on? Anythin' excitin' to report so far?"

"I think it's obvious this is where Captain Ironwood and the warriors in his company last saw the Sorcerer," announced Loken. His hooves stomped the earth as his unicorn eyes glanced about, searching for signs of the Sorcerer as his ears swivelled about, listening for hidden danger.

"Indeed, and over there…" responded Halen, pointing to the eastern edge of the clearing they had now gathered in. Marching over to a large oak tree surrounded by a shedding of blackened leaves, the Elf disappeared on the other side as he called out to the others, "And this is where that fiend struck, attacking us in a bid to facilitate his escape."

While the warriors kept a watchful eye, Rose and the others joined Halen. They gasped in surprised to see the damage inflicted on the grand, old tree. The thick, deeply fissured bark was visibly scorched where the trunk was burned straight through to the heartwood, as though struck by a great bolt of lightning.

"If this is not the work of the Sorcerer, then I have no idea who, or what, possesses this kind of destructive power," said Rainus.

His left hand ran lightly over the wound of the tree as he murmured in Elvish a healing incantation. With these arcane words, the oak began to weep a prodigious quantity of clear liquid. The sap oozed up from beneath the charred bark, attempting to seal this wound to prevent an infection or an infestation by insects from penetrating into the already damaged heartwood.

"That's truly amazin', Lord Silverthorn," marvelled Harold, his fingertip touching the drying sap that would eventually harden into a protective coating of pitch. "Quite miraculous indeed!"

"Thank you, but this was no miracle," said Rainus. "I merely sped up the tree's own natural ability to heal."

"Let us stay on course, Harold," urged Myron, motioning for his friend to cease with this trite conversation.

Harold nodded in response, gesturing the knight to continue on.

"So, Captain Ironwood, this is where you last saw the Sorcerer?" questioned Myron.

"Yes," answered Halen, as he jabbed a thumb over his shoulder. "He fled that way, to the east, after he discharged that great ball of light at us."

"And this was no ordinary light from a flame that would do this," assessed Tag, as he inspected the level of destruction the oak tree had endured.

"As you can see by the extent of the explosive damage done to this oak, it was something far more powerful than merely throwing a burning torch at us," stated Halen.

"A dangerous magic was used here, I'm sure of it!" insisted Harold. Scratching his head in thought, he suddenly realized in his dash to catch up to this party, he had forgotten to don one of his many headpieces he always travelled with. His face reddened, suddenly feeling strangely exposed.

"Did the Sorcerer use the Dreamstone to do this?" asked Tag.

"From the fleeting glimpse we were afforded during our pursuit of that maniac, the flash of light appeared to be discharged from an obsidian crystal mounted atop a staff," answered Captain Ironwood.

"Dragonite had one just like that," reminded Loken.

"What's an obsidian?" questioned Harold.

"It looks like a piece of black glass, but it is an ebony crystal formed within the heart of a volcano's fiery furnace," explained Halen. "Unless the Dreamstone had transformed, somehow through the powers of dark magic, I am more inclined to believe it was something other than the magic crystal."

"That makes sense to me," responded Tag. "Even for the Sorcerer, it would be foolish to brazenly wear or openly display the Dreamstone, lest it draws the attention of others desperate to claim it for their own devices, evil or otherwise."

"Yes," agreed Loken, his unicorn head bobbing in agreement. "And with this in mind, there's nothing to say Dragonite draws on the crystal's powers, disguising it by melding its powers to that of his weapon for this very reason."

"Do you honestly think the Sorcerer is that cunning?" questioned Rose.

"More desperate, than cunning, I'd say," answered Loken. "He will do what he can to retain its power and to keep the Dreamstone away from you, my lady."

"I suppose you are right," said Rose.

"Of course I am right," snorted Loken. With indignation he tossed his mane upon hearing her tone tinged with doubt. "It'd be no different than you traipsing by a band of cutthroat thieves as you travel the countryside. I'm sure even you, Princess Rose, would have the good sense to hide away all you consider precious, than to openly flaunt your valued possessions before those willing to kill you for them."

"I am no fool," grumbled Rose. "Of course I'd be discreet."

"From this point forward, we advance with utmost caution," said Myron. He removed his shield from the stallion's saddle. Securing it to his forearm, he hefted this shield as he peered eastward. "Dragonite will not hesitate to dispense more of his powerful magic."

"You heard Sir Kendall," said Rainus, removing his shield to fasten it onto his left arm. He pointed to the six warriors closest to him. "Gentlemen, shields and swords at the ready. Take the lead with Captain Ironwood. The rest of you, arm your bows and follow immediately behind. The six with shields shall provide you with some cover, freeing you up to take aim, should the Sorcerer show his face."

With these words, Halen Ironwood and the six warriors strapped on their shields before mounting up; while the remaining six prepared their bows to launch an offensive, should Dragonite appear.

"And you said the Sorcerer vanished into the east?" asked Rainus, as he hopped onto his horse.

"Yes, my lord," answered Halen. "He did so on foot, fleeing with unnatural speed for one so decrepit."

"Mount up," Myron ordered his comrades. "We shall take up the rear, so we are not in the line of fire should these warriors let their arrows fly."

"An excellent plan, but can I be the one to ride the unicorn this time?" asked Rose, staring longingly at Loken's adopted form. "I've always wanted to ride one of these beautiful creatures."

"I am not a novelty ride, like one of those wooden animals at the fair to be ridden for your enjoyment, my lady," snorted Loken, tossing his elegant equine head in a visual display of protest. "I may look beautiful now, but trust me, if you should get on my back, it will only wear on my good nature, turning me quite ugly in the process."

"But I promise to be a much lighter load for you to carry than to lug around a hulk of a man like Harold," argued Rose.

"No disrespect to you, my lady, but yes, lighter in weight is true, but you shall prove much weightier in the way your testy demeanour is sure to wear me down should I be subjected to your constant whining and complaining along the way."

"But suppose I promise not to speak while I ride?" offered Rose, thinking only of how regal she would look atop a majestic unicorn.

"Tempting as it is, I hardly think your mare is up to the task of carrying such a large passenger should you trade rides with Harold! I can picture this man's feet dragging along the ground once the poor mare's back bows beyond repair from his great weight."

"Master Loken is right, Princess," said Harold. "It wouldn't be fair for your little mare to be burdened this way. I'm better off ridin' this fine, spritely unicorn."

"Besides, I am making an exception in this case," added Loken. "I am not some beast of burden and I *do not* make it a habit of allowing people, not even royalty, to ride on me, whether I take on the form of a horse, unicorn or any other creature you see fit to harness and saddle."

"Fine!" grumbled Rose. Sensing she was not about to get her way, she stomped over to her ordinary horse. She silently sulked while Tag gave her a leg up into her saddle.

With all in his company mounted up, Rainus gave the orders to advance. "Captain Ironwood, lead the way. Do so with utmost care. There is no telling where the Sorcerer is lurking about."

Halen nodded, steering his horse to the east he led his men in a wedge formation. With eyes fixed to the ground before him, he scrutinized the earth for signs of Dragonite's passing. Here and there, he picked up scant traces of footprints and the odd, broken twig or fresh leaves scattered on the forest floor. The clues continued steadily eastward, forming an obvious trail left by the fleeing villain. For Captain Ironwood, he knew this was not the work of one of his people. The Elves were much too light on their feet, always careful in how they tread through the forest than to leave such reckless signs of their passing.

After escorting the party on for just over a league from the clearing where they had almost ambushed Harold and the unicorn embodiment of Loken, Halen raised his left hand. He signalled for all to stop as his steed emerged at the edge of the forest where rolling grasslands sprawled out before them.

"The trail ends here," announced Halen, as he hopped off his mount. Closer to the ground, he was in a better position to examine their surroundings for clues, no matter how small.

Following Captain Ironwood's cue, all dismounted from their horses to join him in the search for evidence left by the Sorcerer.

"Be careful where you tread," cautioned Rainus, as his far-seeing eyes scanned the territory inhabited by the Trolls. "We must take care not to destroy signs of Dragonite's movements, if we mean to hunt him down."

Fanning out from this point, after several minutes of intensive searching, they found nothing. Not even the bridge over the creek that separated Rainus' domain from the Land of Small yielded clues as to whether the Sorcerer continued his eastward escape.

"I do not know how he did it, but all traces of that fiend ends abruptly at the edge of the forest," determined Halen.

"There is nothing down here either," called Tag, from where he and Rose searched the banks of a creek at the foot of the bridge. Hoping he'd find Dragonite hiding beneath this wooden structure, he had drawn his sword, just in case.

"Perhaps the Sorcerer had doubled back on us, like some tricky animals will do," offered Harold.

"Then we would have ran smack dab into him on his return," countered Myron.

"Then maybe he just plain old disappeared on us," said Harold.

"It is looking that way," said Rainus. In pensive thought he rubbed his chin, perplexed by the abruptness with which the clues had ended.

"Then again, he may have re-entered the forest, but circled around us, giving us a wide berth to avoid an encounter," responded Myron.

"Or perhaps this is just an elaborate trap," said Rose. "Suppose *he* is the one hunting *us*!"

"It wouldn't be the first time," responded Tag. "However, if this is a trap, Dragonite would have sprung it by now. I'm sure of it!"

"Well, I am reluctant to believe that necromancer just vanished into thin air," said Loken.

"If he has not used magic to disappear from our eyes, then how else did he vanish?" questioned Rose.

Loken glanced down at the rushing creek. "There is nothing to say the Sorcerer had not taken to the water to conceal his tracks."

"He travels through this?" asked Rose. She and Tag glanced about, searching for signs of where Dragonite had entered.

"Perhaps I should have my men split up?" said Rainus. "Some follow this creek southward, while the rest head north. If the Sorcerer wades through this water on foot, then those on horseback would surely catch up to him."

"I have a better idea," said Loken.

"I am all for better ideas," responded Rainus.

"We just need to search for him from a different perspective," offered the Sprite.

"How so?" asked Rainus.

In a flash of light, the Sprite morphed from a great white unicorn into a majestic golden eagle. Spreading his wings wide, Loken launched into the air as he answered the mortal. "From a high vantage point, and with these sharp eyes, if Dragonite is about, I will spot him before he can see me."

"Stay safe, Loken," called Rainus, waving as the Sprite's raptor form took flight. "And should you spy on the Sorcerer before we do, do not approach him. Return with news of his position; we shall advance as one."

"Very well, Lord Silverthorn," replied Loken. With his wings pumping, he ascended until a warm bank of air rising up from the grasslands gently lifted him.

As Loken soared, gliding into the azure sky veiled by patches of gossamer clouds stretched thinly across the brilliant sun, Tag stood by the creek. With a hand shielding his eyes from the glare of sunlight, he watched Loken floating effortlessly on the winds, surveying the lands from high above.

"Suppose the Sorcerer vanished using the powers of the dark arts?" asked Rose, as she knelt by the clear, cold water.

"It's possible, Princess," answered Tag, kneeling by her side.

She waited for a moment, making sure the creek was not about to run black. Rinsing her sweaty, grimy hands that had grown numb from clenching the reins for so long, she washed them before pressing her cold, clean hands to her neck to cool down.

"It sounds to me like he is using the Dreamstone somehow to augment his powers," said Rose, blotting her hands dry while dampening down the wisps of windswept hair from her eyes.

"It would appear so." Cupping his hands to scoop some fresh water, Tag splashed it onto his face and neck, shivering involuntarily as icy drops trickled down his chest and back. "But if he had the power to disappear like that, then why not do that from the start? Why bother leading us to the edge of the forest?"

"Because he is Dragonite!" snapped Rose. "As if anything that madman did ever made sense."

"Keep your voices down," urged Myron, as he stared off to the rolling, forested hills to the east where they had initially met the Troll, Tiny Goatswain, during their first excursion into the Land of Small. "Even if we cannot see the villain, there is a chance we will hear him."

Harold nodded in agreement. He pressed an index finger to his pursed lips, motioning for Tag and Rose to cease talking and follow Myron's order.

"Lord Silverthorn," whispered Myron, as he waved the Elf over to the bridge he was standing on.

"What is it?"

"Do my eyes deceive me or is that smoke I see to the east, rising from those yonder hills?"

Rainus shielded his eyes from the glare of the sun.

"Well?" asked Myron.

"Your eyes serve you well, my friend. That is indeed smoke. As thin as it is, something burns in the Land of Small."

"What do you think it is?" asked Tag, rushing up from the edge of the creek to join Myron and Rainus. He stared intently at the thin, grey wisps of smoke curling up in a faint column from the distant, treed hills.

"It could be nothing more than the remnants of a cooking fire," answered Rainus. "Then again, it could be proof Dragonite continues eastward, unleashing more of his brand of destruction along the way."

"Or," said Rose, with a dreary sigh, "it is a trap devised by that evil Sorcerer to lure us away from the relative safety of the Enchanted Forest and closer to his former stronghold in the Bad Lands."

"Sounds excitin'! Should we check it out?" asked Harold. He grabbed the rail of the bridge that creaked under his weight as he joined his comrades.

"We shall refrain from acting in haste," answered Rainus, turning his gaze skyward to search for the Sprite. "That is what we will do."

"So, we'll wait for Loken's return?" Harold wondered aloud as he turned his eyes to the infinite blue skies.

"It would be the most prudent thing to do," said Myron. "There is a chance Loken knows what that smoke is about."

"Very well," said Harold. With a nod, he gingerly stepped off the creaking bridge that seemed to moan in protest under his weight.

"It makes sense," said Rose, nodding to Harold. "Whether it is nothing or especially if it is a trap designed to capture us, why rush off?"

"Look!" Rainus pointed at a dark speck spiralling downward. "Loken returns."

Riding the winds, Loken folded his wings close to his body. The large, primary flight feathers whistled, flattened against his eagle form as he sliced through the air at a terrifying speed, diving toward his comrades.

The three standing on the bridge were forced to duck as Loken's eagle form skimmed low over their heads. His broad, powerful wings opened wide to slow his descent as he thrust his clawed talons forward to brace for a landing. With surprising ease, he made his mark, gracefully alighting upon the bridge's narrow handrail.

With a ruffle of feathers and a flap of his wings, under a bright show of light, Loken assumed his typical form.

"Hold on, Harold! Wait here," ordered Rose. Like he was an overgrown dog, she motioned for him to stay. "We do not want to break this bridge. We may need to still cross it, depending upon the news Loken has to share with us."

Harold nodded in understanding. He paused at the foot of the bridge with Halen and his troop as they waited for further instructions from their leader.

"So, what news have you, Loken?" asked Rainus. He stood to one side, making room as Rose squeezed in between the Elf and Tag to hear firsthand from the Sprite.

Loken drew a deep breath, gathering his thoughts before dispensing the information he had gathered during his aerial surveillance.

"Did you see where the Sorcerer heads off to now?" queried Rose. "Will we be able to catch up to him?"

"I scanned the lands for as far as I could see," said Loken.

"And?" Tag prompted him to share more.

"From my superior vantage point, I saw not one trace of the Sorcerer, nor could I determine in which direction he now travels. It is as though that fiend had simply vanished."

"Well... that little exercise you had conducted was all for naught," grumbled Rose.

"Not entirely, my lady," countered Loken, as he paced along the handrail.

"How so?" asked Myron.

"Loken saw the smoke," surmised Rainus. "The one we had spied upon."

"Indeed, I did, Lord Silverthorn."

"Go on, Loken," urged the Elf. "What did you see? Has Dragonite razed the Trolls' village? Is it the remnant of a great fire we see now?"

"By the wisps of smoke rising through the dense cover of the trees, it appears to be the dying flames of the Trolls' campfire. There are no signs that their village had been attacked and burned."

"So, nothing to worry about," said Rose.

"What I saw gave me great reason for concern, my lady!"

"Who cares if those giants were busy burning their meal? That is hardly news to be concerned about," countered Rose.

"True," admitted Loken, pointing to the sun floating high in the sky, "but consider this, my lady; it is nigh on to the noon hour."

"So what? Then it is all the more reason not to worry, being the lunch hour is almost upon us."

"*So what?*" Loken snorted at Rose. "The real concern is that I did see not one Troll in or about their camp. They were nowhere to be seen!"

"Perhaps they are tending to their goats," said Tag.

"If you recall, young master, the Trolls do not take to their chores when the sun is at its height and most intense," reminded Loken.

"Oh, yes! Hence that coating of blue mud to protect their sensitive skin from the sun's burning rays." Tag nodded in understanding.

"Yes, but even slathered in mud, they tend to restrict their activities to the morning and evening hours if the sun is strong," said Loken.

"So they slopped on an extra dollop of that disgusting mud to deal with their chores now," said Rose. "I still fail to understand what the big deal is."

"The big deal is the Trolls are *nowhere* to be seen, Princess. Blue mud or not, I could not see even one of those behemoths and they are very hard to miss."

"That is definitely odd and rather troubling," admitted Rainus.

"Perhaps the Trolls are hiding somewhere?" offered Rose.

"Really, my lady?" groaned Loken. "When I took to the skies, even from way up yonder, my eagle eyes were more acute than those of an Elf's. I would easily spot those huge beings, even if they were attempting to hide!"

"Loken has a point, my lady," said Myron. "It is nigh on impossible to conceal one of those ginger-haired behemoths on these lands unless they took to hiding beneath the earth!"

"And if they did take to hiding underground, there would be signs; great mounds of excavated earth due to this activity," reasoned the Elf.

"Strangely enough, Lord Silverthorn, to the immediate north of their village, I spied upon a half dozen hills of earth," stated Loken. "They looked relatively fresh from what I saw."

"You're saying these hills were not there before?" Tag scratched his chin in thought as he pondered this news.

"That is exactly what I am saying. Other than a single oak sapling that appears to be strategically placed atop each hill, there were no other plants, not even fast-growing clover or dandelion weeds growing upon these great mounds to indicate they had been there for any duration of time. And from my vantage point, the earth was still dark in places, as though freshly dug."

"The Trolls have either taken to planting oak trees for the wood or for the acorns, or perhaps those giants did take to hiding underground and those were piles of excavated earth," said Rose.

"If the Trolls have taken to hiding, it cannot be a good sign," said

Tag. "Their sheer size alone makes them formidable to the normal adversary foolishly wishing to take them on."

"Do you suspect the Sorcerer had laid siege to the Trolls?" queried Rainus. "Their size would hardly be of concern to that madman, if he uses dark magic against them."

"It makes sense, for that lunatic is hardly a *normal adversary*, if you get my meaning?" said Tag. "If Dragonite means to lash out at all those who came to Princess Rose's aid during our initial quest, I am confident Tiny and his brethren will not be exempt from the Sorcerer's vengeful nature."

"It fits the pattern," said Myron, giving Tag a thoughtful nod. "The Elves, those in the Fairy's Vale and now the Trolls... I sense these behemoths have all fallen victim to Dragonite's wrath, too."

"If that is so, then why has he not vented his wrath on *me*, and me alone?" asked Rose.

"I would say he means to make an example to all that if anyone should come to your aid, they shall incur his wrath to its fullest measure," answered Rainus.

"I can understand that, but what about me?" questioned Rose. "Why has he not attacked me yet?"

"Perhaps the crazed necromancer is saving the best for last?" offered Tag, his words matter-of-fact.

"Well, I suppose that makes sense, after all, I am the *best*, but still... the not knowing is rather unnerving to me."

"I believe Dragonite means to use these acts of vengeance as a means to torture you, my lady," said Loken. "He takes certain pleasure in tormenting you. By subjecting you to witnessing what he will do to those who even contemplate helping you, he lashes out with complete and utter malice."

"Yes, and with this in mind, we should hasten to the east," said Rainus. "We should make it our business to see what had become of the Trolls."

"Oh, huzzah!" crowed Rose. Her tone was rife with cynicism. "As though those big galoots cannot fend for themselves!"

"Come now, my lady," responded Myron, with a disapproving shake of his head, "although they are great in size, you know as well as I do those Trolls were rather meek. Even the sight of their own shadow put them on edge."

"How can that be so?" questioned Harold, scratching his head in thought. "If they're as large as they are in the tales I've heard when I was a wee tot, how can one that big be scared of anythin'?"

"By mortal standards, would you not say you are large compared to most other men?" questioned Rainus.

"Yes, Lord Silverthorn. In truth, I've been told I'm freakishly large."

"So, even with your immense size, you cannot think of a single thing that frightens you?" asked Rainus.

"Well, I suppose I do find puny folks a little unnervin'."

"You find Dwarves unnerving?" Rose giggled at Harold's admission.

"No! I've never had the privilege of meetin' a Dwarf before. I was speakin' of puny folks, as in children, more precisely, toddlers. There's somethin' not right about how those wee things squeal, drool and stumble about like small, drunken sailors! I find it especially disturbin' when they chase after me to start chewin' and droolin' on my ankles."

"Aha! So you can relate to these giants, my friend! The first time we met them, they were frighteningly large in our eyes," explained Tag, "and yet, they were so meek, and perhaps not the most intelligent beings in this realm."

"How meek?" asked Harold.

"So much so, they were afraid of the night. I had to make up a little story for the leader of the Trolls so he would not be so fearful when darkness settled on the lands."

"Oh, my! Even I'm not that scared of the dark, except for what's lurkin' about in it!" confessed Harold.

"Just like with you and the Trolls, small children just take some getting used to," responded Rose.

"I suppose, but what now?" asked Harold.

"We head to the east, into the Land of Small," answered Rainus, turning back to reclaim his mount from Captain Ironwood.

"We're headin' into Troll country?" gasped Harold, his eyes opening wide with wonder as this quest continued to point him toward places he had only ever dreamed about. "We're goin' to see the Trolls?"

"If we are lucky and nothing evil has befallen them, we will," replied Tag.

"And how shall I follow?" asked Harold, looking to Loken for an answer as the Sprite alighted upon the ground near to him. "Will I be ridin' on a unicorn again, Master Loken?"

In a great flash of light, the Sprite transformed.

Harold squealed in terror, falling to the ground as the others struggled to contain their panicking horses in the presence of Loken's adopted form.

The large man cowered in the great shadow cast by this shape-shifting being, now backlit by the brilliant sun.

"What the bloody hell are you supposed to be?" cried Harold. In a panic, he scrambled away on all fours to get away from the transmogrified Sprite.

"He has assumed the form of a magnificent gryphon," answered Rainus, marvelling at the sight of this creature.

Loken bowed his proud head adorned with crests of feathered ear tufts resembling those on a Great Horned Owl, but on a much grander scale. His sharp, hooked beak, like that of an oversized eagle, clattered in agitation at the mortal's frightened response as he explained, "A unicorn outside the Enchanted Forest will only draw unwanted attention and possible attacks from those wanting to capture such a beast. Now, as a gryphon, none in their right mind would even dream of coming near to me, plus, I will be hard to spot high up in the sky."

"Word's familiar, but just what is a gryphon?" asked Harold. He cautiously stood up before the unusual beast that was standing even taller than the unicorn he had ridden. "I mean no offence, but it looks to me like you're a monstrous mix of several different creatures mashed together!"

Loken's feathered forelegs were now armed with the curved talons of a bird of prey. Beyond his massive shoulders the dense covering of mottled feathers ended to reveal sinewy muscles sheathed beneath a coat of short, straw-coloured fur and hair. The long, straight back, supported by strongly muscled hind legs equipped with the powerful, clawed feet of a lion, terminated with a long, rope-like tail. Tufted by longer, coarser, darker hairs, this tail lashed about to display his growing impatience. Stretching open his expansive wings, the shadow cast by Loken's immense gryphon form enveloped Harold in darkness. Cocking his feathered head from side to side to better see Harold, Loken's piercing eyes served to unnerve the man.

"The gryphon is a majestic and powerful creature," stated Rainus, as he nodded in approval. "With the body of a lion and the head of an eagle, it is said to be the king of all beasts with dominion over land and in the air."

Gazing upon the regal creature, Harold stammered, "Y- you know what? I think I can keep up with you folks just by runnin', so I won't need to be flyin' about with Loken... in this form in the wide-open skies... so far from the earth. "

"Nonsense! If you wish to continue on this quest, it is the only way to keep up," reasoned Rainus. "If you do not wish to return to Driven Hill, you must ride with Loken."

"And an additional pair of eyes can be most helpful while surveying the lands," added the Sprite.

"I suppose." Harold sighed in resignation.

"Good! Now, hop on and we will be on our way."

Harold cautiously approached the gryphon. Positioning himself at Loken's side, he crouched down, taking a deep breath before launching himself off the ground. Gathering his courage and strength, he leapt up and onto Loken's back. Harold groaned, landing clumsily on this sturdy frame that did not budge under his weight.

"Watch the wings!" snorted Loken, pressing these folded appendages tighter against his body.

"Sorry," apologized Harold. He winced upon hearing the crunching rustle of feathers being crushed beneath his dangling legs.

Grabbing hold of both fur and feather, he tried to clamber onto Loken's high, broad back. For a moment, Harold flailed about, struggling to throw his right leg over Loken's lion-like hindquarters.

Unable to watch anymore of this undignified display, Halen marched over. Grabbing Harold's left leg, the Elf hoisted him up so the reluctant mortal was able to position himself comfortably on his winged mount.

"Loken!" called Rainus, raising his hand to garner the Sprite's attention as he turned away to take flight. "Remember what I said! Should you spy upon the Sorcerer, do not confront him. Return to us with his position. We shall proceed as one to capture that fiend."

"No worries, Lord Silverthorn! We'll be trollin' for Trolls, not lookin' to capture the Sorcerer on our own," promised Harold.

"We shall not stray too far ahead," said Loken. "And as Harold said, we shall be seeking the Trolls, not looking to land ourselves in trouble!"

Sensing his passenger was properly seated, Loken's easy gait accelerated into a powerful sprint.

Fear and adrenaline coursed through Harold's veins as Loken galloped straight for the small bridge. The clatter of claws and talons striking against the planks of wood resounded through his body as this gryphon gathered speed.

The wind snatched the scream from Harold's mouth. He held on with all his might. With knees locking around Loken's sides, Harold leaned forward, burying his frightened face in the mass of feathers as his arms locked around Loken's neck.

Thundering forward, upon reaching the apex of the bridge, the Sprite pushed off, leaping into the air with his wings thrown wide open. Catching the wind, Harold was jerked upward as Loken's feet launched them into the sky.

Peering over to one side, Harold's eyes widened in horror. He was lifted higher and higher, the ground shrinking below him with each thrust of Loken's wings.

"Don't look down," he gulped, as he squeezed his eyes shut once more.

Harold yelped in fright as Loken banked to his left, catching a rising current of warm air. With the wind whistling over his wings, Loken levelled out. He glided on this thermal, circling effortlessly against this infinite canvas of blue. This aerial sensation nauseated Harold, his stomach churning. Gulping down a great breath, it combined with the refreshing wind blowing against his face. Harold slowly exhaled, relaxing his muscles and moving with Loken, rather than resisting this flight.

He leaned forward as Loken abruptly climbed higher into the sky. Wrapping his arms tightly around this gryphon's neck, Harold held on for dear life as powerful wings flapped with the slow, steady beat of a great heron fighting to gain altitude.

Tag watched in awe as Loken's adopted form and his reluctant passenger ascended ever higher. "I had no idea Loken had the power to take on the shape of mythical creatures."

"We knew these magnificent beasts when they roamed free and shared this realm with us," responded Rainus. "For mortal man, that was an eon ago. So long ago, in fact, they have been relegated to the deepest recesses of mankind's memory to exist only in their mythology."

"Are you saying that gryphons still exist?" asked Tag. He thought back on old tapestries decorating the walls of Rose's palace. Many were adorned with kings and knights of yore, regaling admirers with tales of great hunts and the killing of dragons, unicorns, gryphons and other such fantastical creatures.

"These animals were few to begin with, making them even more desirable for those, especially royalty, hunting them for sport," replied Rainus. "Through the ages, whenever mankind hunted a creature to extinction, and then they realize the error of their ways too late, it seems easier to explain away this sudden absence by saying these creatures were nothing more than mythical, magical beasts than to accept the blame that they were hunted to death."

"So they now live on, but only in folklore?" queried Tag.

"Rumour has it, and it is yet to be substantiated, but there are some who believe a gryphon or two still exists, somewhere," said Rainus, his words coy.

"I hope it's true," said Tag. He watched Loken in graceful flight. Shielding his eyes with his hands, he was in awe as the pair glided before the face of the sun.

"Look at it this way, young sir," responded Rainus, with a playful wink. "Loken can only adopt the shape of creatures, no matter how ordinary or exotic, if that animal still exists."

Tag smiled as he said wistfully, "That would be amazing to fly like that, to ride the wind, as free as an eagle. Maybe Loken will allow me a ride the next time he touches down."

"Oh, dream on, Tag!" snapped Rose, as she struggled to steer her reluctant mare toward the bridge. "If that Sprite refused the honour of allowing *me* a ride when he was a regal unicorn, do you honestly believe he will allow you, a lowly knight-in-training at that, to take to the air on his back as the scary beast he is now?"

"It's possible," said Tag, with a shrug of his shoulders, "after all, I'm not you."

"And just what is that supposed to mean?" grunted Rose.

"It means we move on from here," interjected Myron, putting an abrupt end to their verbal jousting.

With his heels gently prodding the stallion on, the knight coaxed his mount eastward. The steed followed the Elves on their horses as they plodded through the creek to cross over into the Land of Small.

Before Rose could convince her mare to take to the bridge, her horse instinctively followed Myron's stallion. She held on, grasping the reins tightly. Removing her feet from the stirrups, she lifted her legs up high so her leather trousers and boots would not get wet as the mare splashed through the water.

Seemingly to spite her, Tag easily steered his gelding toward the bridge, coaxing his horse on to show he was in complete control of his mount.

Upon hearing the dull thud of iron-shod hooves stomping over the wooden planks, Rose glanced over her shoulder to spy upon Tag and his horse. The pair crossed over the bridge, and both were the drier for it.

"This way," said Halen, as he took the lead.

The captain advanced with six riding in a wedge formation once more, their shields held forth to create a defensive wall for the warriors armed with bows riding immediately behind them. As an added precaution, Rose and Rainus travelled in the middle while Tag and Myron took up the rear. And circling high overhead, with wings opened wide, Loken glided on the thermals as they began their search for the missing Trolls and to hunt down the Sorcerer, if he was indeed lurking about.

As they neared a large wooden bridge, Rose called out, "I know where we are! I recognize this place."

Hopping off her mare, she walked up to the gate they had repaired when they were here last. This gate was used not so much to keep trespassers out of their lands as it was to keep their goat herds contained, preventing the voracious animals from wandering off to ravage the Enchanted Forest.

"There used to be a big bucket that hung from this rope," announced Rose, lifting the coarse, ragged segment still tied to the gatepost.

"That is odd," said Rainus. "Why a bucket?"

"I suppose to the Trolls, because of their great size, it was more of a tin cup suspended from some twine," explained Rose, lifting the end of the frayed rope to show the Elf. "They used the container to collect tolls from those wishing to cross to the other side."

"There used to be a sign here, too," noted Tag, his hand patting the fence post where now only a bare, rusted nail head protruded. "It said *'Tolls for Trolls'* in only the way those behemoths could spell."

"This was also where we first met up with Tiny Goatswain," reminded Myron, as he dismounted to join Rose and Tag.

"The Troll was on the bridge, standing guard?" questioned Rainus.

"No, more like hiding *under* the bridge to avoid the worst of the noonday sun," answered Tag. Abandoning his gelding to Rose, he clambered down the bank to the shallow, but wide river to spy beneath the bridge spanning over this rushing body of water.

"Tiny!" he called. "Where are you?"

Peering into the shade provided by this large, wooden structure, the Troll was conspicuously absent. All Tag could see was the flattened bed of fern fronds and reeds Tiny had used to rest on, cushioning his body against the stony riverbank.

"He's not here," announced Tag, as he scrambled up the bank to join the others gathering at the foot of the bridge.

A dark shadow suddenly glided over them as a boisterous shout filled the air. All glanced up to see Harold and his airborne mount. They ducked as Loken descended, flying in low over their heads. A great billow of air filling those wings was followed by the loud clatter of talons and paws striking upon the planks of wood.

Harold opened his eyes once the wind ceased swirling around him. It was a sure sign he was on solid ground again. More often than not during his introduction to aerial travel, this reluctant passenger kept his eyes closed, especially when Loken banked sharply while riding the thermals, flying Harold higher than any man with common sense should dare go.

Knowing he had been delivered safely back to earth, Harold threw his right leg over Loken's rump to slide off onto the bridge. As though his bones had melted and his muscles were reduced to jelly, he stumbled about, struggling to find his land legs once more. Grabbing hold of the handrail, he leaned heavily against it. Harold leaned over the bridge, retching loudly as the sight of the churning water and the sensation he was still flying through the clouds caused him to vomit.

"Stand back, people! Do not get too close," warned Rainus, watching with concern to see this mortal spew forth like a human geyser. "He is stricken with that dreaded illness that afflicted my people!"

"I think he is just ill from his ride," assessed Myron.

"No worries," moaned Harold. His swished some saliva about before spitting into the river to be rid of the sour taste left in his mouth. With the back of his trembling hand, Harold wiped away the threads of spittle as he regained his bearings.

"How do you fare?" asked Myron.

"I'm thinkin' that man isn't meant to fly like a bird. It really does take some gettin' used to, that's for sure."

"I can only imagine, Harold," said Myron, nodding in sympathy.

"He can complain, but I assure you, it had nothing to do with the quality of the ride," insisted Loken, snorting as his monstrous, feathered head bobbed in response.

"So, what did you see from way up high?" asked Rose.

"When I opened my eyes, you folks looked very puny," answered Harold.

"Well then, no point in asking you," grumbled Rose, as she turned to the Sprite. "What did you see, Loken? Were there any signs of the crazy Sorcerer?"

"Or how about the Trolls? Did you see them?" questioned Tag.

"For now, the lands are strangely quiet," answered Loken. "At first glance, I saw nothing to cause me concern."

"I sense a 'but' in there," determined Rose.

"A big but," assured Harold, nodding in confirmation.

"Though I saw nothing that would normally cause me alarum, it was what I *did not* see that was truly unsettling," answered Loken.

"Was Dragonite breaking bread with the Trolls?" asked Rose. "That would be unsettling!"

"It was nothing like that." Loken unleashed a trouble sigh. "What was unsettling was that with this second flight over the lands, I can say with all certainty that the Trolls are truly missing."

"Could they be hiding?" asked Tag.

"If they are hiding, it would be from the Sorcerer," replied Loken. "And if that is the case, they've done an excellent job of it."

"Well, from the peek I had when I felt inclined to open up my eyes, I'd say those great hills of earth Loken spoke of before were not some monument to oak trees," said Harold.

"What would you say they were?" asked Rainus.

"To me, I'd say they're more like huge mounds of excavated earth," said Harold. "Could be from diggin' out tunnels or a cave."

"So, you believe the Trolls have taken to hiding underground?" asked Myron.

"It sounds rather bizarre, but think on it, Sir Kendall," urged Loken. "Harold could be right on this matter. The Trolls are huge beings to begin with. Trust me when I say it would not be an easy undertaking to hide them – *anywhere*!"

"So, still no sign of Tiny and his brother Trolls?" asked Tag.

"Not one," answered Loken. "The only thing I spotted of their possible presence was that smouldering campfire. I'd say it is safe to assume that fire was left to burn out late in the morning."

"Perhaps the Trolls have fled well beyond their borders," offered Rainus. "Even though they would be on foot, in this span of time, they could be well beyond the borders of the Land of Small."

"It makes more sense these beings would flee than hide, if they were in danger," said Myron.

"Yes, but if they fled, wouldn't it make sense they'd gather their belongings, including their herds?" asked Tag.

"The goats are still penned up in their acreage," said Loken. "By the condition of the trampled vegetation, those eaten down to the roots and the shrubs plucked clean of twigs and foliage, these creatures have been waiting to be moved into another field."

"I hardly think they would leave their stinky goats behind," said Rose, with a doubtful shake of her head.

"I tend to agree, my lady," said Rainus. "Those creatures were the Trolls' main source of commerce. Something is definitely not right."

"So, what do we do now?" asked Harold. "Do we turn back?"

"No," answered Myron. "We venture on."

"I recommend we first tend to the goats," suggested Rainus.

"If you expect me to milk those filthy creatures, you can forget it!" protested Rose, her nose wrinkling in disgust.

"I was referring to moving them to greener pastures so they do not starve," responded Rainus. "There is no telling how long those goats have been secured in that plot of land, nor is there a way to determine when the Trolls will be back to tend to their needs."

"Oh," said Rose.

"Sounds like a plan," said Myron. "Loken, where did you see the goats?"

Loken's head turned to the northwest. "Less than a league from here, not far from those hills of earth I was telling you about."

"Ah! It is perfect!" exclaimed Rainus. "We shall kill two birds with one stone.'"

"I'm not keen on killin' any birds, especially little songbirds," said Harold, shaking his head in woe. "Unless it's one of 'em tasty grouse or pheasant that's perfect for roastin', I'm really hopin' no birds will die needlessly."

"Fear not, good sir," assured the Elf, as he motioned his men to mount up. "I meant to say that after we move the goats to greener pastures, we should take the opportunity to investigate the mystery of those newly formed hills Loken had discovered."

"Excellent!" exclaimed Harold. "That sounds much better than killin' a bird or two!"

"I am glad you approve." Rainus responded with a nod. "Halen, please lead the way. Loken, take to the air once more. Keep a keen eye out for potential danger."

The Sprite nodded as he trotted up to Harold. "Hop on. Hold on tight."

"Again?" groaned Harold, his hand rubbing his queasy stomach that had only now settled down.

"I hardly think you will be able to keep up with our horses," reminded Tag.

"And in light of the Trolls' mysterious disappearance, it is not safe to be wandering through these parts alone," cautioned Myron.

"I get your point." Harold sighed in resignation. Using the handrail, he hoisted his bulk onto the Sprite's gryphon form. He yelped in surprised as Loken suddenly wheeled about, galloping at top speed along the length of the bridge.

Harold's eyes squeezed shut. His heart jumped to the back of his throat as he shrieked involuntarily. Fearing his mount was about to crash head-on into the gate securing the far end of the bridge, the mortal cowered low over Loken's neck as he held on for dear life. Just as the Sprite neared the structure, his wings opened wide. Catching the wind, his powerful legs pushed off against the planks of wood. Loken clipped the top of the gate, clearing the obstacle with a mighty thrust of his wings in the nick of time. The noise of wood pounding beneath Loken's urgent strides no longer sounded.

As the wind whistled around Harold, causing his heavy cloak to billow and flap wildly about his shoulders, it was obvious they were airborne once more. Harold dared to open one eye. Glancing down, he saw his comrades shrinking away below him. His hands were balled into clenched fists, his knuckles turning white, the higher they climbed.

"Time is wasting away," said Rainus, watching as Loken and his passenger circled once more. "Let us proceed. Halen, take the lead."

With a respectful nod, the captain mounted his steed, steering the horse to the northwest as the others followed close behind.

"Remember, people, keep a watchful eye at all times," reminded Halen. "There is no telling what danger is lurking about."

As Loken rode the winds, gliding in large, sweeping circles high above to allow the others to catch up before he ventured on, those on the ground galloped on, following in the Sprite's general direction.

The well-worn trail utilized by the Trolls through these woods, though only narrow enough for these large beings to walk in single file, was wide enough to allow Halen and his men to ride in defensive formation.

As Halen reined in his steed, the horses following behind slowed accordingly to an easy canter, and then a leisurely walk.

"Do you hear that cacophony of noise?" asked Halen. Raising his left hand, he clenched it into a fist, motioning for all to come to a stop as the woods terminated into a large, open field. "It is an assault on one's senses!"

"That dreadful racket is the sound of those bloody, bleating goats!" announced Rainus, steering his horse forward to come abreast with Halen's mount as they assessed what lay before them. "They seem to be in want of something."

"They seem to be in distress," determined Myron, hearing their loud, plaintive cries as he urged his horse into the open.

"Distressed, or not, I am not liking the sounds coming from over there," said Rose, standing up in her stirrups to peer beyond the formation of Elves blocking her view.

With a sweeping glance of the countryside beyond the woods that provided cover, Halen saw nothing indicative of danger.

Whispering words of Elvish, Halen prompted his horse forward. Venturing forth from the cool shade of this forest, Rose basked in the warm glow of the autumn sun as she followed behind the Elves maintaining their formation. She shielded her eyes with one hand, watching as Loken banked in a wide circle, floating down closer to earth upon spying his comrades in the open.

As the party neared the fenced plot of land, goats jockeyed for position along the fence, all the while bleating excitedly to see potential salvation coming their way. Hoping for fresh grass or hay to munch on, the animals pressed up against the rails, heads and horns protruding in a neat row from between the wooden rails as the animals snorted and bleated in welcome.

Repulsed by their tremulous cries and lolling tongues, Rose grimaced in disgust.

The goats' enthusiastic display came to an abrupt end. The herd froze, some toppling over, uncertain of the danger posed by the mysterious, fleeting shadow gliding over them.

The gryphon dropped from the sky, winging away from the goat pasture. As quickly as Loken landed, Harold scrambled to feel solid ground beneath his feet. Wobbling to and fro, he stood with his feet wide apart and his arms extended, rocking about as he struggled to regain his balance.

Myron rushed up to his wavering friend. "How do you fare this time?"

"Better than before," admitted Harold, slowly exhaling a great breath. "But still, I'm really thinkin' man isn't meant to fly, at least, not like this."

"Not going to retch?" asked Myron.

"Nope! Got complete control of my faculties this time."

"Good," praised Myron.

With a hardy pat of congratulations on Harold's shoulder, they watched as the large man keeled over like a falling tree. With a loud *'thud'*, he hit the ground like a great sack of potatoes tossed into a root cellar.

"Good gracious!" gasped Myron, extending a hand to help his friend. "I thought you said you were not feeling ill?"

"I said I was not goin' to *retch*, but I said nothin' about havin' my land legs back just yet."

Tag dashed to Myron's side, helping him to prop Harold upright once more.

"That looks like it hurt," said Tag. The young man was forced onto his knees as Harold's large hand rested on his shoulder, using him to haul his hulking form back onto his feet. "How do you feel?"

"It could've been worse," answered Harold, wavering slightly, "at least I broke the fall with my face."

"So, none the worse for wear?" asked Myron.

Harold waved off his friend's concern with one hand as he used his forearm to wipe away the dirt, dust and dried pellets of goat dung that clung to his face upon impacting the ground.

"I'll be fine!"

"Yes," agreed Loken, "and this time, this fellow was enough at ease that he actually opened his eyes on more than one occasion! Plus, he didn't have a death-grip hold on me for most of the ride."

In a flash of light, the Sprite assumed his typical form. Hovering before Harold's dazed face, he could see the mortal just needed a moment to regain his composure now that he wasn't floating high above the earth.

"It wasn't quite as terrifyin' the second time around," admitted Harold, "but I'm thinkin' that I should walk around a bit, if you're fine with that."

Myron glanced over to Loken. "What say you to that, Master Sprite?"

"I'll continue to fly, but for the rest of you, travelling on foot will do for now, as the hills of dirt are just east of here, well within walking distance."

"Phew! That's a relief," responded Harold.

"Perhaps we can all walk for a bit; give our legs a stretch and our horses a rest," suggested Tag.

"A great plan!" Harold nodded in agreement. "But what about these goats?"

The momentary panic created by the arrival of the monstrous gryphon, and its just as sudden departure, caused the goats to congregate along the fence line once more, demanding to be fed.

Rainus scrutinized the secured pasture. By the trampled, muddy terrain devoid of greenery, it was evident these ungulates had grazed on every blade of grass within this enclosed parcel of land. Every edible piece of vegetation, even the thistles bristling with sharp thorns, had been yanked from the ground. With a vigorous shake to remove the loose earth from the tangle of roots, all parts of the plant were devoured, leaving nothing to waste or to regrow.

Even the shrubs and trees within this enclosed area did not go unscathed. The agile and nimble-footed goats climbed onto branches strong enough to bear their weight, stripping the shrubs and young trees bare of leaves and twigs. The smaller animals, unable to access these higher branches, resorted to gnawing on the bark.

"Well, the Trolls managed to do a fine job of keeping their herds contained, but this is rather ridiculous," noted Rainus. He watched as several goats thrust their heads between the gaps of the split-rail fence. Having plucked up all the greenery within reach on this side of the barrier the Elf was standing on, the hungry animals strained to reach the Elf's cloak to make a meal of it. Other goats began to nibble and gnaw on the rails and fence posts, grinding bits of wood between their molars in hopes of finding some sustenance from the obstacles that prevented them from accessing greener pastures.

"Either they're very hungry, or they're tryin' to eat their way out of there to get at us," decided Harold. The only animals that appeared to be well fed were the kids that were still nursing, growing plump on the rich milk provided by the nanny goats.

"It's evident these animals need to be moved to another pasture," determined Tag. With a sense of purpose, he climbed over the rails. "This can be easily rectified."

"Have you taken leave of your senses, Tag?" asked Rose. "Those goats will eat you alive!"

"They eat greens, not flesh," insisted Tag, as he cut straight through the enclosure toward the closed gate into the neighbouring pasture. "I'll release them to where there is plenty to graze on."

"Famous last words, Tagius Yairet!" warned Rose, shaking her head in disapproval as though her friend was foolishly and brazenly tempting fate.

She watched as the entire herd proceeded to follow behind Tag like he was nothing more than a bag of oats on legs waiting to be spilled and consumed.

"No pun intended, but I *kid* you not when I say you shall die an embarrassing death!" shouted Rose.

"You worry all for naught. I'll be fine! They're only goats, after all!"

From the farthest corners of this enclosure, the animals began to stampede toward Tag. Those closest to the young man began tugging, nipping and nibbling on his cloak as he held it tightly against his body. Unbeknownst to Tag, the old billy goat, the patriarch of this herd, was muscling its way through the crowd, and with head down and horns presented as though it wanted nothing more than to butt heads with this intruder, the goat made its move. Rather than charging forward, the tightly packed herd milling around Tag prevented the billy goat from doing what it does best, ramming its horns into potential adversaries or contenders looking to take over its herd.

"Look out!" shouted Rose. She raced along the fence to warn him. "There's one deranged looking beast coming straight for you!"

Tag glanced over his shoulder. From the corner of his eye he spied the sturdy set of curved horns homing in on his backside. The ram's intentions were palpable, even though its momentum was greatly hampered by the goats crowding around Tag, all tugging on his clothing in hopes it was edible.

With an angry bleat sounding across the enclosure, the herd suddenly cleared a path. The agitated billy goat picked up speed, charging directly toward Tag.

"*Run!*" hollered Rose, waving him on to the gate.

"*Don't run!*" hollered Myron, waving at Tag to stop. "It'll only make the ram want to chase you down."

"*Drop to the ground!*" shouted Rainus. "*Drop and roll about!*"

"What's that supposed to do?" called Tag, frowning in confusion at the Elf. His steps faltered as he debated on which course of action to adopt.

"I don't know," answered Rainus, his shoulders rolling in a shrug. "It was something different! I was just curious as to how the old goat would respond should you do so."

Tag groaned as he proceeded to dash toward the gate, shouting for the animals to get out of his way. Just as he dodged around one goat, another spun about directly in his path. Unable to manoeuvre around fast enough, Tag stumbled, tripping over the animal as it bleated in protest of this unprovoked assault. The young man was sent flying, landing hard on the ground. With his pride more battered than his body, he propped himself up on his elbows. Tag's heart skipped a beat. He could feel the tremor of the goat's pounding hooves as it charged toward him.

"Play dead!" shouted Harold, thinking that Tag would never reach the fence to clear it in time.

Whether he was about to be trampled by hooves or butted by those horns, Tag knew neither fate appealed to him. Scrambling to his feet, he brandished his sword, waving it about to ward off the goats impeding his way as they congregated by the gate, waiting for it to be opened.

"Get out of the way!" hollered Tag. Tripping over a stubborn kid refusing to be separated from its mother, his sword fell from his grasp as he hit the ground again.

"Look out!" cried Rose.

Tag jumped onto his feet, his eyes searching for his downed sword, but it was lost amidst the goats milling about. He didn't have to look to know the billy goat was bearing down on him. With no escape, and no weapon to drive the animal off, he didn't know which side of his body to present that could better withstand the impact against this living battering ram. Turning sideway, in hopes it would minimize the target he presented, Tag cringed as his eyes squeezed shut, waiting for this collision to be over with.

A frightened squeal and the sounds of hooves skidding to a stop caused Tag to open his eyes. To his astonishment, a large, black wolf bounded over the fence, landing just before Tag.

The great beast growled at the billy goat. Baring huge fangs, its lips curled back in a threatening snarl. The wolf was ready to attack.

Overcome, the billy goat's legs stiffened in response. Rather than running off in fear, with a plaintive bleat the goat fell over onto its side. This seemed to cause a chain reaction as animal after animal responded in the same manner, keeling over as though they had fainted from fright.

"What's happenin'?" asked Harold, staring in bewilderment at this odd spectacle. "Are they dead?"

"They only appear to be dead," answered Rose. She breathed a sigh of relief to see Tag remained unharmed thanks to Loken's quick action.

"Are you sure?" asked Harold.

"She is quite right, my friend," responded Myron. "For some reason, these goats have a tendency to faint, for lack of a better word, when they become frightened."

"I've been around goats before, but I've never seen any of them drop over like this."

"It could be that the goats are using this ploy because they are not as fleet-footed as most prey animals," explained Myron. "I believe they are hoping the predator will refuse to scavenge off an old carcass, preferring to dine on what it can kill, to ensure freshness."

"We've been witness to this earlier in the year when we first encountered these beasts," added Rose. "Easily startled, instead of running off, they toppled over, fainting when we tried to chase them away."

"Like an opossum feignin' death," determined Harold, deciding these animals were so clever in waiting for danger to pass.

"I suppose so." Rose shrugged with indifference.

"Brilliant!" exclaimed Harold, slapping his thigh in delight upon learning this bit of information. "Who would've thought goats could be so clever?"

"There is nothing brilliant about these smelly, noisy creatures, especially when they rampaged through my forest, unsupervised by the Trolls, as they devoured everything green in their path," said Rainus.

As Loken assumed his typical form once more, they watched the stiffened legs begin to twitch with life as the goats came to their senses. Tag thanked the Sprite for intervening, sparing him from being battered by the ram. Searching through the downed animals, he found his sword beneath the prostrate body of the young kid he had initially stumbled over. Lifting the little goat by one of its stiff legs, he reclaimed his weapon. Wiping the dust from the blade, he sheathed the sword in its scabbard as he stepped over and around the downed goats to finally reach the gate.

Stepping up onto the first rail of the fence, he stretched; reaching up to unfasten the thick rope used to keep the gate in place against the fence post. Swinging the barrier open, he used the same rope, tying the gate to the fence to hold it in place so the goats could exit into fresh grazing grounds once they were mobile again.

Climbing over the rails, Tag joined his comrades. "Are you ready to move on?"

"Ready when you are," answered Myron, passing the gelding's reins back to Tag.

"This way," said Loken. "We do not have far to go."

"Make yourself useful, Harold." Rose passed him the reins of her mare. "Bring her along, will you?"

Harold was happy to be of service, especially here on the ground than riding through the clouds. "It'll be my pleasure!"

He gleefully followed behind her as Halen escorted them back to the woods while the Sprite took to the air.

"Over yonder!" called Loken, pointing through the stand of trees. "There are the hills I spoke of."

"I see them," said Halen. He motioned the warriors forward, hastening their pace to keep up with the Sprite.

Rose was made to run to keep up with her comrades. She joined Halen and the warriors as they spread out, inspecting the huge mounds of earth that amounted to small hills.

"What do you make of these formations?" Myron asked Rainus as they scrutinized the piles of earth before them.

"I would have to say they are not natural," answered the Elf, crumbling the soft, moist earth between his fingers and thumb. "Judging by the condition of the soil, I would say this is the freshest mound."

"I agree," said Myron

"But what are they for?" asked Tag. "Obviously, Tiny and his people created them, but for what reason?"

Rose proceeded to climb the hill in question. "I am inclined to believe they are monuments to honour some oak deity. Why else plant a single sapling upon the very apex of each mound?"

"Are you sayin' it's a tribute to an oak god of sorts?" questioned Harold, watching as she clambered to the top to examine the young oak tree that was not unlike the others on the surrounding mounds.

"Why not?" answered Rose. "It makes sense to me!"

"That is just plain silly, Princess," dismissed Tag. "How would you know if they prayed to some kind of tree god?"

"And how would you know if they did not?" countered Rose, grabbing onto the sapling as she reached the top.

"Because I read. From the literature I've seen in your palace's library, I don't recall reading about a Troll god, particularly one that has anything to do with oak trees," answered Tag.

"Perhaps it is a new belief they adopted," said Rose. Her eyes searched about for danger, making the most of this high vantage point.

"Whatever the case, I recommend you get down from there, Princess," urged Myron. As he glanced about, a strange feeling of foreboding caused the hairs on the back of his neck to stand on end. "I have a bad feeling these were created by the Sorcerer."

Rose cried out, falling to her knees as the ground beneath her began to tremble violently. Earth and rocks shifted, churning underfoot as she was hoisted skyward.

"It's a trap!" she screamed. Her hands scrambled to hold onto the uprooted sapling.

14
The Living Dead

This churning mound of earth erupted. Rising before them, it forced Halen and his fellow warriors to leap back. They knew immediately this was no ordinary earthquake, for the ground beneath their feet remained still. Only this great hill was moving, coming to life before their startled eyes.

Instinctively, they armed their bows, preparing to down a potential new foe, should their captain give the order to fire.

As the sapling Rose clung to toppled over, she came tumbling down. She ceased her screaming; clamping both her eyes and mouth shut to prevent dirt and dust from entering as she fell.

Tag's foot came up. The heel of his boot rested on Rose's hip, preventing her from bowling him over as she landed at his feet.

Harold struggled to keep the horses from bolting in fright as he yelped, "What the bloody hell is that?"

Myron brandished his weapon, motioning his friend to stand back.

"Look out!" cried Harold, his trembling finger pointing through the cloud of dust to the apex of this hill. "A flamin' bush!"

This *flaming bush* sprang into full view, pelting them with flying clots of soil as it became fully unearthed. This vibrant reddish-orange shock of hair, like sheaves of grain bundled upright for drying, was attached to a large head that poked through the earth like a giant potato.

"Tiny?" Tag's eyes opened wide in surprise.

He abandoned the dirt-covered princess, dashing over to where the Troll rolled over from his side onto his back, propping himself up onto his elbows to confront those disturbing his slumber. He had been curled up in a tight ball, buried beneath this mountain of earth and it was evident by the blue mud streaking his face this Troll had either been weeping or had been caught in the open during a rainstorm.

"Master Yairet? Is it really you?" Tiny wiped away the soil encrusting his eyes to better examine the puny being standing before him. "I can't believe it!"

"What are you doing here, hiding beneath all this dirt?" asked Tag.

"I wasn't hidin', little master. I'm intendin' fer this ta be my final restin' place."

Tiny's words were matter-of-fact; delivered in the slow drawl typical of his people. He blinked hard as he glanced over at the two mortals rushing up to Tag's side while Harold and Rainus, as well as his company of Elves, maintained a safe distance; bows at the ready should the Troll be under a foul spell that would compel him to attack.

"That makes no sense, Tiny," responded Tag. He fanned the air as the dust swirled, settling on and around them. "Only the dead are granted a final resting place. You are far from dead."

"Well, little master, fer the moment I'm like the livin' dead, fer lack of better words ta describe my predicament."

"Your words are sounding rather ominous," said Tag. "What do you mean by this?"

"In my way of thinkin' I'm as good as dead now. Jus' takin' care of the whole messy bizness of burial while I can, cuz ain't no one else gonna do it fer me."

Myron and Rose approached the Troll while Harold continued to stand by Rainus' side. The large mortal stared up in slack-jawed awe, his mouth agape as he took in the Troll's massive size, the coarse, red hair piled high upon his head and the naturally pale complexion that showed through the faded streaks of blue mud and traces of dirt clinging to his skin.

"Oh, my! I don't mean to be rude, but there's really nothin' at all *tiny* about you, Master Troll!" exclaimed Harold. He meekly inched closer to Myron's side.

"My name ain't really got nothin' ta do with my size in general, 'cept that I was the smallest in my clan an' even smaller than my *little* brother." The Troll sat upright to address the mortal, sending more loose earth cascading down his chest and belly.

"Well, that makes perfect sense to me," said Harold, nodding politely as he introduced himself to the behemoth. "My name is Harold Murkins. It's a pleasure to meet you."

"Pleased ta meet ya, Master Murkins, an' the pleasure's all mine." Tiny nodded his large head in cordial greeting, only to shower the mortal with more loose earth. "I know the Elf Lord an' this young master, but who're these other puny folks in yer company?"

"You big buffoon! I am Princess Rose!" She snorted with

indignation, while shaking the clumps of dirt from her hair.

Tiny frowned in confusion. "You don't look like the little princess I know."

"That is because I am not dressed as a proper princess should be, but I am indeed Princess Rose of Fleetwood!"

"Trust me when I say you will quickly come to recognize her shrill, harpy tone and her condescending manner," warned Tag.

Tiny nodded in understand, realizing it was not a feminine looking boy in trousers scowling angrily at him.

"My apologies, Princess! An' what of you, good sir? Can't say I recall ever meetin' you."

"We have met, Tiny! I am Sir Myron Kendall, but when we were last in your company, you knew me as Cankles Mayron."

The drying mud cracked, creating deep furrows along Tiny's forehead as his brows knitted into a frown of confusion. For a lingering moment, he stared at this mortal standing before him.

"You do not recognize me for much has changed since the last time we were here."

"No... *the* Cankles Mayron? The scrawny stick of a man with the kind an' generous heart as big as his head?"

"I don't know if I am *that* kind or generous, but thank you." Myron bowed his head in humility.

"You're lookin' so different, but I thought I recognized yer voice! Well! This is a pleasant surprise, if ever there was one! Wasn't expectin' ta see yer faces again, my friends."

"Oh, great!" muttered Rose. "How is it that I am recalled for my shrill voice and temperamental temper, while this knight is remembered for his kind heart? There is something not right about this!"

"It is common sense," responded Tag. "When our youth fades and our memory falters, even if one cannot recall the name, one is always remembered by the acts of kindness that defined our character."

"Enough with your lessons on high morality!" Rose dismissed his words with a wave of her hand as she addressed the Troll. "Tell us, Tiny Goatswain, just what are you doing in this great heap of earth, for this is an odd place to hide."

"Tiny did state this was to be his final resting place," reminded Loken, hovering before Rose's scowling face.

"So, this wee Sprite's travellin' with you folks, too?" questioned Tiny, his eyes squinting as he stared at Loken as he darted into the air.

"Indeed, I am!"

"Hush, Loken! Allow the Troll to speak," she urged.

"Like the Sprite said, an' as I told ya all before, Princess, this is ta be my final restin' place fer all eternity."

"It still makes no sense, Tiny," said Tag. "What you say implies that you are dead, but it is obvious to all that you are still very much alive. We can all see that!"

"Think of me as one of the livin' dead. Alive fer now, but I'll be dead in a matter of time." Tiny's massive shoulders rolled in a shrug to send more earth clinging to his clothes to come loose.

"Granted, we must all eventually face death, and you appear to accept it with dignity, but there is no reason for you to embrace it prematurely, my friend," said Myron.

"How do your brethren Trolls feel about your premature burial?" questioned Rainus, as he motioned his warriors to put away their bows. "Surely they do not approve of your actions, especially Umber."

"Don't rightly know, Lord Silverthorn. An' my little brother has no opinion on this matter."

"How can you not know?" questioned Rainus. "I hardly think they'd approve of your actions and I have no doubt Umber is still in need of your wisdom and guidance."

"They're not here ta give their thoughts on this matter an', as it is now, Umber is in need of nothin', Elf Lord."

"Then tell us, where are they now?" questioned Myron. "Perhaps we should consult with them."

"They're all… dead," gulped Tiny, forcing down the lump catching in his throat.

"What?" gasped Tag.

Tiny responded by unleashing a melancholy sigh as he glanced over to the other great mounds.

"Are you saying these are their burial mounds?" asked Rose, with a gasp of surprise.

Tiny's eyes welled with tears. "Hence the memorial acorn trees ta mark their graves. I had ta be the one ta bury 'em, even my little brother."

"How can that be?" questioned Myron, noting the other hills of even greater size, each capped with a single oak sapling to mark a gravesite. "Do explain, Tiny! What happened here?"

"Well… the other day Umber an' the others were alive, an' then, the next thing I knew, they were all dead."

"Good gracious!" Rainus motioned his warriors to take a cautionary step away from the behemoth. "Did they fall ill? Were your brethren overcome by a mysterious sickness?"

"Nope, as best as I could tell they were all fine when I last saw 'em."

"When did you last see your brother Trolls, alive that is?" asked

Tag, bewildered by these strange words.

"I'm weary with grief an' easy ta confuse, little master, but best as I can recall it wasn't yesterday, but the mornin' before."

"You are the sole survivor of an attack?" questioned the Sprite, as he landed on Tiny's nose.

"I'm the sole survivor, all right, but I'm still not sure what happened," answered the Troll, going cross-eyed as he stared at Loken. "They were busy preparin' a mornin' meal while I went ta tend ta the goats, movin' 'em inta another pasture fer grazin'. Wasn't gone fer very long an' when I returned ta join 'em fer breakfast, they were all keeled over! It was like they had fallen asleep where they sat."

"That is odd," noted Rainus, listening intently to this tale of woe.

"It is more than odd," said Myron, with a shake of his head. "To me, it sounds like murder!"

"It was the strangest thing, my friends," said Tiny, as this memory evoked great tears that forced Rose to leap out of the way to avoid being splashed by big drops of salty Troll tears. "At first, I believed 'em ta be sleepin'. When I went ta wake my little brother, Umber wasn't movin' or even breathin'. I kept shakin' him, but nothin'. He was good an' dead, but was nothin' good 'bout it!"

"*All* your people are dead?" questioned Rainus.

"Couldn't wake 'em. I went from one ta the other, puttin' my big ol' ear on their chest. There wasn't even a thumpin' of their hearts. No breathin', nothin'!"

"Are you positive?" asked Rose. She puzzled over how would one even attempt killing these gargantuan beings.

"I ain't the smartest bein' in the world, my lady, but even I could tell they were dead."

"I don't mean to be insensitive during your time of grief, Tiny, but do you know what took their lives?" asked Tag. "Was there any obvious signs, say, of a struggle?"

"If you're askin' if I found blood on 'em or somethin' suspicious like that, there was nothin' like that at all! Jus' somethin' that looked like foam comin' out of the nose an' mouth of each one of 'em."

"*Poison!*" declared Rainus, speaking with all certainty. "It had to be poison!"

"Are you positive?" asked Myron.

"What else can it be?" said Rainus. "Perhaps that fiend is ramping up his actions. There is a chance he decided that making the Trolls deathly ill would take too long for his satisfaction. I sense that madman had concocted a highly potent poison to use on them."

"It is an art that Sorcerer is familiar with," stated Loken. "The right kind of poison, dispensed in the right quantity, can most certainly kill any being, great or small. Used in tandem with the powers of the Dreamstone, I suspect he had found a devious and clever way to enter the Trolls' settlement to dispense the poison."

"It would not surprise me if he did so in the cloak of darkness," said Tag. "He slipped in, and out, during the night. Going unnoticed by all as they slept."

"It is possible," agreed Rose, "but how is it that Tiny survived being poisoned?"

"He did say the others were in the midst of preparing a meal while he was tending to the goats," reminded Tag. "There's a chance this deadly concoction had been slipped into their food or drinking water."

"If they had been partaking in this meal, even sampling it while they waited for Tiny to join them, it would explain why they are dead and he is not," said Loken.

"Did you not eat or drink anything, Tiny?" asked Myron, searching the Troll's distraught face for an answer.

"Don't remember when I last ate. Since I got back an' found 'em all dead, I've been too busy ta think of food. Spent all of yesterday buryin' 'em as Troll custom dictates, then at dawn this mornin', I buried myself, so I could join 'em in the afterlife. But who's this fiend you're speakin' of?"

"We have reason to believe Parru St. Mime Dragonite, is behind this horrific crime," answered Rainus. "He means to exact his revenge on you."

"Fer joinin' forces with you Elves in comin' ta their aid when that crazy Sorcerer attacked her an' her friends in his domain?" asked Tiny.

"It is apparent you and your kin were on his list of enemies for doing just that," answered Rainus.

"That necromancer has been making his rounds, dispensing his brand of vengeance as he moves about in secret," added Loken.

"This is my fault. I'm ta blame fer Umber an' the others gettin' killed!"

"Do not bear the blame for the actions of a demented soul," reasoned Myron, saddened by Tiny's words.

"But I was the one ta convince my kin ta join in the fight against the Sorcerer an' when I think 'bout it, I was the first ta throw a boulder at that madman an' his army of mimes."

"Myron is quite right, Tiny," stated Tag. "You cannot be held responsible for the deeds of that madman. If anything, this only confirms our suspicions that Dragonite is out for revenge."

"That can't be good!" gasped the Troll, as he struggled to recall the days leading up to this tragedy. "But how can that be? We ain't seen signs of the Sorcerer in our domain. Haven't even seen any of his crazy little mimes skulkin' about."

"Dragonite moves in secret. He moves alone," replied Myron. "We believe he delves into the forbidden arts to mask his movements and to hide his intentions."

"Dark magic?" asked Tiny, as fear gripped his heart.

"And then some!" Rose spoke with all certainty.

"Well, as all is lost, can you kind folks at least help ta bury me back under all this earth?"

"You want to give up? Be left to die?" gasped Tag.

"It's not that I want ta, little master, but what else is there left fer me ta do?" Tiny lay back down in his shallow grave, waiting for the inevitable. "If you folks won't help me, then leave me in peace. Leave me ta the bizness of buryin' myself again."

"This is too tragic!" groaned Rose. Her heart sank, feeling true sympathy for the lone Troll.

"Don't rightly know which is more tragic, Princess. Ta be one of the dead or ta be the only survivor. I'm alone now. No point in carryin' on all by my lonesome. I'll never manage on my own. The nights will only be lonelier an' scarier now without Umber an' the others fer company."

"Were you serious when you asked that we bury you, so you can be left to die?" asked Myron, mulling over this morbid request.

"Yep, an' if it's not too much trouble, if you can plant that little oak sapling atop once more, I'd appreciate it."

"This is madness, Tiny!" declared Tag. "We are certainly not going to bury you alive, nor will we leave you to suffer in loneliness."

Rose leaned into Tag's ear as she whispered, "I know you mean well, but we already have one big buffoon in our company. We do not need a second, even bigger one, following us everywhere."

"What's she sayin'?" asked Tiny, leaning forward to better hear this hushed exchange of words.

"Princess Rose just said she'd love for you to come along with us, but as we're hunting down that murderous scoundrel, your obvious presence will only serve to alert the Sorcerer that we are near," answered Tag.

"I said no such thing," muttered Rose, only to be jabbed by Tag's elbow for her silence.

"That's very kind of her ta say, but she's right. If we're forced ta hide, it could prove ta be difficult fer me, thereby placin' all of you good folks in danger. Best ta leave me here ta die... alone an' lonely cuz that's ta be my fate."

"It doesn't have to be, my friend," said Myron.

"What are you talking about?" asked Rose, her brows furrowing with concern as she cast a baleful glance at the knight.

"Yeah… what are ya talkin' 'bout?" questioned Tiny, leaning forward to listen to his words.

"I have a possible solution," said Myron, as he motioned Rose to allow him to speak.

"I'm listenin'!" Tiny cupped a grimy hand around one of his ears. "What solution are ya speakin' of?"

"One that will solve this matter of loneliness and squelch your desire to be buried while you are still alive."

"Might not agree with your solution, but I'm always willin' ta hear ya out, my friend."

"Brilliant! Absolutely brilliant!" Rose grumbled as she spurred her mare on. "I thought the point of this quest was to hunt down the Sorcerer, not to herd smelly goats about the countryside."

"The hunt for the necromancer will resume as soon as we deliver Tiny and his herd to the Land of Big," explained Tag, watching as the Troll guided the ungulates eastward.

With the cranky billy goat tethered on a long lead so the rest of the herd would instinctively follow, Tiny's gargantuan frame carved a straight path through the woods, making it easier to travel for both goats and horses following behind him.

"But if we had only remained in the Enchanted Forest, utilizing the clever trap Myron suggested, that Sorcerer would have been caught by now," said Rose.

"Don't you think that's exactly what we would have done, had the Sorcerer *not* moved on from Lord Silverthorn's domain?" responded Tag, his tone tightening with agitation.

"Was the idea not to *lure* him into this trap?"

"Yes, but luring him would require that madman to be in the generally vicinity in the first place. It was evident Dragonite is moving eastward, continuing on this course."

"So, this journey is two-fold," determined Rose.

"Yes! There's no harm in checking on the Dwarves, as they are likely to be the next on Dragonite's list of enemies to be punished for helping you," reminded Tag.

"I suppose there is a chance we will still encounter that demented soul during our travels."

"There is always that chance, Princess, and we shall proceed with due care, but yes, it is only right to make sure the Dwarves have not met the same fate as Tiny's people."

As Loken took to the air, ever watchful for Dragonite's presence, Harold, with staff in hand using it as a shepherd's crook, kept the stragglers moving each time they stopped to graze. Fanning out behind Harold and the goats were the mortals and Elves on horseback, pressing the herd forward.

As they approached a meandering stream, the herd faltered; watching as Tiny stepped over while the billy goat bleated in protest as he was led through the water. The goats at the front of the procession balked at the prospect of following, even as the patriarch of the herd splashed through the stream, clambering onto dry land.

Seeing the animals come to a standstill, Harold manoeuvred through the herd, careful not to make any sudden moves lest he startle the goats, causing them to faint.

Reaching the front of the herd, Harold made clucking sounds with his tongue. Tempting the animals with a handful of oats and gently prodding them with his staff, the goats reluctantly trekked across the stream.

As the last of the herd crossed over, one young kid hesitated as its mother waded to the other side without him.

Knowing they needed to keep moving, Harold picked up the baby goat, draping it over his neck like a fur stole. Its little legs dangled over his shoulders as Harold crossed over the stream, picking up his pace to catch up to the rest of the herd as horses and riders surged forward. As the mother goat began to bleat, distressed to see she had lost her offspring, Harold deposited the kid next to her. The female goat nudged her baby on, pushing it toward the centre of the herd.

With Tiny's lumbering gait, those on horseback followed at a steady pace while the goats, bleating in discontent, were made to trot, ambling along on this easterly journey.

"Those mountains look familiar," noted Myron. He glanced ahead as the sun's rays shone just above the treeline to illuminate the jagged peaks.

"They certainly do," said Tag, as he studied the rugged terrain rising up before them.

"So, we're now in the Land of Big?" asked Harold.

"Yes," replied Tag. "We have been for a while."

"Call me a dolt if you want, young master, but I fail to understand," confessed Harold.

"Understand what?" asked Tag, guiding his mount next to the large man.

"Unless my eyes are foolin' me, these mountains you speak of in the Land of Big don't look any *bigger* than those of the Cascade Mountains in Fleetwood. Just like the trees and animals livin' in the Troll's Land of Small looked no different from those back home or in the Enchanted Forest. It all looked very normal to me, in my humble opinion."

"It is all about perception," answered Tag.

"What do you mean?"

"What the young sir means is that to us, all these things look to be 'normal' for beings of our size," explained Myron.

"Oh… so for the giant Trolls, what seems to be normal sized to us folks, looks really small to them," surmised Harold.

"Yes! Just as these same things all appear to be very large to the much smaller Dwarves," added Tag.

"Well, that's wonderful then!" exclaimed Harold.

"How so?" asked Rose.

"I was startin' to believe there was somethin' wrong with me," admitted Harold. His index finger spun by his head. "I was beginnin' to think I was goin' a little loopy in my noddle, but it's all makin' sense to me now."

"Good for you," she answered with tepid interest.

"Never mind her," said Tag. He smiled in understanding as he nodded in Harold's direction. "Princess Rose took a while to make sense of it, too."

"And now, we are well into the Land of Big," announced Myron.

"So how do we find the Dwarves?" queried Harold.

"Easy! They live where they work," answered Tag. "Just ahead are the mountains that hide the wealth the Dwarves toil over."

"I never had real reason to deal with the Dwarves, so I know not the way," admitted Rainus, steering his horse between Tag and Myron's mounts.

Rose frowned, puzzled by his words. "I thought your people were in the business of buying silver, gold and precious gems from the Dwarves, rather than partake in the drudgery of mining for these items yourself to make your fabulous pieces of jewellery?"

"We fare better above ground, in our fair forest, than to toil in the misery of dark, dank places in search of riches. Of course, the Dwarves supply the raw materials we desire, but they make it their business to deliver these items to my domain. Consider it the price of doing business with my people."

"So you've never travelled to these parts?" asked Tag.

"I have travelled here, and beyond, on numerous occasions, but I never had reason to delve *into* their caves."

"That makes good sense," said Rose. "It was a very odd thing to be under the earth... no sun... no fresh air... only the light and stink of burning torches."

"That is why I would not even know where to begin to look for the way into their community. Rumour has it, the way is a massive vault into one of these mountains, cleverly hidden away from those meaning to rob them of their wealth."

"This vault is really just a large doorway into the mines and their underground community," said Myron.

"Do you recall which mountain holds the entrance?" asked Rainus.

"Yes," answered Myron.

"The entrance is clearly marked," added Tag.

"With proper signage?" queried the Elf. "That is rather foolish! One might as well post directional signs reading: *Rob us, please! This way to untold wealth!*"

"Tag means to say these signs are ancient runes that mark the presence of the doorway into the Mines of Euphoria," explained Rose. "And if he was correct in deciphering them, it included a vulgar rhyme of a riddle, for those wishing to gain entry."

"Oh, my!" exclaimed Rainus. "That is rather brazen of those little people, to boldly disclose the entrance for the whole world to see."

"Truth be told, Lord Silverthorn, these runes Princess Rose speaks of *were* concealed, the entrance cleverly hidden by natural means, at one time," explained Myron.

"And now?" Rainus stared inquisitively at the knight.

"And now, more than these runes, there is a more obvious sign of where this entranceway is," informed Myron.

"What can be more obvious than runes chiselled into the granite face of a mountain? Are these runes protected by magic? Visible only in the light of a full moon or the glow of fireflies?"

"Oh, no! It is nothing like that," answered Tag. "Mind you, once the Princess was done, these runes were effectively ruined, standing out like a sore thumb, moonlight or not!"

"I fail to understand," said Rainus, bewildered by the young man's words. "What did she do?"

"The way was once hidden by a heavy curtain of vines, but Princess Rose made sure to be rid of it," responded Tag.

"She cut down this natural concealment?" Rainus stared with dumbfounded amazement at this mortal cursed with destructive tendencies.

"No, she burned it down," said Tag, with a shrug of his shoulders, as though this was to be expected of her.

"By accident!" declared Rose, as she heaved a disgruntled sigh. "It was quite by accident, I tell you!"

"And by a strange twist of fate, it became a fortunate accident at that," added Myron.

"How so?" Rainus failed to comprehend how the destructive powers of fire could not lead to certain disaster.

"When we first came by this way, we searched high and low. We had a general idea of where to look, but we had no way of knowing for sure how to locate the doorway into the mine in question," replied Myron.

"We had no idea just how close we were camped to it, until the Princess accidentally set fire to the steep face of the mountain," said Tag.

"I see," said Rainus. "Vegetation grows slowly on the scant soil clinging to a granite slope. I am sure there has been little change and minimal growth since this *accident*."

"What do you know?" announced Tag, as they followed Tiny around the bend of a trail to come upon the sheer face of a mountain. "It is still as charred as she had left it!"

Rose's eyes rolled in frustration. Her cheeks burned with embarrassment, and with the way she felt at this very moment, it was almost enough to ignite the trees around her ablaze as she endured Tag's teasing.

She stared up at the looming rock face and sure enough, blackened remnants of burned vines dangled lifelessly. The only evidence these plants had any hope of reviving were bits of greenery struggling to grow from the base of the charred vegetation. Here, near to the roots that remained relatively unharmed during the fast, but intense flames as the fire raced up the mountainside, there were signs of life as new leaf buds and tendrils emerged. These new growths held promise, but it was not enough to veil the entrance to the Mines of Euphoria.

Before the imposing, monolithic slab of solid stone, flattened by chisels and worn by the elements, Tiny and his goats came to a stop. He waited for the others to catch up.

"I see what you mean about this blackened face making the runes more visible," noted Rainus. He scrutinized the pale grey words chiselled into the granite, now more pronounced against the dark soot coating the flat slab. It left the engraved runes, as well as the intricate geometric patterns decorating the entranceway, untouched and completely exposed for all passing by to see.

"So, the question is: How do we enter without setting off the booby trap?" asked Tag.

Harold began to snort, attempting to stifle his laughter as he giggled a single word: "Booby…"

For a lingering moment, Rainus stared at the large mortal before turning his attention back to Tag and Myron.

"There is a trap?" queried the Elf. His anxious eyes searched the runes for clues.

"You are standing on it," answered Myron.

"I am?" Rainus glanced down to the ground.

"We all are," said Rose. "It is really quite large for what it is."

"Once it is set off, this trapdoor drops," added Tag, the heel of his boot tapping on a slab of granite concealed beneath a thin layer of earth and moss. "We'd be plunged into immediate darkness."

Staring up at the Troll whose weight exceeded all of theirs combined, and then some, Rainus cautiously backed away. He motioned Halen and his warriors to retreat with their horses, as Harold tried to drive the goats back so they wouldn't fall victim to this trap.

"Are we safe now?" queried Rainus.

"When the Princess said the trap is quite large, she was not exaggerating," warned Myron. "If it should go off, then we'd all be taking a terrific tumble, as well as a good number of these goats."

"And Tiny would go down, too, but he'd get stuck as it was designed to trap a troop of mortal men, not Trolls," added Tag.

"This is one big trap indeed!" Rainus nodded. "Perhaps there is another way in."

"We can go through this way," assured Myron, staring at the vault-like door. "It is just a matter of knowing how."

Rainus scrutinized the runes.

"I take it, you can read these words?" asked Rose.

"I am proficient in most languages, arcane and ancient, including old Dwarvish. It is a warning of sorts."

"Tell her what it says," urged Tag, pointing at the message before her. "She didn't believe me when I told her before."

"It is old Dwarvish, indeed," stated Rainus, as his discerning eyes studied the runes, "the most basic form of their written language."

"Basic, you say?" snickered Rose, as she teased Tag. "That would explain how you were able to decipher this warning!"

The Elf proceeded to read aloud:

"All who stand before this den,
Must bring a gift, if you want in.
If your hand is empty and your hat is doffed,
Then think again, just bugger…"

Rainus' words trailed off as he muttered, "Oh, my! These Dwarves are a cheeky lot!"

"Brilliant!" exclaimed Tag. He slapped his thigh in delight. "Word for word, I was right the first time I translated these runes for you, Princess!"

"No need to boast about this feat. Lord Silverthorn stated these runes were '*basic*' to begin with," snorted Rose. "If you are genuinely brilliant and seeking a feat truly worth boasting about, you will find us safe passage through this door, not like the last time when we quite literally *dropped in* on the Dwarves."

"Hey! I wasn't the one to set off the trap!" growled Tag, as he pointed to a circular pattern. It was the only round design carved into the doorway and conspicuously obvious to all. "You were the one to do that, when you pressed on that *thing* to trigger the trapdoor!"

"Again, it was an accident," argued Rose. "I told you before, I was merely looking for a door knocker or chime to let the Dwarves know we were here and wanted in."

Tag rolled his eyes. "And I told *you* before, you were being preposterous! A door chime? Really?"

"Pardon me, wee master," said Tiny, as he waved at the young man to garner his attention. "The Princess is right."

"Right about what?" asked Tag, as he stared up at Tiny.

"There is a doorbell, so ta speak. Press an' it hits a brass bell on the other side ta let the Dwarves know they have a visitor."

"You jest!" gasped Tag.

"I'm doin' no such thing."

"Where is this doorbell?" asked Myron.

"It's right here! Right in front of us," answered Tiny.

Myron, and those milling around at the Troll's feet, stared at the ornately carved doorway.

"I see nothing," said Myron.

"I bet it is the one I pressed the first time," said Rose, reaching for the slightly recessed circular pattern Tag pointed out. "I just need to press it harder!"

Tag seized her by the wrist, shouting, "Don't you dare!"

"Master Yairet's right, Princess. That's the button fer the trap," explained Tiny. "I suppose it's better ta say that the doorbell is right up here, in front of me."

All glanced up, searching the vertical face of granite to where Tiny pointed at an ornate, diamond shape that was carved into the geometric designs to look like all the others decorating the doorway. It fit the pad of his stumpy index finger perfectly!

"What? That makes no sense!" muttered Rose. "Why put that thing way up there, where not even the tallest of men can reach it, even with a siege tower?"

"In my way of thinkin', my lady, the Dwarves are used to doin' business with the Trolls," determined Harold, "hence the welcomin' doorbell is exactly where Tiny and his kin could easily get to it, than to have it way down here where we are."

"I mean no offence, but I believe those wishing to plunder the Dwarves' wealth stored in these mountains will most likely be mortal men," reasoned Rainus. "That would explain the positioning of that distinctly shaped triggering mechanism. It is perfectly logical."

"This doorbell, like the door itself, was designed to allow the Trolls easy access in and out of this mountain. Tiny need not stoop to enter," noted Loken, as he flew up to alight upon Tiny's shoulder. Sure enough, directly before him was the doorbell that was obvious now at this high vantage point. "It is all very logical, really!"

"Well, not to me!" grumbled Rose, as she stared up at the Sprite and the Troll. From where she stood, this doorbell appeared to be flush with all the other designs carved into the granite. "If that really is the doorbell you claim it to be, then prove it."

"Oh, me!" shouted Harold. Like an overgrown child, his meaty hands flew up, waving about, as he jumped up and down to garner Tiny's attention. "Let me! I'd love to push that doorbell, if you allow it."

"Makes no diff'rence ta me, my friend," said Tiny.

Loken launched off his shoulder, taking to the air when the Troll suddenly reached down, grabbing the excited mortal by the scruff of his neck. With that heavy bearskin cloak Harold wore, he looked like a cub when the mother bear picks up her offspring to carry it away.

Lifting Harold up to the diamond-shaped pattern in question, though this seemingly oversized *button* was the perfect size to accommodate the tip of a Troll's index finger, both of this mortal's big hands easily fit onto it.

Harold's eyes shone with delight as he rested the palms of his hands onto this diamond-shaped carving.

"Go on then," urged Tiny. "Let 'em Dwarves know we're here seekin' an audience with 'em!"

Dangling from between the Troll's index finger and thumb, Harold forgot his precarious position as he set his sights on this task. His heart raced in anticipation, eager to hear the delightful chiming of bells sounding from the other side of this granite door. He pushed against this diamond, but his first attempted yielded not a sound, not even a *'ping'*.

"It's easy 'nough fer me, but you'll really have ta put yer shoulder inta it. Push harder!" Tiny placed Harold onto his opened hand, thinking it would provide this mortal with greater traction.

Bracing the soles of his boots against this rough, calloused palm, Harold drew a deep breath as he mustered his strength.

"*PUSH!*" hollered his friends waiting below.

"You heard them, Harold," said Loken, as he hovered by the mortal's head. "Give it a go!"

Harold nodded. Pressing his hands against this large *button* once more, he grunted like a bear pushing over a stump. A little puff of dust gushed into the air as this piece of granite shifted slightly.

"Again," ordered Loken, his wings fluttering with excitement. "You can do it!"

With a great roar, Harold threw all his weight against this diamond. The grinding of stone against stone as this piece of granite suddenly gave way, sliding into the doorway. The delicate tinkling of silver bells did not follow. Instead, an alarmingly loud *'BONNNG'* resonated through the barrier as this stone struck soundly against a large, brass bell. The sound sent Harold tumbling onto his backside. As this bell was struck, in turn, it bashed against a slightly smaller bell, and this one bounced against the rim of an even smaller bell, all suspended in a row behind this moveable piece of stone.

Harold and his comrades below had assumed the bells Tiny referred to were small, Dwarf-sized bells. Instead, just like this massive door, it was designed for the Trolls. And should these bells sound off, they were loud enough that the booming peal would be heard deep in the Dwarves' subterranean dwellings.

To Tiny's ears, these chiming bells probably sounded delightful, but to all those in his company, they slapped their hands over their ears as the sound waves produced by the bells rattled through the mountain to resonate clear through their bodies. The horses squealed in alarm, straining against their reins to escape while the herd of goats suddenly keeled over, fainting with fright.

"See! There is a door chime!" exclaimed Rose. She pulled her hands away from her ears to rest them on her hips as she assumed her *I-told-you-so* stance while scolding Myron and Tag. "And here, you two basically pooh-poohed me for even suggesting such a thing!"

"Yes, yes! So you were right, Princess!" Tag admitted sheepishly.

Rainus motioned for Halen and his warriors to stand back. He stepped over the stiff-legged goats scattered about, creating a regular obstacle course to overcome to reach his comrades waiting before the massive door.

"So, now what?" asked Rainus. "Do we push it open? Enter at our own risk?"

"The door pulls out," said Tiny. "But it'd be rude ta just walk in. Fer now, we wait fer the Dwarves ta welcome us in."

"Ha! I was even correct about this door opening outward," snipped Rose, recalling how Tag and Myron had battered their shoulders and bruised their collective pride trying to ram their way in before she accidentally set off the trap floor.

"True, my lady, very true!" conceded Myron.

"Hush!" ordered Rainus. Cupping a hand to his ear, his head tilted toward the door. "I hear something."

His keen sense of hearing detected scurrying footsteps rushing toward this great barrier.

"I hear nothing," whispered Rose, straining to hear what Rainus heard through the thick slab of granite.

"Listen," urged Tag, pressing an ear to this door. "I hear noises... footsteps, I'm sure."

Harold yelped in surprise as Rose jumped back with a start while the goats, having just staggered back onto wobbly legs from their latest bout of fainting, keeled over once again. They dropped to their sides as a loud, metallic 'boom' thundered through this barrier. This noise was followed by the high pitched, resonating squeal of rusted cogs turning to slide back a massive iron bolt that kept the granite vault sealed, preventing potential intruders from penetrating this mountain keep.

"Stand aside, folks," urged Tiny. One hand waved his comrades back while the other pushed aside the stricken goats like they were nothing more than errant pebbles that could possibly impede the opening of this massive door.

The sound of metal was soon replaced by the grating of stone against stone as the seemingly impenetrable monolith of solid granite creaked open, but just barely.

With no doorknob to grasp, the tips of Tiny's fingers grabbed onto the exposed lip of this granite slab. With a loud grunt, he pried it wide open, the hinges hidden within the doorframe squeaking to be oiled.

In the gloom of this mountain chamber, a single torch burned brightly as a deep voice boomed and echoed from within.

"Enter!"

"Go on," said Rose, waving Myron and Tag to go first. "You heard the Dwarf. Enter!"

"Hello! Is that you, Giblet Barscowl?" called Myron, squinting as his eyes focused in the deep shadows of this chamber.

"Who's askin'?"

Myron called out, "Salutations, Master Barscowl! It is I, Sir Myron Kendall! I come with friends, so have no fear. Step into the light of day so I may greet you properly, my friend!"

"I know the Troll, fer it's him I opened this door."

"These are dangerous times, Master Dwarf," responded Myron. "How did you know it was Tiny?"

"Only the Trolls know where the door chime is located an' only they are tall 'nough ta reach it. That's how I knew, but I don't know your name. You're a stranger to me!" This deep voice from the dark growled in agitation.

"You once knew me as Cankles Mayron."

These words were met with profound silence.

"I stand before you with friends, old and new," said the knight, as he bowed his head in respect and humility.

"That may be so, but you, sir, look nothing like the Cankles Mayron I once knew."

Myron turned sideways. Sucking in his stomach to take on a gaunt silhouette, his shoulders slumped and his back adopted a slovenly slouch.

"Glory be! It *is* you!"

Giblet Barscowl stepped out of the shadows as he motioned for his men to stand down. In response, they reluctantly lowered their shovels and pickaxes.

Passing to his brother Dwarf the horn he spoke through to sound more imposing, Giblet marched over. His strong, meaty hand, covered in grime from a day of hard work, was extended in warm greeting.

Grasping Myron's wrist, Giblet's bushy brow furrowed into a frown as his braided beard and moustache bobbed up and down, as though he was chewing on a wad of gristle, as he scrutinized the mortal.

"No offence, but what the heck happened ta ya, my friend?"

"Much has happened since we were last here, but trust me when I say I am still me, just different, but still the same."

Giblet's brows arched up in pleasant surprise as he marched over to Tag, greeting him like he was an old comrade. "Good ta see ya again, young master! I see ya brought a whole mess of friends this time."

"And for good reason, Master Barscowl," responded Tag.

Giblet glanced over to Rose as he spoke, "And just who might you be, young sir?"

The Princess' face burned with embarrassment as she grumbled at the Dwarf, "I am Princess Rose!"

"Ya don't say!" gasped Giblet. His eyes squinted in the light of day, as he stared at this slim figure. Clad in trousers, riding boots and with hair pulled back and plaited into a braid, it was an easy mistake to make. "Well... what do ya know? It is you, my lady, jus' dressed as a man! I see both you an' Cankles, I mean, Sir Kendall, have undergone a transformation of sorts."

"Yes, yes!" sighed Rose. "And I am not dressed as a *man*, I am dressed for travel in inclement weather."

As she corrected the Dwarf, Harold eagerly stepped forward to greet this diminutive being.

"Greetings, Master Dwarf! It's an honour to meet your acquaintance." Harold bowed his head in polite salutation to the leader of this underground community. "I'm Harold Murkins, but you can just call me Harry."

"Hairy? I hardly think so, sir! Even our women-folk are hairier than you," chortled Giblet, as his eyes travelled up this mortal's body to look upon the tallest mortal he had ever seen.

"Just call this fellow Harold," insisted Rose.

"Harold, it is! So, you're either a very large human or a very tiny Troll."

"I've been told I'm large for my size, but I'm definitely no Troll."

Giblet nodded in agreement, and then his eyes shifted over to the Elves in their company. Gingerly stepping over the fainted goats that were scattered about, he approached Rainus.

"Well, Lord Silverthorn, it's a pleasure ta see ya again, but I'm no fool. It don't take a genius ta know it's not a social call that brings ya ta the Mines of Euphoria."

"You are wise, Master Barscowl," said Rainus. He bowed his head in respectful greeting to the Dwarf.

"A solitary Troll, a gaggle of Elves, a shape-shifting Sprite, an' a trio of mortal men in the company of a cursed princess? It's as obvious as this beard on my face, Lord Silverthorn! So tell me, what ill tidings do ya bring on this day?"

"Since you ask, I will not mince words. A harbinger of death has set its eyes to the east," answered Rainus, his words foreboding. "We are in aggressive pursuit. Our presence in the Land of Big is two-fold."

"Two-fold? How so? Explain yourself, Lord Silverthorn."

"Allow me," offered Myron.

"Go on then," ordered Giblet. He listened intently as his eyes scrutinized this unlikely party that included a herd of goats.

Myron drew a deep breath, collecting his thoughts before launching into their tale of collective woes. As he shared in the details of the events that delivered them to this very spot, all the while, Rose kept interjecting that it wasn't her fault.

Giblet Barscowl was silent as he mulled over this disturbing news.

"What say you, Master Barscowl?" asked Myron. He struggled to read the expression on the Dwarf's face that was masked by a liberal growth of facial hair, grime and a heavy helmet that squatted low over his generous brows.

"I say that I can appreciate you folks comin' all this way ta make sure my people are safe from the Sorcerer, an' we've been most fortunate that our community is an impenetrable fortress, but why the Troll an' his goats? What's the purpose of Tiny being here, especially when he's not here ta deliver that fine cheese?"

"I ain't got nowhere else ta go, Master Dwarf," answered Tiny, heaving a dismal sigh as he contemplated a bleak future.

Myron raised his hand to the Troll for silence, "Allow me to speak, Tiny."

"Look here, my friend, I sympathize with the poor soul's plight. An' though I've got nothin' against Tiny an' we're all very fond of that cheese an' promise ta resume doin' bizness with him once he's up ta producin' more of it, what was the point of bringin' Tiny an' his goats here?"

"Tiny is here because of your reputation, Master Barscowl. You are a wise leader, reputed for your compassion and good, old-fashioned common sense," praised Myron.

"I am?" In pensive thought, Giblet tugged on his beard as he pondered these flattering words.

"Absolutely!" assured Tag, stepping forward to lend weight to Myron's complimentary words. "Here is an opportunity for you to assist this poor Troll *and* help your people at the same time."

"Explain," ordered Giblet. He leaned against the handle of his pickaxe. "I'm willin' ta listen."

"When we came upon Tiny, he was quite prepared to die than to live a lone existence," said Myron. "Needless to say, if this should be his fate, there will be no cheese to speak of."

"Hold on here… I have a feelin' I know where this conversation is goin'," sighed Giblet.

Tag said nothing in response. In a gesture to invoke sympathy, he merely gazed with sad eyes at the Dwarf, and then peered up at the despondent Troll.

"Are you suggestin' fer the Troll ta live here?" questioned Giblet. "Amongst my people?"

"Yes, in this very mountain!" exclaimed Tag, as he peered through the great entrance. Inside the massive chamber, Giblet's men were quite literally dwarfed by the sheer size of this cavernous room that could easily and comfortably accommodate several of Tiny's height.

"My mind is boggled," said Giblet. "How would it even be possible?"

"Was this great entrance and chamber not designed to accommodate the Trolls?" asked Tag.

"Yes, but ta conduct bizness within so we weren't made ta do so while exposed to the elements an' whatever manner of danger that lurks, waitin' ta prey on us folks of diminutive size."

"Think on it, Master Barscowl! Here is an opportunity for you to provide this Troll, the last of his kind, with a safe haven and your quality company," said Myron. "Tiny's sheer size alone will provide you with safe passage should you wish to travel beyond Lord Silverthorn's domain to sell your precious metals and gems."

Giblet scratched his beard as he mulled over this idea. "Never considered sellin' in foreign countries, especially because of all them bandits an' brigands waitin' ta rob us along the way should we venture beyond our usual trade routes."

"Well now, here's your chance to expand your horizons and build on your reputation as the purveyor of the finest quality gems and precious metals," said Tag.

"A great Troll like Tiny can strike an imposing figure, standing guard as you venture to new lands to conduct business. His presence alone will keep you and your riches safe from marauding thieves," insisted Myron.

Giblet's eyes turned skyward as he glanced up at Tiny's hopeful face. His size alone would indeed strike terror in the hearts of potential robbers hoping to steal from them.

"True 'nough, Myron Kendall, but what about these goats?"

"Those animals come with the Troll," stated Rose.

"We're miners, not farmers, Princess. I hardly think they'll take ta life in our caves an' tunnels. An' I doubt our gardens will be safe with these ravenous beasts eatin' everythin' in sight. It's hard 'nough fer us Dwarves ta tend to our veggies with eagles an' other predators waitin' ta swoop down on us, an' we certainly can't afford ta have these goats gobble up our foodstuffs or we'll starve before the comin' of spring!"

"Tiny can keep watch over your people as they tend to their gardens," offered Rose. "As for the goats, they can be kept in enclosures to keep them out of your growing plots."

"Plus," added Tag, "areas grazed and cleared over by these goats, and enriched with their dung, can make for more productive gardens."

"And not to forget the meat they can provide once their milk runs dry," said Myron.

"True…" said Giblet, as he considered these words.

"And you did say your people love the Troll-made cheese," reminded Rainus. "Now, you will have access to fresh milk *and* that famous cheese you are so fond of!"

The Dwarf watched as the goats scrambled about, recovering from their most recent fainting spell. He then stared up at Tiny. The Troll was standing silently, wringing his hands in woe as he waited for Giblet Barscowl's decision.

"Well, I can't deny our roasted veggies served up with that magical, melted cheese or cooked up in a creamy sauce is jus' the most exquisite thing ta tease one's taste buds!" Giblet's lips hidden beneath his luxurious beard and moustache smacked together just thinking about these delicious combinations.

"If it helps, in short order, my men can help your people construct fences to contain the goats," offered Rainus, glancing over his shoulder at Halen and the warriors in his company.

Scratching his chin, the Dwarf considered this offer.

"What say you, Master Barscowl?" queried Rose. "I am confident Tiny will prove to be most helpful in other ways we have yet to think of, should you find it in your exceptionally large and generous heart to take him in."

"You can well be right on that count, Princess," determined Giblet. "But more than the fine cheese an' the protection Tiny's great size can provide us, whether it's tendin' ta our garden or travellin' afar ta sell our goods, when ya really think about it, it'd be a bloody shame ta turn the poor soul away, now that he's all alone in the world. Can't have that!"

"Excellent!" exclaimed Myron, patting Giblet on his back for making a decision based on compassion, as well as pandering to his practical side. "This will prove to be mutually beneficial for both your people and Tiny!"

"We can build a simple fence in no time, if we set to work right now," offered Halen.

"Fences need posts an' posts need holes ta be dug," said Giblet, nodding to Halen Ironwood. "You an' your men can take care of the wood fer the fences an' my men can dig holes jus' as quickly where you'll be needin' 'em!"

"Brilliant!" cheered Tag. "A collaborative effort will see these goats secured in no time."

"An' I know the perfect place for the goats just south of here, away from our gardens, should those critters make an escape!"

Giblet thrust a grimy finger and thumb into his mouth. With a loud whistle, seven Dwarves marched out of the chamber; pickaxes and shovels at the ready. Giving them instructions, he waved his men off to escort Halen and his men to a clearing to serve the purpose of containing the goats while keeping them well fed.

"Harold, do be a lamb," said Rose. "While we see to Tiny, settling him into his new home, will you keep a watchful eye on these mangy beasts?"

"Don't mind at all! In fact, I'll keep both eyes on these little critters," said Harold, as he accepted from Tiny the rope that kept the billy goat tethered.

For a moment, they watched as Elves and Dwarves marched off to take care of the business of constructing a simple, but effective, split-rail fence. Halen and his men seemed focused on the task, but the seven Dwarves appointed to this task ranged from being deliriously happy to downright grumpy for being made to dig holes for fence posts, rather than setting their tools against rocks for the treasures hidden within.

"Follow me, my friends!" called Giblet. "Let's get down ta the bizness of gettin' Tiny settled."

Loken's wings fluttered as he darted inside, flying in large circles as he admired the tall, vaulted ceiling carved into this massive chamber.

"Watch your heads," said the Dwarf, with a loud chuckle as he laughed at his own joke.

"You are very funny!" giggled Rose, glancing behind to see Tiny as he passed through the entrance. He easily cleared the top of this doorway with a Troll's hand span to spare.

"Thank you, dear Princess! Contrary ta what most believe, Dwarves have a delightful sense of humour! Our wit is as sharp as the tip of our pickaxe!"

As Tiny was the last to enter, the Troll called out, "Master Barscowl, should I shut the door for now?"

Giblet turned about to address the Troll. He squinted to see Tiny's gargantuan form backlit by the bright daylight.

"With Lord Silverthorn's warriors an' my men at work out there, it's best ta leave the door ajar for now," answered Giblet. "Leave it open a crack, jus' 'nough for 'em Elves an' that big mortal watchin' over the goats ta fit through."

"Are ya sure?" asked Tiny.

"Absolutely! We'll secure it once everyone's done fer the night an' safely inside."

"As ya wish, Master Barscowl!" said Tiny, his voice echoing through the chamber. Wrapping a hand around the edge of the door, rusty hinges squeaked as the Troll pulled the slab of granite closed, leaving a gap the width of his hand to allow Dwarves and Elves to slip through when their work was done.

Except for Loken's golden aura glowing bright in the highest point of the domed ceiling, all in the chamber were swallowed up in the gloom. The single torch Giblet carried when they first arrived now burned in the wall sconce by the doorway. The flame continued to burn intensely, but the torch's light was diminished by the seam of daylight glaring through the gap of the door, creating a single column of light shining against the south wall of the chamber while the rest of the cavity was immersed in darkness.

"Oh, my! It's rather gloomy in here," noted Rose.

"I can remedy that," said Giblet.

Scuttling by the Princess, he clambered up five rocks of graduating sizes that formed steps to reach the sconce where the torch continued to burn. Hopping down from the lowest rock, Giblet marched over to a low, narrow trough. Holding the torch just so, a single flame licked at the oily residue in the trough.

Rainus gasped in surprise and delight as this flame burst to life, a narrow channel of fire racing along, following the south wall of this chamber to end at the Dwarf-sized tunnel carved into the east wall. Trotting across the chamber, Giblet touched the flames of the torch to light up the trough lining the north wall. The flames burned brightly to illuminate this entire cave.

"Sweet mother-of-pearl!" gasped Rainus. "I was not expecting anything like this."

"I did tell you about the large size this chamber," reminded Myron.

"*Large?* Large is not the word to do it justice. This is... is... *EXCESSIVELY HUMONGOUS!*" Rainus' declaration echoed through the chamber as he stared across the expanse that was as large as the largest Troll abode and just as tall, too!

Hexagonal in shape, like one of the cells made by bees in their hive, it was reinforced by six mighty, granite pillars at the vertices of each angled corner of these six walls. Adorned with ruby, sapphire and diamond gemstones; each glittering pillar rose up, arching gracefully as they followed the contours of the domed ceiling to come together at the very apex for added strength. The main entranceway was west facing, and directly across, carved into the east wall was a smaller tunnel made to accommodate the inhabitants of this subterranean community.

"I truly get the sense you have never been in here before, Lord Silverthorn," surmised Rose.

"As I said before, I never had reason to," answered Rainus. His eyes stared in awe at the majesty of this architectural wonder rarely seen by outsiders.

"This particular mountain was the perfect size an' composed of jus' the right kind of rock that's strong, but easy fer us Dwarves ta carve out such a chamber," explained Giblet.

"And I can see your people are master carvers! This is nothing short of magnificent," praised Rainus.

The Elf's discriminating eyes admired the intricate designs adorning the jewel-studded pillars of granite lining the walls at precise intervals. In between the pillars, the walls were just as ornate. Unlike the Elves' proclivity for flowing, twisting floral patterns, the Dwarves were more inclined to carve geometric designs. It was not so much because they felt elegant, floral scrollwork was too feminine for their liking, but more so because granite is not as forgiving as wood, thereby lending its natural composition to more linear patterns for the chisels the Dwarves worked with.

"Thank you fer your kind words, Lord Silverthorn, but this is nothing! Your people understand wood, while we make our livin' out of carvin' what's around us," said Giblet, watching as Tiny stepped over him to sit near the east wall to rest, as he'd be going no further, unable to fit into the tunnels riddling the mountain.

"But how did your people manage to carve so high into this mountain?" asked Rainus. He stared up to the ceiling that was so tall, only Tiny's fingertips could reach its highest centre, if he held his arms straight up.

"My great grandfather an' his kin had the help of Tiny's ancestors in carvin' out this chamber fer both their benefit. I've been told the Trolls helped to removed the boulders an' rubble, an' when it came ta carvin' out the tall ceilin', them Trolls quite literally lent a hand or two, like scaffoldin' so they could reach way up there."

"And now, Dwarf and Troll come together once more for the mutual benefit of both," said Tag, nodding in approval to Tiny and Giblet.

"Roomy enough for a Troll and well lit, too," said Rose. "The Dwarves are safe; Tiny has a new home; his goats are being fenced in as we speak. I do believe our work is done here!"

The flames burning in the oil troughs suddenly danced, guttering with frenetic energy as a great gust of wind blew through the gap of the door. All shielded their eyes as smoke and dust mingled, swirling around them. They were consumed in darkness as the flames were extinguished.

Knowing Tiny was fearful of the dark Loken hovered near to him.

His glow provided a source of light for the Troll as he cowered in the far corner of the chamber while his comrades blinked hard, staring through the settling dust. Their eyes adjusted to the gloom that was pierced by the single, elongated shaft of daylight that lit up the south wall once more.

"What the heck is that?" asked Tag, squinting as a great shadow rose up before them.

This dark form stretched across the wall, growing larger as Myron and Tag unsheathed their swords while Rainus armed his bow. Before them the dorsal spines running from the top of the creature's head down its neck grew large. A pointed snout contorted as the mouth opened wide. Huge fangs protruded as a forked tongue flicked forward.

"Dragon!" shouted Giblet. He hoisted his pickaxe as he motioned Rose toward the passage that would take them deep into the mountain, a passage too small for a great creature to access should it attack. "Get back, Princess!"

The dragon growled, and then to the surprise of all, angry words rumbled from its open mouth as it snarled, *"Prepare to die!"*

15

An Exercise in Futility

"A talkin' dragon!" cried Tiny.

Mortified by this menacing shadow gliding toward them, ever expanding in size against the wall, the Troll cowered.

"A dragon doesn't speak!" declared Myron, staring in stunned disbelief at this strange manifestation.

"Not unless that dragon is a Pooka!" warned Loken.

Scrutinizing the monstrous shadow looming large before them, their eyes followed its shape as it narrowed down to the true source of this threat.

"There! Over there!" hollered Tag. He pointed to the set of stone steps Giblet Barscowl had used to replace the torch used to light the oil troughs. "That's no dragon!"

Backlit by the defiant glare of the retiring sun flooding through the gap of the massive door, there it was! Protruding just above the highest step to cast this mysterious shadow against the wall was a hand. And upon this hand was a tatty, old sock puppet fashioned in the shape of a dragon.

"Hey! It is nothing more than a child's plaything!" snapped Rose. She was more than incensed she had been frightened by a toy. "The only thing I hate more than a mime is a sock puppet! Seize that troublemaker!"

As Loken dove down, joining his comrades as they charged across the chamber to secure this intruder, the lowly sock puppet disappeared, ducking behind this stone structure. With the speed of a frightened rat scurrying for its life, the shadowy figure darted toward the door that had been left ajar. As though shielded by luck, a careless stumble allowed this culprit to dodge the arrow Rainus let fly. The projectile missed its mark, piercing through cloak, but just skimming by these bony shoulders. The steel bodkin ricocheted upon impact. The shaft snapped from the force, shattering as it struck against the rockwork. An explosion of wood splinters and feathers fledging the arrow were sent flying in all directions.

"Quickly!" ordered Myron. "After him!"

Dashing across the chamber to apprehend the mysterious stranger as he exited, with a loud *'BANG'* an invisible power slammed this great granite slab shut. The force was so powerful, the displaced air rushed through the chamber. Like a great breath blowing out a candle, the swirling gust of air extinguished the torch burning near the door as well as the flames in the oil troughs.

Other than the tiny orb of light that was Loken floating high above them, their world was immersed in an unnatural darkness. The gloom was as foreboding as the stifling silence that now enveloped them.

"I'm scared!" whimpered Tiny. Trembling, he pressed his back against the far wall.

"Stay put, folks!" ordered Giblet. He gingerly made his way through the darkness toward the stone steps. "Give me a moment ta relight the torch."

Loken's wings thrummed as he flew toward Giblet's voice. He glowed brightly, offering the Dwarf a source of light to safely make his way across the chamber without bumping into his guests or stumbling into the oil trough.

Just as Giblet reached the first of the stone steps, a thunderous *'BOOM'* resounded through the chamber. All fell to their knees as this percussive blow caused the brass bells to clash together. It was as though a massive boulder was catapulted, smashing against the face of the mountain. The impact echoed through this chamber, rumbling through the air.

"What the bloody hell was that?" gasped Myron, as he steadied Rose on her feet.

No sooner than he spoke, another bone-rattling *'BOOM'* caused the entire mountain to shudder.

"We're under attack!" shouted Rainus.

"Retreat!" hollered Giblet, as he stumbled away from the steps. "Into the tunnel!"

"What about Tiny?" asked Tag. He stared at the frightened Troll.

"He must leave through that door!" said the Sprite, staring at the slab of granite. "There is no other way out for him."

Knowing the Troll was too scared to save himself, Loken glowed brightly as he flew into action.

The mountain suddenly groaned.

Before he could morph into a Troll as big and as strong as Tiny to force this door open, the mountain shook under this assault. Hairline fractures crackled, racing along the walls and ceiling like this granite formation was now as delicate as an eggshell.

"Look out!" cried Myron. He shoved Rose toward the tunnel, but it was too late.

With a thunderous roar, the earth beneath their feet shimmied violently. While Tiny huddled against the northeast wall, the others fell to the ground as rocks and boulders cascaded down in a landslide from near the top of the mountain, sealing them into this crypt.

Inside the chamber, the brass bells came crashing down as huge rocks broke away, falling from the ceiling directly over the granite door to add to the debris on the other side to further block their way. As Giblet took cover, crouching next to the stone steps, Loken was buried beneath the rocks. The falling rubble and swirling cloud of dust instantly snuffed out his light.

Without the glow of Loken's aura, they were swallowed up in utter darkness. The only thing to be heard were the sounds of coughing; the clinking of stones coming loose, falling onto the jumble of rocks; and the tinkling of sandy sediment settling on the debris piled against the granite door.

From the darkness a voice called out. Echoing through this claustrophobic chamber, it was muffled by the veil of dust hanging heavy in the air. "Is everyone safe?"

"I'm not hurt," whimpered Tiny, speaking in a whisper in case the echoing of his words brought down more rocks. "Scared though."

"Princess? Myron?" The voice called again. "How do you fare?"

"Tag?" Rose coughed and sputtered. "Wh- where are you?"

"I'm over here," he answered, blindly reaching toward the sounds of her panicked voice. "Myron? Lord Silverthorn?"

"We are both unhurt," answered Rainus, as he helped Myron onto his feet.

"Master Barscowl?" called Tag. "Loken? Are you safe?"

Tag's words were met by ominous silence.

Suddenly, the sounds of rocks being pushed aside echoed through the chamber as Dwarvish words of profanity accosted their ears. Partially shielded by the stone steps he had crouched against, Giblet Barscowl erupted from the rubble pile.

"You're alive!" cried Rose, staring into the darkness toward the sounds of the Dwarvish cursing.

"It takes more than this ta do the likes of me in, Princess!" snorted Giblet, brushing the dust from his raiment as he adjusted his helmet.

"But where's our spritely friend? He was near ta me when the ceilin' fell."

"Loken!" Tag's hands cupped his mouth as he called.

"Where are you, Loken?" shouted Myron.

"I hate to be the bearer of bad tidings, my friends, but I watched as the Sprite's aura was extinguished by the falling rocks," said Rainus, pointing to the entranceway even though none could see. He strained to focus his sight, but in this suffocating darkness not even his keen Elf eyes could see his hand as he pointed.

"I fear Lord Silverthorn is right," added Myron. "If Loken survived, we'd see his aura glowing brightly, especially in this profound darkness. He'd be as bright as a torch's flame in the darkest of dungeons."

"This ain't natural," whimpered Tiny. "It's darker than the darkest night in the dead of winter in here."

"We need light," said Tag, as he rummaged through his pockets. "Perhaps Loken is just trapped; stuck in a gap amongst the debris."

"Do you have a flint?" asked Rose, blindly groping about to find the others.

"I always carry flint," answered Tag. "I just need to find it."

"Hurry, will you?" she called.

"Hold on… Here it is." Tag fished it out of his trousers' pocket with one hand as the other hunted about for the hilt of his dagger. Sliding his feet over the ground so he wouldn't tread on or stumble over strewn rocks and stones, Tag cautiously pushed aside the debris as he made his way to the oil trough lining the south wall, for it was the closest to him.

As the dagger's blade clashed against the piece of flint, tiny sparks sprang forth, floating into the trough to ignite the oil once more. With an audible *'whoosh'* a line of flames raced along the wall of the chamber once more. However, instead of an even line of steadily burning oil, wherever rocks and rubble clogged the trough, it produced gaps in the flames.

"Oh, my!" gasped Rose. She blinked hard as her eyes adjusted from the overwhelming darkness to the bright glow of firelight that pushed back the shadows. Glancing about, the devastation was far worse than she had anticipated.

"Not good! Not good at all!" grumbled Giblet, squinting as his eyes scrutinized the walls and ceiling for the true extent of damage. Not only did a landslide seal the granite door from the outside, rocks that had crumbled away from the ceiling over this entranceway added to seal their fate. Glancing to where Tiny huddled, his strong back plastered against the northeast wall near to the tunnel, he motioned to the Troll not to move upon spying the hairline cracks that spread, radiating like the web of a drunken spider, down the ceiling and along the wall behind him. "Ya best stay put, Tiny. Ya may well be the only thing holdin' up that side of the chamber."

"No worries, Master Barscowl, I'll stay put," promised Tiny, pressing his back firmly to the wall. "Beside, it's not lookin' like we're goin' anywhere anytime soon."

"How about the tunnel?" asked Rose, jabbing a thumb over her shoulder to the east wall near to where Tiny sat. "We, at least those who are not Troll-sized, can escape, if we use that tunnel."

"There?" asked Tag, glancing behind her to the exit leading into the subterranean Dwarf community. "I think not."

Rose turned about, gazing over to their only hope of escape. "Oh, no! We are truly and surely trapped!"

"Indeed, we are." Rainus nodded in confirmation, "but at least we are still alive and unhurt; a far better fate than what Loken was dealt."

"Now I'm really scared," Tiny moaned. "What happened ta our little friend? He wasn't crushed, was he?"

"There is no way he could have survived beneath all this," said Tag, abandoning Rose to join Myron in searching through the debris.

"I have a terrible feeling that you're right, my friend, but the least we can do is give Loken a proper burial," said Myron, tossing aside a rock from where he had last seen the Sprite.

"I hate to sound morbid, but I'd say Loken *is* already buried," stated Rose. "If anything, as it is now, we are *all* entombed in this crypt, along with the Sprite's body!"

"I meant to say Loken deserves our respect," corrected Myron. "It is wrong for us to abandon him beneath this rubble to be forgotten by all. Once we find him, then we shall consider our options to escape this place."

"It sounds like you have a plan," determined Rose.

"Not at this very moment, but I have every intention of finding a way out, once we recover Loken's body," answered Myron, as he helped Tag lift a large rock from the pile.

"Fair enough," conceded Rose. Tiptoeing through the scattered rubble, she joined Myron and Tag in their search efforts. "We better make haste though, should this entire chamber collapse on us."

While Myron, Tag, Rainus and Rose picked through the debris, Giblet Barscowl made his way to the tunnel. With pickaxe in hand, he tapped here and there on the rocks and boulders that clogged this opening. Each time he tapped, with a hand cupping his ear, he'd cock his head, listening intently.

"It's gettin' warm in here," whispered Tiny.

The Dwarf glanced up to see great beads of sweat gathering on the Troll's furrowed brows, and then he studied the flames that flickered. "It's jus' gettin' a bit stuffy, that's all. Jus' breathe easy an' keep doin' what you're doin', my friend."

Tiny pressed his back firmly against the wall as he nodded. He had no way of knowing that when the Dwarf mentioned it was getting stuffy and to 'breathe easy', what Giblet Barscowl really meant was that they were indeed entombed in this chamber. And should he begin to panic, accelerating his breathing, there was a good chance they'd die of suffocation before they could escape or be rescued.

"Any sign of the wee Sprite, yet?" called Giblet, as he clambered onto the heap to tap on boulders piled high against the entrance of the tunnel.

Rainus helped Myron remove a slab that fell from the ceiling, as he grunted a sombre response, "No, Master Barscowl."

"Are you sure this is where you last saw Loken?" asked Rose, as she tossed a fist-sized rock over her shoulder.

"I am positive this is where the Sprite was hovering just before the ceiling came down on him," answered Rainus.

"We must keep searching," insisted Tag. "Loken is here, somewhere amongst all this."

"If that were so, we would have uncovered him by now," stated Rose. "One thing is for sure, had Loken survived, we would have found him, or at least the glow of his aura shining through by now."

"Are you saying we should give up?" grumbled Tag. Not even affording her a glance, he shoved aside a large rock, refusing to stop this grim task.

"I am saying, it is far better for us to focus all this energy to save the living than to waste time searching for the dead."

As she spoke these words, unseen by Rose, a tiny flea crawled out from between the cracks in the rocks. It wasn't until it hopped, landing on the back of her hand, did she take notice.

"Ewww! Disgusting!" cried Rose. Just as she was about to flick away the tiny creature, Myron seized her by the wrist.

"Wait, my lady!" he ordered.

In a blink of light the parasite morphed before their eyes. Loken took to the air, hovering before his comrades. He was completely unscathed!

"Thank you, Sir Kendall!" said Loken, his aura glowing brightly once more. "It would have been tragic to survive this cave-in, only to be mistakenly killed by Princess Rose."

"Thank goodness, Loken!" exclaimed Tag. "We thought you had been crushed to death!"

"Had I not transformed when I did, I would have been deader than dead," stated Loken. "I am sure of it!"

"But to turn into a detestable flea?" groaned Rose, shuddering involuntarily as her skin crawled. "I swear you did this deliberately to put me off!"

"By its very design, a flea was the perfect choice in this circumstance," explained Loken, as he alighted upon her open hand. "Being so tiny, and being flattened vertically to allow easy travel through thick hair and fur, it allowed me to find a safe sanctuary in the cracks amongst the rubble."

"I suppose it makes sense," admitted Rose, watching as Loken launched off her hand. He took to the air once more to revel in his freedom.

"Of course it does," assured Loken. "I am alive, after all!"

"We're all alive," grunted Giblet, annoyance knotting in the back of his throat, "but it means nothin' in the grand scheme of things! There's no gettin' out of here. There's no escape!"

"No escape?" gasped Tiny. The shattered wall he leaned against creaked as his body shifted. "Did I hear ya correctly, Master Dwarf?"

Myron raised a hand to the Troll, motioning for calm as he spoke, "Fear not, Tiny. There must be a way out. The Dwarves designed their underground communities with multiple exits, should a cave-in occur. Is that not so, Master Barscowl?"

"Should one exit be blocked, in theory, there's always another way out" explained Giblet, pointing to the sealed, granite door, and then to the tunnel across the chamber, "In this case, theory and practice fails. We are utterly trapped."

"Utterly trapped?" repeated Tag, as he and the others picked their way through the rubble toward Giblet. "Is there no way we can dig ourselves out?"

"While you were searchin' fer Loken, I was checkin' out this mess," said Giblet, tapping his pickaxe on a boulder. "As miners, we developed ways ta evaluate situations like this."

"And you have determined that we are doomed to die," groaned Rose.

"Hush, Princess," ordered Myron. "Tell us what you have discovered, Master Barscowl."

"By strategically tappin' an' listenin' ta the sounds the rocks make, one can determine the extent of the collapse."

Tapping on several rocks, each time the pickaxe made contact they gave off a heavy, dull thud.

"If there were just a few rocks an' boulders blockin' the way, I'd hear more of a hollow, ringin' sound resonatin' back. In this case, when I tap, it sounds like hittin' a solid wall. The damage ta this tunnel is far greater than I had first thought."

"Unbelievable!" grunted Rose, as she gazed at Tag and Myron. "Get to work! Hurry up and devise a plan to get us out of here before we die of starvation and thirst!"

"Death shall come faster than ya think, Princess," warned Giblet. The flames burning in the trough guttered, wavering ominously. "Now that the chamber is effectively sealed, fresh air is in limited supply."

"Master Barscowl is correct," said Rainus. "I neither feel nor hear the slightest draft whispering through this chamber. It will only be a matter of time before we run out of air."

With a sigh of resignation, Tag plopped down on a large rock. He contemplated their collective fate. "I don't know what is worse, being instantly crushed to death or to suffer a lingering death by suffocation."

"Oh, shut it!" snapped Rose. "As you and Myron are tasked with keeping me safe, you shall put your brains together; think of a way out of here! As long as you both live and breathe, it is your duty to get me out of this tomb!"

"I can remove those rocks at the door an' try ta push it open," offered Tiny.

"Brilliant!" praised Rose. She shook an admonishing finger at Tag and Myron. "For shame! You have both been out-thunk by a Troll!"

"Stop!" shouted Giblet, his hands frantically waving at the behemoth. "Don't ya be movin', Tiny! Stay right where ya are."

"But Tiny is big enough and strong enough to push open this vault," insisted Rose. "I am sure of it!"

"True 'nough, Princess, but – "

"He has more strength than all of us combined, and then some!" added Rose. "We can help remove the debris to clear a path for Tiny. If it is just enough to force that door open, at least enough to get some fresh air in here, it will be enough to keep us alive until the others come to our rescue."

"Sounds like a plan, Princess, but consider this," argued Giblet. "I know this mountain better than any of you. Jus' as the Elves know how wood can split or shatter dependin' on the tree it came from and how it's cut, Dwarves know how rocks can crack an' shatter, in the same way."

"What are you saying?" probed Rose.

"I'm sayin', Princess, if Tiny moves from there, that wall he's holdin' up will come crashin' down on us."

"Are you positive?"

"Of course, Master Barscowl is positive," confirmed Rainus. "Even I can see those fractures in the wall behind Tiny are potentially devastating. Should the Troll sneeze, even that will be enough to see us buried alive!"

"So, it's as bad as that," sighed Tag.

"Bad, indeed!" said Myron. "So, we can either admit defeat, commiserate in our shared misery and accept death, or we can use this time to figure a way out."

"Either way, we're trapped in here," reminded Giblet. He marched across the chamber, clambering over the mound of rubble resting against the door. Removing his helmet and taking up his pickaxe, he tapped the slab of granite. Pressing an ear to the door, he listened.

"I have good news an' bad, my friends."

"I'm all fer some good news, Master Barscowl," said Tiny.

"Me, too!" said Rose. "Do tell!"

"The good news is, on the other side of this door, our friends are workin' tagether ta do what they can ta dig us out of here."

"Huzzah!" cheered Rose. Her eyes ablaze with renewed hope.

"And the bad news, dare I ask?" queried Tag.

"The bad news is, from what I can tell, there's so much earth, rocks an' boulders that came down, I hardly think they'll get ta us before we run out of air."

As though his words were a dark omen of things to come, the flames burning in the oil trough guttered once more, twisting and flickering in a menacing dancing.

"We're doomed!" wailed Rose. "Why now? Why, when my life had finally taken a turn for the better? When I'm betrothed to the most handsome and eligible prince of the free lands? Woe is me!"

"Woe is *me*, if you don't stop whining!" snapped Tag, clamping his hands over his ears.

"How dare you? I am a princess! You have no right to speak to me with such disrespect!"

"True enough," said Tag, "but in the face of death, we are all equal."

"Well then! Do something about it, for I have no desire to be equal to any of you, except perhaps Lord Silverthorn, given my limited choices!"

"I am flattered, Princess, but insulting present company and panicking will do nothing to help our cause," stated Rainus.

"I have an idea," said Loken, his aura glowing brightly as he hovered before the Elf.

"Do share," urged Rainus. "We are severely limited in the way of options. What is this idea?"

"Princess Rose is correct," said Loken. "Because of his great size, logically, Tiny is the only one strong enough to force that door open."

"But Master Barscowl warned us should Tiny move, that wall, and not to forget the ceiling it is attached to, is likely to collapse on us," reminded Rose.

"I do not doubt the Dwarf's words, but there's nothing to stop *me* from becoming as big as a Troll. Stand aside people!"

All dashed to Tiny's side, hoping to find some safety in his shadow as the Sprite's aura flashed with light.

Tiny was dumbfounded to see his spitting image standing before him. "Look! It's me! Oooh, I'm such a handsome Troll!"

"You stand corrected, Tiny. I am not you. I am merely your likeness. Now stand back, all of you!"

With a sideway sweep of his foot Loken's huge Troll form easily brushed aside the rubble that had trapped him as a flea.

"Hold on!" ordered Giblet. He dashed forward with his pickaxe. "That's all right an' good what ya plan ta do, Loken, but let me first warn those on the other side ta stand clear, so they don't get hurt in the process."

"How do you intend to do that?" queried Myron. "I hardly think they'll be able to hear you shout through that great slab of granite, not to forget all the rocks and boulders piled up against it now."

"No talkin' required, my friend, jus' some strategic tappin'," explained Giblet, holding forth his trusty pickaxe. "It's the way us Dwarves communicate through the tunnels an' chambers, instead of wastin' time an' energy yellin' back an' forth."

Taking up his tool, the Dwarf tapped out a code known to his kinfolk. Each of the three short sentences ended with the tip of the pickaxe dragging down sharply against this granite surface, punctuated by a quick, sharp tap, like it was an exclamation mark to emphasize the urgency of this message. Pressing an ear to the door, the Dwarf listened for a response that his warning was heard and understood.

Satisfied, Giblet backed away, making room for Loken.

"They took heed of my warnin', so yer free ta go at it," said Giblet, his stout, little legs scrambling to deliver him to the others waiting by Tiny's side. "Be quick about it, before the flames die out an' we suffer the same fate!"

Nodding his big, lumpy Troll head, Loken set to work. Resting his hands against the cold granite, he pushed, but the door would not budge. Brushing the dust from his hands, he repositioned them, plying his right shoulder to this solid surface. With a loud grunt, Loken pushed harder. This time, only a faint puff of dust seeped through the seam between the door and the mountain, but other than that, it remained securely shut.

"Is it working?" asked Tag.

"I hope so," answered Loken. "Just stand back. I'm going to take a running start; try to ram that door open."

Rose huddled against Tiny's side for added protection as the Troll drew his knees up to his chest, allowing his doppelganger more space to take a short run at the barrier.

Taking advantage of what little room there was, Loken's heels dug in as he turned his right shoulder toward the sealed vault. With a great roar, his Troll form rushed at the west wall. As his rounded shoulder slammed against solid granite, the air gushed from his compressed lungs. His body appeared to fold, giving in to the impact before the door did.

Instead of crashing open, another puff of dust gushed through to outline the entranceway. All Loken's effort did was to allow a fine dusting of earth to settle in between the door and its frame to further seal the entranceway and any access to fresh air.

"Try again!" ordered Rose.

Loken rubbed his aching shoulder, backing up for another attempt.

Again, he charged. Groaning in pain, his shoulder rammed the impervious granite. The impact reverberated through the chamber to send rocks, pebbles and dirt already loosened from the initial attack to shower down upon the Sprite.

"The way is completely blocked," announced Loken. "Even as a Troll, it is too much."

"So now what?" Rose drew a deep breath between her gritted teeth, struggling to control the rising tide of panic threatening to overwhelm her.

"I will try one more time," responded the Sprite.

"But you said it was too much," reminded Tag.

"Yes, in the form of a Troll. I will give it a try in another form. Stand well back, people. I'll need more room."

Before Tag could ask what he had in mind, Loken's giant form was enveloped in a brilliant flash of light that momentarily vanquished the deepest shadows from the darkest recesses of this chamber.

Tiny's eyes grew wide with surprise. He gasped as all in his company shrank back against the northeast wall, making room for a monstrous reptile unlike any they had ever seen.

"Good gracious!" exclaimed Myron. "What are you?"

"I've adopted the shape of a dragon that inhabits the lands in the far northern reaches of the Fire Rim Mountain Range."

"No disrespect, Loken, but I am long-lived and have had the misfortune of venturing through those lands to the north," said Rainus, "and in all my travels, never had I seen a beast like the one you are now!"

"Yes," added Rose. "A dragon has wings! You have none, at least ones big enough to count as wings. And you look much too squat and heavy to take to the air, if you did have them!"

"These dragons have no need to fly. They dwell *under* the earth, deep in the mountains," explained Loken. As he shrugged, massive plates of scales rolled over his mountainous shoulders where the bony, vestigial remnants of what had once been wings, protruded slightly. Lowering his armoured head, he determined his best approach to tackle the granite slab. "This *squat* anatomy you speak of, this heavy armour of scales to deflect falling rocks and these powerful claws and limbs are adapted specifically for digging and to take advantage of a subterranean lifestyle."

"I see now! I was never one for travelling beneath the earth, so that would explain why I had never seen a dragon such as the one you are now," decided Rainus.

"I suppose there is no need for wings if there is no need to fly," said Myron.

"These spade-shaped paws and stout legs are perfectly designed for digging. And this skull is like that of a mountain sheep's, double-layered to absorb an incredible amount of shock, so my head is now like a great battering ram!"

"Let us see what you can do," said Rose. Impressed by this formidable reptilian form, she eagerly motioned for Loken to bash down the sealed entranceway. "And though you are the ugliest looking dragon I have ever seen, if you get this door open, you will be the most beautiful ugly dragon ever!"

Loken rested his flattened, wedge-shaped head armed with a double-hulled skull squarely against the slab of granite. The flames guttered, twisting and shrinking as his dragon form drew a deep breath, bracing for the task ahead. Setting his heavily clawed feet into the earth, he set to work, pressing as hard as he could. His effort was rewarded with a puff of dry soil coming loose from between this door and the stonework framing it as more sediment settled, further sealing them inside this chamber.

"Well, so much for that," muttered Rose. "You are indeed still an *ugly* dragon."

"I am not yet done," snorted Loken, as he backed away from the door.

With a mighty roar, Loken charged. As he neared the barrier, he reared up. With a thunderous crash, his armoured head smashed against the granite. The mountain groaned under this assault, rattled to its very foundations, as Rose and those trapped with her were pelted by stones and showered with dirt and dust coming loose from the already damaged ceiling.

For a moment, Loken reeled, sending his friends scattering to the far walls as he staggered about, rattled by the impact that resounded to his very bones.

"Well, the door is no more open than it was before," sighed Rose. "Too bad, ugly dragon."

"But it was a valiant attempt," praised Myron.

"Yes, and an exercise in futility, if ever there was one," assessed Rainus, his words matter-of-fact.

"All it's done was ta help seal our fate," said Giblet. He knew by the flames, gradually shrinking in size, it wasn't going to be the lack of oil, but rather the absence of air, to eventually extinguish the fire.

"If I cannot push this door open with all the debris against it, then I am confident if I were on the other side, as a being as large as Tiny or in the form I am now, I can easily remove the boulders and rocks, pushing them aside so this door will open," said Loken.

"Brilliant!" exclaimed Rose. "But *you* are on *this* side of *that* door! Trapped in here with the rest of us."

"We just need to get Loken on the opposite side to help the others dig us out," said Tag.

"How do we do that?" asked Myron.

"We need to dig a hole, one big enough to get Loken through," answered Tag.

"I have made a life out of digging holes an' tunnels, young sir," explained Giblet. His wiry brows furrowed beneath the rim of his steel helm as he considered this mortal's words. "With jus' one pickaxe between us, there's no way I'd dig through ta the other side before this air runs out."

"I shall be the one to dig beneath this door," decided Loken. "With claws like these, I can easily excavate a tunnel to the other side."

"You do realize that while Harold is likely to run, the Dwarves and Elves on the other side are likely to attack you on sight," cautioned Rainus. "While we know it's you, all they will see is a frightening monster emerging before them."

"Worry not," said Loken, prodding the ground as he tested for the best point to execute his plan. "I will deal with this matter when the time comes. The most important thing is to dig out of here, and to do so with haste."

"Then get to it, my friend," urged Tag. "We shall see you on the other side."

Loken nodded, "Just stand clear. Dirt is about to fly!"

Having shaken off the brain rattling effects of using his skull as a battering ram, Loken's dragon form lumbered to the door. The stout, sharp claws arming his spade-shaped forepaws set to work. As his front paws dug, shovelling the loosened soil beneath him, his powerful feet scooped and pushed the excavated earth behind him. Immersed in this task, the nictitating membrane of each eye was drawn obliquely. These translucent third eyelids allow limited vision, but served more to protect the eyes from flying debris.

Like a giant mole burrowing feverishly through soft, loamy earth, Loken disappeared into a great, black hole.

"How long do you think he will be?" questioned Rose. She peered into the darkness, listening to the sounds of Loken hard at work.

"It shall depend on how much of the mountain had come down to block the way," said Rainus.

"Yes," added Giblet, "if we're lucky, he'll jus' pop up on the other side, if the trapdoor hasn't collapsed, but if the landslide is as great as I believe, he'll have ta dig accordingly. An' based on my preliminary tappin', he'll have a whole lot of diggin' ta do ta break through ta the other side."

"So, there is a chance we shall die; suffocating before Loken is done," said Rose, unleashing a dismal sigh.

"We're gonna die?" gulped Tiny.

"We shall all die, eventually, for it is the way of the world," responded Rainus.

"Jus' might happen sooner than we'd all like," grunted Giblet.

"I'm not likin' that at all," whimpered the Troll. He drew his knees up to his chest. Huddling in a pathetic heap, he contemplated his fate as the hope of a second chance at a new life continued to slip away.

"Suppose we go down into this tunnel and help Loken dig?" offered Tag. "We can speed up the process."

"Your intentions are good, but such actions can prove disastrous," cautioned Myron. He listened to the sounds of dirt being shovelled and pushed about. "Efforts to aid Loken will only see us get in his way. Either that, or we shall be buried by all that flying earth being excavated."

"So what now?" asked Rose. She watched, the flames in the oil troughs flickering ominously as Giblet proceeded to cut off the oil supply to the trough along the north wall.

"We wait," answered Myron, as the chamber dimmed. He sighed as the flames were extinguished to reduce the use of oxygen.

"We just sit here?" she groaned. "Wait to die should Loken fail to break through in time?"

"No need to panic just yet, Princess," responded Tag, motioning her to remain calm. "We still have plenty of air."

Rose watched the shrinking flames in the remaining oil trough. The amber tongues lapped at the dwindling air, twisting as it burned with defiance.

"So I exaggerated," admitted Tag, with a shrug of his shoulders. "There is air, it's just not as much as I first thought."

"Great!" snapped Rose. "From this moment on, breathing is forbidden unless it is absolutely necessary!"

"You want us to hold our breath?" Tag stared with raised eyebrows at her. "Are you mad?"

"You are bloody right, I am mad!" Rose shook an angry fist at Tag. "And I hardly think I am being unreasonable with this demand, as it was not my idea to come to the Land of Big in the first place!"

"You may well indeed feel mad in here," said Tag, his fist thumping his chest, and then smacking his forehead in frustration as he continued on, "but without a doubt you are crazy in here."

"If that is so, it is only because you are making me crazy!" Rose's index finger spun by the side of her head.

"Now, now!" said Rainus, waving an admonishing finger at the young mortals. "If we are to die, at least we should do so with our dignity intact."

"What is so dignified about suffocating to death in this hole in the ground?" snapped Rose.

"We're not really *in* the *ground*, Princess," responded Tiny. "I'd say we're more like inside a *mountain*. It's kinda the same, but diff'rent nonetheless."

"I'd say we should all jus' shut our gobs an' stop wastin' precious air," grumbled Giblet. He carelessly tossed his pickaxe to the ground in resignation.

"Listen up, people!" Myron stood upon a rock to garner their attention. "No pacing! No fidgeting! No talking, unless it is to share an idea that will see us out of this chamber!"

With these stern words, a silence fell heavy upon the comrades, making the air all the more stifling as they endured this shared misery.

"Hey… I have an idea, and it could well be our last resort," said Tag.

"Go on," urged Myron. "What is it?"

"We should call upon the Dream Merchant for his help."

"Why? Why now?" Rose glared at Tag. "Is it because you finally admit this was all his fault to begin with and you'd like to give him an earful?"

"No! I say this now because Silas Agincor is the only one with the power to wish us out of here before it's too late."

"He will not come," insisted Rainus. "Need I remind you that he has forsaken his magic to pursue a career in the literary arts?"

"What a bunch of malarkey!" grunted Rose. Her hands flew up in utter frustration. "Since when did fabricating lies, distorting the truth and passing them off as stories be considered an art?"

"It is all very subjective, is it not?" responded Rainus, with a judicious nod.

"That is neither here nor there at this moment," said Tag. "Time is running out! If Loken's efforts fall short and there is a chance Master Agincor can be summoned before it's too late, why not call on him?"

"I agree with Tag," said Myron. "At this point, we have nothing to lose, except our lives. Even if he does not answer our call for help, at least we tried everything at our disposal."

"Does summonin' that old codger require the person ta be asleep?" queried Giblet. Collecting his pickaxe, he swung it like a club. "If so, I volunteer ta hit one of ya on yer noggin jus' enough ta help put ya ta sleep real fast!"

"There will be no need to knock a person unconscious." Tag motioned the Dwarf to put his tool down. "Princess Rose just needs to recite a special incantation to summon the Dream Merchant."

"Well, that's mighty handy," said Giblet. "Recite away, good Princess, recite away!"

Frowning in displeasure as she sat upright, Rose gathered her thoughts.

"You remember this summoning incantation, right?" asked Tag, searching her troubled eyes that grew a deeper shade of amethyst whenever she became agitated or worried.

"Of course I do!" She waved off his concern. "It is not as though I am some brain-addled dolt of a fool."

"Very good then!" exclaimed Myron. "Just don't forget the magic word."

"Oooh!" gasped Tiny. "I'm bettin' that word would be *hocus-pocus* or *abracadabra*!"

"One would think!" responded Rose, as she stood before her comrades. "But neither one is the magical word Sir Kendall was speaking of."

"But they're the most magical words *ever*," insisted Tiny, scratching his head of wiry, red hair as he pondered this mystery. "Come ta think of it, they're the only magical words I've ever heard ta be spoken by magicians."

"Yes, if one does not possess true magic and is only capable of tawdry tricks of illusions to fool the masses," said Tag. "We are speaking of *real* magical powers possessed by a Wizard, not cheap tricks conjured up by a magician."

"Well, then wee master, I must know," said the Troll. "What is this special word? What has the power ta summon the Dream Merchant? Do tell!"

"Please," replied Tag.

"Yes, do tell, please!" begged Tiny.

"That was the word, you fool!" scolded Rose.

"Please?" repeated Tiny. He frowned in confusion.

"Yes." Rose nodded.

"Ooh, I'm supposin' it's right up there with *thank-you*," decided the Troll, as he considered the power of this single word.

"If not magical, it is still oh-so civilized!" declared Rainus. "The world would be a much better place if people just remembered to use these two words more often."

"Before we waste anymore air with talk, I recommend the Princess use this opportunity to summon the Wizard," said Myron.

"You heard the man," responded Tag, as he took a step back from her. "Recite that incantation and don't forget to say *please*."

"Very well," said Rose, as she cleared her throat. "Just cover your ears, people!"

"Because the incantation will unleash a terrifyin' magic, one so powerful it'll deafen us?" queried Giblet, clamping his grubby hands over his ears.

"No, more because this incantation is an atrocious little rhyme that does little to speak of the Wizard's true powers," answered Rose. "If anything, whatever poetic licence he has, it should be revoked because of this."

"Just say the words, Princess!" urged Tag.

Rose raised a single hand to him, motioning for silence. Giving all in her company a stern look of reproach, she waited until she was confident they were not going to mock her. When she was ready to proceed, Rose drew a deep breath as she searched her memory for the precise words used to summon Silas Agincor.

"Oh, great Wizard, the Merchant of Dreams, *please* answer this wish to put an end to my schemes!" Rose took great care to enunciate each word of this incantation.

"An' *thank-you*," chimed in Tiny. "Won't hurt ta say that, too!"

"Yes, please *and* thank-you." Rose added for good measure.

For the longest moment, the trapped friends waited with great anticipation, watching for signs of the Wizard's arrival.

Instead of a great show of light, there was only foreboding silence hanging heavy in the ever-growing gloom as the flame burning in the oil trough continued to sputter and shrink. The tongues of fire lapped feebly at the diminishing supply of oxygen.

"See... No Wizard," said Rainus, with a dismal shake of his head.

Rose said not a word. She passed by Tag, using her booted feet to push aside rubble to clear a narrow space on the floor. Once she was done, she lay down. Crossing her hands over her chest, she closed her eyes in silent repose.

"What are you doing now?" asked Tag, staring in bewilderment at her.

"I am surrendering to our sorry fate. If I am to die, I shall do so with grace, plus, I shall look lovely *and* dignified in doing so," answered Rose, peering up through one opened eye at her friend. "If we should ever be discovered, I shall look like a beautiful princess cast into a deep slumber that I shall never wake from, rather than a wretched mess who died like a hysterical fool that refused to accept death like a real hero."

"Good grief, Princess! There is no grace, nor is there dignity, in giving up at this moment," argued Tag.

"And just who are you to say?" grumbled Rose. Refusing to heed his words, she was resolute, smoothing out her cloak before resting her hands over her chest once more to welcome an eternal slumber.

"Obviously, I speak as one with more grace and dignity than you," snorted Tag. He extended his hand to her. "Now, enough with the dramatics. On your feet!"

"Why should I? This is hopeless! All is lost."

"Really?" snapped Tag.

"Go away! Sulk somewhere else! Leave me in peace!"

"Are you truly intent on accepting death so readily, my lady?" questioned Myron.

"The Dream Merchant never came, even though I remembered to say *please* and threw in a *thank you* for good measure. What else is left for me to do?" Rose opened her eyes to find Myron hovering over her.

"Hmph!" grunted the knight, as he turned to Tag. "She does sound serious, my friend."

"Indeed," Tag responded with a judicious nod. "We should help her."

"I am hardly in need of an intervention."

"It would appear so," said Myron.

"I say we help the good Princess," offered Tag, his hand reaching across his body for the hilt of his sword. "No point in her taking up more air than necessary. If she's so intent on meeting her end, as her friends, we should help speed her along."

Rose's eyes narrowed, staring suspiciously at him upon hearing these words.

"Hold on there, Master Yairet!" Rainus stepped forth to speak his mind, a hand resting on Tag's arm to stay his sword. "It would be a foolish deed to bloody your blade for this cause. This is not the way a princess should die."

"Very true!" agreed Rose. She was pleased to see the Elf speak some sense to Myron and Tag.

"Instead," continued Rainus, "we shall have the Troll step on her! One quick stomp, and it will all be over in the blink of an eye! Tiny will need only to wipe his foot clean of the mess and your blade shall remain untarnished by rust brought on by the staining of blood."

Rose leapt up onto her feet as she scowled at her comrades. Stamping her feet, her balled fists trembled in anger as she confronted them. "You three want to kill me?"

"There are times when you make it so very tempting," mocked Tag, his hand pretending to throttle her from sheer frustration. "But no, I do believe we'd rather have you alive and here, than haunting and harping at us from the great beyond."

"How dare you?"

"What the lad is trying to say in his less-than-eloquent way, by your very words and actions, you really have no desire to die," explained Myron. "You just required some motivation to keep you going... to lift your spirits, so to speak."

"Well, you are all doing a poor job of it!" scolded Rose.

"They gotcha back on yer feet, Princess," piped in Tiny, "rather than havin' ya smooshed beneath one of mine."

"The Troll's got a point," added Giblet.

"So I am back on my feet!" snapped Rose. "We are still no closer to leaving this place."

She was suddenly bowled over as a great flash of light flooded the chamber with its brilliance.

16
Deeper into Danger

Shielding their eyes from the dazzling glare, they brandished their weapons. Fearing the Sorcerer had returned to complete his act of treachery, the comrades prepared to attack. The brilliance subsided immediately; branding their retinas to create ghostly blobs of phantom light that followed every movement of their eyes as they strained to focus on the form taking shape before them.

"What is the meaning of this? Was I summoned to be killed by you reckless fools?"

"Silas Agincor?" called Rainus. Squinting, he blinked hard as his eyes adapted to the returning gloom. The Elf lowered his bow, recognizing this voice before he could fully make out the wild tangle of silvery moustache that became one with his long beard.

"Of course it is! But what are you doing here, Lord Silverthorn? This is an unlikely place to find a wood Elf." Glancing about, he was momentarily baffled to appear in this place.

"Lord Silverthorn came to be here because of us," said Tag, as he and Myron stepped forward to greet the Dream Merchant.

"Tagius Yairet? Myron Kendall?" Silas spun about on his heels upon hearing Tag's voice. "Good gracious! What brings you here to the great Dwarf halls, and in the company of a Troll, at that! My mind is thoroughly boggled!"

"Tis an odd assortment of comrades, indeed," agreed Myron, "but we are here for good reason, my friend."

Silas' back straightened as he mulled over these words. "More odd than the company you keep is how you managed to summon me. Only those wishing to return a Dreamstone have the power to use that particular incantation."

"That would be me," responded Rose, as she stood up. Shaking the dirt from her riding coat and trousers, she unleashed a cloud of dust to float around her.

The Wizard scrutinized the non-descript figure before him. His hand waved about to dispense with this dust fog as he spoke, "You sound strangely familiar, young sir."

"And you are just strange," Rose muttered with indignation. "For an all-knowing, all-wise Wizard, how can you *not* know a princess when you stands before one?"

"Oh, my!" gasped Silas. "I do not recognize your manner of dress, but I do recognize that demanding tone."

"Do not mistake me for Tagius Yairet!" snapped Rose.

"I did no such thing, Princess Rose," insisted Silas, bowing his head politely, but only because protocol demanded it. "You are unmistakably... *you!*"

"Enough with the banter!" grumbled Giblet, pushing his way between Silas and Rose. "Master Agincor is here now! Someone tell the Wizard why he was summoned, if it's not already obvious to him."

"I am hoping it is because Princess Rose has something that is mine. Do you wish to return the magic crystal to me?" queried Silas, his brows puckered into a frown of disbelief that she had finally succeeded in securing the Dreamstone.

"Not quite..." admitted Rose. Her eyes were downcast, staring sheepishly as the toe of her boot nudged about a small pebble.

"For pity's sake!" grunted Silas. With a heavy heart he leaned against his staff that was now more of a walking stick than an instrument of power. "If not to return the Dreamstone to me, then why am I here? Have you gotten yourself into trouble deeper than you can dig yourself out of?"

"I suppose you can say that." Her eyes glanced about the ruined chamber, from the sealed doorway to the collapsed tunnel, in case the Wizard had failed to notice their dire predicament.

Bracing his sturdy dragon legs against the floor of this freshly dug tunnel, Loken mustered all his strength.

His first two attempts at pushing through to the surface had failed; the weight of the fallen boulders and earth proved too much. This time, failure was not an option. Growing desperation drove him on. As the air feeding this tunnel via the great chamber grew stifling, like breathing through a thick, damp veil smothering one's mouth and nose, he was forced to act quickly. Even in this dragon form, Loken knew the air supply was fast depleting. This time, if he did not break through, he doubted there would be enough air to allow him to extend this tunnel by another two or three horse-lengths, for he knew the faster he dug and the more energy he expended, so too, did he use more air to fuel his efforts.

Pressing his broad, rounded back and shoulders against the ceiling of the tunnel that was only as wide as his dragon form, Loken drew in a deep breath. Steeling his nerves for what was to come, he exhaled as the spiny ridges of heavy scales protecting his back bit into the soil. His legs straightened like massive pillars, thrusting hard to press his body against the roof of this passage. To Loken's surprise, this time the earth crumbled, giving ever so slightly, but it did shift, rising up like the start of a giant molehill. It was just enough for him to know he had cleared the weight of the debris field created by the landslide. He was now in a position to dig to the surface, toward fresh air and to freedom!

"Do you hear that?" asked Halen Ironwood.

He stood upright, dropping the rock he was in the midst of removing. The captain motioned for Harold, as well as the Elves and Dwarves working side-by-side to stop labouring.

"Hear what? I don't hear a thing!" grumbled the agitated Dwarf nearest to the captain.

"Silence! Listen carefully," ordered Halen, cupping a hand to his ear. He cocked his head to the ground immediately beside them as he strained to identify this sound. "I definitely hear something!"

The irate Dwarf muttered in response, "It's gotta be them Elf ears of yours, Cap'n Ironwood, 'cause I hear nothin'!"

"Stop bein' so grumpy an' listen up, ya miserable dolt!" ordered his fellow Dwarf with a much brighter disposition. "You should be happy the cap'n has a keen sense of hearin', detectin' what them dirt clogged ears of yours can't."

"Oh, lovely! Don't be bashful! Let them insults fly!" snapped the agitated Dwarf. His bearded jowls wobbled from the percussion as his face was assaulted by the slap of a grimy hand.

"Ya heard Cap'n Ironwood! Shut yer gob an' listen up or I'll smack ya again!" ordered Slappy, raising his hand in threat once more to the miserable Dwarf. It was enough to make the other six Dwarves, as well as all those in their company, cease their bickering. They stood in silence as Halen Ironwood stepped off the debris field to better investigate the strange noises he had detected.

"I swear I heard something," insisted Halen. "I am positive it was the sound of digging."

"You're mistaken," whispered Slappy. "Master Barscowl is a fine miner, one of the best when it comes ta diggin', but there's no bloody way he can singlehandedly dig a tunnel by his lone self from there ta all the way here."

"What makes ya say he's workin' alone? Ain't nothin' ta say our brethren aren't hard at work by his side," responded another Dwarf. He scratched his backside as he considered the possibilities. Though his eyes glinted with life, it was questionable whether there was much intelligence behind that stare.

"You dope! If our men had joined 'em in the great chamber, there'd be no need ta dig a tunnel out!" snapped Slappy, struggling to keep his hands from lashing out in frustration.

"What do ya mean, Slappy?" questioned the intellectually challenged Dwarf with the drooping trousers.

"I mean ta say, if our brethren had joined Master Barscowl in there, there'd be no need ta dig a new tunnel, they'd just exit from the one that brought them inta the chamber!"

"Oh... I suppose that makes sense."

"Of course it does!" grunted Slappy.

"Hush!" Halen raised a hand for silence. Using the heel of his boot, he gingerly pressed the ground beneath his feet to test its soundness. "There is something odd going on here."

"What is it, Captain Ironwood?" whispered Harold. He gently placed aside the large rock he had removed from the rubble pile.

"I am not sure," answered Halen. He listened as he continued to test the earth. "All I know is that the ground sounds different here... Like it is hollow and – "

Halen yelped in surprised. The earth he had tested gave way, swallowing him up in a black abyss.

"Sweet mother of pearl!" cried the Elf nearest to Halen. Watching as his captain disappeared, he stumbled back as the ground abruptly heaved before him.

Just as this Elf scrambled back onto his feet and his fellow warriors dashed toward the gaping hole in a bid to rescue their captain, the Elves fell. They rolled away as the earth shuddered, erupting skyward in an explosion of soil, roots and rocks.

"What sorcery is this!" cried the grumpy Dwarf. He and Slappy brandished their pickaxes. Together, they raced forward just as Halen Ironwood was unceremoniously thrust up from the expanding hole. There he was, clinging to the spiny scales on the back of a terrible beast bursting forth from the bowels of the earth.

"*Run away!*" cried Harold, stumbling over the rubble to flee this treacherous creature.

"*Kill it!*" shouted Slappy. Hoisting his pickaxe, he was poised to attack.

"Wait!" ordered Halen. He clung to this scaly back with one hand as the other motioned for all to stop.

In spite of their captain's order, the Elves armed their bows. Nocking arrows, they prepared to unleash their fury on the oddest-looking dragon they had ever set eyes on.

"*STOP!*" demanded Halen. Scrambling to dismount, he landed on the ground between the beast and the many arrows pointed at the creature as it clambered out of the crumbling tunnel. "Do not shoot!"

Instinct propelled by fear took hold over all as the dragon's full, menacing size became apparent. Instead of heeding this command, the Elves let their arrows fly as the Dwarves charged forward, weapons held high to lay siege to this monster should it disappear once more with the Elf captain.

"*NO!*" shouted Halen. Raising his hands, he motioned for them to halt.

Drawing his sword, the broad edge of Halen's blade managed to deflect several arrows, each delivering a harsh '*clang*' as bodkin met forged steel. His eyes squeezed shut as the arrows he missed whistled by him, the projectiles slicing through the air to strike their intended target.

Both Elves and Dwarves were knocked off their feet as a bone-rattling din, as loud as a clap of thunder, rumbled through the night air when a blinding flash of light erupted behind Halen. He dropped to his knees. The sword tumbled from his hands as he shielded his eyes from the dazzling brilliance as the arrows shattered upon colliding against this strange force.

Glancing back, Halen spied upon the massive hole, now devoid of the odd-looking dragon. In its place, Loken flitted about drinking in the fresh, cool autumn air. His golden aura intensified. He was never so glad to be free of the stifling darkness that was the tunnel he had dug.

Pleased to see Loken alive and well, Halen's attention turned to the people sprawled about on the mound of excavated earth. Two figures stood above the tangle of bodies.

Rainus calmly brushed off the dust from his raiment, scanning his surroundings as he gained his bearings while Silas peered down. He shook his head in disbelief and disappointment at the state of the dazed

Dwarf and the mortals he had rescued.

Rose rolled onto her stomach, slowly pushing herself up onto her trembling hands and knees. Gasping like a fish out of water, she sucked in the fresh air, filling her lungs. She revelled in the fact that she was alive.

"The Dwarf, I understand, but I'd have thought you three would be accustomed to this mode of transportation by now, considering how often I've rescued you and how brief this *jaunt* was," commented Silas.

"You didn't give us time to brace ourselves," muttered Tag. He slowly sat up right, shaking the fog in his head. He blinked hard, glancing over to see Myron slowly rising onto his feet.

"It was not as though the Wizard had an abundance of time," reminded Myron.

"Very true!" exclaimed Silas.

"I am just relieved to be under these starry skies once more," said Rainus, as he nodded to his captain.

"And you are alive!" Halen sighed in relief, embracing Rainus in a brotherly hug. His brows furrowed with concern. "But wait... Where is the Troll?"

"No need ta worry, Cap'n Ironwood," responded Giblet, as he struggled to upright himself. "Tiny's safe for now. We were forced ta leave him behind. The brave soul is currently supportin' the walls an' ceiling, allowin' us ta make good our escape."

"Thank goodness you are all safe!" exclaimed Halen. He was happy to see his comrades again and more than a little surprised to see the Dream Merchant in their company.

"Luck and fate conspired to spare us all," stated Rainus.

"But what happened?" asked Halen.

"*I* happened, that's what!" declared Silas Agincor, proudly stepping forward to greet Captain Ironwood. "It had nothing to do with luck or fate!"

"*You* caused this great landslide?" responded the Elf.

"Oh, no!" Silas shook his head, as he scrutinized the boulders, rocks and earth piled high against the granite door. "As mighty as my powers are, the only thing I am responsible for is rescuing Princess Rose, and all who had been unwittingly embroiled in her latest misadventure."

"I will tell you what happened!" offered Tag, watching as Loken zipped away, flying high into the air to search for lingering danger. "We were attacked!"

"By whom?" questioned Halen.

"Did you not see the catapults launched to hurl boulders at this mountain?" queried Myron, frowning in confusion. "Were you busy fencing in the herd? Too busy to see?"

"We were in the midst of fencing the goats in when we heard a thunderous boom resonate through the air," informed Halen. "We came running, but I assure you, Sir Kendall, there was no such attack."

"No flyin' boulders ta speak of," confirmed Slappy, pushing between the Elf and the mortal to greet Giblet Barscowl. The two Dwarves clasped right hands as their right shoulders bashed together in glad tidings. "What there was though were great flashes of light."

"Two of 'em ta be exact," whispered a shy Dwarf, retreating into the knot of his brethren when all eyes turned on him for more information.

"Yes, brilliant balls of light, as bright as lightning, struck the mountainside," added Halen.

"But they weren't bolts of lightnin', that's for sure," insisted Harold, as he threw his meaty arms around Tag and Rose, lifting them off the ground in a great hug.

"It was the work of Parru St. Mime Dragonite!" insisted Rainus. "It had to be!"

"Impossible!" declared Silas, with a defiant shake of his head. "We all know that murderous villain is dead! I saw with mine own eyes when Tag ran his sword through that madman before he vanished. It was his last and dying act, allowing him to steal away with my Dreamstone."

"That is what we believed at first," said Rose.

"What has changed?" queried Silas.

"Events have come to light that warn us the Sorcerer has returned," answered Tag.

"I am truly baffled by your words, young sir. How can this be so?"

"I'll be happy to explain," said Tag. Inserting a finger and thumb into his mouth, he whistled for the Sprite to return. "First though, we must get that door open and brace the wall Tiny is holding up in order to free him. Loken would be perfect to help with earth removal once he morphs back into his dragon form."

"With a fresh supply of air, he'll be fine, but the poor Troll doesn't take well to being left alone in such gloomy confines," added Myron. "He's sure to panic, if he thinks he has been abandoned."

"Then let us waste no time," urged Silas. "Tell me what you know while we work together to clear this debris."

"It would be easier if you were to just wish it away," said Rose.

🍂🍂🍂

"So... There you have it, Master Agincor." Tag's words were punctuated by a dismal sigh.

"This was not what I had expected, and now that I am here, I feel my presence only thrusts us deeper into danger," whispered the Dream Merchant. He glanced over to where Rose, exhausted by the day's calamity, had fallen asleep by a roaring campfire.

He and Tag moved aside, allowing Giblet Barscowl and seven other Dwarves to march by with a long piece of timber that was cut down, hewn and stripped of branches by Halen and his men. It was hoisted upon their stout shoulders to be carried into the mountain. Inside this ruined chamber, Harold helped the Dwarves set up these logs to brace the damaged wall so Tiny was free to move away from it without fear it would collapse on him.

"Tag speaks the truth," said Myron. "From all we had seen and endured thus far, we have no doubt it is the work of that necromancer."

"It would appear so, but a sock puppet? That makes no sense," Silas wondered aloud. "Dragonite always fancied himself a mime man, the self-appointed patron saint of mimes, to be exact."

"Come now, Master Agincor! You are speaking of Dragonite," responded Tag. "Did that crazy Sorcerer's words and actions ever make sense?"

"His forces, as ineffective as they were, had scattered since our last confrontation to the north," reminded Rainus. "When the Sorcerer disappeared, grievously wounded as he was, I have no doubt his mimely minions, left to their own devices, had long since deserted him. Thinking he had died, the rabble of mimes were forced to abandon Dragonite's ill-fated, ill-conceived plan to elevate these street performers of ill-repute to the grand status of respected entertainers worthy of the professional stage."

"Well, as you claim you had seen neither hide nor hair of his followers during your travels, it could well be the Sorcerer has experienced difficulty in recruiting these mimes once more to do his bidding," assessed Silas. "I suspect they have lost faith in their *illustrious*, but demented leader."

"That could also explain that damned sock puppet," said Myron. "I suppose, if one's mind is already addled, an imaginary friend is better than no friend at all."

"For all we know, that puppet could well be the voice of reason for that madman," determined Silas.

"Or the voice that prompts Dragonite on to take the treacherous course of action he has embarked on," said Tag. "The way he carried on through that cursed toy when he first appeared to us was nothing short of disturbing."

"Whatever the case, the Sorcerer must be stopped," reminded Rainus. "It is apparent Dragonite seeks revenge, lashing out at all he believes came to Princess Rose's aid from the start."

"It appears so." Silas nodded in agreement.

"Then it begs the question, why did that demented soul not seek vengeance on you from the start?" questioned the Elf, as he eyed the Wizard. "In my mind, if I were Dragonite, you would be the first on my list, perhaps a close second to Princess Rose, if I was seeking revenge."

"It is a well known fact Dragonite, for years since the Council of Wizards stripped him of his greatest powers, has craved the magic encapsulated within a Dreamstone. It is the one thing that can restore him to his full might without the council's unanimous consent."

"Then why not you to start with?" asked Tag. "After all, you did say long ago that you were the one to bring Dragonite before this council in the first place. That being so, one would think you'd be high on, if not at the top, of his revenge list."

"I can only assume that Dragonite was waiting to recoup his health and strength. Learning to fully harness the powers of the magic crystal, he resolves to strike out at those he considers easier targets first, than to challenge the one that shall only knock him off his high horse once again."

"He is biding his time; testing his powers before retaliating, where you are concerned," said Tag. "That makes sense."

"Of course it does, my good lad," responded Silas. "Even though I had forsaken my magical powers to focus on the true power of the written word, I still pose a deadly threat to Dragonite, should we be forced to clash."

"I tend to agree with you," said Rainus. "There is a possibility the Sorcerer has been honing his newfound powers on us, as a precursor to confronting you, Master Agincor."

"Yes, practice does make perfect," agreed Silas. In pensive thought, his fingers preened his silvery beard.

"Does that mean you are willing to help us bring him to justice? Force the Sorcerer to answer for his crimes?" queried Tag.

"Though I feel more at ease these days with a writing quill in my hand than this staff of power," sighed Silas, as the crystal mounted atop glowed softly, "I am here now. It would be grossly negligent of me to shirk my responsibilities in allowing that madman to run amok."

"Brilliant!" Tag's spirit was buoyed by this prospect. "Under Myron's tutelage, I've been training hard, preparing for battle, should the occasion arise. And now, with you by our side, we will be unstoppable!"

"All of you should be commended for your courage in assuming this undertaking with Princess Rose," praised Silas, bowing his head in respect to Tag and his comrades.

"We are eager to see the Sorcerer undone for his wicked acts," stated Myron.

"My people will be avenged, and the deaths of Tiny's brethren will not be in vain," added Rainus.

"We are all highly motivated to end Dragonite's reign of terror," assured Tag.

"And what of Princess Rose?" queried Silas, watching her face grimace as a troubling dream tormented her.

"What of her?" Tag's shoulders rolled in shrug.

"How does she fare these days? Is she as driven as you are? Or does she still whine and gripe, angry that she is made to undo what she had brought unto herself?"

"Old habits die hard," answered Tag. "If she were able to stay behind at Pepperton Palace and have us do her bidding, she would have. Tending to plans for her upcoming nuptials would be more to her liking."

"Mind you," said Myron, "the same level of coercion was not necessary this time. I truly believe Princess Rose desires to reclaim that Dreamstone; to return it to you, so these tragic events will come to an end."

"Well, I'd be a fool to believe she could change overnight, and as hard as it is to break old habits, new ones can be just as hard to adopt," surmised Silas.

"Very true," admitted Myron.

"But nuptials, you say?" queried Silas. His brows arched up as he glanced over at Tag, and then at the sleeping beauty. "She has found a proper suitor? One that is a perfect match even with her *discriminating* taste?"

"Perfect, indeed!" sniffed Tag.

"I sense irony tinged with a hint of bitter sarcasm in your tone, young sir." Silas frowned with concern upon hearing his words.

"Oh, do not get me wrong, Master Wizard," responded Tag, "Princess Rose and the prince she is betrothed to are the *perfect* match, in every sense of the word!"

"Tag does not speak in jest," stated Myron. "It was nothing short of uncanny, and strangely so, to see Princess Rose with her intended husband."

"Brilliant!" exclaimed Silas. "And who is this princely suitor to charm her, enough to win the lady's heart and hand in marriage?"

"It is Prince Percival," answered Tag, as he snorted in derision. "King Maxmillian's pride and joy, the heir apparent to the throne of Axalon."

Silas gasped, his jaw dropping. He blanched upon hearing this name.

"I take it you are well acquainted with this particular royal," noted Rainus, as he scrutinized Silas' face.

"I have had the misfortune of becoming acquainted with the young man when he was a small princeling and yet, so very full of himself."

"How so?" asked Myron.

"He was *self*-indulgent, *self*-serving, *self*-righteous and spoiled beyond belief or reason back then, and rumour has it, age has not tempered these sorry attributes."

"Did I not say they were perfectly matched?" said Tag.

"Good gracious!" gasped Myron, as he motioned Tag for silence. "When you first encountered Prince Percival, you did not gift him with a Dreamstone, did you?"

"I refused him, but that prig of a prince would have seen fit to steal it from me, if he could."

"Why would you indulge Princess Rose by gifting her with a magic crystal, but not Prince Percival, when they are two of a kind?" queried Tag.

"Because it was my sworn duty to insure all those I had conducted business with when I was the Dream Merchant abided by the rules of engagement. In her case, Princess Rose, even to this very day, attempts to make good on her promise. Prince Percival on the other hand, felt he was above abiding by any rules or conditions. And in the case of one of my magic crystals, rules and conditions, if not enforced and adhered to, can be an extremely dangerous thing."

"The age-old adage, absolute power corrupts absolutely comes to mind," determined the Elf.

"True enough, Lord Silverthorn, but absolute power in the hands of one already corrupt, or easily corrupted, is far more dangerous," responded Silas. "Prince Percival's refusal to abide by these rules, and the restrictions I felt necessary, made it a deadly proposition. I could sense his evil intentions, even at his young and impressionable age. Even when I demanded an exorbitantly high price to make the deal binding, it did not serve as a deterrent."

"And what was the price?" asked Tag.

"As power and wealth were at his disposal, and he wanted for nothing, I asked for something that was priceless."

"Being?" questioned Tag, eager to learn more.

"I asked that he forsake the love of his mother, the good and kindly Queen of Axalon. Though King Maxmillian desired a son, as he longed for an heir to retain the throne within his family, there was never a true bond between father and son. The Queen, however, loved him as a mother truly loves her child, prince or not."

"He was willing to trade away her love, just as Princess Rose gambled away the love of her parents?" asked Tag.

"There lies the difference, young man. That monster was willing to *kill* her for it, if it helped to prove he had the proper ambition to possess the Dreamstone."

"So you declined," determined Myron.

"I had entered his nocturnal thoughts, and believe me when I say they were the stuff of nightmares rather than the usual pleasant dreams of an innocent child. Being privy to his dark thoughts, I refused outright when it became clear he had the potential to dream up some truly horrible wishes to get what he most desired."

"Then you were wise to end his foolishness," said Rainus.

"I thought so… Tragically, the Queen passed away nary a week after that encounter. The circumstances, as I understand them, were all very suspect."

"You believe he killed his mother?" Tag's eyes were wide in surprise.

"What else am I to believe? When the lad offered to do away with his mother to prove he was worthy, his cold and calculating words, as well as the eerie timing of her death, were more than just a little unsettling to me. It was said she became deathly ill, but there are whisperings to this very day that the Queen was poisoned."

"Murdered?" The word snatched at the back of Myron's throat. "By her own flesh and blood?"

"I'd say so, but what makes it all the more troubling was his demeanour after her passing. Like the spoiled child he was, he railed at the world. When I failed to return to gift him with one of my magic crystals, he swore vengeance against me for refusing him, after all he had done to appease me."

"This is rather sinister," said Rainus.

"What was truly sinister is that Prince Percival was a mere child back then, not even in his teenage years. Since that time, his father had foolishly indulged his every whim to compensate for the lack of a mother, quite literally grooming him into a man with this princely veneer. However, when you peer beneath the surface, there is a true monster lurking under this contrived, public persona."

"This is not good." Tag's back straightened as he mulled over this news. "Princess Rose is spoiled and can be very demanding indeed, but she is no monster."

"Yes," agreed Silas. "And yet, she is about to bind in matrimony to one."

"I can't have that!" declared Tag. "If that fiend is capable of poisoning his own mother, he is more than capable of murdering a princess he cares little for, in order to inherit a kingdom to expand his power and double his realm."

"So you are proposing to put a stop to this sham of a betrothal before it goes too far?" asked Myron.

"Absolutely!"

"And how do you intend to do that?" queried Myron.

"I will tell her the truth."

"You will do no such thing!"

"Why not?"

"She will spurn your version of the truth, Tag." Myron shook his head. "She will accuse you of being jealous, of standing in the way of her happiness… She will do everything, but believe in your words of warning."

"But I am her friend! She barely knows that sod of a prince!"

"And she is a young lady besotted by love!" reminded Rainus. "She is cursed with this human attribute where she is blinded by the very notion of love and is sure to act accordingly. A fool to be sure!"

"How can this be love?" snorted Tag. "They had just met, and only for the briefest of moments."

"It is better to say she is beguiled," explained the Elf, "and in her youth, mistakes infatuation for love."

"Yes, yes!" agreed Silas. "It is a common occurrence amongst the young, but even the old and especially the lonely long for it. I admit that in my youth, in spite of possessing wisdom beyond my years and great powers, I, too, had fallen victim to all the joys and angsts of this most troubling of emotions."

"You?" gasped Tag, his brows arching up in surprise.

"What can I say? Cinyah Morningstar, as I knew her in days gone by, was a comely young maiden whose beauty alone ensnared my foolish heart."

"It sounds as though you have endured the foibles and follies of this emotion," noted Rainus, giving the Wizard a thoughtful nod.

"Endured and barely survived!" groaned Silas, with a dismal shake of his head. "In my youth, I was not exempt from this emotion… or what I had believed was love, but when one is enraptured by this feeling, there is a tendency to become deaf *and* blind to all else."

"But if I tell Princess Rose what you revealed to us, about how Percy purportedly killed his mother, surely she will listen."

"She may well listen, but she will not hear it," warned Myron. "Alas, she will tell you it is nothing more than a rumour, and she will not fall victim to hearsay. She will not allow words of jealousy to stand in her way of matrimonial bliss."

"As much as she drives me insane at times, she is still my friend! I refuse to allow her to endanger her life by marrying that monster! Now I see why he so willingly agreed to marry Princess Rose, even after his insulting remarks to her." Tag's face reddened as he fumed. "I sense he has a secret agenda, one far more sinister than to become the consort to the future Queen of Fleetwood."

"I have had the misfortune of dealing with Prince Percival. Where his motives are concerned, I have no doubt your senses serve you well, young sir," said Silas.

"Then you will help me break this sordid news to Princess Rose." Tag's eyes gleamed with hope as he peered over to the Wizard.

"Sir Kendall is quite right," warned Silas. "She will only denounce you, if you speak of rumours surrounding the Prince's mother and the nature of her untimely death. What you need is a confession or undeniable proof of his involvement in all of this."

Rainus interjected, "In my humble opinion, it will take Princess Rose hearing such an admission straight from the Prince of Axalon to believe he is capable of such treachery."

"So what now?" Tag's shoulders drooped in defeat as he mulled over their cautionary words.

"That shall depend on a number of things," answered Silas.

"Like what?" asked Tag.

"Is she set to marry Percival upon her return to Axalon?" queried Silas.

"As it stands now, she requested that her parents approve of this pairing, but a formal notice of this intent to marry must be reviewed and approved by her first, before it is delivered to her parents."

"Then we have some time."

"Time for?" asked Tag.

"Time to complete this mission; to capture Dragonite first, before we deal with the sticky matter of her impending marriage to this other monster."

"But we can tell her now," said Tag, "than to allow her to cling to this hope of marrying that murderous cad she finds so charming."

"Master Agincor is quite right, Tag," said Myron. "Though we are sworn to an oath of duty to protect Princess Rose, she is but one. The lives of many are in danger, if Dragonite is not stopped immediately."

"Are you saying she is less important than the others?" questioned Tag.

"I am saying, if we are prudent in how we deal with this mission, then we have a good chance of stopping the Sorcerer *and* saving the world and the innocent lives of many, including Princess Rose's life, too!" answered Myron.

"But —"

"But, nothing!" stated Rainus. "My people shall be avenged, as will Tiny's! Princess Rose is not yet formally engaged to Prince Percival, so the nuptials are on hold until then. I say, while Dragonite is near to us, we take action now."

"Wise words, Lord Silverthorn," praised Silas, nodding to the Elf. "We strike while the iron is hot!"

How Far North?

Rose yawned. Rubbing the sleep from her eyes, the vigorous rolling of stiff shoulders was followed by a long, slow stretch to shake off this drowsiness. She squinted, shielding her eyes from the glare of the sun shining low on the horizon. It peered from between the mountains to send shafts of golden light stretching lazily across the forest floor. Her eyes followed these beams to spy upon the Wizard as he tended to a pot of tea brewing over the open fire.

"So, where have you been?" Rose's voice tightened with agitation upon seeing Silas Agincor so early in the day.

"And a good morning to you, my lady! I have been here. I have not left since you summoned me."

Rose abandoned her bedroll, sitting down to break fast with Silas while Tag and Myron readied their horses. Behind them, an army of Dwarves marched in and out of the chamber, removing debris Harold helped to load into their wheelbarrows. Inside, Tiny used his height and large hands to act as scaffolding, lifting the Dwarves high against the cracked, domed ceiling and damaged walls, so they can make the necessary repairs to ensure the chamber was structurally sound once more.

"I meant to say, where have you been prior to last night? What have you been doing since we last parted company from the Devil's Tears to the north?"

Though the Dream Merchant was not dressed in his usual, gaudy robe festooned with a plethora of brightly coloured moons and stars embroidered throughout, in her opinion, he was still tragically lacking in style.

"And why did you not appear before me as you had previously; stylishly dressed and with youthful, princely good looks, instead of looking like… *this*?"

"This?" repeated Silas. Bewildered, the Wizard frowned as he glanced down at his present attire.

"Yes, that!" She scrutinized his apparel that consisted of a moth-eaten, conservatively grey hooded robe held together by a frayed, leather belt tied about his waist and a pair of worn out, scuffed up leather boots.

"What about it?" Silas' shoulders shrugged in response.

"Last night when I summoned, why did you appear before me as your usual self, minus the ghastly robe decorated with those stars?" questioned Rose.

"I told you before, I am no longer the purveyor of dreams. I wished to shed my former life. As a teller of tales, I thought this attire was more fitting."

"How so?"

"Dressed conservatively, as I am now, I am revered. My reading audience treats me as a respected author." Silas' words were matter-of-fact as he passed to her a tin cup filled with freshly brewed tea infused with the fragrant, wild rosehip.

"I hate to be the bearer of bad tidings, but your manner of dress only screams of your lack of imagination, never mind your woeful sense of fashion." Rose nodded her thanks, wrapping her hands around the cup to absorb its warmth. She blew on the hot beverage, sending delicate tendrils of steam swirling into the chilled, morning air.

"That is your opinion."

"And my opinion, especially when it concerns one's manner of dress and more importantly, fashion, is respected throughout the kingdom of Fleetwood and beyond."

"If it is of any consolation, I admit to donning my Wizardly robe during the rare times I am in need of inspiration when my writing muse is slow to rise to the occasion."

"I find no solace in your words, but is it true what you had said?" With words tinged with doubt, she stared through narrowed eyes at Silas.

"I have said many things, my lady. You must be specific. What do you speak of?"

"That you had forsaken your magic to become an irrelevant author spinning silly tales."

"I hardly describe my tales of rousing adventure to be silly, and yes, instead of using *this* to make magic," Silas hoisted the staff armed with his crystal for her to see, "I have been conjuring another form of magic – grand tales made to fill one's soul and expand one's mind!"

"That makes no sense," grumbled Rose, peering over the rim of the cup as she sipped.

"I have been weaving a powerful magic; using words to create stories of high adventure meant to uplift the heart, stir the imagination and withstand the test of time, lasting for an eternity. What is more powerful than that?"

"There is no magic in mere words! There is no power in a writing quill and a jar of ink," snorted Rose.

"I beg to differ, Princess, for with ink and writing quill I have the power to create mighty kingdoms that can rise or fall in a heartbeat. I can introduce to the world inspiring heroes larger than life and subject them to all manners of treachery that will steal away the very breath of my readers! I have the power to force my characters to walk on a razor's edge; their lives hanging in the balance, so they may rise victorious or fall in utter defeat, all at my creative whim! But more importantly, as well as entertaining the masses, stories have the power to open minds and open eyes to greater possibilities! There is nothing more magical or powerful than this!"

"I believe you are padding your ego to justify the abandonment of your true calling."

"So you say, but think on this: A wise friend once said a man who never reads is destined to live only one life, while a man who reads a thousand books can live a thousand lives. I believe this to be true."

"It sounds rather profound when you put it like that, but I still believe you are lending far too much credence to this new undertaking, as a way to justify shirking your responsibilities as a mighty Wizard."

"And you, young lady, do not give enough importance to books and the benefits of reading," sniffed Silas, as he sat next to her. "I have learned that only the wise and the scholarly appreciate the true merits of a well-written story and what opportunities abound for those actively engaged in the business of reading, even if it is purely for pleasure."

"Well, you are certainly entitled to believe what you want, but I recommend we change the subject for now."

"Fine by me," agreed Silas. "And speaking of new subjects, I do believe congratulations are in order."

"But I have yet to recover your Dreamstone." Rose frowned in bewilderment.

"I was referring to your impending nuptials."

"Oh, that! It has yet to be formalized, but if all goes my way, by the spring or early summer of next year, I shall be a married woman!"

"But that is so soon and you are still quite young!"

"I think not! I will have you know I am quickly approaching my seventeenth year! King Maxmillian was quick to point out that my youth and beauty shall fade faster than I desire, but soon? When I know it is true love tugging at my heart strings, why delay the inevitable?"

"And if one pulls hard enough, those strings will snap. You shall feel love's cruel sting," grunted Silas.

"And just what do you mean by that?"

"Love, or what you perceive to be love, is akin to a wild beast that is difficult to tame. It is like trying to ride a dragon. You are young and have yet to understand what true love entails."

"And you are an old, curmudgeonly Wizard, one who knows nothing about love, true or otherwise!"

"I beg to differ, Princess! I was young once. I, too, believed I was in love in another time and in another life."

"Being in love with *yourself* does not count."

"I was speaking of a fair maiden I once adored with every fibre of my being!"

"You mean to say a homely spinster, one who was dealt a poor hand in the game of love, so she settled for the likes of you."

"I mean *fair*, as in beautiful… She was as lovely as an Elf maiden and as spritely as a Fairy, with raven-black tresses and enchanting eyes that shone a dazzling emerald green. She stole my very breath away the first time we met. I was absolutely beguiled by her loveliness…"

He stared off dreamily, his mind wandering off to another time and place in his long life.

"Go on! Tell me more." Rose poked Silas' arm as his words trailed off. "Give me a name, so I will know she was real."

"Her name was Cinyah Morningstar – Cinyah the Beautiful, some called her. Others knew her as Cinyah the Enchantress, and enchanting she was."

"More beautiful and enchanting than me?" Rose frowned in displeasure, for she believed she was the fairest in all the lands.

"We are speaking of another time, well before your grandparents were even a thought."

"Fair enough. Go on then."

"As I was saying, Cinyah was beautiful beyond words, but what lay beneath this perfect exterior was a controlling, conniving, possessive soul, one that wanted to cleave to me completely, body, mind and soul!"

"Why did you not marry her, if this was true love?" queried Rose.

"Did you not hear me? She wanted to *own* me, to control every aspect of my life in the guise it would be for the benefit of both!"

"What was wrong with that, if it was such a beneficial pairing?" Silas' hands quaked in frustration as he stared at her. "You are a lost cause."

"Lost in love, that is!" The mere thought of Prince Percy sent her heart a-flutter.

"Mark my words, Princess Rose, I know enough that love can wax and wane over time. Once the dizzying rapture of love's spell should fade or be tested, if there is no mutual respect and true friendship to solidify the relationship in trying times, then one should not marry, for it is respect and the devotion of a true friendship that shall endure and strengthen these bonds of matrimony."

"I pity you." Rose shook her head in sadness.

"Pity me? Because I came to my senses before I fell victim to her treacherous charms?"

"No, Master Agincor. I pity you because I sense a tinge of envy, for I was destined to find true love, while you allowed your chance for happiness to slip away."

"I *ran* away! I headed for the hills as fast as I could to get away from her enchanting, but manipulative ways."

"Hush, now!" ordered Rose, pressing her index finger to Silas' quivering lips as he fumed in agitation. "Do not let jealousy consume your heart! Be happy for me."

"Why would I be happy to see you rushing into matrimonial bonds with a young man you barely know?"

"Granted we met only once, Prince Percival is my perfect match!" insisted Rose.

"So I've heard!"

"Oh! So your equally jealous friend has been speaking ill about my engagement?" determined Rose. Her eyes narrowed as she glanced over at Tag as he readied her mare's saddle.

"Trust me when I say I speak for the both of us: Tag and I are *not* jealous of you."

"Of course you are, as is Tag! He was green with envy as he watched my charming prince fawn all over me."

"As a trusted friend, the young man is genuinely concerned for you."

"I think not! Tag is just jealous I am willing to follow my heart in the pursuit of true love," insisted Rose.

"Never lose sight of what you have to pursue what you want," cautioned the Wizard, as he glanced over to Tag and Myron as her friends watered their horses now that their work was done.

"Will you stop speaking in riddles?"

"Will you stop speaking like a fool?" Silas snorted with indignation.

"Sounds like you two are engaged in a rousing debate," said Tag. He knelt by his pack to share in some bread, cheese, and dried fruit with his comrades while Myron fetched his water flask to quench a thirst that would not be satisfied by hot tea.

"I would hardly classify this conversation as an interesting debate, let alone a rousing one," grumbled Rose.

"Yes, especially when there was nothing to debate about to begin with," added Silas.

Rose scooted over on the log, making room for her comrades as she turned to Myron. "So what is the plan for today? There is a plan, right?"

She squealed in fright as Rainus Silverthorn abruptly dropped down from the tree to land next to her.

"Of course we have a plan," announced the Elf. He greeted her with a polite bow.

Startled by Rainus' sudden appearance Rose blotted away the tea she splashed down her front. "What were you doing up there?"

"I was watching for the return of our little friend. With this mountainous terrain, it is easier to spot Loken's approach from a higher vantage point."

Rose placed her now empty cup at her feet while Tag handed her a chunk of bread with shavings of hard cheese scattered atop. "And did you see the Sprite?"

"I followed his movements through this forest until he disappeared from my sight as he ventured northward, but that was last night. When I was up in the tree just now, I was watching for Loken's return."

"And while you watched, you were busy devising a foolproof plan, right?" asked Rose, as she nibbled on her austere meal.

"The immediate plan is to wait for Loken to join us," answered Rainus. He accepted the tin from the Wizard, picking it up with the same daintiness as if the hot beverage was being served in a delicate, porcelain teacup.

"That is no plan!" Rose's delicate brows puckered into a disgruntled frown. "In fact, that is a *non-plan*, if ever there was one."

"Hear Lord Silverthorn out," urged Silas, as he discreetly tipped the contents of a silver flask to top up his serving of tea. "Allow him to speak."

Rose complied. She sat back, slowly chewing on a mouthful of bread as she listened.

"While you slept, Loken has been on the move," revealed Rainus. "He spotted our nemesis late last night, and was attempting to follow

Dragonite to his lair. Once we know where that scoundrel is hiding, we will have the opportunity to corner and capture him."

"And Loken has yet to return?" asked Rose.

"Once he does, the real planning shall begin," vowed Rainus.

"Go on," urged Rose. "Tell me more."

"Last night was the closest we had come to that fiend since this quest began," said Rainus. "Once we pinpoint where Dragonite has skulked off to, we will be in the proper position to begin planning our strategy to capture the necromancer, and do so with certain success, now that Master Agincor is here to assist us."

"But Loken has been gone for a long while now," reminded Rose. "Suppose he has met with misfortune?"

"Loken promised to maintain a safe distance, and do not forget, he is a master of disguises," said Silas. "He has the ability to move about in secret, undetected by all, if he so desires."

"If anyone can get close to Dragonite, it will be Loken," averred Rainus. "You worry all for naught, my lady."

"You watch, Princess," urged Tag. "Loken will return any time now."

No sooner than the young man spoke these words, a black dragonfly bedazzled with splashes of deep blue and endowed with crisp, iridescent wings zipped between Rainus and Myron. The insect alighted upon the log, coming to rest next to Rose. Before she could shoo away or swat at the insect, in a flash of white light, it morphed into Loken.

"You little imp!" scolded Rose, staring down at the Sprite.

"Would you have preferred a dragon that flies over a dragonfly?" queried Loken. He hopped onto the palm of Silas' hand that was presented to him.

"Of course not! I just fear that one day, I will be your sorry end, and it will be quite by accident, should I fail to recognize you first."

"I make no apologies, Princess. As a dragonfly, the fastest flier in the insect world by the way, I travelled unnoticed and was able to wing my way back here much faster than had I done so as a Pooka."

"So, what did you see?" questioned Silas, holding Loken before present company.

"And did that villain see you?" queried Myron.

"I was very careful," stated Loken, his feet dangling over the edge of the Wizard's hand as he addressed the mortal's concern. "By night, I adopted the form of the tiny sparrow owl. I was able to see sufficiently in the darkness, and with the ragged edges of the flight feathers to buffer the wind, it allowed me to fly in silence, but still,

I deliberately maintained a safe distance. If Dragonite sensed he was being followed, he showed no sign of it. Not once did he glance back as I trailed behind him."

"Excellent!" said Tag. "What can you tell us? Share in the details, my friend."

"The pertinent details, that is!" insisted Rainus.

Loken nodded in understanding. "As I said before, I maintained a discreet distance from that villain, following behind him as he skulked northward. I spied on him, watching as he took refuge in a cave."

"How far north?" asked Myron.

"On horseback, at an easy canter, it would not take long at all. I'd say his lair is less than four leagues from where we stand now."

"So, we can ride, rather than walk?" asked Rose, hoping aloud.

"It would be far more expedient to do so." Loken nodded.

"I agree riding the horses will be faster than to walk," said Myron, "however, the noises of their hooves will resound through these mountains to forewarn of our coming."

"Sir Kendall is quite correct," agreed Rainus. "Though I am much lighter on my feet than you mortals, to walk is far more quiet than to take the horses, charging northward only to send that cockroach scurrying off to disappear to who-knows-where."

"I understand your concerns," said Loken, with a nod of his head, "but rest assured, my friends, the lands north of here are blanketed by dense layers of soft moss, topped by a thick mantle of fallen leaves. Even a large stag, one with twelve tines on its great rack of antlers, I had spotted on my return moved in complete silence. Its hooves were thoroughly cushioned by the thick layers of moss and leaf litter."

"The Sprite is wise," praised Rose, wanting nothing more than to ride her mare than to walk the distance. "If the way is safe to travel on horseback, why not? It will be much faster, and if Dragonite did take refuge in this cave to seek solitude in sleep, if we move with haste, we can catch him unawares."

When Rose's suggestion was met with silence, she pursed her lips into a sad pout. Her amethyst eyes deepened in hue, adopting that pleading, puppy-dog expression that used to melt her father's stubborn heart, squelching any hope he had of dispensing punishment on her whenever she misbehaved.

"What say you, Master Agincor?" questioned Tag, ignoring her pleading eyes. "Shall we walk? Or shall we ride?"

"Time is of the essence," interjected Loken. "We have no idea how long the Sorcerer will remain in his lair before he moves on, disappearing once again, and perhaps, forever."

"Maybe he is exhausted," said Tag. "There is a chance he will sleep for a good long time."

"By his plodding gait, I'd say it is fair to assume Dragonite was even more exhausted than I am now. On numerous occasions he was forced to stop and rest before limping on to his hiding place."

"Aha!" exclaimed Rose, with a knowing smile. "That fiend will be so deep asleep, he'll not even hear our approach, should we descend with an entire army and a giant of a troll to boot!"

"So you hope!" grunted Tag.

"Are you positive the way is conducive to riding our horses in relative silence?" queried Silas, holding Loken up to his face as he addressed the Sprite.

"Absolutely! Mind you, with Tiny's heavy, lumbering gait and should Lord Silverthorn proceed with his entire battalion, as small as it is, there is a chance with so many horses taking to the trail, they can potentially wear thin the ground cover, alerting Dragonite of our approach."

"Then we can move forward without them," insisted Rose. "And Tiny can remain behind. He can stay to help the Dwarves make repairs to that mountain chamber."

Tag protested, "Without the numbers to ensure our safety and guarantee that fiend's capture? I think not!"

"But if we use the element of surprise that you and Myron are always so keen on incorporating into your strategy, there is no need for Lord Silverthorn to bring his entire troop," insisted Rose. "Or are you both going back on your words about the virtues of this particular tactic?"

"The element of surprise always works in the favour of the wise strategist, when it comes to planning an attack," assured Myron.

"Well, there you go then!" declared Rose, as she beamed with delight. "We sneak up on the Sorcerer *and* move with haste on horseback, while taking only those we need. Problem solved!"

"She does present us with a sound option," said Loken, as he nodded in agreement.

Rose's eyes narrowed in suspicion as she stared at the Sprite. "What is going on here? Since when do you so readily agree with me? Are you under a spell?"

"I hardly think so! As for agreeing with you, there is a first time for everything, however, I am but one. With that said, in my humble opinion, your logic was sound, Princess," responded Loken, nodding in approval.

Rose sat upright as she boasted to her comrades, "At least there is one amongst us smart enough and bold enough to speak the truth."

"It is unbecoming to gloat," scolded Tag, with a shake of his head.

"Why? Because my suggestion was so spot on?"

"Because it was just plain rude, especially for one of your standing," rebuked Tag. "And I know you! You just don't want to walk the distance."

"Why walk when it is safe to ride? Just admit it, Tag! You are being miserable because I am right!"

Myron raised his hands, motioning for silence as he spoke. "In light of the information Loken shared with us, there is no reason why we cannot take to our horses, arriving at Dragonite's lair in a timely manner. And if we use utmost caution, approaching with stealth and taking advantage of the element of surprise, we should be able to secure him without a battalion of Elves to do so."

"Plus," added Loken, raising his tiny hand to gain their full attention, "from what I saw of the entrance to this cave the Sorcerer had ducked into, if the size of the opening is any indication, I get the sense that the chamber is not very big at all. For all of us to enter, as well as the Elves in Lord Silverthorn's company, it can prove dangerous, especially if there is no room to manoeuvre or we are forced to exit with haste."

"I suppose you have a valid point, Loken," admitted Tag.

"Hey! *I* was the one with the good and valid point," grunted Rose, her thumb jabbing at her chest so there'd be no mistaking whom she was speaking of. "Loken merely added more reason to what I had already said, so you would see the logic in my suggestion!"

"Princess Rose has spoken," announced Silas. He lurched up onto his feet, sending Loken launching off his hand into the air. "We ride, and we do so in secret."

"We leave now?" asked Rose, inwardly pleased that she was taken seriously for once.

"We leave when I am ready to do so," answered Loken, hovering before her face.

Rose frowned upon hearing these words.

"You, Princess Rose, had the opportunity to sleep through the night while I was hard at work! If you expect me to guide you and your party on to Dragonite's secret lair, it will only happen after I have had the opportunity to steal away with some sleep, if I am to have my wits about me as we venture forward."

"Fine!" snapped Rose. "Find some rest, but do not be long."

"I will be as long as I see fit. Just know that I will get you there with time to spare, once I am well rested."

With an indignant rattle of his wings, Loken flew off to find a secluded place to sleep, away from the bustle and noise of voices and the din echoing from the mountain as Troll, Dwarves, Elves and mortal man toiled to repair the great chamber.

"Farewell, my friends," bade Giblet Barscowl. Removing his helmet, he tipped his head in respect to Princess Rose and her comrades. "Stay well out of harm's way, ya hear me?"

"That is the plan," assured Rose, hoisting herself onto the mare's saddle as Harold gave her a leg up.

"If all goes accordingly, we shall return sooner than later," promised Rainus. "I will gather my warriors then."

"And when ya do, your men will be ready ta journey home with ya." Giblet nodded in gratitude. "For now, their help here is greatly appreciated."

He moved aside, allowing his brethren Dwarves to march into the mountain chamber. Hoisted upon their shoulders was another beam of sturdy timber hewn by the Elves that Lord Silverthorn elected to leave behind with the exception of Halen Ironwood.

"You are welcome, Master Barscowl," said Rainus. He steered his mount about as Halen took the lead to follow Loken northward. "My men will help to defend your fortress, if need be, should the Sorcerer elude us; doubling back to launch another attack."

Giblet nodded in appreciation as he glanced over to Harold and the packhorse appointed to this mortal. Without Sassy to take on this role, the mare was in a cantankerous mood. Loaded down with the necessary supplies and equipment for the trek, the mare snorted in displeasure.

"Are ya positive ya don't want ta stay here, my good man?" asked Giblet. "You'd be a great help ta us, if ya don't want ta go traipsin' off in search of danger."

"I have a quest to complete and a duty to uphold to Princess Rose," said Harold. "I'm plannin' to continue on with them."

"Well then, good luck ta ya," said Giblet, bowing his head in respectful farewell.

"Worry not, Master Barscowl. I plan to keep my friends safe," vowed Myron.

"Good intentions should keep ya on the straight an' narrow; focused on the task at hand, Sir Kendall," responded Giblet, "but I mean it when I warned ya ta stay out of harm's way. Even if that demented Sorcerer ain't leadin' ya directly inta a trap, the caves an' tunnels in those northerly mountains were abandoned fer good reason."

"What do you mean?" asked Rose. The blood in her veins chilled upon hearing these ominous words. "Are you saying the Dwarves delved too greedily and had unearthed a terrible monster from the bowels of the earth?"

"Heck, no!" grunted Giblet. "Them mines not only failed ta yield a profitable load, they're downright treacherous."

"How so?" queried Myron.

"Let's jus' say a good sneeze would probably be 'nough ta bring the worst of 'em tunnel-riddled mountains crashin' down."

"So, we are to be careful of collapsing tunnels?" asked Tag.

"Yep! Cave-ins an', not ta forget, gapin' holes where the cave floors gave way. Stumblin' inta one of those will likely mean fallin' ta yer death."

"We shall heed your warning," responded Silas, nodding in gratitude to Giblet before turning his attention to the Sprite. "Loken, show us the way."

Perched on the palm of Halen's hand, he launched into the air, his wings trembling with nervous energy.

"Come! Follow me," urged Loken, waving his comrades on.

Lengthening shadows meandered across the lands as the westering sun sank lower in the autumn sky. Loken delivered his comrades to within a quarter of a league of the Sorcerer's lair. Though their trek was uneventful, as they neared Dragonite's mountain hideaway, Halen raised his left hand, motioning for all to halt.

The Elf dismounted as he said to the others, "From here, we leave our horses and walk in."

"But we have travelled unimpeded so far," whined Rose, reluctant to abandon her mare. "Why can we not ride the rest of the way?"

"Captain Ironwood is quite correct, Princess," said Rainus, as he hopped off his horse. "Even if the way is carpeted with moss and leaves to muffled their hoof beat, we should take no chance these horses will get spooked, creating enough of a commotion to alert Dragonite of our approach."

"Fair enough," conceded Rose, heaving a disheartened sigh.

"I'm glad you agree," said Tag, "for we have no time to waste arguing with you."

"I was not planning to argue, I was just trying to save us some time."

As she swung her right leg over her mare's rump to dismount, she almost clipped Harold in his head as he rushed to her side to help her dismount.

"Will you get out of my way," she snapped. Hopping down, she removed her left foot from the stirrup.

"Sorry, Princess," apologized Harold. "Was just tryin' to help."

"I don't need your help, but if you insist on being useful, take these reins, secure our horses so they'll be here on our return."

"As you wish!" said Harold, taking the reins from her hand.

"These days, I wish for nothing," muttered Rose, staring anxiously at the mountain looming before them.

"It is unfortunate this attitude came to you too late in life." Silas unleashed a dismal sigh.

Rose said nothing, merely rolling her eyes in response.

"This way," coaxed Loken, his wings thrumming with excitement. "Follow me! It is not far from here."

"Quickly, then," said Myron, securing his stallion's reins to a sturdy tree branch. "Let us move on. Take your weapons. Keep your voices down as we advance."

Rose nodded in agreement, but she elected to leave her longbow on her saddle.

"You must be feeling mighty confident that you will not be attacked," noted Rainus, staring at the bow he had gifted her.

"As lethal as this bow is elegant, I am more competent with my sling," admitted Rose, patting her weapon of choice and the suede pouch containing the steel balls hanging from her belt. "And because of the bow's great length, I am concerned it will only hamper my mobility as we have no idea how tight the confines are within the mountain."

"I understand," said Rainus, checking the quiver to make sure it was fully stocked before slinging it over his shoulder. "It is second nature for me to take this wherever I go."

"Whatever your weapon of choice, arm yourself," ordered Halen. "We go now."

As Loken flitted between the trees, retracing his trek to deliver them to Dragonite's hiding place, Elves and mortals trotted along behind him.

Loken came to a stop, alighting upon the branch of a dense, sprawling thorn bush. Pressing a finger to his lips, he motioned for silence.

"It is just over there." Loken jabbed a thumb over his shoulder in the direction of the lair.

Halen motioned for all to stand back as he cautiously peered between the tangled branches. Seeing no cause for alarm, he whispered, "All is quiet."

Loken hovered over Halen's left shoulder. "As I said before, the Sorcerer was exhausted after his long night, forced to beat a hasty retreat after the mayhem he caused. I'm positive that madman is still fast asleep, even as we speak."

"That'd be a lucky thing," whispered Harold, as he peeked over Halen's head to peer through the shrub.

"We have never been the lucky sort," muttered Tag.

"Lucky or not, we advance while we can," said Silas.

"Remain behind me," ordered Halen. He boldly ventured forth, his silent steps leading the way as Loken took to the air. Urging them on, the Sprite zipped ahead of the Elf to prove there were no hidden traps guarding the way to the lair.

With cautious steps they crept toward the entrance of Dragonite's hideaway.

"This is it?" asked Rose. Her brows furrowed in confusion.

The very top of the opening was nothing more than a hairline fracture in the rock face. Her eyes followed it down, watching as it gradually widened before her. It was as though a giant, Troll-sized chisel was slammed into the mountainside or a powerful force of dark magic was used to riven solid rock. This jagged opening gradually expanded, widening the most at the base, but standing before the entrance, she determined it was barely the width of her narrow shoulders if she shrugged.

"This is no cave," grumbled Rose, as she scrutinized the entrance. "This is nothing more than a big crack in the mountainside."

"This *crack* will lead us into a cave and on to finding the Sorcerer," reminded Loken, hovering before the opening.

"I take it, you did not venture inside," assessed Myron, peering into the suffocating darkness beyond the reach of day's light.

"I'm no fool! If there is a trap beyond this opening, it can prove disastrous had I entered. What would have happened if I flew directly into danger, unable to forewarn you of a potential trap or to lead you to this very place?"

"Good point," said Myron. "We best advance together; watch each other's backs."

"But suppose there is a deadly trap lying in wait?" asked Tag, pulling Rose away from the opening in case she accidentally set it off.

"Then find it!" snipped Rose, brushing Tag's hand off her arm. "I can throw you in there myself, if that helps."

"No need for that, Princess," said Myron. "And this is not the time nor the place to start bickering."

Ignoring her biting words, Tag knelt down, picking up a sizable rock. Hefting it in his hand to get a feel for its weight, Tag approached the cave, taking slow, deliberate steps. Pausing for a moment, he tossed the rock into the cave, sending it flying in an arc to disappear in the all-consuming darkness.

Startled by his action, everyone, including Tag, jumped back, wishing to be out of harm's way should something terrible happen. They listened, hearing the rock strike with a clatter against a wall before landing with a dull '*thud*' onto the cave floor.

"Seems to be safe to enter," surmised Tag, peering into the darkness.

"How can you say that?" Her tone was incredulous. "For all we know, especially with your aim, the trigger for this supposed trap is just above or below the trajectory of your throw."

"I believe I have a solution that will determine if this entrance is safe," declared Halen, walking off to a nearby tree.

Scanning the ground, he found a long, sturdy branch to suit his needs. Halen unsheathed his dagger, deftly stripping it of twigs and dried leaves as he returned to the cave.

The group took several more steps away from the entrance, fearing an explosion or worse, as Halen swept the branch from the top of the crack down to the bottom. Nothing untoward happened, however, Halen was not yet convinced. Thrusting the branch into the entrance so his entire arm was inside, Halen waved the branch up and down, then side to side. Satisfied, he pulled his arm out of the opening, tossing the branch aside.

"No traps," declared Halen, his words spoken with conviction, "at least, not at this opening."

"So, how do we even enter when the way is so narrow?" queried Rose, as she turned to the Wizard. "Can you not use your powers to enlarge the entrance?"

"I can… My magic is somewhat rusty of late, but it is still as powerful as ever."

"Rusty… Powerful…" repeated Rainus, his perfect brows furrowing with concern. "These two words spoken in the same sentence do not fill me with confidence, Master Agincor."

"I say we err on the side of caution," recommended Myron. "If the Wizard's powers are as potent as ever, but he is lacking in control, there is a chance the way will be sealed off, rather than widened."

"Nor do we need to forewarn Dragonite of our coming, should this magic be explosive, and not in a good way," added Halen.

"With that said, I recommend we just squeeze on through," said Rainus.

"Are you serious?" grumbled Rose, as the Sprite hovered before her face.

"Just work your way in," answered Loken.

"Easy for you to say," sniffed Rose.

"And you actually saw the Sorcerer enter this way?" queried Tag, as he scrutinized this opening.

"Absolutely! I watched as that lanky fiend made his way inside with minimal effort."

"I am proportionately and perfectly lean, not lanky," declared Rose, "but even at that, how are we to fit through?"

She eyeballed the opening, mentally measuring and comparing it to the width of her shoulders that were about as wide as her hips.

"Just find a way," urged Loken. His wings rattled in agitation as he darted inside to be swallowed up by the gloom. "It cannot be that hard."

"We can fit, squeezing through if we turn sideways," suggested Tag.

"Quoting Princess Rose: Easy for you to say," muttered Silas, patting his protruding paunch.

"Suck it in, old chap," advised Rainus. With an affable grin, he patted the Wizard's belly. "If you approach the opening sideways as Tag suggested, squatting down a bit to where it widens to accommodate your *robust* figure, we should be able to push you through to the other side, if need be."

"I suppose that will work," said Silas, unleashing a dreary sigh at the thought of becoming a contortionist just to fit through. "Mind you, I can just use my magic to *wish* myself in there."

"Like you did when the Princess summoned you to the Mines of Euphoria?" queried Myron.

"Yes!"

"That brilliant flash to herald your arrival is sure to flood the cave and tunnels within to announce your presence," warned Rainus.

"Not a good idea," said Myron.

"So, I am to wedge my poor, old body through by conventional means."

"With a little effort it'll work," assured Tag, presenting his right side to the entrance. "I will prove it by going first."

As he wedged his shoulder through, Halen snagged Tag by the arm, yanking him away.

"Allow me to go first," offered the Elf.

"But you said the way is safe," responded Tag.

"The *entrance* is safe, but we do not know what awaits us beyond this opening," answered Halen. Fishing out from the folds of his cloak a rectangle of flint, he struck it with the dull side of his dagger's blade. The sparks sprang forth on contact, dancing about as they fell onto one of the two pitch smothered rags wound tightly on the end of green, hardwood sticks Harold held for the Elf. As the flame grew, it spread onto the second torch.

"There we go!" said Halen, taking one of the torches from Harold as the flames grew, burning steady. "We now have light in the gloom to come."

With sword in one hand and a burning torch in his other, Halen crouched down until the opening was wide enough to accommodate his head and broad shoulders. Turning sideways, he exhaled, holding his breath to compress his torso as he wedged his left shoulder into the entrance first. Wiggling his way through, he disappeared inside the mountain.

Outside, Rose and the others waited for the captain's order to proceed. Peering through this crack they watched the light of the flame swell and gutter, dancing on the end of the torch as Halen glanced about, inspecting the cave for potential danger.

"It is safe," assured Loken.

Halen spun on his heels, turning the torch toward the small voice in the darkness. He spied upon Loken hovering in the darkest recess of this cave that was taller than it was wide.

"So far," agreed Halen. He returned to the entrance, whispering to his comrades, "It is safe to proceed. I suggest Tag come in next and Harold comes in last to carry the other torch for those taking up the rear. Once Tag is in, I shall hand off my torch to him."

"Don't you need to see, Captain Ironwood?" asked Harold.

"You mortals will need the light cast by the torches more than I do. The eyes of an Elf are much sharper than yours, even in the dark of night," answered Halen. "Lord Silverthorn and I should be able to see quite adequately."

"Plus, I have the light of my crystal, if it is needed," added Silas, holding forth his staff.

"Quickly then," said Tag. He turned sideways, working his way into the mountain to join Halen.

Rose glanced over at Silas, Rainus, Myron and Harold. She mentally assessed whom of these four would provide her with the safest position, if danger should strike. Though Harold had quite literally saved her life twice so far, did he have the skills to truly protect her, preventing her from getting into a dangerous position to begin with? And what about the Dream Merchant? Though he was armed with his crystal, Silas was the first to admit his skills were wanting of late.

As there was no question of Myron's tenacious skills with his sword and Lord Silverthorn's accuracy with his bow, Rose decided on the most prudent action to adopt: to fortify her position by having the great Elf follow behind Tag, and then insert herself between Rainus and Myron. This way, with Tag and two warrior Elves before her to counter danger and the others following behind her to repel an attack, or at least provide distraction in the way of becoming worthy and honourable sacrifices should danger sneak up from the rear, she was sure to be safe. At least, as safe as she can be, given their current circumstance.

Pleased with her strategy, Rose motioned for Rainus to proceed as she ducked in front of Myron to secure this position.

After Rainus made his way through, Rose angled in through the opening fairly easily compared to the others. Myron proceeded behind her, followed by the Wizard.

As Silas exhaled, and then held his breath while pulling in his paunch of a stomach, he grunted and groaned, wedging his form through the entrance.

"I am stuck," wheezed Silas, as he squeezed out what little air was left in his lungs in a bid to streamline his form.

Myron took the staff from the Wizard's hand, passing it on to Rose, so he and Silas could clasp each other's wrist. Calling through the opening to Harold, "On the count of three, you push, I'll pull."

Even though the knight couldn't see Harold with the Wizard blocking the way, the large man nodded in understanding as he braced one beefy hand on Silas' shoulder.

"One... Two... Three!" counted Myron. He pulled as Harold simultaneously pushed to force the Wizard inside.

With a grunt of exertion and a groan of discomfort, Silas popped through into the cave like a cork popping off a bottle of well-aged wine.

"Well, that was rather unpleasant," muttered Silas, rubbing his belly that weathered the brunt of the abuse.

"At least you're in," said Tag, holding the torch aloft so the Wizard could see he was fine.

"Make room," urged Harold. "I'm comin' through!"

Within their cramped quarters, Rose returned to Silas his staff as she took a step back. She watched as Harold's large hand reached through the opening first, only to come to an abrupt halt. His upper arm was jammed in the opening. He squirmed about, crouching as low as was physically possible for a man his size, in a bid to access the wider section of the entrance. Where the Wizard was plump around his midsection, Harold's tall stature and stout, barrel-shaped body was not designed to enter such a narrow portal of this height. No matter how much he held his breath, sucked in his midsection and crouched, there was no way to make his size more compact.

"This is not going to work," said Myron, as he and Tag released their grip on Harold's arm.

"Unless we parcel you up and drag you in here in pieces, there's no other way through," added Tag.

"Wait!" Harold backed up; removing his shaggy, bearskin cloak he cast it aside. "Surely this will help."

With as much effort and gusto as the first time, Harold rammed, wriggled and forced his way in, but his body managed to work in no more than a hand span further from where he first got stuck.

"You, my friend, are just too large to fit through," said Myron.

"Suppose you pull while someone pushes me in from behind?" moaned Harold, his breath stifled by his already compressed ribcage.

"And how do we do that?" grumbled Rose. "We are all in here. There is none to push you in."

"This is impossible," said Rainus, with a sigh of resignation. "And we are losing valuable time."

"Maybe if I tried holdin' my breath more while all of you grab my arm and yank me through."

"Brilliant! We shall pull your arm clean from its socket," muttered Rose. "You can lend a *hand* as we proceed with your limb while leaving the rest of you stuck, blocking the way."

"Princess Rose is correct." Halen's words were matter of fact. "Your sheer size alone prevents you from entering. And there is nothing to say we will not encounter passages that will prove to be even more challenging during our pursuit."

"But- but- I want to help," cried Harold, ramming his chest into the opening, but making no forward progress.

"There, there, Harold!" said Myron, as he pushed his friend out and free of the narrow gap. He peered through to see his friend standing in the sun, his eyes squinting in its brilliance. "You can still be of great help, even if your adventure ends here."

"How?"

"Time is of the essence," answered Myron. "Return to our mounts, tend to our horses while we are gone. If fate and luck conspire in our favour, we shall not be long."

"Very well," said Harold. He leaned down, passing the torch on to Myron as he called through the opening to Rose. "Take care, Princess. Stay safe, as I won't be there to save your life, if you find yourself in danger again."

"Worry not, Harold," assured Tag. "We will keep her safe, plus, the Dream Merchant is here to aid us."

"This way," invited Loken, eager to move on. "Follow me."

With a heavy heart Harold peered through the crack in the mountain, watching as whispered voices faded away and the light of the torches dimmed, melting into the darkness.

Standing upright, Harold snatched his cloak from the ground. He brushed off the dust and pebbles that clung to his vest when he struggled to force himself through.

He groaned in frustration as a wooden toggle that had been dangling from his vest and further stressed by his efforts fell away. This toggle glanced off the rock face surrounding the entrance. It dropped, bouncing off the ground to disappear through the opening.

"Darn it all!" cursed Harold.

He tossed his cloak aside as he dropped on all fours. Peering in Harold spotted the wooden toggle. It had rebounded off a rock to land beyond the entranceway that prevented him from entering in the first place.

"There you are!"

Harold thrust his hand in, but it was beyond his reach. Sprawled out on his belly, he used his elbows, digging them into the ground for traction to worm through the widest point of this opening.

"Gotcha!" Triumphantly plucking up the toggle between his finger and thumb, Harold glanced about. His eyes struggled to focus in this gloomy cave.

"This is lovely," whispered Rose, as she crept along with her comrades. The narrow entrance led them to the first of many mineshafts riddling this mountain.

Myron glanced over his shoulder as he addressed her. "We are sneaking through an abandoned mine in search of the Sorcerer. Explain how this can be lovely?"

"Do you speak in jest?" queried Rose, genuinely mystified by his foreboding words.

"I do not," answered Myron. "You best explain yourself."

"I will! So far, there have been no traps, no showering of disgusting glow worms, no huge beast of a monster conjured up by dark magic to devour us, and best of all, no mimes!"

Overhearing this conversation, Rainus whispered, "All true. So far, this trek has proven to be uneventful."

"Unnervingly so," agreed Silas. His eyes darted about, searching for signs of danger.

"Just give it some time," chimed in Tag, as he followed behind Halen. "Something bad always seems to happen."

"Look here, people! I am attempting to remain positive," grumbled Rose. "Just because it has been uneventful thus far, it does not mean it's a bad thing."

"All I am saying is that we've never been graced with an abundance of good luck," said Tag. "The last time we were in a tunnel not unlike this one and I had mentioned the good fortune that at least we had a torch, suddenly and seemingly out of nowhere, a great draft snuffed out our light."

"Hush!" scolded Rose, watching as the flame of the torch he carried abruptly guttered to cast strange shadows against the walls of the tunnel. "Are you tempting fate?"

"I am trying to keep you safe by preventing you from being lulled into a false sense of security," answered Tag.

"I think not!" grunted Rose.

"I think you both should keep your voices down," recommended Halen, pressing a finger to his lips as he shot them a baleful glance over his shoulder.

"What is that?" asked Myron, staring into the darkness beyond the large Elf.

Halen stopped. His eyes squinted as he stared ahead beyond the shadows held at bay by the torchlight.

"What can it be?" questioned Rose.

"It appears to be a single shaft of light," whispered Halen.

"I concur," said Rainus, with a nod. "But where is it coming from?"

"It can well be a trap," warned Silas.

Rose pushed ahead of Rainus only to smack Tag on his arm as she scolded him, "You jinxed us!"

"Ouch!" yelped Tag. "I did no such thing! Besides, it could be nothing at all."

"Hush, both of you!" ordered Myron. "Let us focus on what is ahead of us. Steady your tongues; keep close to Captain Ironwood."

Tag nodded in agreement as Rose rolled her eyes in response.

Halen's focus remained fixed straight ahead, searching for hidden danger as he motioned for Tag to hand him the torch.

The young man complied, passing it on to the Elf as Loken hovered just before Halen.

"Well?" whispered Rose, straining to see. In the pitch-blackness this beam pierced through the darkness to shine down, forming a small pool of light on the floor. "Can you see what it is?"

"Obviously, it is a stream of light up ahead," whispered Halen, gingerly making his way forward. Glancing about, by the way the torchlight expanded from the close confines of the tunnel, the passage opened into a small cave. High in the ceiling, the light burned through a hole no larger than the circumference of a ha'penny. It pierced through the chamber at a slight angle to shine a spot of light on the centre of the floor.

"That is mighty peculiar," noted Silas. He strained against Halen's arms that stretched across the entrance of the cave to block their path, preventing them from entering recklessly.

"Peculiar, indeed," agreed Halen. He raised the torch on high to illuminate the darkest recesses as the Sprite flitted about. "It could well be a trap."

"Fret not, Captain Ironwood!" insisted Loken. "It is nothing more than a crack in the mountain. We are blessed to have even this small amount of natural light to see by. Consider it a singular beacon of hope!"

He flew toward this brilliant beam as Rainus called for him to remain close by.

Just as Loken flew into the light, he was suddenly frozen in time and space, suspended before his comrades' startled eyes. The Sprite abruptly convulsed with violent spasms, and just as suddenly, his body grew limp. He dropped, falling from this light beam to land on the dark ground below.

"What just happened?" gasped Rose, her eyes straining to see where Loken fell to avoid accidentally treading upon him.

"Light! We need more light!" called Tag, motioning Halen to lower the torch as he dashed forward.

Holding it forth to the cave floor, the Elf took a cautious step forward to search for the downed Sprite.

"Where did he go?" asked Silas, as he joined his comrades.

"I'm sure he dropped straight down," said Tag, his eyes scouring the dimly lit floor for Loken's telltale aura or his shimmering wings. "Unless a great draft caught him, blowing him down the other side into that tunnel, he should be here."

"What the heck is this?" asked Rose. Between her index finger and thumb she picked up what appeared to be a tatty old, wool sock where Loken should have fallen.

"Good gracious!" exclaimed Rainus. He snatched it from Rose's hand.

"What is it?" asked Halen.

Rainus spun about to show his comrades. Jamming his hand into this sock like it was a mitten, he thrust it before their startled faces. "It is an abandoned sock puppet!"

For Rose, Tag and Myron, it was a familiar sight to behold, but Halen and Silas were momentarily stumped. The Elf and Wizard stared in bewilderment at the tattered sock embellished to look like a dragon with one of its button eyes dangling precariously by a frayed thread.

"This is the sock puppet we told you about, Master Agincor," reminded Myron.

"I suppose it is not quite as bad as having a mime as a minion," said Silas, staring at the less-than-ferocious dragon.

"Never mind that!" snapped Rose. "Loken tricked us!"

"What are you talking about?" asked Tag, watching as Rose snatched the sock puppet off of Rainus' hand.

She proceeded to throttle the toy, cursing beneath her breath, "You rotten, little miscreant! How dare you?"

"Get a hold of yourself!" demanded Tag. He grabbed Rose by her left wrist as her hands wrung the sock as though she was strangling the toy. The loose, wooden button of an eye swung violently to and fro as she shook it. "This is *not* Loken!"

"Of course it is!" insisted Rose. "This *is* the little troublemaker! He's working for Dragonite again."

"I assure you, Princess, the young sir speaks the truth," stated Rainus. "This cannot possibly be Loken."

"It is, I tell you!" The loose button eye whipped about once more as Rose shook the puppet at Rainus' agitated face.

"Loken possesses the power to only assume the shape of a *living* creature," explained Tag, as Silas nodded in confirmation. "He cannot transform into an inanimate object like this sock puppet."

"That despicable fiend!" cursed Rose. "How dare Dragonite resort to trickery?"

Rose threw the sock puppet onto the ground. As the crumpled toy suddenly writhed about, crawling away like a wounded animal, her boot slammed down. Furious, she began to trample underfoot the ratty puppet, grinding the wool fibres into the earth with the heel of her boot to crush whatever magic was left in it.

"Take that!" growled Rose. With a final, defiant stomp she screamed as the cave floor collapsed beneath her feet.

As she tumbled backwards, Tag lunged for her flailing hands. Their fingertips met in a glancing touch, their hands sweeping by each other in a frantic bid to grab hold. He blanched, watching in horror as Rose fell, following behind the trampled puppet that disappeared into the blackness below. Tag dove down, snagging her by the left ankle of her boot.

"Ooow!" Rose moaned.

Her fall came to a violent halt. Her back slammed against the stony wall, knocking the wind from her lungs. She felt Tag's grip through her leather boot as his hand tightened around her ankle. She glanced up to see Tag sprawled out on his stomach, holding on to her for dear life. She sighed in relief, but just as suddenly, she squealed in horror, peering down to see she was dangling head first into a gaping black hole that continued to crumble around its edges.

"Hold tight!" hollered Tag.

"To what?" cried Rose. She felt the blood rushing to her head, pounding in her ears with every frightened beat of her heart. "Just don't let go! Don't let me fall!"

In a panic, her frantic struggle caused Tag to lurch dangerously over the ledge.

"We've got you, Princess!" hollered Myron, as he and Halen sprang into action. They threw themselves onto Tag, piling on to keep him from going over while he clung to Rose by her boot.

"No! Oh, no!" yelped Rose. "I'm slipping!"

"I've got you!" promised Tag. He wrapped his other hand around the ankle of her boot now that Myron and Halen were bracing him. "I won't let you fall."

"My foot! It's slipping out!"

Tag could feel her leg tensing as she fought to flex her muscles so the crook of her foot remained in the boot as she dangled precariously.

As Halen and Myron held onto Tag, Rainus crouched next to them, reaching down as he called to Rose, "Take my hand!"

This order was tantamount to Rose standing straight-legged, bending at the waist to reach her toes with her fingertips. She was never this flexible, and never had a need to be, and for her, it was hard enough just to sit upright at the dinner table.

With a grunt of exertion she folded at the waist, straining with all her might to reach Rainus' outstretched hand while the Wizard's hand knotted around his cloak should she pull the Elf over with her.

Rose could feel every muscle in her midsection burn as she struggled to reach the Elf's hand.

"Try harder!" shouted Rainus, leaning down into the growing chasm.

"Hurry! Grab her!" ordered Tag. He could feel Rose's entire body trembling in his grip as he struggled to tighten his hold on her boot.

"I can't do it!" cried Rose.

With this admission of defeat Tag felt her muscles grow limp from exhaustion. She screamed in fright as her foot slipped out.

Tag's mouth gaped open. In utter horror, he stared at the empty boot in his hand.

18
Sin

"NO!" cried Tag.

Forced to witness Princess Rose's descent into doom, his thundering heart was pounded by a tidal wave of despair. He tossed the empty boot over his shoulder as he groaned in disbelief.

"Oh, my…" sighed the Wizard. With a whispered incantation, the crystal glowed, swelling with light. He lowered the luminous stone atop his staff into the deep, dark chasm.

"I can't look!" gulped Tag. He rolled onto his back, staring dismally at the craggy ceiling. "I warned her we were never the lucky sort."

"Speak for yourself!" snapped an angry voice.

"Look!" urged Silas. He pointed down with the tip of his staff.

Tag rolled back onto his stomach. At first glance he saw only the deep hole that seemed to disappear into the very bowels of the earth; a bottomless pit bathed in inky darkness well beyond the reach of the light emitted by Silas' crystal. And then he saw her!

"Behold! Princess Rose!" announced Silas.

Tag gasped in surprise to see luck and fate had indeed conspired in her favour. She had landed on a narrow ledge not even seven feet below!

"Thank goodness, you're alive!" exclaimed Tag, as he peered down at the dishevelled Princess.

"No thanks to you!" sniffed Rose. She slowly stood up, pressing her back against the stony wall.

Tag and Myron reached down, each extending a hand to her.

"Quickly, Princess!" ordered Myron, his hand opening wide as he reached down. "Your luck may not hold for much longer. Take our hands before that ledge collapses!"

"Are you saying it will not hold my weight because I am too heavy?"

"I am saying that ledge you stand on now is probably about as stable as this cave floor," grunted Myron. "Now, quickly!"

Rose reached up, balancing on the tip of her one, still booted foot while trying to keep the wool sock on her other foot off the ledge to keep from soiling.

Clasping Tag and Myron's wrists as they took hold of hers, they hoisted her up. Just as she planted her feet on the ground, she screamed as Tag and Myron yelped in surprise. Halen and Rainus grabbed them by their shoulders, hauling them back with Rose still in their grip. They tumbled backward just as the edge of the hole collapsed beneath their combined weight.

"Phew! That was close!" exclaimed Silas, watching as his comrades floundered about at his feet.

"Master Barscowl did forewarn us of the dangers in these mines," reminded Rainus. He and Halen hopped lightly onto their feet before helping the others onto theirs.

"I recommend we proceed with due care," said Halen, picking up the torches to hand off to Myron and Tag.

"Proceed! Are you mad?" gasped Rose, the colour returning to her ashen cheeks as she scolded the Elf. "I do believe this was fair warning to turn back!"

"There is no turning back now, Princess," insisted Tag, as he picked up her boot, passing it to her.

"No disrespect to Captain Ironwood, but you are as crazy as he is determined," admonished Rose, snatching her boot from Tag's hand. Steadying herself by grabbing his shoulder, she struggled to hold the boot upright as she thrust her foot back inside.

"I prefer to believe the young sir and it is our responsibility to see the Sorcerer brought to justice," answered Halen.

"Well, there are no rules stating one cannot be simultaneously crazy *and* responsible," muttered Rose. "I just think it is crazy to proceed and just as *irresponsible* to do so, in light of this trap that was almost my tragic end."

"That was not a trap," stated Rainus. "We were forewarned just how treacherous this place is."

"Are you saying it was my fault?" asked Rose, her eyes narrowing in resentment as she glowered at the Elf.

"Pretty much!" snorted Tag, coming to the Elf's defence. "I don't know how you do it, but you always manage to find holes to fall into or cliffs to tumble over. But Lord Silverthorn speaks the truth about this mountain."

In a heartbeat, her attention jumped from Rainus to Tag, punching the young man's shoulder for speaking up.

"What Lord Silverthorn was trying to tell you, Princess Rose, is that stomping on that bewitched toy caused you to fall through the cave floor," explained Silas.

"And it had nothing to do with your weight." Myron was quick to interject, should the Wizard's comment serve to fuel her ire.

"Fair enough, but if that sock puppet was not Loken, then what happened to him?" asked Rose.

"That is a good question, of which I have no answer at this time," responded Silas, as he cogitated on this troubling mystery.

"One thing is for sure," said Rainus, "if Loken could not be persuaded to lure us to this place, then the Sorcerer was forced to use dark magic to bring that puppet to life, making it appear in the likeness of the Sprite to do so."

"It was enough to fool us," said Tag.

"For such an exacting double, it would have to be a very potent dark magic to do so," stated Silas.

"That alone speaks loudly that we should turn back," insisted Rose. "If not, then we shall be playing directly into Dragonite's hands."

"Then what about Loken?" asked Tag.

"What about him?" said Rose.

"Suppose the Sorcerer holds Loken prisoner? What if he is being tortured as we speak?" Tag pretended to pluck off tiny wings from an invisible Sprite.

"I hate to be the bearer of bad tidings, but I suspect Loken is dead for Dragonite to resort to using that stupid puppet in his place," said Rose, her words more matter-of-fact than remorseful.

"That is a real possibility." Myron nodded. "However, I believe our little friend is still alive. He is being held against his will."

"How do you hold captive a Sprite, especially a shape-shifting Pooka?" argued Rose. "If Loken is alive and being held in a cage, even if the bars of his prison were tiny enough to keep his puny Sprite form contained, he would simply use his powers to shrink into a flea or something equally small to escape. If not that, he'd morph into a great creature, one large enough to break free and warn us of the dangers, but not without devouring Dragonite first, of course."

"Princess Rose does have a valid point," stated Halen. "I suspect the little fellow met an untimely demise. Even if Dragonite threatened Loken with his life, or worse, threatened the life of his ladylove, as he had done so in the past, it would have been the Sprite to lure us here, not an enchanted sock puppet come to life."

"Very true, but if Dragonite has been restored to his full powers, thanks to the Dreamstone, and relies on his skills in the forbidden arts, there is a way to hold a Pooka, rendering Loken powerless," warned Silas.

"But if Loken is alive and refuses to do Dragonite's bidding, then why use magic to hold him captive?" questioned Tag. "It would be less trouble to kill him."

"My thoughts exactly!" exclaimed Rose.

"I have a feeling he means to use Loken to lure us into his trap, having failed at securing Princess Rose as his hostage in the Mines of Euphoria," reasoned Rainus.

"There you go then! All the more reason not to proceed," insisted Rose.

"And had you been the one to be taken hostage, would you not want us to risk life and limb to rescue you?" asked Myron.

"Of course, but I am a princess! You and Tag had taken a sworn oath to keep me safe, so there you go!"

"Yes, but on this quest, we are all equal," reminded Myron. "Loken is deserving of the same consideration."

"Princess or not, would you not expect us to come to your rescue, had you been captured?" asked Tag.

Rose heaved a dreary sigh, muttering in defeat, "We must do the right thing."

"The right thing is the *only* thing," stated Tag.

"Yes, and find solace in knowing there is still a chance Dragonite is unaware of our presence," reminded Rainus.

"Oh, yes, that element of surprise!" An air of sarcasm tainted her words. "If the Sorcerer is profoundly deaf, I am confident he did not hear a thing when the earth collapsed, crashing down beneath my feet into that bottomless pit."

"The integrity of this entire mountain is in question. I am confident tunnels collapse and floors disintegrate on a regular basis," said Halen.

"Very true," agreed Rainus, as he pointed to Silas. "And to add to this element of surprise, Dragonite is unaware Master Agincor is now in our company, for I doubt Loken would reveal this, even under the threat of death."

"A crumbling mountain and a Wizard that prefers to make *magic* with words," grumbled Rose. "I am not brimming over with confidence at this moment."

"Take heart, Princess," said Myron. "In all this time Dragonite had been sneaking about, evil was always one step ahead of us. This time, *we* are the ones sneaking up on *him*."

"Oh, huzzah!" Rose tossed her hands up in feigned celebration. "So, now what?"

"I recommend I take the lead as we venture on," offered Silas. "Though looks are deceiving, I am quite light and spry on my feet. I shall use the tip of my staff to probe the earth before us to make sure it is safe to tread on as we advance."

"An excellent idea!" praised Rose, ushering him forward. "Do proceed!"

"Stay close," ordered Silas. He muted the light emitted from his crystal, dimming it just enough to see a few paces before him than to flood the way as a brazen visual cue of their presence.

Cautious and ever alert, Silas crept into the adjoining tunnel. Using the tip of his staff to sweep, poke and prod the ground, much like a blind man using a staff to feel his way forward, the group advanced. Before long, they came to the end of the tunnel. They stood in profound silence, awestruck by the sight to behold their eyes.

Exceeding the size of the great hall in Pepperton Palace that had played host to the country's grandest and most extravagant galas, this chamber's height far exceeded it, too. The ceiling was so high it was lost in the deep shadows above. It could have gone on forever, but in bold contrast, a narrow crack in the ceiling, a gap of approximately the width of two hand spans, allowed filtered light from the outside world to seep through. The only way of determining the height of this ceiling was to estimate how high this crack was.

The meagre light provided by Silas and the flames of the torches were only enough to illuminate the immediate area where they stood at the mouth of this vast chamber. As they ventured forward, more was revealed to them. Massive pillars rising from the ground stretched up to the ceiling. Each column was decorated with Dwarvish runes and intricate, geometric patterns typical of this race.

One corner of the chamber lay demolished where several pillars collapsed, mixing in with the debris of a past cave-in. Where these columns once proudly stood, shattered buttresses that had supported these structures jutted from the floor to leave the integrity of the chamber greatly compromised. The beauty and grandeur of these feats of architectural design, now flawed by destruction and neglect, filled Rose and her comrades with a sense of foreboding.

Halen and Rainus peered up to the crack in the centre of the ceiling. Their keen eyes spied the faint glow of the earliest stars against the twilight sky.

Directly below this crack was a very large puddle. Noticing this accumulation of water, Rainus gestured for the others to follow him.

Tiptoeing to the water's edge, Rainus leaned over, staring at his reflection as he contemplated the nature of this water. He determined the pooling rainwater had fallen through the crack, stagnating in this inky black pond. For a moment, he wondered if something evil lurked just beneath its surface. He suddenly recoiled as the overpowering smell of ammonia wafted into his nose, assaulting his senses.

"What is that horrible stench?" Rose gagged as she drew the edge of her cloak over her mouth and nose. Her eyes watered as she cried out, "And why is the earth moving?"

Shielding their mouths and noses to filter out the stink that grew stronger the more they tread on this floor, Rose watched in horror as the ground beneath her came alive. It undulated, writhing as if disturbed by their presence.

As Silas intensified the glow of his crystal, the swell of light illuminated their immediate surroundings, revealing more of the towering pillars and rubble. Giant cockroaches scattered, darting to the dark recesses of the pillars and scurrying into the debris to escape the glow of the orb. The Princess froze. She glanced down as the '*crunch*' and '*pop*' of maggots and beetles underfoot, feeding on the carcasses of dead bats and the layer of bat dung covering the chamber floor, sounded beneath her boots as she stepped.

"*AAAH!*" shrieked Rose.

Amplified by the acoustics of the chamber, Rose's shrill cry sent thousands of bats into flight, exploding forth from the ceiling. Her scream was drowned out by the clamour of leathery wings as the bats swarmed, flying in a sweeping circle before exiting through the crack in the ceiling.

"Well, that was disgusting!" groaned Rose, shaking her head in case a bat had become tangled in her tresses.

With words muffled by the cloak still drawn across his face, Tag scolded her. "Those bats would have remained on their roost, had you not screamed like a girl."

"I am allowed to scream like a girl because I *am* a girl! What was your excuse?"

"I *did not* scream," insisted Tag.

"Hush!" ordered Rainus. "And that was me, by the way. Those bats took me by surprise."

"No point in laying blame," whispered Halen. He pressed a finger to his lips. "Undoubtedly, those bats were already restless. I can see by the opening in the ceiling that dusk has already settled upon the lands."

"All the more reason to move with haste," said Myron. Dousing out his dying torch that was producing more smoke than light at this point, he snuffed it out in a heap of bat dung that writhed. Fleeing beetles and maggots sizzled on contact with the heat, adding to the suffocating stench already hanging heavy in the air. Directing Silas to take the lead once more, Myron urged the Wizard on.

With the light of the sputtering torch Tag held aloft, the deep gloom of this subterranean chamber seemed to press in on them from all sides. Silas whispered an incantation, causing the crystal atop his staff to glow brighter.

"More light, please," said Rose, noticing how Tag's torch sputtered, the flame ebbing with his every movement no matter how slight.

"This will do for now," responded Silas. "As long as you remain close, this light will be sufficient."

"We don't need to send out a beacon to announce our presence," reminded Tag.

"True, but I'd like to be able to see where we are going," whined Rose.

"Just stay close to Tag," urged Myron. He manoeuvred around her to strategically position himself behind Silas, should the Sorcerer strike.

"Yes, as long as we can see danger and can act accordingly, that is all that should concern you, Princess," added Rainus, as he and Halen took up the rear.

Rose knew there was no point in arguing. She plodded on. Following so close behind Tag, to his annoyance, she would occasionally clip the heels of his boots.

As they exited the chamber, they crept behind Silas, following him into a dark tunnel as he made his way forward. The only sounds to be heard were the steady beating of their hearts and the rhythmic drip and splash of water falling from the cracked ceiling that grew fainter as they ventured on. Rounding a bend in the tunnel, Tag's torch finally burned out, the last of its flame flickering in defiance as he tossed aside this light source as a trail of smoke remained, wafting lazily through the air to be dispersed in their wake as they advanced into the darkness.

Before Rose could complain, Silas drew his staff closer. Whispering words of an incantation, the light within the crystal swelled in small increments.

"That is a slightly better," whispered Rose, inching closer so she could take advantage of the sense of safety exuded by this inviting glow.

"You're so close to me," complained Tag. He could feel her warm breath tickling the nape of his neck. "Why don't you just climb on my back? I'll carry you."

"Well, thank you!" said Rose. She smiled in delight, waiting for her friend to lean forward so she can clamber on. "I never thought you'd offer."

"I was speaking in jest!"

"Oh…" Rose sighed in disappointment. With a heavy heart, she trudged along.

As they rounded another bend in this winding tunnel, Rose and her comrades could sense the path before them had a slight grade, tilting deeper into the heart of the mountain.

"How much further?" whispered Rose.

"That will depend," answered Silas.

"On what?"

"It shall depend upon what unfolds before us, Princess." Myron answered for Silas. "We go on until we can go no further or until we capture the Sorcerer, whichever comes first."

"Well, something better happen soon," grumbled Rose. "Traipsing through these never-ending tunnels is getting tiresome."

"Be careful what you wish for," cautioned Tag.

"I no longer wish for anything! I was merely speaking my mind."

She bumped into Tag as Silas suddenly raised his hand, motioning for all to halt.

"What do you see?" asked Myron. He peered over the Wizard's shoulder as Silas stared into the darkness beyond the glow of his crystal.

"Nothing at this moment," whispered Silas. "It is more what I hear than what I see."

Rainus and Halen's ears pricked up as they listened into the deep dark before them. Their keen ears detected a change in the acoustics that resonated with their hushed words.

"A large chamber," whispered Rainus, as Halen nodded in confirmation. "But there is something different about it."

"Remain here," ordered Silas. "I shall venture forth; check for possible dangers first."

"I will accompany you, Master Agincor," offered Halen. "The rest of you, stay put."

"Will you be taking our only source of light?" asked Rose, staring longingly at the crystal glowing atop Silas' staff.

"Of course. How else will we see?"

"Then how will *we* see?" questioned Rose, disturbed by the thought of being abandoned in all-consuming darkness.

"If you remain here, there will be no need to see where you are going," reasoned Silas.

"In the pitch black?" gulped Rose. "With no light? Not even from disgusting glow-worms?"

"As long as you don't go gallivanting off, you'll be fine," assured Tag.

Rose merely snorted a disgruntled huff. "Well then, I suppose I shall stay put."

"An excellent plan." Silas nodded in approval as he waved Halen forward to commence their exploration.

"If we do not meet with misfortune, we shall not be long," assured Halen.

"Then, do not meet with misfortune," urged Rose, watching as Silas and Halen turned away to venture down the tunnel, into the unknown.

"Just don't wander off," Silas called over his shoulder. "Wait for us here."

"I am not stupid. In fact, I will sit for now. So fear not, I will not be the one to tempt fate," vowed Rose. Sliding down against the tunnel wall, she folded her legs beneath her as she sat on the cold, hard ground.

"Brilliant! It will give us one less thing to worry about," said Tag, as he leaned against the tunnel wall next to her.

Rose, Tag, Myron and Rainus watched in silence as Halen and Silas' silhouettes, backlit by the Wizard's crystal, became one with the deep shadows.

"Do you believe the Sorcerer is near?" whispered Rose. Her muted words echoed, seemingly suspended in a blackness that was deeper than the darkest winter sky on a moonless night. This all-consuming darkness made her feel isolated and vulnerable. She needed the reassurance her comrades were still close at hand, even if it was an agitated, but familiar, voice scolding her. "That he is lurking about close to us?"

"I suspect so, Princess," answered Myron.

"I believe in order for Dragonite to conjure magic, the kind of magic to bring that sock puppet to life in the form of Loken, and to control it, he must be close to us," added Rainus.

"If that be the case, should we not arm ourselves? Just in case?" queried Rose, her hand blindly groping about to feel for her sling.

"At the risk of injuring each other in this stifling darkness, I would not recommend it," answered the Elf.

"So, we should just sit here? Wait for danger to take us by surprise?"

"Be patient," urged Tag. "Our friends will be back soon. Once they return, we shall proceed accordingly."

Sensing it was his way of telling her to hush up, Rose sat quietly for as long as she could. Overcome with the tedious boredom of waiting, Rose began to softly hum a tune. It was a love ballad she felt appropriate for an orchestra to play at her wedding gala, should she survive this quest.

"Will you stop it!" snapped Tag. He shifted about, shaking his right leg.

Though she could not see her hand even if it was before her face, Rose glanced up toward the sound of this agitated voice. She was surprised Tag did not take as much pleasure in the sweet tone of her voice as she did.

"Stop humming?" asked Rose.

"Stop fondling my leg, that's what!"

"Are you mad? Why would I do that?"

"Whoa!" yelped Tag. An invisible hand gingerly climbed higher up his leg, tightening its grip on his thigh. "You're getting too friendly for my likening, Princess. Keep your hands to yourself."

"Not even if you paid me and provided me with a long stick would I touch you, and if you do not stop with this foolishness, the only place you shall find *both* my hands will be around your neck, throttling you!"

"Before you accuse me, I am over here, against the far wall," whispered Myron, holding up both hands even though none could see them.

Tag froze as this touch stopped at mid-thigh. "Lord Silverthorn... Is that you?"

"Me? My hands are busy elsewhere."

"Busy? Just what are you doing?" asked Rose, staring into the darkness where she assumed the Elf was standing.

"If you must know, I am adjusting my codpiece as we speak. All this walking has caused some uncomfortable chafing, so I am adjusting the *family jewels* before we are made to journey on."

"That was more than I ever wanted to know," groaned Rose.

"Hey... If this is not the Princess or Myron, and you claim it is not you..." Tag suddenly blanched, and then he shrieked.

Thinking a giant cockroach or monstrous spider was making friends with his leg, Tag jumped about, desperately trying to shake off this invisible presence steadily creeping toward his nether regions.

Feeling this unrelenting touch, in a blind panic, Tag dashed forth. With his arms outstretched before him, he bounced off the walls of the narrow tunnel and into the chamber Halen and Silas had gone off to explore. Tag tripped in the darkness. His moan of pain was drowned out by the clatter of his sword's scabbard as he crashed to the ground.

"Wait!" called Rainus, his hand flapping about, feeling for the proximity of his friends.

"Come!" ordered Myron. By sheer luck, he managed to grab Rose by her wrist. With the other, he used it to trace the contours of the tunnel as he called, "Tag! Stop!"

As the wall of the tunnel abruptly ended, so too, did their chase. Tag yelped in surprise as Myron and Rose tripped over his feet. They flew forward, landing on top of him. Rainus, hearing their cries of astonishment and the *thud* of their bodies falling over Tag, came to a skidding stop. The toes of his boots striking against theirs as the mortals lay in a heap on the dark ground before him.

Tag, Rose and Myron opened their eyes to see the glow of Silas' crystal bobbing through the darkness as he raced toward them.

"What happened?" called Halen. Dashing up behind the Wizard, he spied on his comrades sprawled out upon the floor of this great chamber. "Were you attacked?"

"It was not an outright attack, so to speak, but something sinister was manhandling my leg!" gasped Tag, struggling to knock Rose and Myron from his back.

"For shame, Princess!" Silas shook a stern finger at her. "And here, I thought you were spoken for; engaged to be married!"

"I assure you, it was not me!" Rose clambered onto her feet. "I have better taste than this."

"Taste or not, it was definitely not me," disclosed Myron.

Halen and Silas' eyes narrowed as they glanced over at Rainus. Before they could ask him, Lord Silverthorn spoke up, "Do not look at me! My hands were preoccupied."

"Then what was it?" asked Silas, his brows furrowing in curiosity.

"Whatever it was, I believe I killed it," moaned Tag, as he rolled from his stomach onto his back.

"Oh, my!" gasped Silas. He leaned in closer to shine some light on the squashed object that fell from Tag's leg as he stood up.

"Ewww! It better not be one of those cockroaches!" groaned Tag, shuddering involuntarily.

"What is that thing?" asked Rose.

Between his index finger and thumb, Silas gingerly picked up Tag's flattened victim. "It is no wonder you thought it was a hand fondling your leg, young sir."

They gathered around Silas as he held forth the offending culprit. Limp, bedraggled, and battered from severe abuse, the lifeless, dangling eye hung by a frayed thread. This eye finally fell away. It *'plinked'* as it struck a rock at the Wizard's feet before bouncing off into the darkness.

"It is that loathsome sock puppet again!" snarled Rose, scowling in anger as recognition set in.

"How did it even get here?" wondered Myron. He examined the toy's remaining wooden eye that was now chipped and scratched, undoubtedly from when Rose stomped on it, before being lost in the chasm that almost consumed her, too.

"It is dark magic, I tell you!" insisted Silas.

The sock puppet suddenly writhed. Like an angry, wounded snake, it thrashed about to be free of the Wizard's grip. Lashing out, it snapped with woolly teeth at its captor. In repulsion, Silas tossed it to the ground.

Wrapping his hands around a hefty rock, with no remorse or second thoughts, Tag deliberately dropped it on the bewitched toy before it could crawl away.

Anchored beneath this weight, the ragged edges of the puppet protruding from beneath the rock squirmed, and then convulsed as though in the throes of death. Just as abruptly, it drooped, falling limp as if its life was finally snuffed out.

"Take that, you hexed, little beastie!" declared Rose. In anger, she kicked dirt at the puppet. "There will be no escape for you."

"Yes, none will be giving you a *hand* this time!" quipped Rainus.

"It is odd." Halen rubbed his chin in pensive thought. "How did that ghastly thing get from the bottom of that pit to this very place?"

"I suspect Dragonite still controls it," determined Myron. "It was summoned by its master, crawling out of the depths of that great abyss to answer his call to follow us."

"So the Sorcerer must be near," determined Tag. His eyes glanced about nervously.

"I feel there is dark magic near to us," whispered Silas, as he shuddered involuntarily. "I sense the Dreamstone is close by, too."

"I recommend we move on," said Halen. "The Wizard and I saw nothing untoward in this great chamber. As large as it is, there is nothing here that poses a threat to us."

"There is a tunnel that leads away from here," stated Silas. "Undoubtedly, it shall take us deeper into this mountain, and perhaps on to the Sorcerer's lair."

"Then we move with haste," urged Myron.

With the vastness of this cave and the overwhelming gloom pressing in on them, Silas willed his crystal to emit greater light.

"Come," ordered the Wizard, waving his comrades on to follow. With hushed steps and the light of his crystal to show the way, Silas guided his comrades on. "Stay close to me."

Just as they advanced across the chamber, Rose dropped to her knees. She hastily pushed loose earth up against the base of the rock. Tamping the soil with the palms of her hands, she further buried the lifeless sock puppet, making sure it did not follow them in case there was still a spark of magic left within.

Tag paused, suddenly aware that Rose was not clipping the heels of his boots as she was before.

"Keep up! This is not the time to lollygag." Tag glanced over his shoulder to chastise her, only to frown in suspicion. He watched as a small orb of light floated in the darkness of the tunnel they had come from. In silence, it glided in Rose's direction, only to come to a halt, resting on a boulder near the mouth of the cave.

"Loken?" called Tag. Puzzled by this odd phenomenon, he listened for the familiar thrum of wings as his eyes strained to see through the deep gloom that only intensified behind Rose with each step Silas took away from her.

"What are you talking about?" Rose stood upright, brushing the dirt from her hands. Before she saw the light Tag had spotted, she shrieked in fright. A shadowy figure rushed up from behind, seizing her by a fistful of hair.

"Princess!" cried out Tag. Drawing his sword, he dashed toward her.

Rose's scalp stung as strands of hair were yanked from her head. Clamping both hands over the bony one knotted around her tresses, Rose's struggle stopped. Something cold and sharp pressed against her throat.

"Unhand her!" shouted Tag.

Myron and the others turned with a start upon hearing this commotion. Instinctively, they drew their weapons, running after Tag to confront this danger together.

Dragonite's jagged obsidian crystal mounted atop a crooked staff glowed as it was removed from Rose's throat. This ebony glass abruptly flared with blinding light as the tip of this crystal shard was driven into the earth.

Rose screamed in fright, watching as Tag and the others fell to their knees. The ground quaked beneath their feet, shuddering violently as the earth was riven in two. In a swirling cloud of dust, crumbling rocks and cascading boulders crashed down from the cave's ceiling. Tumbling into the widening divide, the rubble splashed loudly, swallowed up in a churning, belching river of molten, red-hot lava.

As the crack in the earth grew into a widening chasm, Tag raced forward. Driven by desperation, neither the intense heat swelling from below nor the rain of debris crashing down served as a deterrent. Pushing off the edge of the precipice to leap to the other side, he cried out in surprise.

Halen seized him by the scruff of the neck. With a powerful heave, he yanked the mortal away from certain death.

"You will never make it!" shouted Halen. Pulling Tag onto his feet, he steadied the lad as the earth moaned, rolling beneath their feet in ferocious protest to this dark magic. "Even I cannot clear this distance at a full run. It is too great!"

Clambering onto his feet, Silas shouted, "Stand back, my friends! I shall deal with that necromancer, once and for all!"

Levelling his crystal at his nemesis, Silas fell upon his knees once more; his weapon forcefully yanked free of his grip.

He and the others watched in dismay as it flew from his hands. This invisible force hurled Silas' staff across the divide to land at Rose's feet as her attacker unleashed a maniacal laugh.

Before Rose could push her assailant off to claim Silas' staff, a foot slammed down. With a loud '*craaack*', the staff snapped in half as the light in the crystal died.

"You pathetic, old fool! You are no match for me, Agincor! You never were!"

"You underestimate me!" shouted Silas, pushing off Myron's hands as the knight helped him onto his feet.

Rose shuddered. Her blood ran cold as this voice hissed in her ears, "Know thine enemy, Agincor. Is that not what you once said to me? It must be hard to hate the one you love."

"There is no love lost between us! A wise Wizard knows better than to have dealings with a necromancer."

"I am wounded by your damning words! And you dare trivialize our relationship? Our long history together?"

"I stand firm on my convictions. No good has ever come from dealing with a Sorcerer, especially one as demented as you!"

"I am no Sorcerer!" This scoffing voice shouted to be heard over the roiling lava. "I am an Enchantress!"

Silas blanched. The colour drained from his face upon hearing this declaration. A moan of anguish squeaked from his mouth as the unsettling chill of recognition clawed at his heart and mind.

"No…"

"Oh, yes!" A gnarled hand reached up, pulling back the hood of the cloak that shrouded this mysterious form in shadow. As it fell away, a ghastly face was revealed to all. "I am an Enchantress of renown!"

Peering over her right shoulder, Rose recoiled. She pulled her face away from the untameable shock of tangled black and grey hairs spilling forth to frame a gaunt, withered, unnaturally pale visage that looked as though it had never been graced by the light of day. Rose cringed in revulsion as she spied upon the profile of a hooked, beak-like nose and a cloudy, milky white left eyeball staring vacantly ahead. As the hag pulled her closer, using the Princess' body as a human shield, Rose flinched in repulsion as the bristling hairs protruding from a warty mole on her assailant's chin brushed against her cheek.

"Ewww! There is nothing enchanting about you!" Rose groaned in disgust.

"Shut your mouth, you wretched girl!" The old crone growled at Rose as she stared at Silas, never taking her one good eye off him. "Remember when I was more beautiful than this princess? Remember when you once cherished the very ground I walked on?"

"What is she babbling about?" cried Rose, as she clawed at the hand still holding her by the tresses

Silas' heart dropped, sinking to the pit of his stomach. With his suspicions confirmed, his body visibly trembled at the sight of this wizened form and hideous face.

"Cinyah Morningstar…" gasped Silas.

"It is *Sin Mourningstar* now, no thanks to you!"

"*Ugly as sin*, is more like it," chided Rose, before rebuking the Wizard. "For pity's sake, Wizard! Where is your sense of taste? You told us the love of your life was beautiful!"

"Stay your tongue, Princess!" ordered Silas. "Or do you wish to tempt fate? For there stands a formidable Witch, if ever there was one!"

"I am a powerful *Enchantress*, not some lowly Witch!"

"Whatever she claims to be, I am just trying to make sense of this!" shouted Rose. "If you truly loved this wretched creature, then either love is truly blind or you prefer to scrounge about in the dregs of the *ugly barrel* to fall for this one!"

"I knew her *before* she subjected herself to all manner of potions and spells in a quest to hold the years at bay; to retain her beauty. This is the result of experiments gone bad!" snapped Silas, struggling to justify his former love. "She was indeed beautiful, but that was many years ago, and the years have been unkind."

"This hag?" Rose dared to say, as she glanced over her shoulder for a second look, only to shudder once again. "I think not! No beauty regimen, no matter how uncouth or drastic, can result in this atrocity!"

"In my youth, I *was* an ethereal beauty!" The old woman hissed in her ear. "Alas, I was single-minded, overzealous even, in my quest for an anti-aging potion, but I failed."

"Indeed! You must have fallen headfirst into a bad batch to look as you do now," noted Rose.

"Shut it!" snarled the Witch. She yanked back on Rose's head so the chords of her neck were pulled taut. "Shut your mouth or I shall slit your pretty little throat!"

The Princess yelped in pain, gagging as the woman growled in her ear. The heat of her breath, like a noxious vapour, hung heavy on Rose's neck, prickling at her delicate skin. The sour reek of failed potions, mingling with the stench of decaying teeth and abscessed gums, wafted from between the woman's thin, cracked lips as she huffed in anger.

"Whoa! Hold on here... this is *the* woman you told us about?" gasped Myron; slow to understand whom Rose and the Wizard were speaking of.

The knight stared in disbelief, watching as the light emitted by the churning lava below illuminated the hag's hideous face as she manoeuvred Rose closer to the edge of the chasm. The rising river of lava bathed the Witch in an eerie, red glow to accentuate every wrinkle, scar, pockmark and wart marring her face.

"I trust that Wizard spoke well of me," hissed the woman, as she shoved Rose closer to the fiery divide. "If not, I will be in a foul mood, indeed!"

"Unhand Princess Rose!" demanded Tag, waving his sword about in hollow threat. "Let her go!"

"Into the lava?" She cackled gleefully, nudging the panicking girl toward the crumbling ledge. "In fact, I can toss the Pooka in, for good measure. Burn them both alive, if you wish!"

She glanced over her shoulder to where she left Loken in a small, iron cage. The Sprite was bound and gagged with a smear of pitch over his mouth to prevent him from calling out to his friends. Somehow, Loken had been rendered powerless.

"Or should I do away with that shape-shifting miscreant first? We can see how quickly he is reduced to cinder, so the Princess can be witness to what is in store for her."

"No! That is not what I meant!" hollered Tag.

"Then say what you mean and mean what you say, for the lives of your friends shall depend on it!"

"Do not act rashly!" urged Myron.

"I can understand the Princess, for she has a way of getting under one's skin without even trying," said Rainus, as he glanced over at the anxious Wizard, "but what grudge does that old crone have with you,

Master Agincor?"

"Yes, other than being a woman scorned after you spurned her?" added Rose, in a desperate bid to deflect the Witch's attention away from her and on to him.

"Scorned?" raged the hag, shaking her prisoner by a fistful of hair. "Not only did Agincor spurn me, he brought my brother to his ruin!"

"If it is a personal matter, then release Princess Rose," demanded Myron. "She has nothing to do with the trouble and strife caused by bad-blood from days gone by!"

"This wretched girl was instrumental in my brother's demise! He said she was the bane of his existence and the cause of his mortal wound."

"Say again!" gasped Rose, twisting about to look upon Sin's wretched face. Her mind raced, desperately searching the annals of her memory for a deadly encounter with an equally ugly male sibling. "I do not ever recall meeting your brother, never mind having a hand in killing him!"

"How soon you forget!" snarled the Witch. Releasing the Princess' head, she grabbed Rose's shoulder, spinning her about so they were face to face.

Rose grimaced with an equal measure of pity and revulsion. From the side, this woman was ugly enough, but face-on, and this close? She was truly hideous, especially the one working eye that glared menacingly at her, burning straight through Rose's soul to strike fear in her heart.

"You undoubtedly remember my brother as Parru St. Mime Dragonite!"

"What?" Rose gasped. "How can that be?"

"All shall be revealed, for I want you to know with your dying breath why you deserve to suffer by my hands!"

"The Sorcerer never mentioned a sister!" protested Rose. She stared in confusion at Silas.

"She was considered the black sheep of the family; a member rarely spoken of by her kin," explained Silas, with a shrug. "Every family has one!"

"More of a black sheep than Dragonite?" questioned Tag. He shook his head in disbelief as he stared at the Wizard. "You mentioned this woman, but you never told us she was a Witch – "

"Enchantress!" declared Sin.

"Or that she was Dragonite's sister!" added Myron.

"Yes!" called Rose, shaking a fist at Silas. "You lied to us, you crazy, old coot!"

"Withholding information is not an out-and-out lie," corrected Silas. "Besides, it is bad enough enduring your ridicule now that you have seen her with your own eyes. Can you imagine if I had told you from the start I once loved Dragonite's *sister*? I would never have heard the end of it!"

"Had you warned us, we could have anticipated this; prepared for such an attack," responded Rainus.

"Bah!" Sin huffed an incredulous snort. "So you say, Elf Lord, but it was obvious you had no idea I was behind the sickness to infiltrate your domain or the deaths of those blasted Trolls!"

"So now, you mean to avenge your brother's death," assumed Silas, unleashing a dreary sigh. "And here, I believed you despised him when he became the self-appointed patron saint of mimes. You were humiliated when he was dragged before the Council of Wizards and found guilty for his crimes against humanity and good taste."

"*Despised?* I loathed him! I hated that idiot of a brother! Who in their right mind appreciates mimes to that degree? He brought shame to the family when he adopted the name *St. Mime,* adding it to Dragonite. Why did you think I changed my surname, if only to distance myself from that fool?"

"Then we did you a great service by ridding you of that demented brother!" declared Tag.

"Indeed, you did! I stole away with his staff armed with this black crystal, but with his dying breath that fool bequeathed unto me a wondrous gift!" The hag reached beneath the bodice of her tattered frock. Holding before her for all to see was the Dreamstone Dragonite had absconded with.

Rose gasped in surprised to see the familiar glow of the Dreamstone as she cried out, "That belongs to me!"

"It is mine now!"

"Truth be told, that Dreamstone is rightfully mine, if Princess Rose wishes to relinquish it," stated Silas.

"Really? And how do you plan to get it back, if I refuse to give it to her?" retorted Sin. She mockingly dangled the Dreamstone for all to admire her coveted prize. "Are you going to use your magical staff, Agincor?"

"Well, I…"

"Well, nothing! It is here! It is broken!" scoffed the Witch, glancing behind her at the shattered staff. "Like you, it is utterly useless!"

"If we did you a favour in killing the Sorcerer, then why all this?" asked Myron, struggling to understand her motive. "Why all this violence and heinous acts of revenge, if not for the overwhelming grief of losing your sibling?"

"Revenge?" laughed Sin, rolling her good eye that gleamed with malice. "If my brother was dear to me, perhaps revenge would be a sound motivator. But this has nothing to do with avenging his death!"

"Then what is it?" Halen demanded to know. "What do you want from us?"

"This Dreamstone will not resurrect the dead! I tried to bring my brother back from the dead, but this crystal will allow me to do everything, but that!"

"Of course it won't!" said Silas. "Can you imagine the madness and mayhem that would ensue should every person granted one of my Dreamstones wished to resurrect a lost loved one?"

"And you said you did not love your brother!" reminded Rose. "Why would you want him alive again?"

"With his dying breath, my brother told me of this magic crystal; what it does and how it works." She held forth the Dreamstone as it throbbed with light. "He promised it to me, if I create a special potion to restore his life. He vowed he would return more powerful, able to complete his mission of bringing respect and honour to the art of mime, while hunting down to kill all those to bring misery to his life!"

"But you said his love of mimes brought dishonour to your family name," said Tag. "Why would you want to resurrect him to complete his life's mission?"

"My brother was more than a little touched in the head when it came to those pathetic fools he tried to pass off as professional entertainers. I have no desire to see his demented dream come true! The horrors!"

"Then why do you want him alive?" asked Rose.

"So *I* can be the one to kill him!" growled Sin.

"Oh, my!" muttered Rainus, with a dismal shake of his head. "It must run in the family. She is as crazy as the Sorcerer was!"

"I am *not* crazy! My fool brother was the crazy one. I am being practical."

"How can resurrecting your brother, only to kill him by your own hands, be practical?" questioned Tag. "If anything, it only speaks of how demented *you* are."

"If you must know, once I return life into that useless corpse I had carefully embalmed, he will be restored to his full power and glory!"

"And then she means to steal away with her brother's powers to make them her own!" deduced Silas.

"Exactly! That fool died before I could steal it away from him! Now, in order to take what should have been mine, I must create a special potion and conjure a binding magic to make it so."

"But this Dreamstone you now possess can make you powerful in your own right," said Rose.

"The act of *wishing* for this or that does not make one powerful," complained Sin. "It is an illusion. I desire *real* power! I want the kind of power that will be the envy of every Witch I know. And I shall tear asunder the Council of Wizards for refusing me a place at their *respected* table! I will drive them to their knees. They shall do my bidding this time!"

"That cannot be a good thing," grumbled Rainus. "Such a threat is usually followed by an attempt for world domination."

"There is nothing wrong with ambition," said Rose, trying to cajole her captor. "But why me? I have nothing to do with this council Silas Agincor is privy to."

"You, foolish girl, will help to make this potion to resurrect my *dear* brother."

"Me? I know nothing about concocting magical potions! In fact, I have trouble just boiling water!" admitted Rose.

"You idiot!" cursed Sin. She pressed the sharp edge of the obsidian crystal to Rose's throat. "I need the blood from the one who had delivered my brother's demise in order to reverse his present condition. I need *your* blood!"

"Wait! She did not kill your brother! I did!" declared Tag, his balled fist thumping his chest in defiance.

"Then I will have your blood!" snarled Sin, her right eye narrowing in contempt as she glared across the divide at the young man.

"No! I was the one!" shouted Myron, as he stepped before Tag.

"What?" Sin's face twisted into an angry scowl as her one good eye glanced from the young man to the knight.

"You heard me," snapped Myron. "I killed that wretched soul!"

"I beg to differ." Rainus boldly stepped forth. "I did it! I was the one to kill that deranged Sorcerer!"

"Do not take credit for that heroic deed, my lord," insisted Halen. "I was the one to murder that madman."

She glowered at Silas. A strange mist swirled over the surface of her blind eye while her sighted one narrowed in utter contempt. "In a bid to confuse me, I suppose you are going to take credit for my brother's demise, too?"

"Me?" responded Silas. His hand rested upon his heart in solemn promise. "Well, I certainly thought about it, but no, I can say with all certainty that it was not me to do the deed."

"Well then, it was most likely you!" snapped the Witch, pointing the tip of the obsidian crystal at Silas.

"Really now, my dear Cinyah, have I ever lied to you?"

"It is *Sin*! And do not try to sweet talk me! In fact, you *did* lie! You once claimed you loved me! You told me that we would be together forever, but you lied!"

"Well, I can understand why!" Rose's words were matter-of-fact. "You are not exactly eye-pleasing nor do you possess a sparkling personality to compensate for that ill-favoured look of yours."

"I told you before, I will tell you again," shouted Silas, "she did not always look this way."

Glancing over her shoulder to stare at the wrinkled visage, the Princess thought that under different lighting conditions and viewed from perhaps another angle she'd see the loveliness Silas once saw in her.

"Really?" asked Rose. "I find that hard to believe."

"Shut up! Stop mocking me! Look at that old gizzard of a Wizard! He is no prize!" shrieked Sin, thrusting the sharp edge of the obsidian crystal to Rose's throat.

"Wait!" hollered Tag. "You said you need the blood of your brother's killer for the potion!"

"I do!" snarled Sin.

"Now, it is an impossible task because you know not who the real killer is!" stated Rainus.

"Ha! Take that!" added Silas, pointing a scornful finger at Sin. "An impossible task, indeed! Perhaps I was the one to do the deed after all!"

"Well then, it shall be a process of elimination. I will begin with the Princess, and then I shall kill each of you, one by one, harvesting your blood as I go."

Rose squealed in fright, hearing the whine and feeling the wake of Halen's arrow as it flew by. The swan feathers fletching the shaft grazed her right cheek as the old woman ducked behind her. The steel bodkin ricocheted off the stony wall as the shaft shattered on impact, forcing Loken to dive to the bottom of his prison to avoid the flying shrapnel.

"Hold steady, you fool!" snarled Sin. "Next time I may not be so lucky, and neither will you!"

Raising her black crystal, she pointed it at Rose's comrades as they gathered along the edge of the chasm. Reciting an incantation, the obsidian glowed unnaturally.

A great bolt of energy exploded forth, clearing the chasm to strike down the Elf. In response, Halen merely angled away to avoid being hit.

Sin snarled. Trembling in rage, it only served to further compromise her ability to aim with any level of accuracy. Unleashing another bolt, she targeted Tag, as he was laughing the loudest at her first attempt. Even though this mortal lacked the natural agility gifted to the Elfkind, Tag merely stepped out of the way. The destructive magic flew in his general direction, but came nowhere near to endangering him.

"That was a pathetic display!" Silas ridiculed her with a hearty chuckle. "You may have my crystal, but even with Dragonite's, you are utterly useless, aiming with that one good eye!"

Sin shrieked in anger and frustration, hurling a ball of energy at the Wizard. The fog clouding her blind eye swirled, like mist rolling over a swamp, as her level of rage escalated. With aging sight in one eye, her depth perception and field of vision were greatly challenged. Even Silas, as physically unfit as he was, simply rolled out of the way, laughing at her futile attempt to obliterate him.

"Stop moving!" demanded Sin, stomping her feet like an angry child erupting into a tantrum.

"But if we move, there is a better chance one of us shall stray into your line of fire!" scoffed Silas.

"*ARGH!* You dare mock me?"

"You are making it easy to do so," he responded.

Muttering beneath her breath, Sin's right eye suddenly clouded over too, as milky white as her blind eye. She wished a terrifying wish that caused the Dreamstone to throb with unnatural light.

With the jagged edge of the obsidian crystal pressed against Rose's throat once more, the Princess managed to glance over her shoulder. From the corner of her eye she noticed the bound and stifled Sprite ramming his shoulder against the bars of his prison, struggling to be free. Rose then glanced down to see the large rock Tag had dropped on the bedraggled sock puppet as it began to rattle about. The earth she had packed around it exploded.

Rose turned her face away, closing her eyes as the flying debris pelted her and the Witch. The rock pinning the puppet was propelled skyward, striking with a resounding *boom* against the ceiling of the cave.

Rose opened her eyes to see a dark shadow rising from the disturbed earth. The sock puppet had come back to life, but this time, it did not appear as a child's toy or in Loken's likeness.

Instead, a great reptile of swirling black sand took shape before Rose and her comrades' startled eyes. They watched from across the chasm as this menacing form swelled in size.

Rose gasped in horror. It was both amazing and terrifying to see this toy transmogrify into a monster as large as a real dragon. Her only consolation was that this conjured beast did not develop a true physical form clad in scales as tough as steel. Instead, grains of sand swirled, churned and spun into the shape of a winged leviathan. The air felt charged and the noise of the rapidly and ever-moving particles sounded like a swarm of angry bees driven from their hive. As its mouth curled back into a snarl, jagged rows of black teeth gnashed together as a throaty bellow rumbled forth. Rose was confident this manifestation was all sound and thunder; there would be no *bite* behind this menacing, phantom dragon.

She squealed in fright as this nightmarish beast lunged forward, its gaping maw sinking into a stalactite bigger than her body. Yanking this calcified formation from the ceiling of the cave, its teeth smashed down, pulverizing stone into rubble and dust.

"Go! Kill them!" commanded Sin, pointing across the divide. So incensed, she was willing to gamble that it was indeed Rose to kill her brother. "Kill them all!"

With a thunderous *whoosh,* massive wings unfolded, casting Sin and Rose in its shadow. The conjured beast launched into the air in a whirlwind of dust. It dove head first into the chasm, gliding over the churning river of lava, completely unscathed by the intense heat swelling from the earth's furnace. With a bone-rattling roar, the monster swooped upwards. As though supported by the rising heat, the dragon hovered before Tag and his comrades. Cocking its massive head to one side, where once there was a single button eye, a burning red orb of fire stared at him.

Tag hoisted his sword, preparing to attack. He was bowled over as the creature's mouth dropped open, a loud bellow blasting forth.

"Damn it!" cursed Sin. In her haste to create this monster, she had imagined the details of its size and shape, but carelessly forgot to wish for this dragon to breathe incinerating fire.

The creature's clawed feet latched onto the edge of the precipice, the earth crumbling beneath its talons as it pushed off into the air once more, heading straight for Tag as he scrambled onto his feet to run.

Myron boldly raced forward, slashing at this monster. His sword sliced through the shadowy form like it was a ghost, but there was the abrasive sound of metal being pelted by thousands of grains of black sand as the blade cut through the shadow dragon's torso.

Completely unfazed, the creature swooped down. Scooping Tag up in its hind feet, Halen and Rainus unleashed a torrent of arrows that passed harmlessly through this dark spectre.

Tag cried out as powerful, curved talons wrapped around his chest and legs.

Racing to his aid, Tag's comrades were beaten down by the force of the wings as the dragon struggled to gain elevation.

"Into the lava!" demanded Sin. "Let's hear that body sizzle! Drop him! Drop him to his death!"

"No!" screamed Rose.

She fought against Sin's tenacious hold. In an absolute panic, Rose didn't even feel the sharp edge of the obsidian crystal lance her throat. Crimson blood seeped from the broken skin as she watched the phantom beast take to the air with Tag in its clutches.

Knowing their weapons were useless, Halen leaped forward. Seizing Tag by his ankles, the Elf struggled to pull him free as Tag, still armed with his sword, continued to slash in vain at this phantom form.

With a powerful thrust of its wings, this swirling shadow lifted man and Elf higher.

"I cannot hold on!" cried Halen, dangling as he struggled to maintain his grip on Tag.

The creature veered sharply, the tip of its right wing scraping against the far wall to send a shower of dirt and rocks cascading down. Just as it flew toward the chasm and the river of lava below, Halen dropped to the ground, ducking as Rainus threw the loop of his rope to snag Tag around his neck and left shoulder.

Halen, Myron and Silas rushed to Rainus' side. Both grabbed hold of the rope as Tag released his sword, letting it fall to the earth. He quickly slipped the loop around his right shoulder just as the noose tightened around him.

All four held onto the length of rope, digging their heels into the ground while Tag groaned in pain and the creature bellowed in rage at this sudden resistance.

With wings flapping furiously, the creature ploughed forward to deliver Tag to a fiery death, dragging his friends along to their doom, too, if they refused to let go.

Seeing her comrades heading straight for danger, anger overrode fear as Rose's blood boiled. Her elbow flew back, striking the Witch in her bony ribs. For a brief instance, Sin's will over the dragon was broken as she wailed in pain from the assault.

The phantom creature unleashed a blood-chilling roar as it released its hold on Tag. Sin cackled as Rose screamed in horror, watching her friend fall from the dragon's talons to plummet into the chasm.

"*HEAVE!*" hollered Myron, scrambling to set his heels in against the crumbling ledge.

Tag screamed in fright, seeing the surging lava rushing toward him as the blast of heat swelled from below. Swinging from the rope like a human pendulum over this red-hot river, he groaned in pain. His body smashed against the cliff wall, bouncing from the impact as dirt and rocks rained down on him from above where Myron braced himself from tumbling in.

"Huzzah!" Rose cheered in triumph. She watched as Tag dangled from his tether, beyond the grasp of a fiery demise as their friends hauled him to safety.

"Damn you!" cursed Sin! "Damn you all!"

Slapping a gnarled hand over the Dreamstone, the enraged Witch focused on controlling the shadowy dragon as it skimmed along the heights of the tall ceiling.

Before Sin could imbue this dragon with the power of a fiery breath to incinerate her foes, desperation forced Rose to act. Clenching her fist, she smashed the Witch on her nose.

Sin shrieked in pain, stumbling back from the blow. She instinctively released her grip on Rose's hair to nurse her battered nose. The Princess was quick to take advantage of her sudden freedom. Instead of fleeing, she lunged at the Witch to send her sprawling onto the ground.

"Take back the Dreamstone, Princess!" hollered Silas, as he helped Myron pull Tag to safety.

Enraged, and in no need of prompting, Rose launched herself bodily at the hag. She landed atop the bony rack of ribs, struggling to pin these lanky arms wildly thrashing about to be rid of her.

Wrapping her hands around Sin's wrists, Rose snapped, "Keep still, you old bag of bones!"

A visceral growl rumbled from the back of Sin's throat as her good eye gleamed with utter contempt for this mortal.

Just as Rose released her grip on the woman's left wrist to snatch up the Dreamstone, Sin shifted her weight, knocking the Princess to her side. Like a writhing, greased weasel impossible to hold, the Witch was on top, straddling Rose's body. Rather than fighting to pin this mortal to the ground, her hands dove straight for Rose's throat. Bony fingers and thumbs wrapped around, throttling the Princess as she gagged, fighting to break this choking grip.

Wheezing, Rose gasped for air as Sin, fuelled by rage, leaned over her, pressing down with unnatural strength for one so wiry.

Rose's mind and body grew numb as her lungs ached, unable to snatch a breath of air. She lacked the strength and coordination to grab the Dreamstone, even as it dangled temptingly before her.

Spots of light danced before Rose's eyes as her world closed in, growing darker with each panicked beat of her heart.

Rose coughed, gasping as Sin's weight was suddenly lifted from her. She squinted to see, forcing her eyes to focus on the great shadow hovering over her.

The Witch shrieked in anger, thrashing wildly as huge hands easily wrapped around her thin arms.

A deep voice boomed, "Don't you go hurtin' my friend!"

Sin frothed at the mouth. Snatching up her staff, she fought to turn the tip of her black crystal against the behemoth of a man. When it became apparent this struggle was futile, she stopped.

The malevolent stare and that scowling face contorting in rage suddenly softened, losing its angry edge even as Harold tightened his grip to prevent Rose's assailant from lashing out.

"You wouldn't hurt a little, old lady, would you now, dearie?" whimpered Sin.

"You're a lady?" gasped Harold. He stared in disbelief at this ghastly face peering over her bony shoulder to glance up at him.

"Of course I am!"

"My momma taught me to never strike a lady, but you're sure as heck not actin' like one."

Like a rabid animal, she snarled. Gnashing her teeth at Harold's startled face, she growled, "Unhand me so I can kill you!"

Instead, Harold tossed her like a rag doll, throwing her against the cave wall. With a moan of pain, Sin bounced off the stony surface, landing beside the boulder where Loken remained trapped in his fortified prison.

"Seize her!" Silas shouted from across the divide. He and the others were forced to the ground as the phantom dragon dove toward them. "Don't let her escape!"

Harold fearlessly charged toward the hag as she scrambled onto her feet. With a demented cackle, she snatched up the cage holding the Sprite.

"Let him go!" yelled Harold, watching as Loken was flung against the bars of his prison.

"Make me!" growled Sin.

With a wave of her staff and a rushed incantation, Sin spun. Her tattered rags swirled about like a small, black cyclone. A thick cloud of dirt and dust whipped around her; pelting Harold to drive him back with its force. Undeterred, the large man closed his eyes, blindly forging on toward the dark whirlwind twirling before him.

"Grab the Dreamstone, at least!" cried Rose. She staggered to her feet, raising her hands to shield her eyes from the flying debris.

The obsidian crystal mounted atop Sin's staff flared with unnatural light as dark magic swelled, pulsating through the air. With this frenetic energy, this crystal became a blur of shadow and light as the ragged cloak and flying dust lashed all around her.

In a final, desperate bid, Harold dove at her, throwing his arms around the villainess. He was consumed by this dark mass, only to come crashing to the ground. He groaned in pain as the Witch, in the eye of this cyclone, was propelled upwards.

Rose watched in disbelief as Sin vaporized, disappearing into the ceiling of the cave. Just as suddenly, the phantom dragon skimming low over Tag and his friends swooped upward to follow its master. Instead of dissolving into the ceiling as Sin did, the dragon bellowed in agony as it smashed into the rocks and boulders above.

"Look out!" cried Halen.

He seized Silas and Tag, shoving them against the wall of the chamber as Rainus and Myron dove for cover. Crouching low to the ground they shielded their heads, waiting for the dragon to come crashing down. Instead, they were showered by black sand that was followed by an audible 'plop' as what was left of the ragged sock puppet, now minus both eyes, fell.

Before Sin could call upon this toy once more, Tag made a dash. Scooping up the quivering puppet, he threw it into the chasm. Lava churned, belching as the wool fibres burst into flames before swallowing it up in the ooze.

"Well done, young man!" praised Silas, as Halen helped him onto his feet.

"Where did that Witch go?" asked Myron. He glanced about to see Harold sprawled out on the cave floor as Rose raced to his side.

"I'm sorry to say she escaped," apologized Harold, calling across to his friends.

"She escaped, but you saved me!" exclaimed Rose, throwing her arms in a grateful hug around the big man.

"I'm gettin' rather good at this!" Harold embraced her, relieved to see that she and the others had survived.

"Your timing was impeccable, my friend!" praised Rainus.

"How did you even find us?" questioned Tag. Staring across the way, he was astounded to see the man.

"Are you foolin' with me, young sir?" Harold smiled with dismay.

"No, he is not!" assured Rose, brushing the dust and dirt from her hands. "How was it even possible? We left you far behind."

"Well, my lady, in your typical fashion you left a trail of devastation great and small, not to forget the trail of torches discarded along the way to follow."

"That was brilliant, my friend!" praised Myron.

"Not really, where the tunnel branched off, I did take the wrong turn here and there, wastin' some valuable time."

"Oh, my!" exclaimed Rainus. "You could have been lost for all eternity."

"The wrong turns led to dead-ends. I merely retraced my steps and kept on goin'. And if you hadn't noticed, sounds really carry through these tunnels. Just had to listen carefully to follow Princess Rose's voice."

"Are you saying I am shrill and noisy?"

"Didn't say that at all, my lady. All I know is that your voice is a distinct *pitch* from the others."

"I can accept that," said Rose.

"But how did you manage to enter this mountain when not even we could get you through?" questioned Halen.

"That openin' was the widest at the ground. By happy accident, I discovered this. I just crawled and wiggled through on my belly."

"Happy accident, indeed!" agreed Silas. "It was fortunate you arrived in such a timely manner."

"Unfortunately, once again, we come away empty-handed," lamented Rose.

"Not quite. That hag escaped; takin' Loken with her, but she didn't get away with this," announced Harold. Dangling from his hand was a chain and upon this chain was the Dreamstone! "I snatched it away from her. Doubt she even knows it's missin' yet."

Rose's mouth dropped as her eyes opened just as wide in astonishment.

"I believe this is yours," said Harold. Offering the magic crystal to her, he placed it in the palm of her trembling hand, folding her fingers around it so she'd know it was real.

"You did it, Princess! You reclaimed the Dreamstone!" shouted Tag. He whooped in victory as his fists pumped the air.

Rose shook her head. "No... Harold did it. He did what I could not."

"The important thing is you possess it once more. Just be grateful it is no longer in the hands of evil," said Rainus.

"And before I forfeit it, I shall use it one last time." Rose held the Dreamstone close to her heart. She closed her eyes as she made her wish.

"Huzzah!" cheered Harold. He was pleased and surprised to see his comrades magically appear before him as Rose's wish came true.

Her friends threw their arms around her, elated as they encircled the Princess in a great hug.

"This belongs to you, Wizard," said Rose, presenting the Dreamstone to Silas.

"Are you sure you wish to return it to me?"

"I have never been so sure of anything in my entire life!" Her words were spoken with conviction.

"Wait, Princess!" called Tag, his hand wrapping around hers. "Are you positive you want to do that?"

"Tag is right. There is a chance it'll come in handy," added Myron.

"This Dreamstone has been a vexation to my spirit. What would I need it for?" Rose's tone was dismissive.

"To save Loken, of course," answered Tag.

"Say again!" Rose's heart sank upon hearing this.

"A little magic is exactly what we will need to rescue the Sprite," said Halen, examining the residue left on the boulder where Loken's cage had rested.

"How so?" queried Silas.

"See for yourself, Master Agincor," replied Halen.

The Wizard marched over to the Elf. He leaned in close, examining the evidence Halen presented.

Peering over Silas' shoulder, Tag asked, "What is it?"

"See this?" Silas' fingertip pressed against the surface where Loken's cage had rested. He thrust his finger before the others, allowing them to examine the residue encrusting the tip of this digit.

"It looks like grains of salt," noted Myron.

"How can this be salt?" queried Tag.

"Yes, it is too pretty," assessed Rose, as she scrutinized the pink-tinted granules.

"This is no ordinary salt, my friends," assured Silas, with a dismal shake of his head.

Rainus seized the Wizard by his wrist. Jamming Silas' index finger into his mouth, the Elf tasted the pink crystals.

Silas yanked his finger free of Rainus' mouth. "Do you mind?"

"Not really," said the Elf. He swished the saliva about from cheek to cheek, allowing the substance to dissolve as he closed his eyes. He focused on identifying the crystals.

"Well?" asked Rose.

Turning his head away, Rainus spat. Wiping his chin with the back of his hand, he answered, "Master Agincor is correct. It is indeed salt, but with an intriguing flavour. It is unlike any salt I had ever tasted."

"That is because this is no ordinary salt," confirmed Silas, wiping his digit dry on his robe. "This particular substance is as rare as it is powerful."

"Are you going to tell us something ridiculous? Like it was made from the tears of a unicorn?" snorted Rose.

"Don't be silly," grunted Silas. "It was harvested from the tears of a Mermaid."

"Are you speaking of one of those half-fish and half-human

monstrosities?" gasped Rose.

"Sea-maiden or Mermaid, if you will," responded Silas. "And they are not monsters, they are just... misunderstood."

"Are you telling us the Witch uses a Mermaid's tears to bind Loken, so he cannot use his powers?" queried Myron.

"Confined in a cage of iron, set by a spell and reinforced with this salt, it is possible. This is one of the most powerful elements known in the world of magic. Because of its purity, it can prove most potent when employed in the forbidden arts," revealed Silas.

"Well, I have this!" declared Rose. She held up the Dreamstone for all to see. "Just as I wished for all of you to appear before me, rather than risking a hazardous crossing of that chasm of doom, I shall simply wish for Loken's safe return to us."

Silas shook his head. "A spell reinforced by this salt cannot simply be undone by a wish. Even I cannot undo it to rescue our little friend."

"I take it, this special salt is so rare because it is difficult to obtain?" assumed Tag.

"Extremely so! And more often than not, it is *harvested* at the expense of the Mermaid's life," answered Silas, with a dismal shake of his head.

"I quail at the mere thought of how that old crone acquired it," said Rainus, shuddering involuntarily.

"Oh, my!" Harold gasped in excitement. "Are you saying there's a Mermaid that needs rescuin', too? We're off on another adventure?"

"There was nothing said of another quest!" scolded Rose, shaking an admonishing finger at the large man.

"You may have reclaimed the Dreamstone," reminded Tag, "but now Loken is in imminent danger for trying to help us help you."

"So this is my fault? I failed again," groaned Rose.

"Not so, Princess!" contested Myron. "To reclaim the Dreamstone was no small feat. You had not failed in this. Just think of the outcome as fate's way of telling you to set a new course, one to change your destiny and to spare Loken's life."

"I am not liking this new course that only serves to reflect on my failure," sighed Rose.

"When you think about it, failure only comes when you simply give up," said Myron.

"Are you giving up now?" asked Tag, staring into her amethyst eyes.

"Well, I did reclaim the Dreamstone..." She stared at the crystal in her hand.

"But what about Loken?" queried Tag. His words prickled at her conscience.

"This is insane!" cried Rose. "I wish to go home now. It is not safe here. This world has become a dangerous place!"

"Beyond the comfort and safety of your palace, the world has always been a dangerous place," responded Silas, "and it is not because of the people with evil in their hearts."

"You are speaking in riddles again!" snapped Rose. "Of course it is! Dragonite was evil! His lunatic sister is evil, twice over! The world is dangerous because of their evilness."

"No, my dear girl, it is because of those who will do nothing about it when they have the power to put this evil to rest, that is the real danger."

Tag glanced over to Rose as she brooded. "What will it be, Princess? Good intentions mean nothing. We need action. You can be vilified by history for your indifference, or you can help make a history to your liking by saving a life, possibly two, with our help and the help of that Dreamstone."

"But we do not even know where that Witch fled to with Loken, nor do we know if indeed she holds a Mermaid captive," stated Rose.

"Every web begins with a single strand. We unravel it by following the clues," said Silas. "Without the Dreamstone, Sin relies solely upon the forbidden arts, no doubt using more of this salt to strengthen her powers. I am confident she will be forced far to the north, where the last of the Mermaids are believed to exist. It will only be a matter of time before we right the wrongs instigated by the abuse of this magic crystal."

"That, by the way, was entrusted to you, Princess," reminded Tag. "So what will it be? Will you quit? Walk away now? Leave us to our own devices when you still have the power to affect changes to make a true difference?"

"So *I* must decide?"

"At this point, we are not going to force you to join us," stated Myron. "This is a decision you must make. You can come with us or you can wish yourself back to King Maxmillian's castle and your intended husband."

"In truth, your quest to reclaim the Dreamstone was fulfilled. Your obligation ends here, if you wish to return it to me," answered Silas. "But for the rest of us, it is a forgone conclusion that we must journey on now, with or without you."

"So I can choose to go home?"

"Yes," said Tag.

"Whatever you decide, choose wisely, Princess Rose, and do so with haste," urged Rainus. "Home to prepare for nuptials or join us one last time to save the world from certain peril."

"How am I supposed to decide on something this big?"

"Life is all about making decisions," reminded Tag. "If you don't know what to do, then consider this: What decision will give you the least regret?"

Rose's shoulders slumped from the weight of this burden.

"So what will it be, my lady?" queried the Wizard. "Your journey ends here, if that is your wish."

"I suppose it does," said Rose, as she stared at her companions' anxious faces, "but I can hardly see all of you managing without me."

"So we journey to the north?" asked Tag, his brows arching up in surprise to hear the conviction in her voice.

"Apparently so," said Rose.

"But first, we return to the Enchanted Forest," said Rainus, as he nodded in approval. "A journey beyond the Fire Rim Mountains will require preparation, if we are to brave the cold and meet with any measure of success."

"An excellent plan, Lord Silverthorn," praised Myron. "First, we need to get out of this wretched mountain as quickly as possible."

"Well, I do have one more wish to use before this day is done." Rose draped the Dreamstone around her neck. "I suppose it would be a pity to let it go to waste."

"A pity indeed! As soon as we leave this place, we have work to do," announced Silas.

"Yes, we do," answered Rose, as she mustered her courage. "One more rescue mission, and then I shall return home to plan my wedding, should we survive."

"And survive, we will," vowed Silas, as he gathered his crystal from the shattered remains of his staff. "Together, we can survive and rise above all."

Accepting her fate, Rose shook her head as she spoke, "Say anything, but promise nothing, Wizard."

The end... is nigh.

YA Fantasy Series
(in reading order)

The Dream Merchant Saga: Book One, The Magic Crystal
The Dream Merchant Saga: Book Two, The Silver Sword
The Dream Merchant Saga: Book Three, The Crack'd Shield
The Dream Merchant Saga: Book Four, Sin
The Dream Merchant Saga: Book Five, World's End

Adult Fantasy Series
(in reading order)

Imago Chronicles: Book One, A Warrior's Tale
Imago Chronicles: Book Two, Tales from the West
Imago Chronicles: Book Three, Tales from the East
Imago Chronicles: Book Four, The Tears of God
Imago Chronicles: Book Five, Destiny's End
Imago Chronicles: Book Six, The Spell Binder
Imago Chronicles: Book Seven, The Broken Covenant
Imago Prophecy *(Prequel to Imago Chronicles series)*
Imago Legacy *(Sequel to Imago Prophecy)*

About the Author

*L.T. Suzuki is a fantasy novelist, script-writer
and a senior instructor of the martial arts system,
Bujinkan Budo Taijutsu;
incorporating six traditional samurai schools
and three schools of ninjutsu.*

Please check out L.T. Suzuki's official website at:
www.imagochronicles.com